To

# TAKEN

Bryan Vaughan

Enjoy!

Bryan

Copyright © 2011 Bryan Vaughan
All rights reserved

ISBN: 978-1-4478-5450-0

To Ree Ann

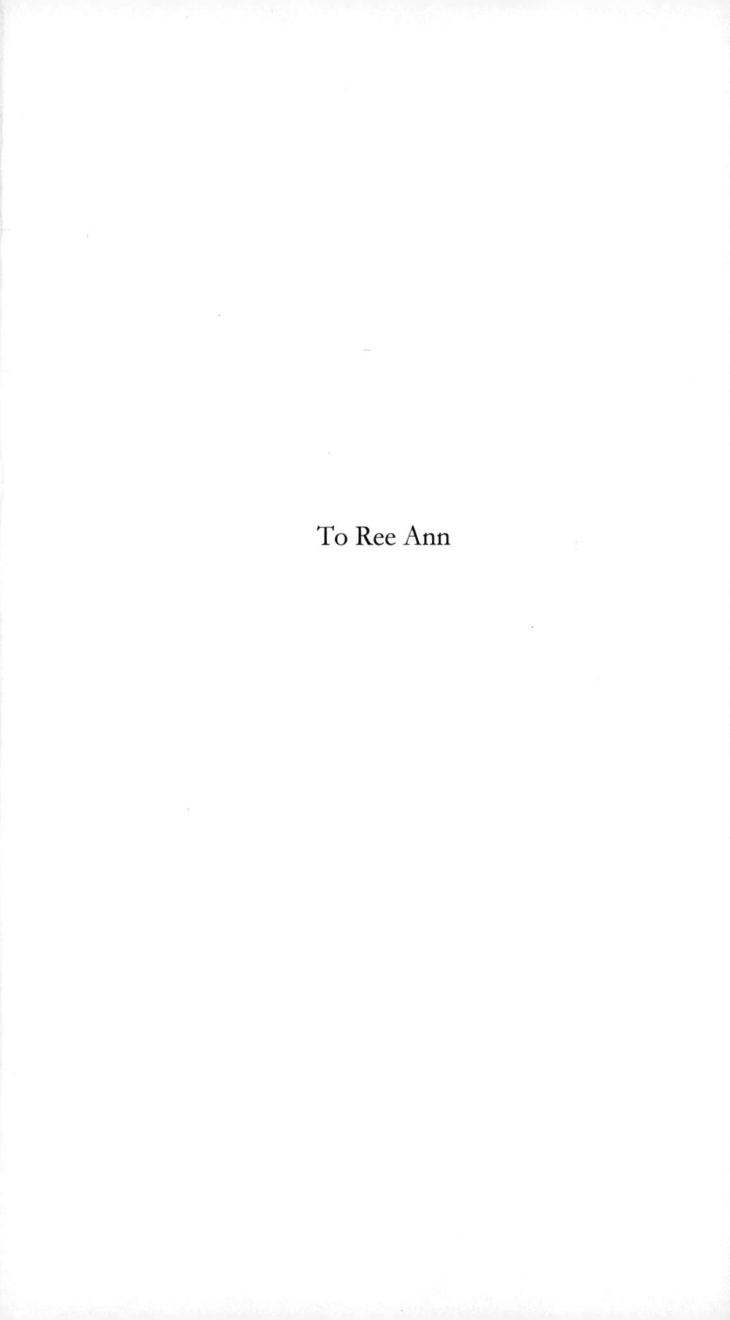

# Beginnings

It was time. So nearly time. The Voice had said so. The Voice was always right. It always had been. And now, it was time. Almost. The final play was about to commence, and a thousand years of planning would come to fruition. But still, patience was required. What were another few days in the span of centuries? He could wait. And watch. And win.

# Chapter 1

She knew it was pointless, but she ran anyway.

It had taken three darkened streets and sixteen rapid, shallow breaths to confirm that the footsteps, slightly out of step with her own, were not an echo.

At three in the morning London was eerily quiet, contrasting the hectic bustle of the day. There was little traffic, no rumblings from the underground trains, and the occasional bus that might happen to rattle by was empty save for the driver and perhaps one or two dozing, lonely passengers. Piles of rags bundled in doorways barely concealed the homeless, shivering in disturbed, meths-clouded sleep.

No one was going to help her.

Roxy knew her pursuer was close behind but whenever she glanced back she saw nothing but shadow. Her lungs burned and her thighs screamed but she sensed that no matter how fast her long legs could carry her, the unseen presence stalking her would be able to reach out and snatch her at any time.

She knew it was pointless, but she ran anyway.

Vomit covered every surface of the tight bathroom and clung to her night-shirt, hands and legs. Roxy sobbed pitifully as pain twisted her body in ways she never thought possible. Tendon-popping cramps cascaded through her in waves. Her fingers were numb, her legs belonged to someone else, and the demon pounding against the side of her head pulled at her hair and set fire to it. Bile rose up, burning her already tender throat, but before she could open her mouth, a wave of darkness brought the relief of unconsciousness.

"Christ Roxy, you're frozen."

Roxy couldn't say anything. Her mouth was gummed up and her throat was raw. She felt hot and flushed, despite the shivering. She'd heard Scarlet knocking, but hadn't had the energy to let her in. Scarlet had let herself and the children into the flat with her spare key and found Roxy curled up in the bath.

Roxy didn't resist as Scarlet stripped off the filthy, blood-splattered t-shirt and dropped it straight into the bin. Scarlet rinsed the mess from the tub, filled it with warm, soapy water and started to wash her gently. To Roxy, every splash echoed like the colliding of immense granite cylinders and the dim uncovered bulb hanging from the grubby flex overhead dazzled her. Scarlet's blouse was lurid and overpowering, a riot of sickly colour ricocheted from its satin sheen. Roxy squeezed her eyes shut, which brought the heavy scent of Scarlet's perfume into focus. It was as if she had poured an entire bottle down her front. Roxy moaned, then realised she could identify separate smells as easily as she could distinguish different objects by sight. She knew exactly what each was and from where it came; the honeysuckle conditioner Scarlet had used to wash her hair that morning, the acrid smell of her own excretions washed away by a bar of coconut-oil soap and the flowery detergent Scarlet had used to wash her clothes, not quite masking an odour of mould from a day or two lying wet on the floor the previous week. She gagged at the bitter tang of Scarlet's lipstick which seemed to be pasted onto her tongue.

Roxy panicked. It was too overwhelming. Scarlet's hands were scorching her thighs and she could feel the pulse thrumming through their fingertips as they massaged the soapy water into her skin. Roxy opened her eyes, and cried out in pain from the blinding light of the low-watt bulb. She jerked back and slipped in the water, cracking her head painfully on the rim of the bath.

"Roxy!" Scarlet tried desperately to grab her, but Roxy barely heard. She was slipping away, not from the pain or the blow to the head, but from sensory overload. It was like an extreme case of the flu where every movement, every sound and even the softest touch ripped into her like a ravenous beast.

# Chapter 2

There was no chance of escape.

The dark figure loomed up in front of her. How had he got ahead of her? She slid to an abrupt halt and turned, back the way she had come. She ran, but seemed to cover no ground. A chuckle caressed the back of her neck. She gasped for breath, her vision swam with hypoxia. She felt a hand grasp her shoulder.

There was no chance of escape.

Roxy awoke in her bed, expecting to see Scarlet and the children at her bedside – their voices were so clear and close – but she was alone in the dark and the door was closed. She could hear Scarlet through two doorways as clearly as if she had been standing next to the bed, telling her two year old daughter Leah and Roxy's sixteen month old Claudia to be quiet. Roxy propped herself up on her elbows and wondered if there was an air duct channelling their voices to her, but she knew there wasn't. She sometimes put Claudia to sleep in her room and had to leave both doors open to be able to hear her if she cried. She swung her long legs over the side of the bed and listened to Scarlet reading to the children.

The only light came from under the bedroom door and the normally cocooning darkness was now as clear as an overcast day. Everything lacked colour, but seemed to have gained something else; a texture of some kind. Roxy gingerly lowered her hands to the bed sheets, noticing for the first time how rough they were. Her fingertips were ultra-sensitive, not in a painful way, but disturbing nonetheless.

Roxy rose to get dressed. Her jeans felt coarse against her skin and her bra cut painfully into her breasts while the lacy cups felt scratchier than ever. She took the bra off and pulled on a soft t-shirt, grimacing at its rasping touch on her shoulders and back. She opened the door, blinked against the bright hallway light and walked into the sitting room.

Scarlet looked up in surprise, "Roxy! How are you? God girl you look terrible, you got no colour in your face. You want a cuppa?" She didn't bother to use the demure Chinese accent of her heritage when she wasn't working, but stuck to her broad estuary, which was even thicker than Roxy's South London glottal stop.

Claudia dropped her bottle of milk and rushed as fast as she could toddle to wrap herself around her mother. Roxy picked her up and hugged her close, pressing her face against her daughter's soft cheek and breathing in the gentle smell while Scarlet headed through the arched doorway into the small kitchen to put the kettle on.

"How do you feel?" Scarlet asked from the doorway, hesitantly.

Roxy looked up and was suddenly, terribly, *aware* of her friend. She smelt so desirable, the strong perfume not quite disguising the sweet aroma of her skin. Roxy felt a stealthy lust rising inside her, and blinked to suppress a sudden urge to leap across the room, take Scarlet in her arms and...what? Roxy shuddered, then looked back to Scarlet with a smile, "I feel great."

Scarlet gave her a sceptical look.

"I mean, I feel a bit strange. I don't feel sick, but I do feel a bit oversensitive," Roxy explained.

"Are you hungry?"

"Yeah, I am actually."

Scarlet disappeared into the kitchen while Roxy played with Claudia and Leah. It was past their bedtime and they were tired, but they knew something was going on and were too excited to settle down. Roxy was happy to play with them though, and kept staring at her daughter, seeing things she had never noticed before. She could smell her scent, clean and fresh and mingled with baby powder, easily distinguishable from those of Leah and Scarlet.

"Here," Scarlet interrupted, holding out a bowl of tomato soup.

"Thanks," replied Roxy, "it smells gorgeous."

The soup had barely hit her stomach when she doubled over and vomited it back up, along with a quantity of stringy red bile. Scarlet snatched the bowl away and guided her to the bathroom, but although

Roxy experienced several more dry retchings, no more fluids came up.

"You're in a shit state," said Scarlet and handed her a flannel. "I'll call in sick tonight. I don't think you should be left alone."

Roxy nodded weakly and crouched over the toilet as Scarlet went to get her phone. Roxy listened as Scarlet prepared night-time drinks for the children and got them settled in bed. Every sound in the small flat was magnified and hammered against Roxy's ears, giving her a headache. Scarlet returned with a glass of water and some dry bread. Roxy waved the bread away, but tried to drink. She found she could take very small sips, just enough to wet her tongue, without her body rejecting it. Scarlet went into the kitchen and returned with a small thermometer. Roxy dutifully put it under her tongue and walked unsteadily into the front room. She was starting to feel a little better, as long as she didn't eat. Scarlet took the thermometer from her a minute later and looked at it with a frown.

"Well that can't be," she murmured crossly, and held it out to show Roxy. It wasn't even registering. Scarlet shook it and clenched the bulb in the palm of her fist. A few seconds later it started to climb up as it was supposed to. Scarlet handed it back to Roxy, who placed it inside her elbow. Once again it failed to register. A shiver passed through Roxy as she handed it to Scarlet, who put it away quickly without meeting her gaze.

"I feel fine," Roxy tried to reassure her, and she did. She was so very awake, she couldn't sit still. Every movement was a joy, made with exquisite precision. She danced around the flat like a cat, ignoring Scarlet's pleas to get some rest, and hopped on tiptoe across the patterned lines of the kitchen linoleum.

Roxy prowled around the room, only half-listening to Scarlet tell her about her latest night-class in business computing, and then leaned on the arm of the threadbare settee and vaulted slowly into a one-armed handstand. She looked back at Scarlet to see that she had stopped talking and was staring open-mouthed back at her. Her disbelief became a trembling panic as she met Roxy's eyes and involuntarily drew back. The next moment, Roxy collapsed in a heavy tumble to the floor as pain wracked her stomach once again and she could do nothing except moan in agony. Scarlet hesitated only briefly before going to her side. Roxy was overcome with emotion and burst into tears. She was scared, excited, unhappy and confused all at once. Scarlet gathered her up and knelt on the floor hugging her.

As Roxy wept into Scarlet's shoulder, a yearning sensation started to filter through her, originating from deep inside her chest and spreading outwards. She turned her head towards Scarlet's neck, and felt a sudden compulsion to kiss her. She'd performed with other girls at some of the strip clubs she'd worked in, as had Scarlet, but that was acting. She had never felt any attraction towards her partners.

Now, she was overcome by the alluring smell of Scarlet's skin, the musky scent of her sweat mixed with perfume and...something else. Roxy could only describe it as blue-ish, like a winter's day just before dawn. Her ears rang with a rhythmic pulsing. She was acutely aware of the way Scarlet's skin rippled as the blood flowed just underneath it. With her chin resting on Scarlet's shoulder, it was easy to shift her head to rest her lips against her warm neck.

Scarlet jerked away when Roxy licked her.

"What the hell are you doing?"

"Hold me, Scarlet," Roxy pleaded in a soft, seductive voice, "you're so warm and soft. I just want to touch you. To feel you."

Scarlet broke Roxy's gaze and shivered, then rose to her feet and dragged Roxy up.

"C'mon Rox, you're sick. You need to sleep."

Roxy protested and pouted, but eventually allowed Scarlet to lead her to the bedroom and put her into bed. She lay awake trying to ignore increasingly troubling hunger pangs, listening through the walls as Scarlet called the hospital. She explained Roxy's symptoms; mood swings, coughing blood, diarrhoea and vomiting, but when she told them that Roxy used to be a heroin addict, the nurse seemed to lose interest. Scarlet argued with the woman for a while as she tried to explain that Roxy was clean now, until she threw the phone down angrily. The nurse's words must have had some effect though, as for the next half an hour, Roxy could hear Scarlet going through her cupboards and drawers, searching for her needles and works. Eventually, Roxy fell asleep.

# Chapter 3

She didn't know pain could be so painful. At first it was pleasurable, erotic, and she drifted on a pre-orgasmic plateau and knew she was going to die. And she didn't care.

Then a chance vision of her beautiful Claudia intruded and she jerked and kicked feebly. She'd be alone. Helpless. A pale, slender hand stopped her screams, and she bit down in frustration. One final act of defiance.

She didn't know pain could be so painful.

Cold blood filled her mouth, sending barbed tendrils of fire exploding down her throat. Her chest erupted in a splintering of agony, as a thousand shards of ice stabbed into her heart and every muscle boiled with acid.

She didn't know pain could be so painful.

Roxy woke with a demanding ache in her stomach, trembling from the slowly fading nightmare. She sat up slowly, clutching herself and gingerly explored the rest of her body to see if anything else was hurting. After a while she decided she just felt hungry. The flat was empty. She was shocked to find that it was already dusk outside, and a look at the clock in her small kitchen made her realise that she had to be at work in half an hour. There was a note from Scarlet on the counter-top, *"Taken the kids shopping. Get something to eat and wait for me to get back."*

Roxy shook her head, knowing she'd go crazy if she spent another night cooped up inside. She scribbled a reply to Scarlet saying she felt great and would be back in an hour, instead of the three she would normally work and then skipped back into her room to dress. She grabbed a kit bag and stuffed a few costumes into it before leaving. The pub was only a few streets from where she lived and she was looking forward to the walk.

The late spring night was beautiful. She felt more alive than she'd done for ages. The breeze caught the back of her exposed neck, making her shiver with unexpected delight. She had only cut her black hair from its mid-back length a few weeks ago, and was still unused to it. Wearing wigs was a little easier, but she didn't think she'd want to keep it this short. It was meant more as a statement – she was cutting herself off from her old life and habits and starting over. She walked over the uneven paving slabs listening to the night. She could hear everything clearly; voices and engine noises carrying further than normal in the descending night air.

She walked lightly, brimming with such confidence that when she saw a group of youths hanging about on the corner up ahead, she marched directly towards them smiling, instead of crossing cautiously to the other side of the road. They stared at her as she approached, their darkly predatory gazes becoming uncertain and hesitant at the expression on her face. She slowed her pace as she neared them and murmured a gracious thank you as they parted to allow her to pass. She could smell their scent as separate, identifiable sources, each tinged with cologne and tobacco in a way that was curiously arousing. She felt drawn to them, savouring the way their breath caught as she looked down at them. She imagined she could hear their heartbeats quicken and she slipped into an exaggerated, sexy walk, thrusting out her breasts and swaying her hips.

Then she turned the corner and the moment was gone. She felt oddly disappointed that none of them had tried to grab her. As she continued down the road she could hear their excited conversation resume, telling each other what they would do to her if she came back, and how much she would love it. She considered going back, but then she caught sight of her destination and the thought slid from her mind.

Clive, the landlord, greeted her on her way in and she threaded her way through the already busy bar towards the ladies toilet at the back. She had performed here many times, and some of the regular customers caught her eye and smiled. This was a local pub, with traditional dark wood features, horse and tack decorations and worn red carpeting. Half a dozen tables with accompanying benches and chairs occupied one side while the other was dominated by the long, sticky bar and a few bar stools. The far end of the room contained a homemade stage, little more than a raised platform three feet high and about five square, set into the corner opposite the entrance to the lavatories.

This was no pole-dancing venue. The girls came out of the toilet where they changed, walked around the bar clutching a glass into which the customers would throw some change – anything from coppers to pound coins, rarely any notes, then climb on the stage and strip to a song from the jukebox. Clive didn't pay the girls anything, telling them they could take home anything they made from tips. He gave them a free drink for every session they did, but as they each performed ten or twelve sets a night, after the first couple of drinks Roxy would have to switch to water or coke to avoid getting too drunk. It was a pretty shabby deal, but it was steady work. Roxy hated it, but it was a step up from what she used to do, and it paid better than waitressing.

Roxy was one of only two dancers that night; the other being a blonde she'd met a few times before. They alternated taking to the stage every ten minutes, and after the first couple of sets each, they took their routines into the crowd, encouraging patrons to pay for the privilege of touching or licking beer from their nipples. Roxy was riding high on the feelings flowing through her and was at her sluttiest best. She dressed as a schoolgirl and sat on the customers' laps, grinding onto them as she moved her hips in slow, wide circles. She came out as a dominatrix in a leather basque and four inch heeled boots, raising her to an intimidating height and forced a young student to kneel before her while she towered over him, pulling his face towards her crotch as she held him in place with a long whip.

Next, she wore a clinging black lacy dress with long satin gloves and shiny high heeled shoes. She strutted lazily through the bar and selected a clean-smelling young man to follow her to the stage. She was wearing a Cleopatra-style wig and teased him by unbuttoning his shirt and trailing the fake hair up and down his chest. She guided his hands to remove her dress, bra and panties until she was left wearing only the gloves, stockings and heels and then laid him down to crawl over his body. The crowd loved it, and the young man's friends cheered with envious encouragement. He was clearly aroused and Roxy made a big show of caressing the bulge between his legs as she ran her tongue up his firm stomach. She could feel his heart pound like a drum when she reached his strong, broad chest, and he smelled so good she thought she would pass out. Her lips parted to kiss his throat then she raised her head and smiled at him wickedly.

His eyes widened with shock, and there was a collective gasp from the watching audience as her canines had seemed to grow into long, sharp fangs. His pulse leapt up rapidly, and it had an immediate effect on her. She felt an orgasmic shudder ripple through her as she dipped her head to his neck and bit him, piercing the soft skin easily. Hot blood rushed into her mouth and she swallowed excitedly, the hungry ache in her belly eager to be sated. The pain eased almost immediately, but she kept her mouth fastened on his neck, slowly sucking more of the delicious liquid from him. He was giving off an intoxicating scent, as fear and desire mixed in his sweat. Roxy inhaled deeply, seeming to gain just as much satisfaction from it as from the blood. He clutched at her tightly, holding her against him as she drank slowly, lingering over every drop.

The sound of the onlookers shouting and whistling snapped Roxy back from her trance. It felt like she had been feasting from his neck for hours, rather than the ten or fifteen seconds it had actually been. She pulled away, and saw blood oozing from two small wounds on the side of his neck, surrounded by a deepening bruise. She licked her lips as she sat up, nearly overbalancing as the pressure in her head shifted, and looked around at the applauding crowd. The young man lying under her groaned in pleasure and opened his eyes to smile up at her. She had just enough presence of mind to blow him a kiss and stood up unsteadily.

Forcing a smile for the patrons, she lowered herself from the stage and passed numbly through the bar with an empty beer glass, her thoughts racing. Behind her, her victim was being helped to his feet and teased by his friends. She was getting more tips than normal, including a couple of notes. No one seemed to have noticed that she had really drawn blood from him. She felt her teeth with her tongue, but apart from a light, salty coating, they felt normal. No fangs, as far as she could tell. She needed to get out of the busy room and be alone to think. As soon as she could, she retrieved her clothes and headed into the toilet.

She pulled off the gloves and wig and leaned on the sink, staring at her reflection in the mirror as she tried to organise her thoughts. Her lipstick was smudged and the harsh fluorescent lights made her skin look pale and unhealthy. She ran her tongue across her teeth again, tasting his blood. It had a bitter, metallic tang to it, but she found herself wanting more, like a craving for salt or coffee in the way that neither really tasted nice, but they seemed to satisfy something deep inside. She curled her lips back and looked at her teeth. They were stained pink, but that was all. She raised her hand and touched them, thinking she must have imagined them changing shape. The gums around her canines were tender and sore. She gripped the sink with both hands. It didn't make sense. The pain in her stomach was creeping back, like a wary scavenger lurking just out of reach of a lion crouched over a kill, but it was bearable; more like a normal hunger than a crippling one. Roxy licked some more blood from her teeth and felt her stomach tighten, but at least it didn't groan. Something was tugging at her subconscious, enticing her to reach for it and bring it forth, but she wasn't ready for it yet and thrust it away.

Then the sink under her hands shattered. Shards of ceramic dug into her palms painfully causing thick, dark blood to flow profusely over her fingers. She gasped and stepped back. The front part of the sink was ruined, and as she watched, it fell away from the wall with a loud crash. She stared at it for several seconds and then the door flew open and Clive was standing there, looking annoyed.

"What's goin' on?" he demanded.

Roxy ran past him, desperate to get away. He hardly moved, just staring at the sink as she burst into the main room. She made it all the way through the crowd to the door before she realised something was wrong. No one seemed disturbed by her mad run, even though she had pushed a couple of people out of her way as she passed. She turned and looked back to see the other girl on the stage dropping her blouse. One of the men she had pushed was leaning over at a very odd angle, both feet fixed in one place. He was still holding his beer. Others were turning to face him, but too slowly, as if they were moving under water. The blouse was falling to the ground like a balloon. The man she had pushed was starting to put his arms out to break his fall. His beer splashed out of the glass like honey, all over an elderly gentleman nearby. Roxy blinked, and everything returned to normal. The man fell heavily to the floor, the blouse landed on the stage and other people she had passed were staggering and looking around in confusion. Roxy turned quickly, pulled open the door and fled into the night.

# Chapter 4

She passed a couple of closed-up shops before she remembered all she was wearing were her stockings and high heels. The crisp night air puckered her skin and hardened her nipples. Headlights appeared up ahead, blinding her, and she quickly turned off the street into an alley beside a shop. Her way was immediately blocked by a high gate. She panicked, not wanting the driver to see her, and grabbed hold of one of the bars and vaulted over it. She landed easily on the balls of her feet on the other side and sprinted into the dark, narrow passage that ended in an unmarked door. Roxy huddled in the grubby doorway and watched the car flash by. She looked up, expecting to see the moon, or a lamp, but saw only heavy clouds, dimly reflecting the city lights. She could see clearly, as if it were merely an overcast day, rather than the dead of night. She bent her head to examine her hands and gasped. The cuts had disappeared. They had healed over completely without scarring. All that remained were traces of dried blood.

Roxy's head swam. She knew she had broken the sink with her bare hands. She glanced at the gate blocking the alley and tried to work out how she had got over it. At school, she had been taller than all the boys and most of the teachers, and to her annoyance, she had always been picked for netball and selected for the high jump. Her personal best jump had been a little under six feet, which was good, but was nowhere near as high as that gate. Then the subconscious thought that had taunted her earlier returned, amidst visions of super-heroes bitten by radioactive spiders, and she remembered the attack two days earlier. He had bitten her. She rubbed her shoulder and smiled at the thought of a radioactive vampire, but then froze as the thought took root. A vampire? It was obviously nonsense. But I've just drunk someone's blood, she thought, and a lot of weird things have been happening lately.

Male voices drifted towards her and she tilted her head to listen. She could hear their words clearly. There were two of them, probably students from the local university, judging from their out-of-town accents. They were heading in the direction she had come from and were talking with barely contained excitement.

"...she's really tall, like, six-two or something," one was saying.

"No shit?" asked the other.

"Yeah, and really athletic looking, short black hair, good looking. Smallish tits though, but nicely shaped."

"And she's on tonight?"

"That's what he said,"

It occurred to Roxy that they were talking about her. They were probably on the way to the pub she had just left. She stood up and wandered over to the gate, expecting them to pass by any moment, but was surprised to see that they were still about twenty feet away. The night air carried their scent ahead of them, as clear to her as a thick, rolling fog. Her legs felt weak as new sensations coursed through her. So many unfamiliar smells were wrapped up in the deodorant they wore. She closed her eyes and found she could clearly visualise how quickly they were approaching by the way the intensity of their smell increased.

She opened her eyes and stared at them. If she stayed where she was they would see her in moments. She didn't want that. Not yet. She reached up and took hold of one of the bars. Very slowly, she pulled and her feet left the ground. As her face drew level with her hand she reached up with her other hand and grasped the top of the gate. She felt no straining of her muscles, no warming buzz that she normally experienced doing chin-ups in the gym. Normally she could do about nine or ten with a lot of effort, using both arms. She wasn't even breathing heavily now. She wasn't breathing at all. She hung there silently, her legs dangling, brushing the bars below. The men were very close now. Roxy didn't want them to see her legs, and pulled herself up to crouch on the top of the gate. The crossbeam was only about an inch wide, but she had no sense that she would lose her balance. The men walked by, and she had a sudden urge to reveal herself, to call to them, to smile and drop down behind them, knowing that their pulses would race and their veins rush with adrenaline. She clamped her teeth together for a few seconds and then they were gone.

She sat perched on top of the gate for several minutes afterwards, listening to the sounds of the night, not trusting herself to move. A few more cars drove by, and then a group of five giggling girls of about fifteen years old or so appeared. Her eyes watered as the heavy cloud of perfume reached her, and she held her breath. She waited for the clogging, dizzy feeling behind her eyes that usually accompanied holding her breath, but it never came. She didn't want to check her pulse. When the girls had gone she stood on the top of the narrow gate and looked up. The tiled roof of the shop was just above her head and she pulled herself up onto it. East London opened up before her as she crept up the corrugated slope to the apex. A light rain started to fall.

Roxy looked out over sentinel ranks of terraces that stretched away for miles, separated by the warm orange glow of streetlights. The air was cool against her wet skin, and the tiles were uneven and slippery under her heels. She slipped them off and stood on the cold surface in her stockings. Her thoughts were wrapped in cotton and she moved more by instinct than reason. She started to walk over the roof in the direction of her home, gripping a shoe in each hand. The sloping, curved tiles felt like level ground and her sheer stockings seemed to grip the surface like thick rubber boots. Every step was placed with careless precision. She reached the end of the terrace and stared across the road at the next row over thirty feet away. She stood for a few moments, unthinking, and then took a couple of steps backwards. She was in the air before she realised she had jumped and landed lightly on the opposite roof.

She started to run, her fractured thoughts flashing too quickly to process so they became nothing more than a blur. She wanted to scream. She started to make reckless jumps, almost daring herself to fall. She wanted to fall, to let the pain wake her up. She vaulted over chimney-stacks and television aerials, somersaulting across alleys and hurling herself across narrow streets.

When she finally stopped and looked around she was overlooking the vast expanse of Victoria Park, over a mile east of where she had started. A wave of nausea made her legs give way. She clutched at a nearby chimney, her shoes long since gone, and clung to it, waiting for her head to clear, then lowered herself to the sloped roof and sat down, listening to the sounds of distant traffic, the soothing tinkle of fountains in the park and a cat prowling through the rubbish bins below. A peace crept over her, isolated from the world below, and she finally allowed herself to think. Something had happened to her. Something incredible that she couldn't explain. Was she a vampire? The thought made her smile. She had visions of having to buy a coffin and stock the fridge with bottles of blood. She shook her head. Too many questions. Well, she'd deal with them later.

She glanced at her wrist and swore as she realised she'd left her watch back at the pub with her clothes. And her tips. And her phone. It was probably about nine-thirty or ten though, and time she should be heading home. Scarlet was probably going out of her mind with worry. That was another thing. What should she say to Scarlet? Oh hi, sorry I'm late, but I was turned into a vampire the other day, and I'm still having trouble adjusting? As she looked around, a whole host of more immediate questions came to her, such as how was she going to get down from the roof, and how was she going to get home without being seen? She was still almost naked, her stockings laddered and ruined. At least the rain had stopped.

She managed to clamber gingerly down a drainpipe and jogged back towards her home through darkened alleys and parks. She wasn't ready to use the rooftops again. She was almost home, padding nervously along one of the smaller streets, when a pub door opened up ahead, and four men came out, laughing and joking, Roxy froze in mid-stride, poised on tiptoe under the full glare of a streetlight. Not knowing what to do, she moved behind the concrete lamppost, putting it between herself and the men. It was too narrow to shield her at all. She closed her eyes as the men turned in her direction and prayed that they wouldn't notice her.

# Chapter 5

The men drew closer, an acrid smell of beer and sweat carried ahead of them by the breeze. Roxy waited for their conversation to falter as they saw her. It didn't. She heard them pass within touching distance, and opened her eyes to watch them walking away. How could they not have noticed her? She didn't wait for the magic to fade, and quickly hurried the last few hundred yards to her home.

"Where the bloody hell do you think you've been?" Scarlet was furious.

Claudia toddled up to her mother excitedly, but as Roxy bent to pick her up she suddenly started screaming and trying to get away. Roxy frowned at Scarlet, thinking it was her shouting that Claudia didn't like, but Scarlet had already calmed down, her anger born only of worry. She stared curiously at Roxy's state of undress. Claudia continued to wriggle anxiously in Roxy's arms, and only settled down when she set her back on the floor.

Roxy stared at Claudia, devastated as she realised that her daughter could somehow sense that something had happened to her, and didn't like it.

"I called Clive," said Scarlet. "He told me you wrecked the sink in the loo. He's keeping the money you made tonight to pay for it. Then he said you ran out, leaving your stuff behind. I didn't believe him, but now I see you," she gestured towards her, letting the end of the sentence hang.

"It's complicated," Roxy started, unsure what else to say, and suddenly aware that she needed to find some clothes.

"Maybe you should see a doctor?"

"No!" Roxy said quickly. She didn't think it was something a doctor could fix, and she didn't want to draw attention to herself until she had to.

Scarlet tilted her head to the side and gave her a frustrated look. "Are you using again?" she accused her, "If I find out you are then so help me God I'm taking Claudia and never seeing you again!"

Roxy shook her head, helplessly, knowing anything she said would only sound false. They had been here before, and both of them knew how well she could lie. Scarlet mistook her hesitation as an admission, and suddenly flung herself at Roxy, screaming. She was not a big woman, short and slender, her eye-line was about level with Roxy's breasts, but that didn't stop her from reaching up and slapping her repeatedly across the face, scratching with her long nails. Roxy staggered back, more shocked than hurt and tripped over the small coffee table, tumbling inelegantly to the floor. Claudia and Leah started screaming, scared by the sudden noise and movement. Roxy lay there, unresponsive, hardly feeling the blows, when the smell of blood caught her attention. Scarlet had scratched her deeply and now a slow, wet trickle was crawling down her face. A black cloud descended on Roxy, obscuring her vision as hatred welled up inside her. How dare she! What right did she have to tell her what to do? She ought to be taught a lesson, feel what true pain was like. She glared at Scarlet, who suddenly yelped as though she'd been slapped and staggered back, open-mouthed. She scrambled away crab-fashion as Roxy stood up, desperately trying to put some distance between them.

The panic in her eyes finally reached Roxy, who paused in confusion. Scarlet reached the crying children and snatched them protectively to her chest, sobbing uncontrollably, a wet stain spreading from between her legs onto the carpet. Roxy sat down, calm now, and called Scarlet's name softly, her voice thick with guilt. Scarlet flinched and ignored her at first, burying her face in the children's bodies, but after a little more coaxing she turned frightened eyes towards Roxy.

"What the fuck are you?"

"What do you mean?" Roxy whispered.

"Your eyes...your teeth..." Scarlet gasped, "are you going to kill us?"

"I...of course not," Roxy protested, running her tongue across her teeth. They felt normal. "What about my eyes?" she was desperate to know what Scarlet had seen.

"They just turned red, your teeth...pointed, like a fucking animal!" She was angry now, her fear turning into an embarrassed rage.

Roxy stared at the floor, feeling her stomach turn to ice. What could she possibly say? "I'm sorry," her voice broke, but she struggled on, "I don't know what happened but I... I've changed. Someone attacked me...bit me. Since then everything has been crazy. I can't keep food down, my senses have gone nuts, I'm stronger..." she trailed off. Roxy realised she was crying and wiped a hand across her face. It came away coated in red tears. Scarlet stared at her strangely.

"Amanda," Scarlet said softly, "what's happened to you?" She never called her Amanda. They had an agreement that they would use their stage names all the time in case they were overheard by customers, and it became easy to continue to do so in private. Scarlet's real name was Seen Won, so Roxy was happy to use Scarlet instead.

"I think I'm some kind of vampire," Roxy whispered. She couldn't bring herself to admit to her other actions that evening.

Scarlet was still holding Claudia and Leah, who were now drifting off to sleep, exhausted from the late night and emotional turmoil. She said nothing for a long time and then looked across at Roxy and said, "So, what are you going to do now? Drink my blood? Should I go and get the garlic and crucifix?"

Roxy looked up, trying to work out if she was being sarcastic. Scarlet had a wary look in her eyes and wasn't smiling. "You believe me?" Roxy stammered.

Scarlet shrugged, "My grandfather used to tell old Chinese tales of monsters that would sneak into houses at night to steal the breath and blood of those sleeping inside. I always assumed they were just stories, but I remember I said that to him once and he got really angry. He actually believed in them and told me that I should too. I thought he was just a daft old man, but after what I've just seen, and what Clive told me, I'm not sure now."

Roxy shook her head, "But I can't be a ...! It's insane. They don't exist." She felt more tears rising and clamped her lips together to hold them back.

"Whatever you are, you've changed Roxy. I can feel it. There's something about you, something scary. Forget about the glowing eyes and pointy teeth, you don't blink any more. It's making my eyes water."

Roxy blinked, just for her.

Scarlet rose from the floor and eased the sleeping children onto the sofa before turning to face Roxy. "Well I can see your reflection in the mirror over there, and I can't see any pentagram signs on your palms, so those myths aren't true." She reached into her top and pulled out a small silver cross on a chain and brandished it at Roxy who flinched slightly, not sure what to expect, but felt nothing and stared back at her. Scarlet shuffled forward, holding the cross as far ahead of her as the chain would allow. Roxy felt her stomach knot in anticipation, but forced herself to sit still and allowed Scarlet to touch the cross to her forehead. Nothing.

"Silver doesn't work either apparently."

"I thought that was werewolves?"

"I think it's vampires too."

"So what now?"

Scarlet shrugged, and bent to pick up the coffee table which had fallen during the struggle. Roxy rose and walked over to look down at Claudia, keeping her back to Scarlet. Every sense she had screamed a warning. If Scarlet wanted to attack, then this would be the time, but Roxy ignored her inner voices. If she couldn't trust Scarlet and Claudia couldn't stand her, then she didn't want to live at all. She bent over Claudia, thinking how beautiful she was when she was asleep and gazed down, wanting her last memory to be of her. Scarlet stood up behind her and brushed past on the way to the kitchen.

"Do you want to try a cup of tea?"

Roxy's legs nearly gave way in relief. She glanced over to watch Scarlet start to fill the kettle and shook her head. "I don't think so."

"Well I need one for sure," Scarlet replied. "I need to go and wash first though. You made me pee my pants."

"Sorry about that."

"Don't be sorry, you're going to be washing them." It wasn't much of a joke, but Roxy smiled gratefully as Scarlet hobbled off to the toilet to clean up while the kettle boiled.

Roxy turned back to Claudia and reached down to stroke her platinum blonde hair, so unlike her own. Claudia stirred, and raised her hand to grab Roxy's finger. Then she smiled in her sleep and Roxy's heart filled with love, knowing that she hadn't lost her. She just needed time. Roxy stayed in that position until Scarlet returned. She didn't feel tired from holding the awkward pose for so long. She could have stayed there all night, but reluctantly she eased her finger from Claudia's grip and sat down on the floor in front of the sofa. Scarlet settled into the armchair with her tea clutched in both hands.

Roxy sat staring into space for a while as Scarlet sipped her tea in silence, both wrapped in their own thoughts. Finally, Roxy said "I need to find out what's wrong with me."

"No shit. What happened?"

"Just after I left Rudi's I realised someone was following me," Roxy frowned, trying to remember details that were skulking just out of reach. "I remember being frightened...running, and--" she reached up to touch the top of her shoulder, "he bit me!" She craned her neck to see the wound.

"There's nothing there now," observed Scarlet.

"No, but, it happened." She said feebly and held out her hands, studying where the cuts had been. "I heal faster now, as well. Maybe it got better?"

"What did he do then?"

"I can't remember. I can't remember what he looked like. I can't even remember how I got home." Roxy glanced at her wrist, and swore softly as she remembered she'd left her watch at the pub. "What time is it?"

"After midnight."

"Do you think I should go try to find him?"

Scarlet shook her head, "Not now. Dawn isn't far off. You might not get back in time."

"I hadn't thought of that," Roxy mumbled. "Shit, this is going to be a pain in the arse isn't it?" They both looked at each other, and then burst out laughing.

For the next few hours they sat and talked about Roxy's "condition" as Scarlet put it, gamely trying out as many vampire myths as they knew. Scarlet knew a great many more than Roxy, whose education stopped at Hammer Horror films and Christopher Lee. Garlic smelled particularly strong to Roxy, but she found she could hold her breath and had no trouble getting close to Scarlet. Silver and crosses they had already tried, although for some reason Roxy's skin did crawl when Scarlet recited the Lords Prayer. She didn't need to put earth in her bed, or to sleep in a coffin, if the last two days were any indication, although she did seem to be comatose during the day. Scarlet threw a handful of rice on the floor in front of Roxy, who just gave her a puzzled look. Scarlet explained that some vampires supposedly felt a compulsion to count the grains. They couldn't test sunlight until the morning, although Roxy was a little reluctant to try that, or a wooden stake for that matter. She was pleased that she could still see her reflection in the mirror – it would have made putting on make-up impossible. She cut herself with a kitchen knife, and they both watched the wound knit itself together before their eyes. She even managed to work out how to extend her fangs at will. Watching it in the mirror was scary, finally bringing home to Roxy that this was for real. Finally, they settled down to talk about her need for blood,

"I...fed from someone tonight," Roxy admitted, and told Scarlet about the incident in the pub.

"Was he okay? He didn't die did he?"

"No, he just looked a bit dizzy, like he'd just given blood I suppose. Maybe I should have offered him some tea and biscuits?"

Scarlet smiled at the joke, but then became serious, "How often do you think you'll need to drink?"

Roxy shrugged. It was impossible to know.

"What about if you get hungry when I'm around? Or Claudia? Are you going to attack us?"

Roxy had been worrying about that too. How bad would it get?

"Well, I can feel when I'm hungry. It can hurt a lot actually. I'll just have to get away from you if I start to feel like that." Roxy didn't add that she was feeling hungry at that moment. It was only a light hunger, as if she'd missed a meal, but she didn't feel the need to attack Scarlet right now.

"I wonder if the guy I bit will become a vampire too?" Roxy pondered.

"Dunno," Scarlet shrugged. "Let's hope not."

They lapsed into silence, and Scarlet tried to suppress a yawn.

"You should go to bed," Roxy observed, not feeling at all tired herself.

Scarlet nodded. "What shall we do?"

Roxy thought for a moment. If she did suddenly fall fast asleep when the sun came up, unable to wake until nightfall, then someone needed to look after Claudia. The question was, was it safe for Scarlet to stay in the same house as Roxy? They decided that Roxy should go into her bedroom and wait for dawn while Scarlet slept on the couch. She would look after the children and then check on Roxy in the evening. The decision made, they both hesitated, watching each other. It would take a lot of trust on both their parts – Scarlet to trust Roxy not to feed from her while she slept, and Roxy to trust Scarlet not to open the curtains or stake her during the day.

Roxy broke the tension with a smile. "Well, goodnight. Don't let the bed bugs bite. Or anything else..."

Scarlet grinned, "Go to bed Vampirella, before I get out the garlic."

"Go ahead, we both know it doesn't work," Roxy retorted flippantly.

Scarlet poked her tongue out playfully and watched her kiss Claudia softly before heading for the bedroom across the hall.

Roxy shut the door behind her and lay down, trying to sleep, but found it difficult to settle. Her mind was dancing with thoughts about what had happened to her, and what she might do the following night. She resolved to head back to town and try to find the man who attacked her. Maybe he hunted in that area often and she would stumble upon him and demand an explanation? She heard Scarlet drift off to sleep, listening to her soft, even breathing through the door. Roxy paced around the room, ignoring her growing hunger and keeping her promise to Scarlet to stay where she was.

Eventually, she saw the curtains start to lighten as dawn approached. A sudden irrational fear gripped her, and she backed away from the window. She wanted to open the curtains and test the sunlight myth, but her body refused to obey. She started trembling, wanting nothing more than to get away from the terrible light. Her eyes started to sting as the room became brighter, and a wave of fatigue overcame her. She fought it for a while, crouched in the far corner of the room, listening to the birds singing and the sound of early morning traffic outside her window, until she could bear it no more. She crawled underneath her bed, covered herself with a quilt and was asleep within seconds.

# Chapter 6

She woke the next evening at dusk. There was no drowsy slumber, no yearning for a few more minutes before she had to open her eyes and get up. She was instantly awake and refreshed. Her eyes flickered open to stare up at the underside of her bed, immediately aware of being hungry. She rolled out and stood in a smooth motion, massaging her empty stomach. She felt as if she hadn't eaten in a week. She sensed that the house was empty and listened quietly for a few moments to check. She could hear the television in the flat upstairs and next door's teenage daughter was on the phone to her friend complaining about her mother grounding her, but that she would sneak out later anyway.

Scarlet was gone, taking the children with her. Maybe she didn't want to be in the flat when Roxy woke up, just in case? Roxy didn't blame her. Even *she* didn't know what to expect from herself. She stripped off her nightshirt and headed for the shower. Her feet were still dirty from her rooftop chase the night before. She noticed that she didn't smell of sweat, but she could pick out several different types of scent clinging to her; beer, cologne, car fumes. The shampoo and soap were very strong and cloying and she made a mental note to buy some unscented stuff as soon as possible. When she had finished washing, she remained in the shower for another ten minutes, the hot water spray cascading over her as she let her subconscious mind organise itself. Very little crossed her surface thoughts during this time, and she finally stirred when the water started to run cold. A sliver of guilt clawed at her, knowing that the hot water supplied the whole building and that the other residents might be a bit pissed off with her, but then she shoved the thought aside. What were they going to do? She was a vampire, right? She got out of the shower, dried herself and brushed her teeth, although the notion of a vampire brushing her fangs seemed slightly ludicrous to her, and she kept breaking out in giggles.

Scarlet returned just as she was dressing, bringing the children with her. Roxy had decided that jeans and a t-shirt would be the most practical outfit to wear that night. Claudia's face lit up as she saw her mother and ran into her arms. Roxy held her tightly and listened to her babbling incoherently about her day.

"Look Rox, I can't afford to keep taking time off," Scarlet started, reluctance evident in her tone. "You can go out tonight and look around, but tomorrow you have to stay home and look after the kids."

Roxy nodded to her, smiling as she bounced Claudia around and listened to her laughter. She knew that Scarlet was in the same dire financial situation as she was. London rent wasn't cheap and Scarlet had already missed two nights on Roxy's behalf.

"I'll make it up to you," Roxy promised, "I swear."

They made small-talk for the next hour and played with the children, cautiously skirting their conversation of the previous night, or any reference to what had happened. Roxy wondered about that, but it was clear to her that Scarlet wasn't very comfortable with the subject, so she didn't force the issue. Roxy put Claudia to bed with a story, and then pulled on her boots and leather jacket and left, waving a casual farewell to Scarlet.

The city seemed alive as she made her way toward the tube station. She almost forgot the burning in her stomach as the bustle of the night sang to her. She skipped down the grimy steps of Aldgate East station, the smell of urine and old vomit almost overpowering. She passed beggars clutching pleas for change scrawled desperately on scraps of cardboard, students tarted up for a night on the town and a group of foreign tourists clutching maps and travel-guides. Once on the platform, she stood by the tiled wall, her eyes flicking restlessly from person to person, drinking in the smallest details now revealed to her. She felt the warm, oily gust of air from the tunnel preceding the train and heard the frantic squealing of rats as they scuttled to safety. On the train she sat alone. People instinctively avoided her, hurrying past to stand near the rattling doors at the far end of the carriage. It occurred to her that she should take the opportunity to find someone to feed from, but hesitated, unsure of exactly how to go about it.

Soon, she was on Tottenham Court Road, just a few hundred yards from where she had been attacked. It had started to rain while she was underground, and as she headed south into Soho. The neon lights from the strip clubs and bookstores made the puddled roads glow like brightly coloured rivers. She was dazzled by the beauty of it all and paused for a time, allowing the rain to fall on her hair and run down her face. Where once she would have hurried past darkened doorways she now lingered, staring into them, the absence of light no more of a hindrance to her than a pane of glass. Shifty, nervous youths haggled for drugs with grizzled men in heavy coats, or slouched in bored groups carving graffiti into dank brick walls with commando knives. It always struck her what a muddled place London was. The lowest criminal elements dealt and fought mere streets away from brightly lit theatres frequented by the rich and privileged. Many tourists had taken a wrong turn and found their exciting evening turn into a nightmare.

Roxy's stomach cramped up and she buckled over with a gasp. She fell to her hands and knees, her vision blurred, and waited for the pain to subside. She heard them walking towards her while she was still on the ground; four men, wearing heavy boots and denim, drawn to the weak woman like hyenas circling a wounded beast.

"Hey girl, you lose your contact lenses?" one sneered, provoking laughter from his friends. One of them raised his foot and kicked her hard in the ribs. Roxy fell sideways, unsure which pain hurt more. She tried to crawl away, not knowing where she was going and not caring, when another kick swept her hands out from under her, sending her face crashing onto the wet concrete of the narrow side-street. One of the men said something to her, but it was meaningless. Her ears were roaring, her wrist throbbed and the sounds and smells of her attackers mingled with the distant sounds of the city and made her dizzy.

"Get her jacket," one said, and another crouched down next to her and grabbed her arm. The slim thread of her patience snapped. Her body suddenly felt hot; a burning sensation flooding from her chest to the tips of her fingers and toes, banishing the pain that had paralysed her moments before. The confusing muddle of sounds from the street faded, replaced with a concentrated awareness of only the four men near her. She could hear every breath, the creak of their boots as they moved, the smell of cheap deodorant failing to cover their body odour and excitement as they crowded around her. She opened her eyes and stood up, a low, feral growl coming from her throat. The one holding her arm struggled to hold her down, but he was no more of an impediment to her than a child. She rose to her full height, almost a head higher than the tallest of them, and bared her teeth. Their faces changed as fear gripped them, and they backed away from her. Roxy followed the nearest one, who had been attempting to remove her jacket, thinking only of his blood and how she wanted the taste of it on her tongue. He pulled out a knife and held it out toward her. She reached out and grabbed his wrist. He was so shocked by the brazen act that he just stared at her before she twisted his hand and gave a little tug. The bones in his wrist shattered like dry spaghetti and he screamed. The others turned and ran as Roxy pulled the shrieking man toward her, making him stumble to his knees.

Roxy held onto him, bent her head to his swelling wrist and bit into it. A steady flow of warm, tangy blood filled her mouth and she swallowed eagerly, barely keeping control of herself. As she drank, the man's cries softened to whimpers, his head hanging down and his other hand scrabbling helplessly at her long legs. He would have collapsed if Roxy hadn't been holding him up. She was lost in a fugue, the taste of his blood fascinating her. It was so different from her first victim. She imagined she could taste changes in its flavour perhaps due to diet, or age, but a deep part of her recognised the main difference. It was fear. The hormones and adrenaline flooding through this one came from a different source – flight, not fight. She could have drunk from him forever, each mouthful promising a further revelation, another facet of his life.

"Okay sister, that's enough," a woman's voice behind her demanded.

Roxy heard, but the words held no significance to her. Then a pair of hands gripped her and she found herself flying through the air and slammed hard into a brick wall, crashing heavily to the ground. She shook her head, trying to work out if she was in pain or not and looked up to see a woman with a bizarre hairstyle leaning over the man she had been feeding from. She had turned his face upwards and seemed to be blowing into his mouth. Roxy stared at the young woman, seeing her features clearly despite the shadows shrouding the alley. The sides of her dirty-blonde hair were shaven to a short fuzz, but from a strip running from her forehead to the nape of her neck, grew fine mop-like strands which hung down either side of her head past her ears. She was dressed in tight jeans and a bomber jacket decorated with dozens of metal badges. The man she was holding went limp and she lowered him gently to the ground before straightening up and turning to face Roxy.

Roxy sat up and eyed the young woman cautiously. She was wearing a warm, friendly smile, but Roxy had not forgotten that she had just thrown her ten feet through the air into a wall.

"Are you okay? You were losing it a bit there."

Roxy nodded, a warm, pleasantly satisfied feeling in her stomach.

"I'm Vicky," the woman offered. "Sorry about butting in there, but you were about to kill him, and that would have been awkward."

Roxy cleared her throat, "I'm Roxy," she said, and stood up. Vicky let out a mock yell as she did so.

"Eek! You're taking off. Come back down here!"

Vicky was only a fraction over five feet, and Roxy loomed over her. Roxy smiled weakly, still not sure enough of her position to relax. Vicky held out her small hand to shake and Roxy immediately noticed its lack of warmth. Another moment and she realised that Vicky didn't smell either. Just a few traces of detergent and city smoke from her clothes. Roxy wanted to ask the obvious question, but hesitated. Of course she was. It would just sound foolish to ask her. Instead, she said, "What happened to your hair? Do you want me to break the arms of the guy who did that to you?"

Vicky frowned and ran her fingers through it irritably before answering, "Yeah I know, it sucks. Thanks for reminding me."

"Why don't you just cut it neater?" Roxy asked.

Vicky looked up at her sideways, "You're new, aren't you?"

"Damn, I knew I'd give myself away eventually." Roxy joked.

"Well congratulations, you got lucky."

"Yeah? How so?"

"You met me," Vicky said simply. "I'm not going to kill you for being a stranger, or screw you around for being ignorant. Some of us vampires really live up to the name you know?"

# Chapter 7

"So we *are* vampires then?" Roxy asked.

Vicky shrugged, "It's as good a word as any. It's a hell of a lot easier to say than Annunaki." She looked over her shoulder at the comatose youth on the floor who gave a small moan, as if on cue. "We should get moving, it doesn't last for long."

"What did you do to him?" Roxy asked as she hurried after Vicky, who was making her way back to the busy main street.

"One of the cooler things we can do. Breathe into their mouth and they pass out for a few minutes. When they wake up, they've also lost the last five minutes or so of their memory. Very useful to cover your feeding." She spoke casually to Roxy as they walked, seemingly unconcerned that she might be over-heard by passers-by.

"Where are we going?" asked Roxy, as they crossed the road.

"Somewhere we can talk. Besides," Vicky smiled impishly up at her, "I fancy a little ride."

Vicky led her to an isolated side street, looking around furtively before making her way towards a shiny new BMW. She raised her hand, punched through the driver's side window and unlocked the door. The air was filled with a tremendous wailing as the alarm system went off. Roxy clutched her ears in pain, her sensitive hearing taken by surprise as Vicky reached in to the car and popped open the bonnet. Then she darted around to the front of the car and leaned over the engine to adjust something. Mercifully, the sound ceased. Then the engine flickered to life and Vicky reappeared, grinning.

"Ready?" she asked, closing the bonnet.

Roxy looked around nervously, then shrugged. In for a penny, in for a pound, she thought, and headed to the passenger side. As she sat down she noticed Vicky pulling shards of glass from between her knuckles and they both watched as the welling blood flow stopped and the cuts healed.

"Neat huh?" murmured Vicky.

"I've seen it already. How much can you heal by the way?"

"Dunno, pretty much anything I think. Unless you get your head chopped off or your heart pulled out."

"So it's true about a stake through the heart then?"

Vicky looked over with a grin, "Not quite, but don't tell everyone." She put the car into gear and pulled away sharply. Roxy reached for the seatbelt but stopped when Vicky glanced at her and rolled her eyes, "Oh, puh-lease. Don't you trust me?"

Roxy felt a little silly, and left the seatbelt alone, although a nagging thought at the back of her mind warned her that peer pressure could be a terrible thing. Ten seconds later she was wishing she had listened to herself. Vicky's driving was wild. She floored the accelerator and wove in and out of traffic, leaving angry drivers blaring their horns behind them. Roxy gripped the seat, expecting to see flashing blue lights behind them at any time, as Vicky screeched around Trafalgar Square, scattering pigeons and pedestrians alike. Roxy saw that she was grinning with delight, but her reactions were good enough to steer them around oncoming traffic without harm. In minutes they were speeding down Embankment heading east and Vicky started to speak.

"So, Roxy," she started, "how long have you been a member of our little club?"

"Um, a few days I think."

"Who is your *parens*?"

Roxy gave her a puzzled look, "My what?"

"Your creator. The one who took you, made you." Vicky explained.

"Oh, I don't know. He just ran off. I think he'd fucked up and was a bit annoyed."

Vicky clicked her tongue and swore softly. It didn't sound promising.

"That's bad, I take it?"

Vicky shrugged and forced a smile, "Maybe. Anyway, as I said I'm Vicky, and I got taken in nineteen seventy-eight by a guy called Antony."

Roxy studied her, noticing for the first time several piercing scars in her ears, nose and lips. She reached up to touch the stud in the side of her own nose, wondering if it and the three in each of her ears would leave similar marks. "What happened to your hair? It's not some vampire fashion I have to follow is it?"

Vicky screwed up her face in annoyance, "Nah. I was a punk rocker. I had the full Mohawk, safety pins in my face, "God Save the Queen" t-shirt and I thought it would last forever." She turned to look at Roxy with a wry smile. "I hope you like the way you look right now, because you're stuck with it."

"Why don't you just cut it back?"

"I used to do that, but every night it reverts back to how it looked when you underwent *nativitas*."

"Nativi-what?"

"Nativitas. It's Latin for 'born' – when you became a vampire. Do you know Latin?"

Roxy shook her head.

"You will. Language changes so quickly that the only way to guarantee that people from different centuries can communicate is to use a dead language, which is kind of ironic in a way, don't you think?"

Although having to learn Latin was probably the most important thing Vicky had just said, all Roxy could think about was her hair. "You mean I'm going to have this haircut forever? It will never grow, and if I cut it, it will grow back overnight?"

"Spot on. The good thing is it will never go grey though, and you can dye it and the colour will stay for ages."

Roxy looked out of the window as the car entered an underpass. "You know, I'm a bit pissed off about that. I loved my hair." Roxy had always intended to grow it straight back, and to be stuck with her current boyish cut struck a deep sense of loss in her.

Vicky gave a humourless chuckle, "You should count yourself lucky. There are some really weird styles out there that look really old-fashioned. Thorkel has to work hard to blend in these days."

"Who's Thorkel?"

"He's the head of my house. Taken sometime around the tenth century I think. He claims to have been a Viking."

Roxy raised her eyebrows, "Shit, that's old. So it's true then? We are immortal?"

"As far as I know. You can still die from injury or sunlight, but not from old age or disease or drowning or whatever. And Thorkel isn't the oldest in the city either. The Abavus is a guy called Catallus, who claims to be nearly a hundred generations old."

"How many years make a generation?"

"Twenty. It's some bullshit points system the elders use. You're not even considered a true vampire until you are three generations. They figure by that time you've gone beyond a human lifespan and have risen above the chattel."

Roxy struggled with the maths for a while, then gave up trying to work out how old Catallus was, instead turning to Vicky, "So you are what, one generation old now?"

"Yeah, pretty much. I've also made it past my first year, so I'm considered posteritas – I have potential, in other words."

"What's so special about one year?"

"Most can't handle the change. They either kill themselves, or are killed by the elders. Another milestone is after a generation, when you see your mortal friends and family growing old, and then after three generations they are dead of old age. All pretty traumatic stuff, which is why the most successful of us are cold-hearted bastards with no ties."

"What else do I need to know?"

"The blood changes us," Vicky continued, "anything is possible if your will is strong enough."

"What do you mean?"

"Your senses, for example, are a gift that all of us share, along with increased strength, resilience and healing. However, no two vampires are alike, and as everyone has different experiences, they will develop unique abilities based upon their personal strength of mind. There are stories of ancients who could fly through the air and destroy cities with a thought."

Roxy remembered the previous night outside her house when the men from the pub had walked past her without so much as a glance. At the time she had been praying for them not to see her. She mentioned it to Vicky, who nodded, "You see? You have started already. Some things, especially for the newly created, are instinctive. A survival trait if you like."

They fell silent as they saw Tower Bridge rising ahead of them, with the Tower of London on the left, floodlit from below to look like a ghostly apparition rising from the earth. Roxy opened her mouth to comment on its beauty, when Vicky suddenly swung to the side as someone pulled out in front of them. Their car fishtailed, its tyres slipping on the wet road with a squeal into oncoming traffic. Vicky struggled with the wheel as a truck bore down on them, horn blaring, and got the car sliding in the opposite direction and onto the pavement. The next thing Roxy knew there was a tremendous bang, and she was hurtled through the windscreen. She bounced off a wall and hit the floor in immense agony as the car spun back toward the road, with Vicky still trapped behind the wheel.

Roxy opened her eyes. I'm alive. I think. Can't feel anything. Can't see clearly either. Is that blood in my eyes? Agh, there's the pain. What's wrong with my legs? They're bent the wrong way. And I shouldn't be able to see my bum should I?

Then she heard laughter and Vicky's face appeared.

"Christ Roxy, you look like shit!"

Fuck you, thought Roxy. I'm fucking dying here and all you can do is laugh. She tried to speak, but couldn't move her mouth. Then Vicky reached down and turned her head the right way around. Roxy's neck started to burn with a dull heat as feeling flooded back into her face, accompanied by an ominous clicking sound. She cried out in pain as Vicky straightened out her legs. The blood flowing down her face cut off like a tap and once again she felt a warming sensation in her legs, mixed with a feeling of intense pins and needles, as her bones and torn flesh knit themselves together. Roxy groaned.

There was another flash of pain as Vicky pulled her into a sitting position, and then it was gone.

"What the fuck?" Roxy stared at her body, cautiously raising a hand to her forehead and feeling a slight fading tenderness, but nothing more. Her clothes were torn, with huge holes in her jeans where she had rolled across the concrete. Drying blood covered her face and t-shirt and small nuggets of glass from the windscreen lay scattered all around.

"Come on sweetie," Vicky hauled Roxy to her feet and started leading her away. Roxy looked back to see several people standing at the side of the road staring at them and winced as a painful hunger swept over her. The BMW was a twisted mess, with its front end crumpled up completely and its wheels twisted, one of them raised off the ground, still spinning slowly and making a laboured metallic rasping. Vicky pulled Roxy into a jog, ignoring the cries of the onlookers behind them and made for the bridge. Roxy followed robotically, dazedly aware that they needed to get away before the police arrived.

They ran for about a quarter of a mile, passing the bridge and Vicky led the way purposefully down a series of streets.

"Where are we going?" asked Roxy.

"We group ourselves into domii, or houses, headed by an elder vampire. Usually everyone in the same house is related to the head vampire; either created by them, or created by one of their creations, et cetera."

"Like a family?"

"Right. Occasionally you get lamia contemptibilis, like you," she continued, giving Roxy an apologetic smile as if she'd said something offensive. "These are vampires with no house. Either their parens deserted them, or died soon after nativitas. In any case, they are alone and generally ignorant of our society."

"What happens to them?" Roxy ventured.

"They get killed usually. Outsiders are not trusted, and without a house to protect you, you're fair game." She turned around and gave Roxy a sinister-looking grin, allowing her fangs to show. She looked suddenly very frightening in the half-light, making Roxy stop involuntarily. Then she laughed, and the moment passed. "I'm just shitting with you Roxy. I'm not going to kill you. There's a guy called Rupert Wolfe I'm taking you to. He's like you, but he's managed to survive long enough to form his own house, made up of other orphans he has scraped together. It's not a great option – his house is still hated – but the alternative is worse."

"Thanks."

"Don't thank me. Just remember you owe me." Vicky gritted her teeth as she said it and Roxy sensed that she was angry with herself for some reason.

"Will this Wolfe take me in then?"

"Well hopefully you won't have to beg too much."

Roxy sighed inwardly. Why couldn't she get lucky, just once in her life? "What's he like?"

Vicky shrugged, walking toward a nearby tube station, "He's an arsehole. He thinks he's some tough nut because he's had a few lucky breaks, but he's just small time."

"Great," Roxy muttered.

Vicky gave her a sympathetic look. "Sorry Roxy. I can't do anything else for you."

"That's okay. Shit happens and I deal with it. So will Wolfe be able to tell me about what I am?"

"Maybe. I wouldn't count on it though. Knowledge is power in this world, and you'll find nobody will tell you anything without wanting something in return. If you want some advice, keep your head down and your mouth shut. There are more laws and ancient traditions that govern us than you'll learn in a hundred years. No one will teach you them, no one will explain them and if you break them, you'll be killed."

# Chapter 8

Rain started to fall as they approached the station, filling the air with the scent of wet grass and concrete. Roxy's thoughts were spinning at the scale of the picture Vicky was painting. She was in way over her head and there was no way out.

They took the tube to Kentish Town in North London. Roxy had dozens of questions, but didn't know how to ask them and besides, there were too many people about, trying not to stare at her tattered, bloodstained clothes. When they emerged above ground they found that the rain was now a torrent, the raindrops bouncing off the ground and drenching the scurrying pedestrians. They ran through the puddle-strewn streets, quickly becoming soaked as they headed for a nightclub several hundred yards from the station. The nightclub, which according to the dazzling neon sign above the door was called Obsession, was owned by Wolfe, and was in a building that had the characteristic glazed terracotta brickwork and high arched windows of a Leslie Green tube station. Large semi-circular windows dominated the upper floor, creating a focal point where people could dance, visible to those on the street below.

A long queue had formed up outside, the customers dressed in a fusion of punk, goth and grunge; dyed hair, torn jeans, leather jackets, tie-dyed shirts, green boots and striped leggings. Sometimes all on one person. Roxy looked at the line of people standing huddled under umbrellas or hunched over with their collars up and swore silently at the thought of having to do the same. Vicky, however, just marched straight up to the door where two very large and very mean-looking men in dark suits were standing. As she approached, they noticed her and stepped aside to let her pass. She jerked her thumb over her shoulder at Roxy and said "Her too," and they were let inside without a word.

It was dark inside and there was a loud thumping coming from upstairs which bored into Roxy's head painfully. Vicky waltzed past the kiosk with a smile and a wave to the woman behind it who was taking the high entrance fees. Roxy hurried to keep up with her, raising her hands to cover her ears. Vicky led the way towards a staircase leading up, taking the grimy concrete steps two at a time. The decor was uniformly black with red lighting, giving the place a surreal, hellish appearance. Ultraviolet lamps made everyone's teeth and eyes glow unnaturally, but Roxy found the atmosphere soothing, especially after the brightness of the tube and dazzling headlamps of the cars. At the top of the stairs was a door and as Vicky pushed it open a wave of noise, heat and sweat assaulted Roxy, who stumbled to the floor in a crumbled heap, clutching her ears and squeezing her eyes shut. She felt herself being lifted and carried somewhere. A moment later the sound lessened. Slowly, the pounding in her head eased and she opened her eyes.

She was lying on a leather settee in a room furnished with a thick red carpet, two cream leather armchairs which matched the settee and a large polished oak desk dominated the wall opposite. There were no windows. The walls were crimson, matching the carpet, which gave the room an oppressive look. Roxy didn't like it very much. Several large, expensive-looking oil paintings in elaborate frames depicted street scenes from the nineteenth century, or sombre men and women in stiff poses. They were gracefully illuminated by uplighters, which also provided the primary lighting for the room. Only a cast iron stand holding four burning candles on one side of the desk provided additional light.

Leaning against the desk was a tall, handsome man with fair, unruly hair, smooth pale skin and an unnerving smirk on his face. He gazed at Roxy with eyes of the clearest blue she had ever seen. He was wearing black leather trousers and a shirt unbuttoned to the navel to reveal his pale hairless chest. To his right stood a short, slender woman. Roxy had to force herself not to stare at her. She had glossy black hair cascading down to her waist, perfect skin the colour of alabaster and dark eyes of a shape she'd never seen before, faintly Asiatic, but too large. You could sink into those dark pools and be lost forever, Roxy thought.

She was vaguely aware of someone beside her, near the door and realised it was Vicky when the man turned his head in her direction and said "What have you brought me, Antonia Thorkelia Victoria?"

Roxy glanced at Vicky, noticing for the first time how dowdy-looking she was, alongside the beautiful pair in front of her, and realised that she must look no better.

Vicky nodded toward Roxy, "Newbie. This is Roxy. She doesn't know her parens and I thought that you might take her in."

This must be Rupert Wolfe, Roxy thought, while he looked her over as if she were something he was considering buying.

He turned to Vicky "I owe you nothing!"

"Of course."

He stared at Roxy a little longer, before turning to the delicate woman at his side, who shrugged.

"Do you wish to be adopted into Domus Wolfe?" he addressed Roxy with an unpleasant smile.

Roxy sensed that this question was loaded with subtle meanings, but she couldn't work out what they were. She had little choice, however. She felt like she was making some diabolic deal when she nodded and replied "I do."

Vicky gave her a faint smile and said, "See you around, Wolfia Roxanne." Then she spun on her heel and slipped out, leaving Roxy to her new family.

# Chapter 9

Roxy looked at Wolfe, who was watching her closely, a sinister smile playing across his lips. The woman fixed Roxy with a piercing stare which seemed to drill right through her, stripping her naked, before she lost interest and turned away.

"My name is Rupert Wolfe, and this," he said, tilting his head in the woman's direction, "is Natalie."

"Hi," Roxy said to Natalie, who gazed back, expressionlessly.

"So then, Roxy," Wolfe lingered over her name, "how old are you?"

"Nineteen...uh, I mean a few days I think."

Wolfe grinned at Natalie, who took a seat in one of the leather armchairs. She was tiny and seemed to be engulfed by the large chair as she curled her feet beneath her. "I guess you're not the baby any more, Nat?"

Natalie looked up at him and parted her scarlet lips in a smile, "Hurrah for that," she said softly, her voice like wind resonating in crystal pipes, with a curious lilting accent that Roxy couldn't place.

Wolfe folded his arms across his chest. "Well then, Roxy. Here's the situation. You are an unclaimed vampire, deserted by your parens, ignorant and confused and lucky to have survived this long. Correct?"

Roxy shifted uncomfortably, "Well I wouldn't necessarily..."

"Without a parens you have no house," Wolfe interrupted, "and without a house you are nothing. You could be killed out of hand and no one would care. You have no rights to feed and nowhere to rest. No one will grant you passage or hospitality, and without introduction, no one will speak to you or for you. You are lamia contemptibilis, infamari, an orphan and a bastard, and no one wants you."

Roxy stared at Wolfe, speechless under his verbal attack. Then he smiled and softened his voice, changing his entire demeanour to one of an understanding, comforting relative, "On the other hand, if you were part of my house you would have the protection of a nomen and the support of your brothers and sisters." He opened his arms towards her and stepped closer. Roxy was fascinated by the way he moved. He reminded her of a great cat, stalking its prey – each movement calculated and deliberate. It took her a few seconds to realise he was still talking to her, "...these things do not come without a price."

"*There's* a surprise," she replied, her attention back to where it should be. She was negotiating for her life. "What do you want?"

"You will swear allegiance to me and in return for your total loyalty I will give you my nomen and teach you what you are and what you can do."

Roxy licked her lips. She had no idea what a nomen was, but she understood the gist of the offer. She'd be accepting him as some kind of leader, and would be forever in his debt in return for protection and education. The thing she didn't know was what kind of favours he would call on her to perform. She had seen many such agreements made on the streets when she'd been homeless, often made by pimps to young, desperate women. She'd managed to avoid making such deals herself through sheer stubbornness, and received punishment because of it, but this was different. Punishment wouldn't mean receiving a beating and robbery, but death by people who didn't fear the law. And if what she had heard about vampires was true, then she could be in his debt for a very long time indeed. Wolfe was staring at her, allowing her time to reach the conclusion he knew she'd reach. He had phrased the offer very carefully, so there was only one reply she could give. Roxy knew it, and hated it, but said it anyway. "Okay, I accept."

He came closer until their faces were almost touching. She could smell his cologne and traces of old blood about him but where hot breath ought to be caressing her lips there was nothing except a ripple of cool air as he whispered, "Are you sure?"

Hell no, she thought. In fact she was sure that this was a very bad idea, but she nodded nonetheless. He pulled away from her.

"Good. Now you need to prove your loyalty, to seal our bargain in the traditional way. In blood."

Roxy looked up at him warily. "Okay."

Wolfe smiled – sharp, pointed teeth visible between his lips making Roxy shiver involuntarily. "Raise your chin and offer me your throat."

Roxy swallowed. Was he going to kill her anyway? She glanced at Natalie, who was staring implacably at the two of them. Is she remembering her own experience? Roxy wondered. Reluctantly, she raised her chin and tilted her head to the side to expose her neck. Her whole body tensed up, ready to flee as Wolfe bent over her. His hand reached up to lightly cradle the back of her head. Roxy felt that any resistance on her part would cause his grip to tighten to prevent her from escaping. The feeling of helplessness made her dizzy as he slowly lowered his mouth to her neck. It took every trembling effort she possessed to remain still as his teeth made contact with her skin, and if it hadn't been for her thoughts jumping suddenly to Claudia, she knew she would have struggled as he bit down and pierced her skin. She was doing this for her daughter. She needed to protect her, and raise her, and she couldn't do it if she was dead. She would accept Wolfe's rules and play his game for now, and for as long as it took until Claudia was old enough to look after herself. She recited this in her head, a mantra to keep the terror at bay. She felt Wolfe sucking unhurriedly, taking a mouthful, then another, before he pulled back, stopping a dribble of her blood from escaping down his chin with a finely manicured finger. Roxy noticed the blood was so dark it was nearly black. It bothered her that she had black blood. Wolfe looked down at her with a smile, "Welcome to Domus Wolfe."

"You will find you'll come to enjoy it, I promise you. No curse ever carried such rewards. We are immortal. The lords of the dead and masters of the night. We bow to no one, and take anything we desire." Wolfe's voice was seductive, and filled Roxy with a sense of awe tinged with arrogance that was hard to ignore.

"Why doesn't everyone know about us?" she asked quietly.

"Ah, but they do, my child, they do. Every year more films and books are produced about vampires and ghosts and werewolves. It isn't that humans do not know about us, but rather that they refuse to believe. Their conscious minds reject us, because they know, deep down, that to admit it is to live in perpetual terror. It is the same blindness that makes people return to their homes at the foot of a volcano after an eruption. This is what hides us more effectively than any efforts on our part. Reveal yourself to a mortal, and before the night is out he will have convinced himself that you must have played a trick on him, and will press you to reveal the truth. But if you convince him utterly with irrefutable evidence, he will shrink from reality. Insane he will become! Even if he manages to resist his inevitable slide, others around him will consider him mad and shun him. The isolation he suffers will then finish the job you started and you will be safe once more." His demeanour changed from that of a serious, learned teacher, to a playful child as he broke into a grin, "I've done it to several people myself. It's great fun!"

Roxy pressed herself deeper into the soft leather sofa and glanced nervously at Natalie who was watching her inscrutably. She was starting to wonder whether Wolfe himself was slightly insane. All her instincts were screaming at her to leave. This was a thoroughly dangerous individual, made even more so by any number of unknown powers he might have. She forced herself to smile and share the joke as he laughed, and hoped that she hadn't done anything to hurt Scarlet by telling her.

"Have you had any dreams?" he asked suddenly, all mirth gone. Roxy took a few moments to follow his mood change and shook her head in confusion. He turned abruptly and strode to his chair and sat down.

"You will return tomorrow, and I shall introduce you to the other members of Domus Wolfe."

Roxy frowned. Scarlet had to work tomorrow and wouldn't be able to baby-sit for Claudia. She opened her mouth to object, but Wolfe continued as he picked up a gold fountain pen and pulled a piece of paper toward him, "In a few days, there will be a gathering of the Houses of London. There I will announce you and throw you to the mercy of the Lords. With my patronage they may allow you to live."

That didn't sound very good at all.

"I can't make it tomorrow," she started to say. Wolfe's face changed, and his suave smile became a feral snarl. He leapt to his feet faster than she could follow and seemed to loom over her from his position behind the desk. The room seemed darker and colder, as if a cloud had passed overhead on a winter's day, and she cowered reflexively back into the leather cushions.

"How dare you!" he shouted, "I have accepted your miserable hide into my house and have taken of your blood. You are beholden to me now. I command you in all things and you will accept my wishes without question. Do I make myself clear?" He glared at her from across the room, but she sensed that he could strike her at any time, regardless of the distance between them.

She nodded hurriedly, "I-I'm sorry," she stammered.

Immediately his mood changed and he sat down as if nothing had happened. The room seemed light and warm again.

"You may go," he said flatly, retrieving his pen without looking at her. "Be here tomorrow, an hour after sundown."

# Chapter 10

Roxy arrived home in the early hours of the morning, glad to be away from the noisy club and its unstable owner. Scarlet had been too tired to ask any questions, for which Roxy was grateful, but she was annoyed when Roxy told her she had to go back the next night.

"Shit Rox, I can't do this for you again tomorrow. You know that. I've got to work. You were supposed to look after Leah too!"

"I know, I'm sorry. I'll work something out." Actually, Roxy didn't have a clue what to do. If she didn't show up there was no way she could go back afterwards. Not to Wolfe, anyway.

"Why don't you go home now and I'll give you a call later?" Roxy suggested.

"Fine," Scarlet sighed, "but I'm not changing my mind on this."

Roxy didn't push the issue and helped Scarlet to get Leah bundled up and leave before sinking into the chair to think.

Roxy woke to the sound of Claudia screaming. The clock showed that it was now nearly three in the afternoon. Roxy was sick with shock and staggered to Claudia's room. She had no idea how long Claudia had been crying, but she'd been trapped in her cot all day without any food. Her nappy was huge, and the bed was wet under her where it had leaked. Roxy picked her up and held her while she stripped it off and murmured soothing words to her. The nappy was full of excrement but Roxy dropped it to the floor, uncaring that it might stain the carpet and hurried to the kitchen to warm up some milk.

Claudia clung to her tightly, digging her nails into her mother's back as she wailed, not yet ready to relax. Roxy gave her a bottle of cold milk while she waited for the kettle to boil and Claudia grabbed it desperately and started drinking immediately. She was so hungry. Her face was red and raw from tears and her throat was swollen from crying all day. She also had a bruise on her head and Roxy guessed that she'd fallen while trying to get out of her cot. How could I have slept through that? She prepared another bottle, and set it in a bath of the hot water to warm up for when Claudia had finished. She really wanted a microwave to save time, but that was just another thing on her wish list she couldn't afford. She held onto Claudia long after she had calmed down, cursing her negligence and quietly weeping pink-tinged tears.

At some point she realised her drowsiness had gone. Claudia had apparently forgiven her, helped by a biscuit, and was clamouring to be let down to play with her toys. Roxy went over to the window. Daylight was filtering through the curtains, and she frowned in confusion. She'd started to think that daylight was the reason for her unnatural sleepiness, as she had previously only woken up at dusk, and had fallen asleep at dawn. Now though, she felt very awake. Maybe shock and maternal instincts were keeping her alert? She reached cautiously for the curtain and had barely parted them when searing pain shot down her arm. She hissed in agony and jerked her hand away, clutching her wrist, which had already turned an angry red colour where the sunlight had touched it. She retreated from the window and sat on the floor, nursing her wrist and waiting for the pain to subside. She kept expecting the wound to heal before her eyes, but nothing happened, and the pain didn't go away either. Eventually she got up and went into the kitchen to wrap it in a bandage, which helped ease the pain somewhat. Happy now? She chided herself, and resolved to stay away from sunlight in future.

She spent the rest of the day tidying up, making dinner for Claudia and going through her mail. The phone company was threatening to cut her off again, and she had a final demand for the electricity. Since she had left her last gig in a bit of a rush she hadn't been paid in nearly a week, and she knew that Clive had taken her tips to pay for what she did to his sink. She needed to find a way of getting some money soon, which didn't look likely the way Wolfe was talking.

She was still trying to work out what to do when Scarlet knocked on the door. It was dusk, but the sky was still light enough to make Roxy nervous as she let her in. She felt a slight, uncomfortable tingle as she opened the door, which made her glad to close it again and retreat from the punishing sun.

"What are you doing here?" Roxy asked once they were inside.

"I tried calling, but your mobile was turned off and your landline has been disconnected."

"What?" Roxy grabbed the red bill from the phone company and read the date. It was nearly a week old and had been delivered when she was sick. Great, she thought moodily. It'd cost her to reconnect, and her mobile was still at Clive's.

Scarlet sat on the edge of the couch without taking off her coat. She was dressed and made up for a gig. "Look Roxy, I've managed to get my mum to look after Leah tonight so that you don't have to. I'm sorry I can't get her to look after Claudia as well, but it was hard enough as it was to get her to agree to have Leah."

Roxy knew that Scarlet suffered a strained relationship with her mother, who didn't approve of her choice of career. It was not as if Scarlet had had many places to turn after her husband left her with the baby and a ton of debt, but her mother didn't see it that way. Roxy knew it must have taken quite a lot for Scarlet to ask her mother to do this, and they had probably argued for a long time.

"I understand. Don't worry, I'll be okay," Roxy assured her. Scarlet didn't look convinced, but nodded and left for work anyway. Roxy changed and fed Claudia and wondered what to do. She would have to leave in the next five or ten minutes in order to meet Wolfe's deadline. There was nothing for it. She would have to take Claudia with her.

When she reached the club just after nine, the neon sign reading "Obsession" was dark and no lights were visible through the upstairs window. She crossed the empty street to reach the club, cradling a sleeping Claudia against her chest and wondered if she had got her days mixed up. The door was closed, so she banged on it with her fist. It was opened a few moments later by one of the bouncers she had seen the night before. He recognised her immediately and stepped aside respectfully to let her in. "Mr. Wolfe is in the downstairs bar miss," he said, and gestured down a dark concrete corridor behind him. Roxy was somewhat taken off-guard – she wasn't accustomed to being spoken to in that way. It was quite charming really, she thought, as she gave him a smile and walked in. She might get used to this.

She stepped cautiously into a dimly lit dance area, smaller than the one upstairs. A dark wooden bar occupied one side of the room, while tables and chairs lurked in the shadows against the other three walls, leaving the middle of the room empty. Roxy counted about ten people in the room, scattered between the bar and tables. They were all staring at her. With a sudden rush, as if she had stood up too quickly, she realised that most of them were vampires. She didn't know how she knew at the time, but later found that it was relatively easy to spot vampires, if you were another vampire, that is. It was the tiny, subtle differences that gave them away; their stillness, for example. Humans constantly move, even when asleep. They twitch, breathe, shuffle in their seats to find a more comfortable position, scratch and so on. Scarlet had already pointed out that Roxy didn't blink very often, which was remarkable of her, as most people wouldn't notice. Rather their subconscious mind would start to get edgy, which they'd misinterpret as fear or excitement.

Roxy stared at each one in turn, identifying seven that she thought were vampires. Nothing was said, but in a single movement, all seven abruptly rose and started to walk slowly toward her. There were two women approaching from the bar, dressed in high heels and spaghetti-strap tops; one blonde, one brunette. Next were three men, one in a suit, the other two more casually dressed. Then a short black woman with tightly-wound corn-row hair and a tall skinny man who reeked of incense and marijuana.

Claudia stirred and woke up, and their attention snapped from Roxy to her. They stared at Claudia with hungry eyes that made Roxy's skin crawl and she backed away a step. As they glided closer the two party-girls started making a low, hissing sound and circled around behind her to prevent her escape. The others spread out in front and to her sides. Roxy tried to speak, to tell them that Wolfe was expecting her, but she found that she couldn't move. The suited man was staring into her eyes and she couldn't look away. They were twin black holes, sucking her in. She could only flinch as cold hands stretched out to paw at her, pulling at her clothes and stroking Claudia's hair. They were all hissing now, their different vocal pitches intertwining to create a dissonant rasping like sand slipping down the face of a dune.

A squeal of fear from Claudia suddenly released her and she shuddered, breaking the gaze of the vampire in the suit. He looked surprised as she lashed out at one of the other men, her body suddenly flushing hot. She caught the man square on the nose with her fist, lifting him clear off the ground as if she had thrown him, but he was moving much too slowly. She recognised that the same thing was happening that had occurred at the pub after she broke the sink. She was moving faster than natural, and her reactions had speeded up accordingly, making everything else seem slower. All except the two party-girls, who seemed to be moving at the same speed as her and reached out as she turned towards the exit. Roxy shrugged them off and sidestepped around the skinny man, who was staring motionlessly towards the still airborne vampire. There was a sudden blur before her eyes, and the other man materialised in front of her. So fast! She tried to dodge around him, but ended up in front of the blonde woman, who grabbed her arm so tightly that Roxy's fingers went numb. Roxy was aware of several upturned heads, their mouths wide to reveal long, sharp fangs poised to bite, when a commanding voice carried across the room from beyond the bar.

"Enough!"

Everyone froze. A second later there was a loud crashing of splintering wood as the vampire she had punched landed heavily on a table about fifteen feet away. Wolfe was standing at the far end of the bar, with the diminutive Natalie beside him. She looked bored and drifted over to a table in the corner as Wolfe strode towards them. The other vampires quailed and withdrew from Roxy at his approach. He glared at them, a pale sepulchral glow seeming to emanate from his eyes and his lips curled back to reveal pointed teeth. The man Roxy had punched rose to his feet behind Wolfe and started to run towards her with a snarl, ignoring the reaction of everyone else. His humiliation had driven all reason from his mind and now he wanted revenge. Roxy braced herself for the attack, but he had only taken a couple of steps when Wolfe rounded on him, grabbed him by the throat and hoisted him into the air before she could blink.

The vampire kicked and struggled as Wolfe brought his free hand up in a lazy arc. Roxy caught a brief glimpse of long, curved nails on the end of Wolfe's fingers before they dug into the suspended vampire's face and ripped it off.

# Chapter 11

Blood rained everywhere and when Wolfe's hand came away holding a scrap of flesh Roxy saw the exposed jawbone and subcutaneous muscles twitching as an agonised scream filled the air. Wolfe dropped the vampire to the floor, who immediately put his hands to his face to support his eyeball which had popped out of its socket and was dangling against his cheek. For a time, the only sound was the whimpering of this creature, which slowly subsided as his face started to heal. Then Wolfe turned to Roxy.

"What is that?" Wolfe demanded, raising a clawed finger toward Claudia, who was clutching Roxy tightly like a monkey in the presence of a snake.

"She's mine," Roxy answered warily, ready to flee at the slightest sign that he would try to take her away. Her body was wound up like a spring, and helplessness filled her as she contemplated her chances of leaving alive against his wishes. He had dispatched his follower with ease and it was clear that the others feared him too. He stared at her for a moment, then broke into a grin, threw his head back and laughed.

"If you've claimed her then so be it!" He turned to the rest, "This is Roxy everyone, our newest sister. No one kills her, or her...pet, without my permission." He was still chuckling as he said this. The others glared at her with hostility and suspicion. Wolfe started to call out their names by way of introduction, but she barely paid attention. She noticed Wolfe didn't introduce the two human women now fawning over Dave, the man with the ruined face, who were obviously not panicked about the extreme violence they had just witnessed or surprised that he had now healed completely. The barman was clearing up the broken furniture, equally unconcerned by the events, apart from his obvious irritation at the mess.

Wolfe turned, and with a jerk of his head, indicated for the other man, James, to follow him to the office beside the bar. Roxy scowled, annoyed that he had left her there alone after only the most cursory of introductions. The others stared at her for a few moments, until the tall, skinny man broke into a grin, raised an imaginary glass to her, and turned back to his table. The blonde woman gave Roxy a strange smile, her eyes lingering on Claudia, before returning to the bar. Her friend followed her immediately, with a slight nod to Roxy. The remaining two approached Roxy. She was several inches taller than the man in the suit, and twice that over the woman. Both stared at Claudia first, before looking up at Roxy. The man gave her a charming smile, flashing dazzling white teeth at her. Roxy was a little nervous about looking into his eyes, but he didn't appear threatening now. The woman wore a thoughtful, guarded expression.

"A pleasure to meet you, Roxy," began the man, holding out his hand, "I am Sanjay and this is Ruth." He had a clear Knightsbridge accent and spoke in a smooth, relaxing tone that made Roxy feel as if she were the only woman in the room and she experienced an unexpected flush of pleasure. She took his hand quickly, not wanting to appear impolite, and immediately felt a seductive tingle race down her arm and caress her from within. She blinked to clear her vision and pulled her hand away. The sensation lingered for a moment, then faded away. He watched her reaction with a knowing smile. Ruth gave her a nod in greeting, but thankfully did not offer her hand.

"Allo Roxy," she said, in a slight French accent, "is this your child?"

Claudia was wide awake now, and was twisting round in Roxy's arms, trying to get a better look at what was going on. "That's right."

Ruth shook her head slightly as she looked at Claudia. "It was a mistake to bring her," she muttered. Sanjay however, reached out a finger for Claudia to grasp and stroked her hair, making cooing noises. Roxy didn't much like the idea of his touching her, so moved away, disguising it as sitting down on a chair. Ruth and Sanjay followed, taking seats on either side of her.

"When were you taken?" asked Ruth.

"Taken?"

"Made, created, became a vampire," she explained impatiently. "We use slang words to describe the creation to avoid awkward questions from mortals who might overhear us. The same goes for feeding and other aspects of our business. We sometimes refer to ourselves as the Taken."

"About three days ago I think. How about you?"

"Nineteen sixty-seven," Ruth answered tonelessly.

Roxy looked at Sanjay, who said nothing. When she prompted him, he merely smiled and said "Ah now, I don't wish to reveal all of my secrets do I? Suffice to say that I was the fourth to join Domus Wolfe."

Roxy glanced around the room. "What about the others?"

Sanjay adjusted his cuffs, "Wolfe found James, his number two, then Ruth, followed by myself." He glanced over his shoulder at the blonde woman, "After that we got Jessica, the darling of the chattering classes, right before Marty. Dave and Sarah came together, then recently Natalie. Now you make us ten."

"Is that a lot? Compared to other houses?"

"We are larger than many," Ruth cut in, "but there are others, both larger and more powerful than us. I do not suppose we will remain ten for long," she turned a baleful eye on Claudia, "the weak and the foolish do not survive long."

Roxy bristled, but couldn't deny that Ruth had a point.

Jessica appeared, followed by Sarah, who gave Roxy a warm, friendly smile. Roxy almost smiled back, but was more concerned with Jessica, whose smile wasn't quite so warm, or friendly.

"What a delightful creature!" she exclaimed, and suddenly reached down to grab Claudia, pulling her out of Roxy's protective arms.

"No!" Roxy jumped to her feet and tried to take her back, her insides twisting and rushing away like meltwater, but Jessica whirled away from her, laughing. Claudia started to scream, which made Jessica laugh even harder.

"Give her back...please!" Roxy begged, noticing Dave sneering at her from across the room, clearly enjoying her discomfort. Claudia screamed louder, kicking and writhing in an attempt to get away, but Roxy was frozen with panic, not wanting to provoke Jessica into hurting her.

"Give her back Jessica," Sanjay stood up.

"Yes, please Jess, it's not funny," Sarah seemed to be upset. Jessica ignored both of them, twirling around on the spot and laughing at Claudia.

"What a gift you've brought us Roxy," sang Jessica. "I hardly know what to say."

Roxy swayed, and grabbed a chair to stop herself falling. She desperately searched for the words that would save her daughter, but she could only silently mouth the words "No, please".

Then Natalie approached and held out her hands.

"Give the child to me," she whispered softly. Jessica immediately stopped laughing, and handed Claudia over to her. Natalie cradled Claudia for a moment, looking at her strangely. Claudia stopped screaming and gazed back. Everyone in the room fell silent, staring at them. Roxy's chest was tight, her legs weak, expecting something awful was about to happen. Then, to her shock and relief, Natalie turned and held Claudia out to her, looking up at her with a slight smile on her ruby lips. Roxy took her in trembling arms, and time seemed to resume again. Jessica turned back to the bar without a word, followed by Sarah, and Natalie was already on her way back to her corner table before Roxy had a chance to thank her. Everyone was acting as if nothing had happened.

Then Wolfe and James emerged from the office. Wolfe walked over to sit with Natalie, but James headed straight for Roxy.

"A word, if you please, Roxy," he said. He guided Roxy a few paces back toward the wall, and then gestured impatiently at Claudia. "What is this?"

"This is my daughter," replied Roxy defiantly, still shaking but her fear now turning to anger. She was expecting a furious reply, so his response surprised her. He simply closed his eyes briefly as if pained and when he opened them again, his voice had taken on a softer, more sympathetic tone.

"You cannot keep her."

"Why not?" asked Roxy stubbornly, not quite ready to let her temper fade.

"Lots of reasons," he said gently. "Firstly, you're dead. Love cannot sustain you any more. Secondly think of the practical problems. You have to sleep during the day. The child will need to go to school eventually, have birthday parties, go to the beach. You cannot take her. Finally, and most importantly, she is mortal. You are not. Mortals cannot know of us. They cannot love us. She will betray you, and that will put us all in danger."

Roxy stared at him, each word cutting into her like a knife. "She's just a baby," he whispered. She knew he was probably right, but the thought of losing her was unbearable. It must have shown in her eyes because James' gaze became one of pity.

"You have to let her go, Roxy. You place her in danger by bringing her into this world. There are many among us who would kill her to get to you, or simply for fun." Roxy noticed his eyes flick towards Jessica, who was staring at them with a disturbing intensity. "Take a few days," he continued, "even a week or so, but do it soon. The longer you leave it the harder it will become. The same goes for your family and friends. Remember you are dead. Let them think it too."

Roxy looked down at Claudia, who was reaching out towards James with a frown on her face, and felt tears threatening. "Fine," she said thickly. He nodded once, then turned away, leaving Claudia grasping empty air with an indignant cry.

Roxy stood there for a while composing herself, and wasn't sure what to do next. Wolfe was talking animatedly with Natalie, not seeming to notice that she wasn't listening. Sanjay and Ruth were at a table with the unkempt Marty, deep in conversation, occasionally casting a glance in her direction. Jessica and Sarah were at the bar and James was crouched next to Dave, who was still sitting on the floor while the two mortal women hovering around him. James was obviously trying to calm him down, but as Roxy watched, Dave raised hate-filled eyes towards her, so clear and unrestrained it made her feel sick. She looked away hurriedly. He would never forgive her, she realised. Not only had she beaten him in a fight, he had been humiliated by Wolfe in front of everyone when he tried to retaliate. She made a mental note not to be alone with Dave if she could help it. Not wanting to interrupt Wolfe, and since Jessica gave her the creeps, she wandered over to the table where Sanjay, Ruth and Marty were seated.

"Mind if I join you?" she asked.

Sanjay rose and pulled out a chair for her in a gentlemanly fashion. Ruth sat opposite her and Marty, who was busily involved in rolling a cigarette, merely tilted his head and said "Evening," before pulling out some more paper to roll another. Well I don't suppose he has to worry about lung cancer any more, she thought idly. Marty offered her one.

"No thanks," she declined, "I never really got into that habit."

Marty lowered his eyes, and she followed his gaze to the needle-scarred hollow of her elbow. Feeling self-conscious, she moved Claudia to conceal them, wondering if they would ever fade now. Marty turned his attention back to his roll-ups, saying nothing. Roxy held Claudia close anyway, unwilling to let her run around freely. She wriggled at first, eager to get down, but was quickly distracted by Sanjay who started playing with her.

Roxy shuffled in her seat, absently running her hand through her hair and realised she had forgotten to spike it with gel as she normally did. I must have had other things on my mind, she thought bitterly to herself.

"What did you do to your hand?" asked Ruth sharply, interrupting her thoughts. Roxy glanced at her bandaged wrist and gave Ruth an embarrassed smile.

"Sunburn, I think."

Ruth's mouth dropped open, and Marty raised his eyes to look at her with an expression of intense curiosity. "You can stay awake during the day?" she asked.

Roxy noticed the calculating look in Marty's eyes, and became aware of a stillness in Ruth and Sanjay, and suddenly decided that she didn't want to admit to that. Was there something wrong with her? Or was it something they found threatening? She shook her head a little too quickly and tried to sound convincing. "No, I think I fell asleep with the curtains slightly open. It was like this when I woke up, under the bed somehow."

That seemed to satisfy them, and Ruth sat back, nodding. "It is instinctive for us to hide from the sun. Do not worry, it will heal eventually. Maybe a week or so."

Roxy nodded, glad to hear that. Anxious to change the subject, she asked "So how many of us are there in the city?"

Sanjay looked up from teasing Claudia, "No one knows for sure, but hundreds at least."

"Hundreds?" It shouldn't really surprise her, she thought. London was a city of over seven million people. If anything, she should have expected more.

"There are twenty recognised houses in the city," Sanjay continued, "essentially different families, each with a territory carved out for themselves. In addition there are dozens of other individuals, who try to stay out of the way. Wolfe has claimed this club and the surrounding area for himself. We are allowed to feed here, and you'll be fairly safe once you get known."

"What about other places?" Roxy asked.

"You take your chances. You'll get to know where you can go and where to avoid. A lot of the other houses don't like us. They consider us pariahs and attack us on sight."

Roxy nodded. It was a bit like the gangs she grew up trying to avoid. Great. She had hated that time of her life. She was about to ask something else when Wolfe shouted across the room to her. "Hey Roxy, get your lanky arse over here!"

She pulled Claudia close and rose from the table. As she did so, Sanjay caught her eye and mouthed "Be careful." As if she needed the warning. She walked over to Wolfe, adding a brazen swagger to her stride. These people didn't respond to weakness. Natalie and James sat on either side of Wolfe, who motioned for her to take the seat opposite. All three eyed her intently as she sat down.

"How are you Roxy?" Wolfe's voice was warm and gracious, but it wasn't reflected in his eyes. Roxy looked away. Claudia was fidgeting and Roxy felt terribly exposed and vulnerable. Wolfe seemed to find her discomfort amusing. James looked on expressionlessly, and Natalie regarded her with an air of mild curiosity. Roxy found herself staring at her flawless, oval face.

"I'm fine." Actually she was confused, scared, bitter and miserable, but she doubted that Wolfe would want to hear that.

"Good. I want to take you to a meeting on Friday."

Great, she thought, more time off work. "What meeting?"

"Well more of a soiree, really. The Primus has called a Gathering. It will give me an opportunity to introduce you to him, and to everyone else." Wolfe smiled. "He might order you killed. I don't know. I'm kind of interested to find out myself."

Roxy stared at him incredulously.

"We are getting a little big, you see," he explained, grinning widely. "Then again, he didn't bat an eye when Natalie joined us. Maybe he has finally accepted that this is the right place for strays like you? Just don't worry about what the other houses are saying."

Roxy didn't want to ask what the other houses were saying.

"Are you hungry?" Wolfe asked.

Roxy swallowed, "Yes." Now that he had mentioned it, the ache in her stomach was hard to ignore. Wolfe picked up an empty glass from the table and placed it in front of him.

"Soon I shall teach you how to hunt for yourself, but for now, this will suffice." He raised his wrist to his mouth, bared his fangs and bit into it. Then he held the wound over the glass and drizzled blood into it. The smell hit her at once. She could feel her body tightening in anticipation, her eyes widening, her teeth sharpening and extending. She watched entranced as the blood level rose slowly in the glass. When he had filled the glass half way, he stopped and licked his wrist before pushing the glass towards her. Wolfe, James and Natalie were looking at her in a strange way, and as she reached for the glass she noticed that Jessica and Sarah were also watching her. She made a bet with herself that more eyes were fixed on her, but she didn't turn to check. She drank the cool blood. It was gorgeous. It sated her immediately, and was just what her body demanded. It was strong but refreshing, smooth but had a meaty quality that eased her hunger. She drank it down and held the glass to her lips long after she had finished, trying to get more dregs from the sides of the glass. Eventually she put the glass down and looked back at Wolfe. Straight into his eyes. She felt no fear, no caution; only confidence and strength. She raised a finger to wipe the last traces blood from her lips and felt that her skin was warm. Her whole body was singing.

Wolfe reached out and retrieved the glass from her with a sly grin. "Did you enjoy that?"

She nodded, needlessly.

"Good. Now I have given, so must you. Give me your wrist."

Roxy held out her wrist immediately. He took it with a cold, firm grip and raised it to his mouth. Roxy gasped as his teeth plunged into her skin and watched as he took a delicate sip of her blood. Then he released her, and sat back, licking his lips. Roxy looked at the two pinpricks of blood on her wrist, an inch apart, and was unable to resist licking them clean.

"I will also need you here on Thursday. Wear something you can run in, and leave the sprog at home."

"Thursday *and* Friday? I can't. I have to work," she protested, the blood making her overly bold. She knew as she was saying it that she should be careful, but she couldn't help herself. The blood was as dangerous a drug as heroin, she realised, and just as addictive. The only difference was she couldn't kick the blood. She needed it to stay alive.

Wolfe rolled his eyes and shook his head with a smile. Then he reached into his pocket and pulled out a loose stack of folded notes and tossed them towards her. It was more than she earned in a month.

"Be there. And don't forget the baby sitter."

# Chapter 12

She seemed to have been dismissed, and left the table, clutching Claudia tightly. People were starting to filter in, staff by the look of them, which meant the club was probably about to open. She didn't feel like hanging around until the music started, but on the other hand she hadn't really learnt anything apart from a few names. She drifted back across the dance floor with a sense that she had wasted her time, when Sanjay appeared at her shoulder.

"Are you free now?" he asked, softly.

"I suppose so," Roxy answered, glancing down at him. "Wolfe just told me to come back on Thursday. What's happening on Thursday?"

"I have no idea. He likes to keep things close to his chest. The only one he talks to is James."

"And Natalie."

Sanjay gave her a puzzled look, then tilted his head in thought and nodded. "Anyway, I know we all have to be here. He told us just before you arrived."

The speakers started to blare out twangy electric guitar chords leading into a Nirvana song. Roxy felt her head throb. Sanjay touched her arm to get her attention, and led the way towards a door marked "NO UNAUTHORISED ENTRY", opening it to reveal a set of descending stairs. Roxy followed him, relieved that the music was now muffled by the heavy door and distance.

The steps were bare concrete, and the staircase was unlit, but dim electric bulbs at the bottom provided enough illumination to see that it led down to the old train platform. She reached the bottom and stepped onto the rough floor of a long, narrow room, about eighty feet long and ten wide. Litter and rubble lay strewn about and huddled in the darker corners. The tiled walls were peppered with faded posters depicting smiling rosy-cheeked people holding spades and "Digging for Victory", or telling the viewer to "Be like dad, keep mum". The name embossed every twenty feet read "South Kentish Town". Where the track should have been there was now a brick wall, mildewed and cracked with age, running the entire length of the room. A deep rumbling noise emanated from behind it, growing steadily louder, which made Claudia squirm nervously.

"What's that?"

"It's the Northern Line. The track on the other side of that wall is still used. It's the section between Camden Town and Kentish Town. Funny isn't it? You probably went right past on your way here tonight."

Roxy looked around, "What is this place?"

"It was once South Kentish Town station," Sanjay explained. "It has been closed since the mid-twenties. During the Second World War, the platform was removed and sealed from the track to make it a bomb shelter. Wolfe now uses these underground rooms as emergency quarters."

Roxy nodded slowly. "Are there a lot of these old stations about?" She asked after the train had passed. She was slightly disturbed that the vibrations had caused dust to fall from the ceiling.

"Dozens. You wouldn't believe how many. And then there are other chambers designed as storage rooms or train depots that were never even used. Some of them we had made for us deliberately and then had the records destroyed. There is a whole city down here now."

He turned towards a door which was protected by an electronic entry lock. He keyed in a four figure number that Roxy couldn't see, and pushed the door open. The room beyond was fairly large and contained a couple of couches, four battered-looking armchairs and two low wooden tables, badly in need of varnishing. A thin, not quite threadbare carpet covered the floor, and the lime-green walls showed faded patches where various posters had once hung. The far corner contained a large television and a DVD recorder. The muted up-lights which Sanjay switched on softened the room's appearance, and the heat pouring out of the heavy radiators gave it a comforting, cosy feel. With the door locked shut behind her, Roxy reluctantly let Claudia down to play, but kept most of her attention on Sanjay, acutely aware that she was alone with him, and far from potential help. Roxy looked round at the room as she lowered herself into an armchair, surprised that Wolfe hadn't bothered to re-furnish it, given the lavish attention he gave to his office upstairs.

Sanjay took a seat on one of the couches opposite to her and said, "I thought you'd be happier down here. The others can take a bit of getting used to. We don't trust newcomers."

Roxy looked across at him, pulling her legs up under her, "Why not?"

"Competition," he said simply. "Each vampire needs to feed and needs territory, like all predators. Someone will always lose out when our numbers increase."

"Is that why Wolfe said that the Primus might kill me?" she asked.

"That, and because you are increasing Wolfe's power. He's probably made it seem like he's doing you a really big favour by taking you in, but really you are the one helping him. All credit to him, he has forged himself a House out of nothing by adopting the cast-offs the other houses throw away, but now he is getting too strong. The other houses don't like it. As far as I can tell it is unprecedented. Before Wolfe, we would have been killed out of hand without a parens to speak for us. Most people, including myself, think that he must have something on Catallus to have got this far."

"You mean blackmail?"

Sanjay gave her a cold smile. "It's the only currency that means a damn. That and what you owe. Everyone owes somebody something. We all owe Wolfe our lives, for example."

"Why are you telling me all this?" Roxy asked, suddenly suspicious.

Sanjay leaned forward, "Ah, you're quick. Good. I've seen Wolfe take in several new vampires now and I remember how it was with me. He will tell you nothing. He will dole out knowledge as if it were his finest jewels, and make you beg for every snippet. After ten years, you might be ready to hold a conversation with another house without embarrassing yourself, but you will not know a fraction of the things you are capable of. Dave and Sarah have been taken for nearly fifteen years now, yet you still bested him easily tonight. Jessica has made Sarah her slave, and Sarah doesn't even realise it. However, I am willing to help you. To teach you in ways that Wolfe will not."

"In return for what?" Roxy narrowed her eyes.

"For a favour, of course." Sanjay chuckled. "You are an investment. I will offer you something you desperately need, and in return you will owe me."

"You're being very open about all this?" Roxy said, wondering if she was missing something.

"Ah yes," Sanjay gave a mock sigh, "I'm afraid that is down to experience. I tried to make the same offer to Sarah when she first arrived, but either I was too subtle, or she was too dim-witted to grasp my meaning. Forgive me if I have tarred you with her brush, but I didn't want any misunderstanding this time. Besides," he continued, "it is not like you can do anything about it anyway. I think it best if all the cards are laid so we can see them, don't you?"

"Especially when they are so heavily stacked in your favour," commented Roxy, icily.

Sanjay smiled again, infuriatingly, "Please do not begrudge me this little victory. I have been waiting twenty years for this. Now, do you accept?"

Roxy studied him. "You're never going to call in this favour, are you?"

Sanjay shrugged, "You never know, do you? I hope I am never in a position to have to, but it is a dangerous world out there, and I am in need of some assets."

Roxy sighed and dropped her head into her hands. She was stuck. She had no doubt that he was telling the truth about Wolfe, and so far she had little else going for her. What the hell, she decided. Right now the benefits outweighed the potential penalties. "All right," she said, raising her head to look at Sanjay, "and you can start right now. What the fuck are we?"

Sanjay gave her a wry smile, "Your very first question is one that I can't answer. But then, no one can. Not with any certainty. We are dead, or undead to be more precise, just like Hollywood says. Caught at the point of death and held there unchanged. Forever."

"Bullshit," said Roxy, "I can't believe that. It must be something else, some sort of sickness maybe?'

Sanjay smirked, "Wolfe, like many others, believe that we are part of the Divine Master Plan, to be evil so that people turn to God to save them. But I've heard all sorts of other theories; that we are the manifestation of selfish thoughts, or the scientists who think it is a recessive genetic marker activated by a virus in the blood, and even a suggestion that we must be possessed by aliens. I don't think we will ever know the truth, so why bother worrying about it?

"I do know we cannot die easily. Destroy the heart and you cripple us, but only sunlight or separating our heads from our bodies will permanently kill us. Anything else and we will heal, although massive damage such as losing a limb will take longer."

"Vicky said we get supernatural abilities, and can do anything. Is that true?" Roxy asked.

"A slight exaggeration, in my opinion. What you can do depends on the kind of person you are, although some things we hold in common. Dave, for example, will never be able to hypnotise a person in the way Jessica or I can. He is far too impulsive. No self-control."

"Is that what you did to me earlier? I couldn't move for a while at first."

Sanjay frowned. "Yes, except that you shouldn't have been able to break free. How did you do that?"

Roxy opened her mouth to speak, but had no answer, so she just shrugged. Sanjay studied her thoughtfully for a few more moments, making her feel uncomfortable, so she looked away towards Claudia, who was exploring the television.

"There is something else you should know," continued Sanjay quietly, following her gaze. "By bringing your daughter you have revealed your greatest weakness. Never reveal any information about yourself to another vampire. Anything that might be used against you. From now on, if any one of us wants something from you, or wants you to do something, all we have to do is threaten her."

Roxy's eyes blazed, "If you touch her..."

Sanjay raised placating hands, "Don't worry. I don't need to now. You already owe me, remember? But I cannot say the same for the others. Jessica, for example, has a vicious streak that you should be careful of. Dave and Sarah were lovers once, taken together while making out on a park bench. After we took them in Jessica hypnotised Sarah, enslaving her and taking her from him. Dave was too weak to prevent it, and now Jessica has Sarah follow her around like a puppy, making her take lovers in front of Dave just to taunt him. Sarah doesn't even know what she's doing. Her mind is so dominated she's like a zombie."

Roxy felt bile rising in her throat and swallowed. "And none of you think to tell her?" she whispered.

Sanjay shrugged, "There is nothing to gain by doing so. Sarah is the weakest of us. She cannot offer anything to compensate for Jessica's anger."

"That's monstrous." Roxy shook her head in disbelief.

"Yes, Roxy," he whispered back, a shadow seeming to cross his face, "we are monsters. And so will you become too, if you want to survive."

Roxy was unable to meet his gaze. No, she told herself, she wouldn't become like that. Never. In fact she should be the one to tell Sarah, and break the spell if she could. However, she found herself hesitating. Jessica would make a bitter enemy and it wouldn't gain her many friends. She'd need to know more about the situation first, which meant waiting. Just like everyone else. She looked across at Claudia and felt her heart sink lower. It was stupid of her to bring Claudia along. Stupid, stupid, stupid! Her mind was spinning, trying to think of a way out of the mess she had made for herself, but her thoughts kept returning to the look in Jessica's eyes when she saw Claudia, and the hate that Dave now reserved for her. So this was it. This was to be her future. Trapped with a bunch of murderous psychos. Forever?

"I have to go." She stood up abruptly. It was too much to take in, and her head was aching again.

"Then I shall see you again on Thursday, if not before. You know where we are, but remember three things and you'll increase your chances of survival a hundred-fold; never reveal yourself to a mortal, never drink from a victim once their heart has stopped beating, and always talk respectfully to your elders."

# Chapter 13

By the time Roxy arrived home, Claudia was asleep against her chest. Roxy changed her nappy, woke her to give her a drink, and then put her to bed and watched her fall asleep. She remained beside her cot for over an hour, watching her little chest rise and fall and listening to her tiny breaths. She had always loved watching her daughter sleep, but now she could stand motionless indefinitely without becoming tired. She had fucked up tonight, she knew. She shouldn't have taken Claudia with her. She had placed her in danger, and now she had to make very sure that creatures like Jessica didn't find out where she lived. It occurred to her to keep her real name secret. Not only because they could easily trace her if they knew it, but they might have strange powers they could use on her. Couldn't faeries enchant you if they knew your true name? Okay, they weren't faeries, but who knew what they could do?

As dawn approached she started to worry about what to do with Claudia. What if she fell asleep again and didn't wake until dusk? She could set an alarm clock, she supposed. Hell, she couldn't even phone Scarlet and ask for help, until she got her mobile back. She put some biscuits and a bottle of juice in

Claudia's cot so that she would have something to eat and drink when she woke up. She also scattered a few toys at her feet and set her alarm clock for midday. It was worth a try. If she could just wake up long enough to change her nappy and give her some lunch, then she could let her play in her room while she slept a few hours more. After that she went from room to room, making sure that all the curtains were drawn tightly and the doors locked, and settled down on her bed to sleep.

It sort of worked. She managed to fall asleep fairly quickly and the next thing she knew she was awake and consumed by an inexplicable anger. She could hear Claudia screaming in the next room, which stopped her rolling over and going back to sleep again. She had to clench her hands into fists and force herself to calm down, otherwise she feared she might do something terrible to Claudia. In the end, it was the memory of her step-father looming over her as a child which brought her to her senses. She had always sworn that she would never end up like him, or ignore her child in the way her mother had treated her. When she hauled herself out of bed and looked at her alarm clock – an old fashioned wind-up with bells on the top – she saw that it was completely mangled as if someone had squeezed it in a vice.

She felt groggy and her wrist still ached from the sunburn, but she managed to get into Claudia's room, clean her up and cuddle her until she settled down. Then she put some food in a bowl and sat her in front of the television with her toys and a drink before heading back to bed. She had long since baby-proofed her flat, so she wasn't worried that Claudia would hurt herself.

She woke up later feeling refreshed, but her wrist still throbbed. It was late afternoon and the light filtering through the cheap curtains stung her eyes if she looked at them directly. She could hear Claudia burbling to herself as she explored the flat. Roxy rolled out of bed and pulled on a pair of black jeans and a white t-shirt. She really wanted a coffee, but she knew she would just throw it back up if she tried to drink it, so she settled for making a cup anyway and letting the rich aroma fill the room as she played with Claudia. Her new sense of smell went on overdrive after she made it, and she started to feel light-headed. She was also hungry again, although she didn't realise until she bent to pick up Claudia. It was her scent that stirred something inside Roxy that, once woken, was impossible to ignore. It was more of a craving than simple hunger, and Roxy had to continually massage her stomach to distract herself from its demands.

She played with Claudia and made her some cereal. She was running out of food for her. She started to make a shopping list in her head, and then scolded herself for thinking about food when she was hungry. The pain in her stomach was growing, becoming a burning coal turning below her ribs. She tried to think of other things, but found it impossible. She paced the small flat restlessly, repeatedly opening and closing the cupboards in the kitchen, looking for something to sate her hunger, but found nothing. She tried to sip a little water, but even the tiniest drop made her queasy. There was nothing in the fridge any of the dozen times she checked, and she inevitably found herself returning to the front room to hover in the doorway and watch Claudia play. She was so warm and rosy-cheeked. Roxy could hear her heartbeat, rapid and light as she pulled her dolls out of her toy box and scattered them about the floor. Maybe just a little? Roxy wondered idly.

She turned away, holding her breath so that she wouldn't smell the sweet bouquet of her daughter's soft skin and pushed her hands against her ears so that she wouldn't hear her excited breaths. The sun was dipping lower outside, but slowly, oh so slowly. Roxy's sight became blurred and her vision narrowed so that all she could focus on was a narrow tunnel directly ahead of her, and every time she opened her eyes, Claudia was sitting at the end of it, smiling enticingly back at her. Roxy licked her lips to try to satisfy her need, and even bit into her own wrist, to taste her blood. That was a mistake, as it drove her stomach even wilder, and she curled up in a tight ball in the hallway by the front door, clutching her belly. She stood up to check on the position of the sun, and caught her reflection in the mirror. Her canines had extended to sharp fangs and her lips had curled up away from them, giving her a feral look. Her skin looked dreadfully pale in the dim light, but it was her eyes that captured her attention. They were wide, the pupils slightly oval, orientated vertically, and her normally deep brown irises were a silvery colour, lambent like those of a cat.

Roxy turned in a trance, her senses numbed as if she was back on heroin, and found herself gliding silently towards the front room. Only a couple of paces and she was standing in the doorway, casting her gaze around the poorly lit room. She didn't have to look for Claudia – she had been tracking her movements subconsciously for hours. Claudia looked up happily at her mother, smiling, trusting. Roxy smiled back, and Claudia laughed. She laughed? Sudden fury overcame Roxy. *How dare she?* Then it struck her that Claudia was laughing at her teeth and shining eyes. She thought her mother was playing a joke on her. Roxy's world spun and she grabbed the door frame to stop herself from falling. She'd been about to do the unthinkable. Claudia's reaction had been so unexpected it had surprised the darkness rising inside. She should have screamed; that was the proper reaction.

Roxy whipped around. She had to leave. The sky was still a murky grey outside, but the sun had passed out of sight behind the brooding rows of terraced housing that characterised towns and cities all across Britain. Roxy whispered a silent thank you to functional, ugly architecture, and slammed the door behind her before running down the street as fast as she could, leaving Claudia far behind.

Now that she was outside and letting the beast within her loose, her senses returned with a startling intensity. She ran, barefoot, in the direction of Bethnal Green, effortlessly passing people who were hurrying home carrying shopping bags or clutching the evening paper. With long strides she covered a large distance in a very short time and turned away from the main roads to hurtle along the back streets and alleys. Eventually she slowed and started paying attention to her surroundings. The noise from televisions blasted out through the windows of nearly every house she passed, cars hummed and horns honked in the distance. The smell of food filled the air as mothers prepared the evening meal for their families.

A cat leapt from under a parked car and turned to hiss at her. Roxy paused and crouched down low, staring back at it. They both sized each other up, and Roxy heard herself hiss in reply. The cat suddenly decided that she was a threat and darted away, but Roxy didn't let it. She jumped forward, covering ten feet in a single stride and landed next to it. Claws scraped across the concrete paving stones as the cat tried to change direction, but Roxy's reactions were so much faster it might have been wading through treacle. She leaned over and leisurely scooped it up in her hand. The cat went berserk, hissing and struggling as she brought it to her mouth and bit into its back.

Hot blood spurted into her face and she pressed her lips against the wound to drink the bitter liquid.

It was weak and unappetising, like a soggy lettuce, and its hairs came off onto her tongue and caught in the back of her throat, making her gag. She dropped to her knees beside one of the cars that lined the narrow road and continued to drink. She found if she sucked on the wound she could drink faster, but it wasn't quick enough. She ended up squeezing the cat to try to get more out of it, but animals are not like tubes of toothpaste. Its ribs snapped and destroyed its internal organs, killing it instantly. She cast it aside carelessly, too busy coughing and spitting up cat hair to care about anything else. She was still hungry.

She heard his footsteps first. Sharp sounds of leather on the pavement up ahead. She looked up, still kneeling and saw that the road was empty, which confused her until she realised the person was approaching from a side street several paces away. Seconds later he came into sight, a young man in his early twenties, with short, fair hair and a curtain-style fringe framing his blue-green eyes. He wore a suit which was a little too large to fit him well, and his shiny new shoes squeaked as he walked. He turned his head toward her.

Do not see me, she willed, and his eyes passed idly over her, then flicked to the body of the cat lying nearby. His pace barely slowed at the double-take, and he strode on. Roxy watched him cross the road and disappear from sight, but she could still hear his heels clicking against the concrete, one slightly lagging the other as if he favoured it. A blister, perhaps? Roxy stood and sniffed the air, catching his scent and licking her lips. Her stomach turned over and her mouth tingled in anticipation.

Hardly understanding what she was doing, she stepped onto the road to follow him. When she turned the corner he was already about twenty yards ahead of her, humming some inane tune to himself. Roxy padded after him, matching his pace, taking deep breaths through her nose to hold his scent in her mind. She picked out his deodorant and the underlying sweat it attempted to mask. It stirred a sensual, almost sexual desire in her stronger than anything she could remember. She could also make out other, less tangible elements mixed with his sweat – pheromones, although she didn't recognise them as such at first. She knew, as clearly as if he had a sign pinned on his back, that he was happy and excited. There was nothing sexual about his excitement though, so he wasn't on his way to or from a date. Roxy increased her pace, her soles making slight slapping sounds on the ground. He turned his head to glance over his shoulder. *I am not here*, thought Roxy, and his unfocussed eyes swept the street behind her. He turned back and continued walking, picking up his pace, and stopped humming. A few moments later, the wind carried his scent to her, subtly changed. If she had experienced desire before, she now felt the fire of lust explode inside her as his pheromones betrayed his unease.

The road was dimly lit by old streetlamps, which cast a milky-white glow in a small puddle at their base but failed to extend further, making the vast expanse of darkness between them seem thicker in contrast. Roxy deliberately shifted her pace and stamped her feet just out of step with his to watch his reaction. He glanced over his shoulder again and scanned the dark street frantically.

"Come on Simon, get a grip," he muttered to himself.

The street was deserted, and lined with parked cars. Roxy lengthened her stride, then launched herself into the air, covering the remaining fifteen yards between them and landing without a sound right behind him. The smell of him was heavy with apprehension but she wanted more. She wanted fear.

"Simon," she whispered in his ear. He stopped and whirled around. It was easy for her to circle around him so that she remained at his back. His reactions were painfully slow.

"Get a grip," she whispered again.

"Who's there?" he called out tentatively. Roxy raised her hand and gave him a little push, sending him sprawling to the floor. He rolled over and started to crawl backwards on his elbows looking around in panic for his attacker, but Roxy had leapt into the air and was clinging to the top of the lamppost above him. She looked up and saw a couple of wires leading to the light shroud. She reached out, suspended by one hand, and pulled at the wires. They snapped easily and the light flickered and died, leaving Simon engulfed in darkness. He looked up and gave a weak cry as he saw her silhouetted against the periwinkle sky. Roxy's lips twisted in a crooked smile as he scrambled to his feet, his fear making her feel light-headed and strong. Her hunger was still there, but she sensed she was gaining something simply from his panic. She watched him run for a couple of seconds, before dropping down after him.

As he turned to look behind him, she jumped, somersaulting over his head to land in front of him. His steps faltered as he looked again, trying to work out where she was, and by the time he looked back, his legs had carried him halfway to where she stood blocking his path, a tall shadowy figure whose shining eyes glittered from a pale face. She smiled, revealing her fangs and he yelped in horror. A rush of strength and power flooded through her and she advanced upon him as he desperately tried to stop and run back the way he had come. She let him get a half a dozen paces before jogging after him. The chase was on.

He ran for his life, panting hard and trying to squeeze as much speed from his dress shoes as he could, his blisters now forgotten. Roxy ran lazily after him, easily keeping pace as he darted across the road, making for an intersection. He threw a look over his shoulder just in time to see her launch herself into the air, vaulting a Volkswagen Beetle on one side of the road and landing on the bonnet of a Ford Escort on the other, only a couple of paces away from him. He let out a whimper and ran on. She could smell the salty tears streaming down his face and a sudden acrid ammonia tang from his trousers.

"This is fun," she giggled.

There was nowhere he could go that she couldn't get him. She could take him whenever she wanted, and the longer she waited, the stronger she felt, feeding off his terror. Another thirty seconds, however, and he started to slow. He had sprinted nearly four hundred metres, but now his body was failing him, his adrenaline reserves sapping. She knew that now was the time to strike, while he still had the strength to scream.

He managed to make it to an alleyway leading to a busy main road before she caught him. She let his spirits lift at the sight of the noisy traffic, believing he might reach the illusion of safety that comes when surrounded by other people, and then reached out and snagged him back, grabbing the collar of his jacket so that his feet slid out from under him and he collapsed to the ground. She was upon him instantly, a hand on his mouth to muffle his screams and parted her lips to show him her fangs. He twitched and his bowels opened, adding to the wet stain in front of his trousers. His arms came up to fend her off but he was so weak in comparison to her that she could hold both of his wrists above his head in one hand. She paused for a couple of seconds, letting him struggle helplessly and realise his vulnerability and the inevitable outcome. He couldn't even beg, as her hand was still over his mouth, but his eyes looked up at her pleadingly, desperately trying to make her understand. She understood very well, however, and it just made her smile more widely. She could wait no longer and lowered her head to sink her teeth into his neck.

She bit deeply, releasing a sudden burst of hot, sticky blood all over her face and neck. The force of it was so strong she couldn't drink fast enough and it showered over her. It was delightful; heavily laced with hormones and adrenaline and hot, unlike the cold liquor that Wolfe had fed her. Wolfe's blood had a deeper, more potent effect on her, but Simon's blood tasted so much better. It was like experiencing a massive orgasm after hours of foreplay; an explosive release of pleasure made all the more sweeter for the waiting. She drank and drank, missing every third or fourth mouthful at first, but eventually the blood slowed and she had to start sucking to draw the fluid into her mouth. Simon had stopped struggling as soon as she had bitten him, wrapped in a paralysis that the bite inflicts on its victims – a survival mechanism to allow the vampire to feed in peace. She could hear his breathing grow shallower, his heartbeat grow weaker and faster, then slower, but she didn't care. All that mattered was the blood. She drank more, having to suck harder as the blood thinned.

She dimly heard his final breath rattling in his throat and the final beat of his heart, but she was distracted by something else. The blood had reduced to a trickle, but something else was beyond it. Nothing physical, but the merest hint of a reservoir of something elusive – a pure nectar shrinking away to hide in the furthermost recesses of his body. She sucked harder, seeking it out, drawing it towards her. It resisted furiously, but a mania had crept upon her which would not allow her to give up. She threw her whole strength into it, clenching every muscle in her body, and it suddenly flowed into her in a rush; something akin to the sensation she had experienced from his fear, but multiplied a thousand-fold. Her body went rigid and she shuddered violently as though electricity was coursing through her.

Images flashed through her head: a birthday party with a dozen pre-school children seated around a long outdoor table laden with jellies, sandwiches, cakes and squash. People's faces flickered across her eyelids, each attached to a name and a relationship – her mother, her father, sister, brother, aunt, school friend, girlfriend, ex-girlfriend, college tutor, sports coach – except they were not Roxy's associates, but Simon's. More images of his life, his memories, flooded her thoughts, drowning her, dragging her under the dark waters of his past. She was Simon now, twenty-one, a student at university, just about to sit her – his – final exams in his astrophysics degree. She was one of the top students and theorems and equations rolled around in his – her – head; Schrödinger's equation, electromagnetic theory, stellar structure, the intergalactic distance scale, the complex mathematics of general relativity and manifold geometry, all jostling for attention. She – he – had just returned from a job interview in the city,

TAKEN 115

to model weather systems for an insurance company which would pay a telephone number salary, and they seemed to like her. Him. She was on her way back to the house she shared with her girlfriend – no, *his* girlfriend – Angela – a biochemist due to graduate this year too. Another shift in perspective and she remembered it was band practise tonight. She played lead guitar in a rock band she had formed with her mates, and she had just got the hang of the solo in the Metallica song they were covering.

Pain lanced through her as she pulled away from his neck and the contact was broken. She sat back on her haunches, bewildered for over half a minute. She had forgotten who she was. Roxy and Simon both clamoured to be recognised, but she couldn't understand, couldn't decide. She couldn't remember. Finally she looked down at her body and saw the blood-drenched t-shirt clinging to the small mounds of her breasts. A few more confused seconds and then Roxy won out. She was female, therefore she must be *her*. She collapsed to the ground, clenching her eyes shut to stop the world from spinning. She imagined she heard Simon's scream of denial as he was cast into the dark reaches of her mind, and opened her eyes. She found herself staring at the side of Simon's head, his eyes glazed, lips slightly parted and already starting to grey.

She could feel Simon's presence in her mind, remember his memories, which were now her memories, but it was no longer overwhelming. She knew that he had thirty pounds in his wallet and she knew the PIN number for his bank card. It took only a few moments hesitation before she reached into his pocket and withdrew it, turning it over in her hands as she sat up. It was black leather and slightly stained with the blood seeping through his jacket. Her fingers were covered in the sticky, drying stuff though, and quickly made it worse. She knew what was inside without even looking; a student ID card, an ATM card, a couple of store loyalty cards and a photograph of Angela. She felt sick, disgusted at herself for what she had done, and for what she was considering doing, and tossed the wallet aside. She wouldn't steal from a dead man. She hadn't sunk that far. Maybe that was how other vampires made their money? Certainly Wolfe didn't seem short of a few quid, but she wasn't ready to become that person. Not yet.

Slowly, realisation crept over her. Simon was lying motionless beside her and the passion that had stolen her actions had departed, leaving her with the consequences, and her conscience. She had killed him. He was dead. A low moan escaped her lips as the enormity of what she had done hit her, and she started to tremble. He would never sit those last two exams. He would never get that first-class honours degree he was predicted, he wouldn't return home to Angela who was anxiously awaiting news of his interview. He was gone, snuffed out never to return. She had even taken his soul. The pure essence she had chased down after he died had been his spiritual self, now denied release and reintegration into the cycle of life and trapped inside an undead vampire. Once again she imagined she could hear his screams, but quickly thrust that notion aside. That he should still be conscious of his condition was too horrible to contemplate.

Then another, more immediate concern struck her. What was she to do with the body? Thick, drying blood coated her arms, face and torso, and puddled around him on the ground. She had missed a lot, apparently. Traffic swept by at the end of the alley, still busy in the early evening. Her thoughts raced, all sorts of possibilities coming to her, mainly from Simon's memories. Acid baths, dismemberment, tossing the body into a dustbin or dropping it into the sewers. He was so much cleverer than her, but having him effectively suggest ways to dispose of his own body was too much for her, so she ran, leaving him there. She needed to get back home, to wash and oh God, to Claudia, who must be going nuts. She had to get rid of her clothes too. There was no way to clean them now, although in the back of her mind she listed a number of enzymes that could do the job. She didn't even know what enzymes were. It was too weird. She ran home, wishing all the time not to be seen, and hoping she wouldn't meet anyone who might make her lose control again. Fortunately she saw no one, and finally shut her door behind her.

# Chapter 14

She spent forty minutes in the shower, the scalding water turning her skin pink, but she still didn't feel clean. Her skin had felt hot when she returned home, in contrast to its coldness over the past few days. She'd felt slightly warm after she'd drank from Wolfe, but only for a few minutes. She remained warm to the touch for the rest of the night, allowing her to feel almost human again. Her once white t-shirt was ruined, but she decided that she could rescue her black jeans. As she towelled herself dry, she noticed her wrist had healed and was no longer tender to touch. Another benefit of a good meal, she supposed.

Claudia was happy when she finally reappeared, and followed Roxy about as she wrapped her t-shirt in a plastic bag. When she threw it in the bin, Simon screamed in her head not to be stupid. He had been a fan of crime dramas and knew that the first thing the police did was to go through the rubbish of a suspect to look for clues. She left it there anyway, stubbornly. It wasn't that she could hear his voice in her head, but rather that she now simply possessed his knowledge. She could still distinguish between what she knew and what he knew, but a cold chill ran through her as she wondered if the lines would eventually start to blur. A person is the sum of their memories, they said, so what did that mean for her? She was already finding herself thinking differently, more logically. Simon had been a scientist and trained to think in a certain way, but she had never been like that. She tended to act without thinking and deal with the consequences later. That attitude hadn't got her very far in life though, she had to admit.

She changed and dressed Claudia and got her something to eat before sitting down and allowing herself to think, something she had deliberately resisted whilst in the shower. Something had happened to her. Not the memory thing. That was unexpected, but she could accept that as another part of being a vampire. Sanjay had warned her not to drink from a person after their heart had stopped beating, but he hadn't told her why. She'd assumed when he'd told her that something bad would happen, perhaps she would die too? It was the reason that she hadn't heeded the warning that concerned her. She had lost control, not just then, but from the moment she left the house, if not earlier. She would never have hunted anyone down the way she did if she was in her right mind. The cruelty of life on the streets had drummed into her that everyone deserved respect and that everyone occasionally needed help. But she had done it, and what's more she had enjoyed it. Something had twisted her thoughts and turned her into a monster.

It was the Hunger. She hadn't eaten for a couple of days, and even then it was just a few mouthfuls from Wolfe's wrist. Now she was feeling well and truly sated, bloated even. It was the first time she had felt full since the night she was attacked. Which led her to her next question, how long would it last? She had come very close to hurting Claudia tonight, and she had to make sure that didn't happen again. Perhaps the thing to do would be to feed as soon as she felt hungry? She decided to keep a notebook to record the times she felt hungry and when she fed. It was a very Simon-like thing to do, but it was still a good idea so she forced herself to do it. She was going to have to learn to live with his memories anyway. She couldn't go on ignoring them or doing the opposite to what they suggested.

Then the final thing that she had been trying to ignore broke through the wall she'd been building. She had killed someone, the ultimate crime in civilised society. Abhorrent and unforgivable. Quite apart from being forbidden by God and that now she might be reincarnated as a bug for the next thousand generations, she was uncomfortably aware that in many of the vampire films she had seen, the curse could be broken as long as the vampire hadn't made its first kill. Of course a lot in those films was nonsense, but not everything. What if this was true? No one she had met so far had mentioned a way to reverse what had happened to her and become human again, but they had all seemed to be pretty happy with what they were. Also from what she understood they wouldn't tell her anyway unless they had something to gain from doing so. Knowing her luck she had lost her only chance for redemption. She suddenly felt angry. Angry at the one who took her, for being careless and leaving her to fend for herself, angry at Vicky for taking her to Wolfe and angry at Wolfe for his arrogance and for teaching her nothing.

A knock at the door made her jump. She leapt up and rubbed her face and hair vigorously before going to answer the door. She double-checked her appearance in the mirror before opening it. She was wearing only a long nightshirt which hung to mid-thigh, and her short black hair was still damp and spiky. Her reflection showed no signs of blood and her eyes and teeth looked normal. Her hands had been scrubbed over and over again, but she checked them again to make sure they were clean. Satisfied, she opened the door. It was Scarlet and Leah.

"Hi Roxy," chirped Scarlet with a hesitant smile.

Roxy couldn't help glancing up and down the street as she let Scarlet in, half expecting to see flashing blue lights. She suddenly felt very exposed and closed the door quickly.

They stood in an awkward silence for a few moments, both trying to pretend they didn't notice by watching the children greet each other.

"Uh, do you want a coffee or something?" Roxy asked, trying to lighten the atmosphere.

"Only if you're having one," she replied, and sat down. Roxy gave her a sideways glance, but Scarlet was in the process of arranging her jacket on the back of the chair, and didn't seem to realise what she had said. Roxy shrugged and went into the kitchen to turn on the kettle. When she returned Scarlet was curled up watching the children play. Roxy sat on the sofa, and studied her. Scarlet looked pale, as if she were ill and there was a looseness to the skin around her eyes hinting that she had not been sleeping well. Her perfume was heavy and cloying, but couldn't mask a sense of nervousness and uncertainty.

"So how are you feeling?" Scarlet asked eventually.

Roxy shrugged, "I'm still getting used to it."

Scarlet nodded absently, "I'm sure you'll be better soon."

"Well I'm not sure about that."

"Yeah of course you will. It was probably just a touch of flu or something."

Roxy stared at her, not quite sure what she was saying. Scarlet was avoiding her gaze and then gave a nervous laugh.

"It was funny to pretend though, wasn't it?"

"About me being a vampire?" asked Roxy, softly.

Scarlet flinched momentarily, then forced a smile and nodded. Roxy hesitated, wondering what to say. Why was she denying the truth now? Sanjay had told her not to reveal her true nature to humans, but no one knew Roxy had told anyone, so Scarlet shouldn't be in danger. Then she remembered something Wolfe had told her. People often couldn't accept the fact that vampires existed and would refuse to believe no matter how much evidence was presented to them. She could see this happening to Scarlet right before her eyes. She was waiting for Roxy to agree with her, to tell her the nightmare wasn't real. Even the smallest assent on her part would allow Scarlet to persuade herself that it was all a trick. Roxy sensed that she could contradict her and tell her that she was indeed a vampire, and Scarlet would nod and accept it, but how long would that last? She would probably still try to reject it, and if Roxy kept forcing the truth on her then she might well lose her mind, as Wolfe had warned. Roxy realised that Scarlet was already suffering from nightmares and broken sleep trying to come to terms with the knowledge. She couldn't do that to her.

Scarlet was her only friend. She had stuck by Roxy in her darkest times, and they had shared many of their secrets and dreams. Roxy wanted – needed – to share what had happened to her. She didn't want to face it alone. But she knew that if she didn't release her now, then Scarlet might deteriorate very quickly and she'd still be alone, only this time she would have destroyed another life. It struck her with a terrible certainty that she would always be alone. Forever. She could never tell anyone and she could never have any friends. She couldn't suppress a shudder of horror and tried to disguise it by standing up and walking to the kitchen to finish making Scarlet's coffee. She paused in the doorway and glanced over her shoulder to smile weakly at her friend.

"Yeah, it was fun to pretend." Then she whirled away into the solitude of the kitchen so that Scarlet wouldn't see her tears.

# Chapter 15

The next evening, Scarlet arrived to drop Leah off for Roxy to babysit while she went to a night-class in computer skills. It was something she had always wanted to do, and had finally saved up enough money to enrol in a local course. Roxy wanted to better herself as well, but had been thinking of something less intellectual and more practical, such as childcare or sports coaching. When Scarlet showed her some of the work she had been doing, Roxy realised with a shock that she could have done it for her. Simon's memories again, his skills. Roxy's head spun. It occurred to her what a powerful ability she now had. No secret was safe from her. If she wanted money, she could have it. She just needed to find a wealthy man or woman and she would know their bank account details. If she wanted to play the piano, find a pianist and voila. She would even get a nice meal in the process. All it would cost would be a little pang of conscience, and didn't they say it got easier after your first?

But she wasn't like that, she reminded herself. That wasn't her. She didn't want it to be, and she made a promise to herself never to kill again. She didn't know if it would be possible to keep it, but she made it anyway. She needed to feel she was in control of something, and the only thing she could ever really control was herself. In the end, that was all that anyone could do. It didn't make Simon's death any easier to bear though. She couldn't forgive herself and she knew that she would mentally beat herself up about it for years. The first is special that way. She harboured a lingering compulsion to go to Simon's house and try to catch a glimpse of Angela, but forcibly thrust it aside. Was it Simon putting that wish into her head, or was it just a sick desire to find out more about his life? She didn't know.

She grew hungry again as the night wore on. Nothing serious, but simply that little niggle that had been ever-present from her turning. She'd thought it was part of being a vampire, but now she knew that the ache could be eased for a few hours, she found it impossible to ignore. She feared she might never get used to it, that even if she sated herself she would always be dreading its return. But how could she feed next time? She couldn't wait until she was really hungry again. It was too dangerous for anyone around her, so perhaps she ought to go out every night, and drink just a little. But how? She felt uneasy about mugging someone in a dark alley. She had no doubt that with her reflexes, speed and strength it would be easy, but she had been mugged before, and it wasn't something you shrugged off quickly. It could cripple a person's confidence and give them nightmares. She remembered Vicky had mentioned something about breathing into their mouths to make them forget, but she hadn't tried that yet. Besides, she would still have to witness their panic and begging while she was feeding, and given her excited reaction to Simon's fear, she might lose control. Perhaps she could break into a hospital and steal some blood? No, she shook her head. There would be cameras, locks and someone might end up dying because of her anyway. Animals? The cat had been disgusting, but other kinds might satisfy her.

Roxy sighed and sank back into the couch watching Leah and Claudia sort blocks, when another possibility occurred to her. Prostitution. It took a while for her to accept the idea, as it meant breaking an earlier promise to herself, but this would be different. She knew how men behaved when they were aroused; they became very open to suggestion, and would happily accept, even encourage her biting them during sex. It had been easy with that first young man, she recalled. None of those watching had realised she was really drinking his blood. She could pick up customers, take their money, feed on them and, yes, even wipe their memories so they didn't realise they hadn't actually had sex with her. And if she felt any guilt at ripping them off, well didn't they deserve it? In her experience the kind of men who visited prostitutes were not particularly pleasant or trustworthy individuals.

It was a slim distinction, she knew, and quickly put out of her mind the lonely widowers and the awkward, anxious teenagers who tended to make up the other sort of clients. It was the lesser of two evils, she thought. They would still enjoy it, in a way, and the money was necessary to maintain the illusion. Yeah, right, she chided herself, but not too severely. She could use the extra money. Roxy held her head in her hands. What a choice? Degrade and humiliate herself or degrade and humiliate another by mugging them? She couldn't think of any other alternatives. She'd have to ask Wolfe, or better yet, Sanjay for advice. In the meantime, there was only really one choice she could make, and she might as well do it that night.

Scarlet returned from her class later, bubbling with happiness and eager to share what she had learned with Roxy. She was finding it fairly easy now, and was clearly enjoying it.

"You should come along, Rox. It'll do you good."

"Maybe," offered Roxy, "but not yet. I still feel a bit strange. Plus I can't afford it right now anyway."

Scarlet patted her arm sympathetically, "Well take your time and get better. If you feel okay next week, we should take the children for a picnic in the park, don't you think?"

Roxy nodded slowly. Scarlet had totally forgotten about her new condition, it seemed.

Scarlet didn't stay long, and after Roxy moved the sleeping Claudia into bed, she started to get ready to go out onto the streets once again. She had left most of her sexy clothes at Clive's and still hadn't got around to collecting them. There were still a few things lying about she could use; fishnet stockings, a pair of high heeled sandals, a short skirt and a shirt she knotted together above her stomach. She applied her make-up heavily and looked at herself critically before she left. You look like a whore, Roxy, she thought with a shake of her head. Well she had found it paid to be obvious about these things, even if it did get you noticed by the police easier. She grabbed a purse full of condoms and loose change and left the house. She didn't need to worry about sexually transmitted diseases any more, but she didn't want to become a carrier and infect someone else. Besides, condoms made the whole business slightly less messy, and would reassure nervous clients.

It had only been ten months since she'd walked the streets trying to get enough money to pay for her next fix, so she had no trouble fitting back in. She even got a few nods of recognition from the other girls. Nothing friendly, just enough to let her know where their patch was and for her to find somewhere else. She found her customer on Commercial Road, a kerb crawler in a red hatchback. He was in his late twenties, but wore a baseball cap which made him appear younger. He looked around nervously and gestured for her to get into his car quickly. Normally Roxy wouldn't have got into a car like that – it was too dangerous – but she wasn't frightened any more. She climbed in and bent over to give him a blow job while he found a quiet street and waited until he brought the car to a halt before she sat up to bite his neck. Once again she was surprised at the force of the blood spurting out from the wound, and found it difficult to get a good seal around it with her lips.

Hot, sticky blood gushed out to cover the lower part of her face and neck until she found the best position to hold his limp, paralysed body. The neck is not the best place from which to drink a victim's blood, despite what happened in the movies. She later found that the wrist or the inside of the elbow were much easier and more comfortable, with the blood flowing at a more manageable pace, allowing her to take her time. She stopped drinking after only half a dozen mouthfuls, conscious not to take too much and erring on the side of caution. The blood welled from his neck as she released him, but eased to a drizzle when she licked the wound. He looked round at her dazedly, his eyes starting to widen in shock as she leant forwards and breathed onto his face. Immediately, his eyes glazed over and he slumped back into the seat, fast asleep.

Roxy wiped the blood from her chin, coating her hands in the process. She sat back, checking her mental and physical state and was pleased to discover that she did not feel hungry, or more importantly, any desire to further drain her victim. She fumbled in her purse for some baby wipes. She normally carried them with her to wipe away other kinds of mess, but they were perfect for cleaning the blood from her face and hands. She was reapplying her make-up when the man stirred beside her and woke up.

"Well look who it is," she greeted him, inwardly sighing with relief. She wasn't sure how much she could drink before doing serious damage.

The man looked at her blearily and then blinked himself to full alertness. "Uh, hey, wow. That was wicked...I think. It's a bit of a blur though." He frowned at her, "Did I pay you yet?"

Roxy shook her head, "Nuh-uh. I was in too much of a hurry to get my teeth into you." She leaned across to him, snapping her teeth playfully.

He reached into his wallet and pulled out a couple of twenties. "Here. Can I see you again sometime?"

"Sure. I'll be around." She took the notes from him, blew him a kiss, and climbed out of the car. She walked away quickly, in case he got any ideas about hassling her, and decided to call it a night and go home. She didn't want to overstretch herself. Better to take baby-steps and see how things worked out.

# Chapter 16

Roxy rubbed her eyes wearily. Claudia had woken her again in the middle of the afternoon. She had moved into the front room and lain on the couch where she could watch Claudia play, and where Claudia could occasionally bring things over to her without Roxy having to do much more than open her eyes, smile and make pleased sounds. It seemed to satisfy Claudia, but Roxy didn't get the rest she wanted. Now it was fully dark outside, and although she felt a little more awake, there was still a part of her that wanted to crawl back into bed until morning.

She turned on the television for the evening news, hoping that there would be no mention of Simon's death. There wasn't, but when the announcer mentioned the date, the last vestiges of fatigue left her. It was Thursday evening. Wolfe had told her to return tonight. A cold hand gripped her stomach from within as she made the decision not to go. Wolfe would be pissed at her, and it meant staying out of his way for years to come. In fact she should stay out of the way of all vampires for the next twenty years or so, until Claudia was old enough to leave home and look after herself. It shouldn't be too hard to avoid contact with vampires. London was big. If she just stayed away from popular areas, especially the tourist spots in the West End, and kept to the suburbs and outer zones, then she would probably never run into one. She had never told Wolfe where she lived, or her real name, so there was no way he could find her. She should move house anyway, as soon as she could, but that was just her paranoia talking, and she doubted that there would be any real need to do so. Wolfe would forget about her soon enough, maybe even think she was dead. A lot of new vampires died in the first few days apparently. Most never made it past their first year. By the time she returned she would have a much better understanding of her abilities and limitations, and be able to stand up for herself. She might not need Wolfe.

In the meantime, she needed to get back into a work routine and get some money coming in. The forty pounds she had "earned" the night before wouldn't go very far. She picked up the phone to call Scarlet, and swore silently to herself when she heard nothing through the earpiece. It was still dead. Muttering obscenities about the family heritage of the phone company, she went to her bedroom to get dressed.

She was just putting socks on Claudia so that they could go round to see Scarlet and arrange a babysitting day, when there was a knock at the door. Roxy shivered. Her lower back muscles clenched and a chill draft caressed her as she raised her head towards the noise. Something was wrong. She rose to her feet, absently smoothing the hairs on the back of her neck and walked cautiously to the door. There was no spy-hole or window in the door, so she had to open it to see who was there. Claudia padded behind her, holding a sock in her hand to match the one on her foot, as if to remind her mother that she hadn't finished dressing her yet.

On the doorstep was a pale man of medium height, who was thin almost to the point of illness. He was wearing a grey double-breasted suit with a crisp white handkerchief poking neatly out of the top pocket. His hair was a sandy-brown and cut in a peculiar style, like a beatle-cut with a very straight fringe that circled his head, to the top of his ears, and shaven below. He was perhaps middle-aged, judging by the lines around his mouth, but his eyes held a weariness that made her realise that he was a lot older. He had a scar threading across his left cheek from the bottom of his ear to his chin. His cheeks were pitted with small circular marks, but they seemed to increase his rugged attractiveness rather than detract from it. She caught a faint musty smell emanating from him, reminiscent of a long abandoned room that had once been damaged by damp and mould. He was holding a slim briefcase in his bony left hand and his right extended towards her in greeting, halfway between a handshake and a wave.

"Miss Harker?"

This is definitely wrong, thought Roxy, her initial hopes that he was a salesman scurrying away as lightning prickles shot down her spine and she was possessed with an overwhelming desire to flee, but his eyes held her rooted to the spot like a mouse facing a serpent. His thin lips twisted into an amused smirk as Roxy tried to untangle the morass of information flooding her brain. He had a strange accent, part west-country, part American. He was a vampire, she realised, and an old one too. Her legs turned to jelly as she realised they had found her. He said something she did not register, and before she knew what she was doing she had moved aside and let him into her house. Claudia stared up at him, pale and frightened, and clutched her spare sock to her chest.

"And this, I presume, is your daughter, the lovely Claudia Celeste?"

Roxy flushed angrily. How did he know that? She was sure she hadn't mentioned Claudia's name to the others. He was about six inches shorter than her, and probably weighed less than she did, but some instinct kept her from lashing out at him. She tried to swallow, but her throat was too dry, so she forced a cough and managed to croak "Who are you?"

"Forgive me, my lady," he said, inclining his head in apology. Roxy was again struck by his accent, and tried to place it. "Forgive me" sounded like "firgave may."

"I am called Reyne, and I entertain no threat to thee or thy offspring. May we be chilled and at ease?" He indicated a chair, and after a brief hesitation, Roxy nodded, slightly confused by his grammar. It reminded her of Shakespeare. She had never understood Shakespeare. He sat down while Roxy gathered Claudia in her arms and sat on the sofa as far away as possible. Claudia was trembling and was as quiet as a lamb, but her cornflower blue eyes were wide and never left him. He rested his briefcase on the coffee table between them and flicked open the catches with a loud double-click which made her flinch. He removed a large folder almost an inch thick and placed it carefully on the table. Then he calmly closed his briefcase and set it neatly down by the side of the chair. Roxy saw that the folder was marked as property of the Metropolitan Police and that her name was stencilled near the top in black ball-point pen.

"Amanda Harker," he began, opening the file casually to reveal a photograph of her taken the last time she was arrested, "also known as Mandy, Roxy, Liza, Rebecca and probably others. Thirty-two arrests over four years leading to seventeen convictions including vagrancy, prostitution, possession of a class A narcotic, possession of a lethal weapon and disorderly conduct." He paused to study the mug-shot of her sporting a black eye and looking sourly at the camera and then looked up at her.

"You have been a naughty little child, have you not?"

Roxy said nothing. There was nothing to say. She wanted to ask where he had got her confidential police file from, but knew he would never tell her.

"All minor crimes really," he continued, "mostly settled with cautions or fines, or mayhaps a number of weeks in the service of the community. Nothing to suggest that you may be a menace to society. Until this," he turned to the back of the folder to reveal a large glossy colour photograph of a body lying in a circle of dried blood. It was Simon. Roxy swayed, her body momentarily weightless as if she was falling from a great height. Several more photographs showed the body from different angles in daylight, including one showing a close up of two puncture wounds in his neck. Reyne lingered a while on this photograph, shaking his head in disapproval.

"What do you want?" Roxy asked. She was finished. How could they have linked her to the death so quickly? As if reading her thoughts, he started to read from a forensic report.

"Eleven bloody fingerprints were lifted from the scene, all of which matched those on your record. Several black hairs were retrieved from the victim's clothing and skin samples from the attacker were found under his fingernails. Moreover witnesses reported seeing the victim being pursued by a tall woman matching your last known description." He paused and glanced at her, "Except for the hair. The cause of death was exsanguination, apparently from a pair of wounds on the victim's neck."

He looked up at her, "Tut tut Roxy, You have been careless. Did Wolfe teach you naught?"

"How do you know about Wolfe?"She blurted out.

"I know all about you, Roxy. I know that you are supposed to be meeting with Domus Wolfe tonight, but that you are planning not to go. I even know what Wolfe is planning for you all this evening."

Roxy opened her mouth to speak, but nothing came out. She sat back, hugging Claudia and desperately trying to think of a way out, but her thoughts had seized up, defeated by the succession of shocks and the implications for her probably very short future.

Reyne gathered the documents back into the file, closed it slowly and deliberately pushed it to one side. "Fortuitously, one of my contacts in the police was alerted to the strange nature of this murder, and arranged to have the matter quietly removed to my care. I can see that none of this ever comes to light. Furthermore, I can see to it that your past records are cast into the fire, such that they never existed nor be uncovered in future days. Anonymity is a most important virtue for our kind, do you not agree?" He smiled at her.

Roxy said nothing, waiting for Reyne to finish, but he remained quiet, watching her. The silence stretched out, and Roxy eventually nodded, unable to maintain the facedown that Reyne had begun. Roxy knew he was waiting for her to ask for help, and though she resented it, she had no choice but to do so. She braced herself as his smile grew wider.

"You are probably wondering how to thank me for this act of kindness?"

Roxy nodded slowly, "Something like that," she muttered

Reyne took on a serious expression, "I require only a minor geas in return."

Roxy had never heard the word geas before, but she got the drift. "Go on," she prompted.

"Wolfe is not everything he appears to be," he continued. "Something queer pervades everything he does. His bastard house of contemptibiliae is an abomination. It would never have been allowed in the past. He has somehow managed to coerce Catallus to stay his wrath and grant legitimacy to his scheme." Reyne's thin lips pursed in anger as he talked and his speech started to deteriorate. Roxy had to concentrate hard to follow what he was saying.

"All of the other domii seem to have turned their heads to their navels where Wolfe is concerned. He must know some great and powerful truth, for he is ne'er strong enough to explain all the concessions he hath received. He is working to a plot, methinks, but what plots lieth therein and surmounting said plot? This I must ken yet I da'ent seek t'er reason."

Abruptly, he stopped and took a few moments to compose himself, rising to his feet and turning his back to Roxy. When he turned and spoke again it was with a calm smile, his accent and dialect once more approaching a modern style. "All attempts to remove Wolfe have so far failed, showing a remarkable amount of luck on his part. Another attempt will be made tomorrow, and I'm afraid that as part of his house, you will suffer his fate. Unless someone were to intervene on your behalf."

Roxy looked across at him, her heart sinking. "What do you want me to do?"

"I need you to act as my eyes and ears in this matter, Roxy. You are to return to him, whilst saying nothing of this conversation tonight, for 'tis twixt thee and I, and observe him in all things to ascertain what secrets he holds."

Roxy had to run through his words a second time in her head before she worked out what he meant. "You want me to be a spy?"

Reyne parted his lips in a smile, showing two long, white fangs, "I do indeed, as you say, wish you to espy upon Wolfe."

Roxy sagged, staring dejectedly at the floor. This wasn't good at all. Now she was trapped in this dangerous society, playing a game which would probably get her killed if she made a single mistake. Reyne started to put the file back into his briefcase, not bothering to wait for her verbal agreement.

"When you find anything, put it in a letter and send it to this address, marked for my attention," he offered her a business card, which she took dumbly. It was a Post Office Box number in West London. He then touched his forehead in farewell, and left. She didn't bother to show him out. Claudia was still clinging to her in fright, and her nappy was full. Roxy glanced at the clock. It was nearly time to go.

# Chapter 17

She arrived at Club Obsession a little after ten, wearing jeans, boots and a plain t-shirt under a denim jacket. She had rushed Claudia round to Scarlet's and begged her to watch her for a few hours. Scarlet wasn't happy about it, but Roxy told her she had been called up to do a gig at short notice and offered to watch Leah the next two days in return, so she'd agreed. The club wasn't open, and Roxy had to knock on the heavy door to be let in. Sanjay opened it. He had swapped his suit for a full set of heavy duty biker leathers. He grinned up at her.

"We were taking bets about whether you would show up. Are you ready for some fun?"

"What kind of fun?" Roxy asked warily, but he simply smiled wider and led her into the ground floor dance hall. Everyone else was already there and Roxy felt a minor twinge of embarrassment about being late. They were all dressed in hard-wearing clothes such as jeans or combat fatigues and leather or denim jackets. Wolfe was even wearing what looked like a chain-mail shirt under a battered leather jacket.

"Roxy," smiled Wolfe, "welcome to the party." He was carrying a broadsword, which reflected the dim red lighting in its mirror finish. She noticed the others were all carrying weapons as well, either swords or long knives. All blades. Dave was carrying a large fire axe. Roxy suddenly felt vulnerable, but sensed that she was in no immediate danger. Wolfe veered towards a table as he approached her and picked up an eighteen inch long curved blade, which he handed to her. It had a blue plastic handle at one end, was single edged and had a hole at the other end. It was the blade from a paper-cutting guillotine, removed from its base. It wasn't balanced in any way, and Roxy found it difficult to handle as she tried a few experimental hacking swings.

"Wouldn't a gun of some kind be better?" she asked.

Wolfe turned toward her expressionlessly and reached into his jacket to pull out an automatic pistol. Before she could react, he pointed it at her chest and fired three times. Roxy took a step backwards, too shocked to do anything else and stunned into silence by the waves of pain washing through her. She looked dumbly down at the holes in her t-shirt. She could smell the blood seeping into the fabric. As she raised her hand stupidly to her breast, the pain was replaced by a sudden onset of pins and needles, and by the time she had pulled out the neck of her top to look at the wounds, they were healed. She looked back at Wolfe, who was calmly putting his gun away. Roxy felt as if she ought to fall over, or stagger or something, but her legs had felt weak only for a moment and were now strong again.

"Bullets won't help us against our enemies," said Wolfe darkly. "You might buy yourself a second or two of distraction, but that is all. Only severing their neck or cutting out their heart will truly kill them. And even then be careful."

Roxy was aware of smirks directed toward her, and forced herself not to look round. "Are you going to tell me what's going on?" She was starting to get annoyed. It probably wasn't a good idea to get annoyed at Wolfe, but she was almost past caring. She was getting sick and tired of feeling out of her depth and nervous all the time.

"We are going to pay a visit to Kate Craven," replied Wolfe, turning to include the others, "who is the materfamilias of Domus Craven. Ha! Craven is a fine name for the cowardly wench!" Wolfe laughed, and a moment later the others joined in. "Tonight we shall punish her for her lies. We will fall on Domus Craven hard and without mercy."

Dave let out a whoop of delight and raised his axe. Jessica grinned and licked the machete she was holding. Roxy noticed that James merely nodded, as if he had heard all this before.

"Roxy, do you have transport?" asked Wolfe. She shook her head slowly, a feeling of dread creeping over her.

"You'll have to ride with one of us then."

"I'll take her," offered Sanjay.

"Good. We leave in five minutes."

The group broke up as they went to retrieve bags or to put on jackets, leaving Roxy standing alone. She watched as Wolfe and James huddled together in conversation, while Natalie pulled on fingerless leather gloves with a gleam of excitement in her normally composed face. Dave was hefting his axe in broad circles around him, as if limbering up. Ruth pulled on a heavy looking vest, like the kind police marksmen wore, and then reached for a loose cagoule to conceal it. Marty was concentrating on rolling a cigarette and appeared nervous, but he held a wicked looking staff with jagged blades at either end in the crook of his arm. Roxy wondered how he was intending to carry it through the streets without getting arrested. Sarah was wide-eyed and chattering inanely to Jessica about how exciting this was, and what did she think of it all, while Jessica blatantly ignored her and filed her nails idly. Sarah didn't even notice. A light touch on Roxy's shoulder made her jump.

"Are you okay?" It was Sanjay.

"What's all this about?" Roxy asked.

"Let's just say that Craven and Wolfe don't see eye to eye."

"How bad is it? I mean, does he really expect us to fight them?"

Sanjay nodded, "More than that. You can't fight a vampire and let them live. It's too dangerous. They live too long and hold bitter grudges. Wolfe intends to wipe out her house."

Roxy stared at him in shock. "You can't be serious? How will he get away with it? Won't someone find out?"

"Probably, but as long as no one remains alive to accuse him, people will look the other way. In fact he'll gain respect because he achieved it cleanly." Roxy looked away. She felt sick.

Sanjay leaned in close to whisper to her, "You have to go through with this Roxy. He will be watching you closely. Remember, he can kill you at any time without fear of repercussion. Be careful."

Sanjay's eyes flicked around and he licked his lips nervously, "There's something else you should know," he said.

Roxy looked back at him, but as he started to speak, he clamped his mouth shut and stared past her at something. Roxy turned to see the diminutive Natalie standing nearby with a strange expression on her face. Lust, perhaps?

"It is time," she whispered, holding Sanjay's gaze for a few moments too long, before turning to follow Wolfe. Sanjay flashed Roxy a frustrated look, and then grabbed a black motorcycle helmet with full facemask and gestured for her to lead the way. Outside the air was chill with a hint of impending rain, and several motorcycles and a sports car were parked in the narrow road. Sarah and Jessica climbed into the Lotus while everyone else headed for their bikes. Wolfe had an old Norton with a sidecar that Natalie rode in. Roxy followed Sanjay toward a huge black and grey Suzuki sports bike with full fairing. It looked too big for him, but he handled it easily enough.

"I don't have a spare helmet," he said as he pulled his on, "but don't worry, I won't crash."

Roxy was more worried about getting pulled over by the police, but she swung her leg over the seat behind him, still clutching her guillotine blade and wondering if there was any way she could get out of this.

Wolfe led the procession through the winding streets of London, heading south and east, and Roxy quickly lost track of where she was. She was unused to travelling above ground through the city, but always enjoyed it when she did, finding herself entranced by the mix of architectural styles crowding the skyline. She wrapped her arms tightly around Sanjay, fearing that she would fall off the back of his powerful bike every time he accelerated. Eventually they were travelling down Whitechapel Road towards Bow, passing uncomfortably close to where she lived. For a few moments she half-expected Wolfe to veer off toward her house, but he kept going, taking them further east to the flyover by Bow Church. There, they turned off and double-backed down the narrow side streets, before coming to a stop under an overhead railway track. It was supported by a series of brick arches, which were closed off by large wooden panels to form workshops. A faded sign painted over a set of double doors declared the place to be a Motor Repair shop.

Everyone clustered around Wolfe on the pavement opposite the main door. Roxy followed, holding her makeshift blade.

"This is it. Remember, no survivors!" Wolfe whispered, a manic gleam in his eyes. "Dave, Sanjay, Ruth and Roxy go round the back and stop them escaping. We'll give you a minute to get into position. Go!"

Dave grinned and set off at a run under one of the arches next to the workshop. Ruth and Sanjay exchanged a quick look, and then turned to jog after him. Roxy hurried after them. On the other side of the bridge was an open area, littered with rubbish, in which several cars and a couple of motorbikes were parked. There was a single fire-door leading into the workshop, which opened from inside, and a couple of small, soot covered windows flanking it. Dave sidled up to it and peered in through one of them. Ruth reached inside her cagoule and pulled out a vicious-looking knuckleduster with a large serrated blade jutting forward from the knuckles. Sanjay wore his biker leathers and helmet and now carried a sword.

He caught Roxy's bemused look and flicked up his visor to grin at her, "Armour," he said, tapping his helmet, "works a treat and stops you losing your head."

As he pulled the visor back down, Roxy suddenly felt very naked in just her denim jacket and jeans. She also felt hungry, but the rising tension of the impending attack made it easy to ignore. They waited in silence, listening to faint sounds of music from behind the door, until a massive crash and splintering of wood shook the night. Dave gave a battle cry and raised his axe to smash at the door, which flew inwards off its hinges at the second swing. Then he was inside, vaulting over the remains, swiftly followed by Ruth and Sanjay. Roxy hesitated, trying to fight down her fear and force herself to follow. She licked her lips, took a deep breath, which felt strange, but still oddly comforting, and took a step towards the opening. Just then Ruth flew out headfirst, face-up, thrown by someone inside. Roxy darted to the side before looking back to see that Ruth was still airborne and slowly drifting to the ground. Roxy recognised that she had instinctively increased her speed and reactions again. Ruth's face was a bloodied mess, her nose and cheekbones caved in and her body limp as she fell heavily to the ground, the rough concrete tearing long grazes in the back of her head. Roxy turned to face a tall grinning man in a leather jacket holding a fire extinguisher in both hands. He threw it at her, but she easily stepped aside, letting it sail past her.

She raised her blade defensively, realised that the man seemed to be moving at a normal speed to her, and wondered if she was also back to normal, or if he was as fast as her. He tried to circle around her, and she concentrated on moving to block him, feeling a tingling throughout her body as she moved, and noticing that he seemed to momentarily freeze in place. The man bared his fangs and reached into his belt to pull out a mini-Uzi submachine gun. Roxy tensed, wondering what he expected to achieve, and soon had her answer as he let out a spray of bullets towards her. Roxy staggered back as what felt like dozens of red hot darts peppered her chest, sending blood spurting out in multiple small geysers. She gasped, nearly dropping her blade from the pain and the agonising pins-and-needles numbness that followed as her body stitched itself back together.

Belatedly she remembered to look at her attacker. He was gone. Roxy frantically searched around, then heard a noise above her. The man was scaling the brickwork overhead. Roxy jumped up, reaching out to grasp the wall a dozen feet off the ground. Her fingers dug into the crumbling brickwork like steel pins, creating small hand-holds and she started to climb after the vampire, awkwardly holding her blade. She reached the top and pulled herself over the wall onto the railway tracks to see the man once again pointing the Uzi at her. This time she had no intention of getting hit, and swung her blade at it, striking it solidly. It clattered to the ground and bounced once before hitting the live rail, causing sparks to fountain up with an unnerving crackle. He snarled at her, unconcerned about the loss of his weapon, and stepped in swinging with balled fists. He caught her square on the chin with a force like a pile-driver, and sent her sprawling along the track.

She landed heavily, her head ringing, and tried to stand. He moved like lightning and was suddenly behind her, kicking her back down, this time face first. Something cracked in her side and a spear of pain forced a scream from her lips. Her body desperately tried to heal the damage but it was taking longer than before, and Roxy realised that she was getting tired. She pulled herself to her knees, distantly wondering if there was a limit to how much she could heal, and once again her attacker struck her from behind, catching the side of her head with a savage kick. She was knocked towards the live rail, and flung out her hands in panic, barely managing to stop her face from hitting it. It buzzed below her nose warningly. There was a screeching sound, and she looked up to see a train turning the bend twenty yards away. Her attacker took a step towards her, but she threw herself forwards, tumbling over the outside rail to put some distance between them. Her body ached. She rose to her feet to face the vampire, who had picked up her blade. She couldn't remember dropping it. They both turned to look at the approaching train, and a sly grin came over the face of her opponent. The train would pass between them in seconds, and Roxy realised that if it did she would lose him.

She jumped, passing right in front of the startled driver, and felt the wind at her back as she landed. The man crouched down, raising her blade defensively as she stepped towards him. Not sure what to do, she levelled a kick at him, which he evaded, retreating back against the low wall at the edge of the bridge. Roxy followed, trying to think of a way to wrestle the weapon from him when she noticed the Uzi lying between the tracks. She started towards it, which spurred the man to action. They both reached it at the same time, Roxy getting her hand to it first. He reversed his arm, bringing his elbow into her face and knocking her backwards. He stood up, a sickening smirk on his face as he now had both weapons, and he raised the gun towards her. Then another squeal of metal alerted them to the presence of another train coming in the opposite direction, this time on the track on which Roxy was lying. The man grinned wider, redirecting his aim towards her leg.

Roxy screamed as bullets tore into her thigh, and desperately tried to crawl out of the tracks. The man let out a laugh and kicked her back, waiting for the train to plough into her. Roxy pushed herself up, getting her good leg under her, no longer feeling the pain in her blind panic and did the only thing she could think of. She launched herself at her attacker, driving him back against the wall, and pushing him over it. Her momentum was too much for her crippled leg to counter and she followed him over, unable to stop. They fell thirty feet to the concrete below, landing close together at the edge of the car park.

Roxy lay on her side, unmoving, her entire body numb, waiting for the pain to come. When it did she thought she would pass out, but her eyes remained open, staring helplessly at the other vampire, who was slowly picking himself up off the ground and bending to retrieve her blade. He looked in pain too, but was healing much faster than she was. She had called on her body too many times that night. She felt a dull tingle and knew she was healing slowly, but there was no way she could recover before he reached her. She couldn't even muster up enough energy to panic. He stepped across her, moving out of her sight.

"You little shit," he gasped, kneeling down behind her.

Roxy heard the sound of the metal blade dragging across concrete as he raised it to deliver a blow to her neck. Roxy closed her eyes. She'd never thought of herself as someone who gave up, but it was just too hard this time. She was beaten.

# Chapter 18

There was a clatter of steel on concrete and a dull thud. Roxy opened her eyes and managed to roll away from him, knowing she was moving too slowly to save herself, but frantic to do something. She saw his body, still with his knees curled under him, but he had fallen backwards onto his ankles. The guillotine blade lay by his hand. Roxy struggled to sit up, blinking against the pain her chest, and stared at the object lying next to him. It was his head. Thankfully his face was turned away from her, but she could see it starting to decay before her eyes, desiccating and turning to dust, collapsing under its own weight. The same was happening to his corpse, which quickly became a shrivelled husk clothed in leather and denim. Roxy looked around fearfully, but she was alone.

Roxy swayed to her feet, wincing as her body complained, and tried to ignore the pins and needles which were painful enough on their own. She glanced down at the body again. "Well I can probably rule out suicide," she muttered, unable to explain what had happened. She hadn't seen or heard anything. A shiver ran down her spine and she decided that she'd rather be with the rest of the house – safety in numbers, and all that. She staggered back to the road where they had parked their bikes, not quite ready to brave the inside of Craven's lair yet. She could hear sounds of fighting from inside and noticed that Ruth's body was gone. She must have healed and gone back in, she thought.

She passed under the archway and was halfway across the road when there was a crash behind her, and she was illuminated by headlights. A car had burst through the double doors, tearing them off and it sped towards her. Roxy tried to move, but her body refused to respond. She had just enough time to see a young blonde woman behind the wheel of the Porsche, before it ploughed into her, sending her bouncing off the bonnet, over the roof and into the gutter, her legs shattered and twisted under her. *For fuck's sake,* was the only thing Roxy thought as another wave of pain overtook her. This time, she passed out.

She came round a few moments later, a dull but persistent ache pulsing through her. She opened her eyes blearily, and saw that the Porsche had crashed into the bridge support. The driver had presumably lost control after hitting her. As she watched, Wolfe came into view from the driver's side. He was holding the woman by her throat. He was joined by James, who grabbed the woman's arms from behind, and then Natalie, who advanced on her with a triumphant smile on her face. She said something that Roxy couldn't hear, and Wolfe and James shifted their grip to move either side of the woman, who was staring at Natalie in abject horror. Roxy watched Natalie raise a hand to stroke the woman's face, an almost loving gesture, then lower it to a point between her breasts. Fortunately Natalie's body blocked her next action from Roxy, but from the sudden movement of her shoulders and the wide-eyed reaction of the woman, she knew what had happened. Roxy almost looked away, but didn't, and so she was still watching as Natalie drew out the woman's heart, raised it to her lips, and bit into it. Roxy felt bile rising, and turned over, expecting to vomit, but could only manage a couple of dry heaves. She struggled to her feet, dimly aware that her legs were working again, and wondered "Hell, just how much punishment can I take?" None of the others were in the street, so Roxy stumbled towards the broken doors, for some reason unwilling to let Wolfe know that she had witnessed the scene.

She pulled herself into the workshop to see Jessica, Sarah and Ruth dragging several dried husks that were once vampires into a pile in the middle of the room. Ruth's face was stained with dried blood, but she was otherwise unmarred.

"Jesus, Roxy," she said in her lilting French accent, "you look terrible. You must be hungry."

Roxy suddenly realised that she was, and curled up in pain as her stomach demanded attention.

Jessica laughed, "Oh poor thing. You'd better get something quick dear, or the Little Death will take you."

Roxy barely heard her. Her ears were roaring, her vision blurred, and she slid to the floor, her legs too weak to support her. Jessica and Ruth exchanged a few more words, which Roxy didn't understand, but the tone seemed to indicate that Ruth was pleading with her about something. After a few more exchanges, Jessica gave up, and said something to someone. Then Roxy felt something soft touch her lips, and a feminine voice calling her. She opened her eyes, and saw Sarah kneeling alongside, holding her wrist to her mouth. Sarah bit into it, drawing blood, and offered it to Roxy.

The smell engulfed her, stirring her into action, and she clamped her mouth around the wound, sucking hungrily at the precious fluid. Gradually the pain in her stomach eased, and her vision cleared. She became aware of other pains, mainly bruises across her chest and legs, which were rapidly replaced by the now familiar pins-and-needles sensation of healing. She continued to suck and drink, unable to break away, even after the pain was gone. She heard Sarah give a frightened moan and tried to push her away, but Roxy grabbed the wrist and held on tighter. She felt hands on her shoulders pulling her away from the exquisite liquor, and thrashed and kicked, desperate not to lose contact with the wound, an animalistic, selfish act which was pure id, crushing all higher thought processes.

Then it was gone, and she was sprawled on the floor, licking her lips. Slowly, her composure returned, and she looked up to see Ruth standing warily above her, and Sarah shuffling backwards on her bottom, clutching her swollen wrist.

"Uh, I'm sorry," started Roxy, ashamed at her actions after they had been trying to help her.

"It is okay," said Ruth, squatting down next to her. "It is normal. It can be dangerous to feed a hungry vampire like that, but I was expecting it. Always make sure there is another present to break the feed."

Roxy looked across at Sarah, who appeared pale, but was smiling again. "Thank you."

"That's okay Roxy. Don't worry, I'm okay.'

Roxy sat up slowly, "What would have happened if I'd continued to drink?"

Ruth's face darkened, and she looked at Sarah. "It would have been bad. You might have sent her into the Little Death instead. We need blood to exist, to continue. It draws more energy to use our physical powers, such as strength, speed and healing, than merely resting, which is why you were so hungry just now, but the end result is the same. Without blood we lose the ability to move, so our bodies collapse into a coma, unseeing and unfeeling, and will remain that way forever, unless someone comes along and drips blood into your mouth."

"So you can still recover from it?"

Ruth nodded, "Yes, but most horrible of all; it is said that you are still aware of what is happening, and are trapped in the helpless shell of your body, unable to call for aid. It is a common punishment for those that deserve more than death."

Roxy shuddered, wishing she had never asked.

"Your body rarely lets you get to that stage though," Ruth continued, "at a certain point, the darkness inside takes over, and hunts for you, turning you into an unthinking monster. That can be dangerous too, as you will attack the first thing you see, which could be a friend."

Roxy remembered her lack of control when she had hunted Simon. It would have been nice to have known that earlier, she thought bitterly. It seemed that people only told you things after you had found them out for yourself.

Roxy rose and noticed Marty sitting quietly in a corner, patiently rolling a cigarette. Beside him lay another shrivelled body in a dress which had obviously once been a woman. She didn't see any weapons near the woman's body. In fact, Roxy realised, very few of the Craven vampires appeared to have been armed. Jessica sauntered over to Marty, her hands on her hips.

"Are you going to help us here, or what?"

"Just a moment," he replied, in his slow, measured voice. He put his finished cigarette behind his ear and then leaned over the body, reaching for something. He unclipped a gold chain from its neck and a couple of rings from its fingers before slipping them into his pocket. Only then did he pick up the body and take it to the pile in the middle of the room, under Jessica's amused gaze. Roxy found it somewhat distasteful, but didn't say anything. She'd done worse things in the past.

"You really are pathetic aren't you?" sneered Jessica.

Marty shrugged, "We can't all have millionaire husbands can we?"

"Then get one," Jessica replied tartly, "you're a vampire, you can do anything you want."

"I have more respect for people than that."

"Meaning?" Jessica's voice was like ice. Roxy flicked her eyes to Ruth, who was concentrating on ignoring the exchange.

Marty glanced towards Sarah meaningfully. Jessica followed his gaze and laughed.

"Sarah doesn't mind, do you dear?"

Sarah had been standing mutely with a slight frown of confusion on her face, but smiled back at Jessica, not really comprehending what she meant, but eager to agree with her.

Marty turned away with a sigh and a shake of his head. Roxy got the impression that this was an old argument they were continuing. Jessica rolled her eyes and turned to Roxy.

"Marty thinks we should try to be more human. He seems to forget what we are now. What do you think Roxy?"

Roxy shrugged, unwilling to be drawn into anything. Jessica narrowed her eyes and gave her a thin smile.

"You'll work it out soon enough dear. If you live long enough, that is."

Roxy stared back at her, holding her gaze for slightly longer than necessary. She knew it was a foolish thing to do, but she found herself unable to roll over and accept Jessica's taunts without some show of defiance. Jessica turned away, her smile growing broader.

"Where are Sanjay and Dave?" asked Ruth, breaking the tension somewhat.

Marty jerked a thumb over his shoulder, gesturing to a door at the end of the room, "They went that-a-way, checking for stragglers I imagine."

Ruth caught Roxy's eye and started to walk towards the door. Roxy followed, happy to be away from Jessica and the pile of dried corpses. Ruth opened the door and crept in, and Roxy copied her, unsure what to expect. She was acutely aware that she was unarmed, and hoped that Ruth would be able to cope with any surprises on her own. Beyond the door there was a storeroom containing crates and boxes of car parts. The smell of oil and grime made Roxy's eyes water. In the middle of the room, sitting cross-legged on the floor with his back to them, was Dave, his axe cradled across his lap and a body laid out in front of him. He seemed to be going through its pockets. Roxy glanced about for Sanjay, and spotted his helmet, carefully placed on a stack of tyres.

"Dave," whispered Ruth.

He turned to look over his shoulder at her, "Ruth," he acknowledged.

Ruth relaxed her guard, and walked in, looking at the body on the floor. Roxy hung back, something worrying her.

"What have you got here?" Ruth asked.

"Roy, one of Craven's brood."

"Where is Sanjay?" Ruth asked.

Dave tilted his head towards the far corner. Ruth and Roxy looked, and saw a pair of feet poking out from between some racking. Roxy circled over to them, and saw what had once been Sanjay, sprawled on the ground, his severed head lying to one side, the skin tightened with age and split in some places. She looked away, but the image of his corpse remained, as if burnt onto her retina.

"What happened?" asked Ruth tightly from beside Roxy.

"We were jumped," said Dave, "he killed Sanjay before I could do anything. I finished it though."

Roxy looked at the body in front of her. It was difficult to tell, but it looked to be reasonably intact, with the only obvious wound apart from the decapitation, being a large cut in the middle of his back. It looked more like an axe strike than a sword strike. She glanced at Dave and found him staring at her challengingly.

Beside her, Ruth clucked her tongue, "It was a pity he took his helmet off before making sure the room was clear, wasn't it?" Roxy guessed from her pointed tone that she had drawn the same conclusions as her.

"A terrible shame," agreed Dave, tonelessly, shifting his gaze to stare at Ruth.

Ruth shrugged and bent to pick up Sanjay's body. "Grab the head Roxy. Get the helmet too; we don't want to leave anything behind."

Roxy looked down at the head and blanched, struggling to fight back a desire to throw up, but decided that she would much rather do that than spend another few seconds in the room alone with Dave. She reached down and gingerly grasped the head by the hair, but shuddered with disgust as it came away easily from the rapidly decomposing scalp. She took a deep breath, which didn't have the normal calming effect she was hoping for, and grasped the head with both hands. She carefully balanced it in one hand as she walked back towards the door, and grabbed Sanjay's motorcycle helmet as she passed. She couldn't get back to the main room fast enough, and dropped the head on the edge of the pile with shudder. It hit the ground with a dry crack and split open, spilling a dark grey dust from within before crumbling away to large, unrecognisable fragments.

"Ewww," exclaimed Sarah from behind her, "poor Sanjay."

"Sanjay's dead?" Wolfe's commanding voice demanded from the shattered double doors. He was flanked by Natalie and James, who was carrying Kate Craven's corpse over his shoulder.

Ruth gestured to the body on top of the pile, "Unfortunately yes. Dave was there if you want to know the details."

Roxy held her tongue about her suspicions. If Ruth wasn't prepared to mention it, it probably wasn't wise for her to say anything either. At that moment Dave appeared, carrying the body of the last Craven vampire under one arm, and holding his axe in the other. Wolfe merely made a dismissive motion and stepped into the room.

"Well it is only to be expected. Still, we took out seven of them with only one loss, so I count that as victory, don't you? And I personally finished off Craven. She won't be bothering anyone ever again." He grinned and gestured to James to dump her body on the pile.

Roxy narrowed her eyes and glanced at Natalie, wondering how she would take his interpretation of events, but her face was its usual impassive mask, slightly bored, with no sign of surprise. Neither was James surprised. Wolfe had obviously told them what he was going to claim as they were walking back from the car wreck. Why would he do that? Roxy wondered. Probably an ego thing, knowing Wolfe.

"Is that all of them?" Wolfe asked, looking at the pile of corpses. Roxy remembered that the body of the one that she had been fighting was still outside

"There's still one more out the back," she volunteered quietly.

"You killed one?" Wolfe's eyes gleamed in delight. Roxy made a non-committal gesture that Wolfe took as an affirmative.

"Excellent. James will see to it. I see you've also already claimed Sanjay's bike, Roxy," chuckled Wolfe, looking at the helmet still clutched in her hand. "I like that, and it's no bad thing. Take it. Can you ride?"

Roxy opened her mouth to protest, then closed it again and shrugged, "I can learn." Ruth stepped over to Sanjay's body and reached into his pocket for the keys, which she tossed at Roxy.

"Good." Wolfe turned back to the group, which had now formed a half-circle in front of him. "Remember, no one talks about tonight. We were never here. For the sake of our newbie," he glanced at Roxy, "I remind you that what we did will get all of us killed if it ever came out. Understand?"

More nods. Roxy nodded too, a cold knot forming in her stomach. She was also getting hungry again. Sarah's blood was not going to be enough to keep her going for long.

"Right," finished Wolfe, "get going. Meet back tomorrow night at the club at ten. There will be a Gathering."

There were murmurs of assent and people started to disperse. James picked up a petrol can and tipped it over the bodies, soaking them liberally, before starting on the rest of the room. Roxy followed the others back to the vehicles. Sanjay's bike looked huge to her. She had never driven a bike before, and the prospect was somewhat daunting. She threw her leg over it, thankful for once of her height and wondered how to start it.

"Roxy," called Ruth from behind her. Roxy turned to see her and Marty approaching. Ruth was carrying Sanjay's sword.

"Take this too," she handed the sword to Roxy, "you'll probably need it."

Roxy looked at it dubiously, wondering how to carry it, and then spotted a long bag running alongside the bike, and slipped it inside.

"Know what to do?" Marty looked over her arm at the dashboard. Roxy noticed the speedometer went up to 200 miles an hour.

"Uh," started Roxy, "not really."

Marty pointed to the ignition, "Put the key in here to start it. The left handle is your clutch, the right is the front brake, your right foot sits near the rear brake and your left foot..."

"Switches the gears," finished Roxy, realising that this was all familiar to her. She gunned the engine and revved it a few times, suddenly aware that she knew how to ride it. Simon. Simon had owned a bike. She felt another pang of regret, mixed with triumph at her new skill and looked at Marty. "I've got it." She pulled on her helmet and released the brake, gently easing away onto the road under Marty's bemused gaze. The bike was heavier than anything Simon had ridden, but she had the size, and the vampire-enhanced strength and balance to handle it easily, after a few initial wobbles. It was like the proverbial riding a bicycle, she decided, a muscle memory that she had never before possessed, but it seemed natural to her. She opened the throttle, her mind threatening to shut down in protest at the impossibility of it, and allowed herself to be lost in the thrill of the ride.

# Chapter 19

She arrived home well after three in the morning. She had meant to go straight home, but found she needed time to clear her head, and the bike ride had helped considerably. She rode all the way across London and back, just following the front wheel of the bike, not caring where she was going.

She would have been home a lot earlier if she hadn't stopped to feed. She found herself passing Lincoln's Inn Fields, and pulled over to drink from a beggar curled up on a bench. She'd struggled with her conscience for a few moments, feeling some kinship with the man, who looked to be in his forties, covered in newspapers and empty cans of Special Brew, but hunger quickly overcame her and she bit into his grimy wrist.

Unfortunately, something else no one had bothered to tell her happened. She got drunk. His blood was so heavily laced with alcohol that it affected her too. She found herself drinking several more mouthfuls than she intended, and when she stood up, she toppled backwards in a dizzy fit. She stumbled to her new bike, giggling quietly to herself as she tried and failed to walk in a straight line, and after several abortive attempts to get the key in the ignition, she leaned over to look at herself in the wing mirror.

"You're pissed," she told herself sternly, then broke out in another fit of giggles. She had never been good at alcohol, but she couldn't remember ever being this badly affected before. She hadn't even drunk very much of his blood really. She was in just enough possession of her senses to realise that trying to ride the bike in her current state would be stupid, so she swung her leg off it, nearly dropping the bike in the process, and started to walk down the quiet streets, pushing the bike and singing softly to herself. Eventually, as she neared Aldgate, she felt clear-headed enough to try again, and managed to ride carefully back the rest of the way home without incident.

She pulled up outside her flat and dismounted, a nagging worry crossing her mind that the bike wasn't really safe there. It had a heavy security chain in the stowage bin, and the key to it was on Sanjay's key ring, but it might still get vandalised in this neighbourhood. Roxy scolded herself. It's not even really your bike Rox, she thought. Stop worrying about it. You never had it before did you? She pulled off her helmet, unloaded the sword, and walked towards her door. She passed a white transit van and almost collided with a startled man in his late twenties, about her height, who stared at her in shock, before mumbling a hurried apology and walking off. Roxy looked down at herself. Her clothes were stained black in the orange glow of the streetlights, covered in dried blood. Several bullet holes riddled her T-shirt, and her jeans were torn away along her thigh and knees. She would have startled anyone, she realised, and hurried up the narrow path leading to her door. She fumbled in her pockets for her key, and was just pulling it out, when her senses came alive again – the prickles down the back of her neck seemed to warn her of danger. She crouched down, turning her back to the door and scanned the street. It was empty.

She sniffed. There. A scent. Male. Familiar. She lowered her head to the ground and it grew stronger. Someone had recently come up her path to her front door. She moved her head to the side, sniffing the ground like a dog, tracing the movements. He had crept over to the window and tried to look in, and peered through her letter box. It was the shocked man she had nearly bumped into. She had caught his scent only briefly, but she recognised it now. She stood up and looked down the road in the direction he had been heading. She couldn't see him, but there was a corner not far away. He could have turned off. She shuffled back to the road, half crouched, following his scent and started jogging after him. Who was he? He was mortal, she was sure. Vampires didn't sweat. She was annoyed and slightly worried, which annoyed her even more. Well she would soon find out, and he'd better have a good reason for snooping around her house, otherwise... She didn't finish her thought, but her blood was starting to sing with anticipation.

She walked on down the road and bent her head down, following the scent trail and only looking up when she turned a corner, or rounded a bend. Then she looked up and blinked in confusion. She was back on the road where she lived, about thirty yards from her flat, and the sky was tinged a definite pink. It was dawn. Roxy frowned. How could that be? She hadn't been running around for an hour, had she? She bent down and searched for the scent. She couldn't find it at first, it was so faint, but as she crossed over the road and it became stronger. It reached its strongest at an empty parking spot not quite opposite her flat, but affording a very good view of it. Someone had parked here for a while. She picked up a couple of fainter trails leading to her house, and then onward towards the tube station, following the path she had taken on the way to Wolfe's earlier that night. Someone had been following her. Roxy looked up at the sky. It was starting to get painfully bright now. She turned away from the trail and hurried back to her flat. What the fuck had just happened? She'd suddenly lost an hour. Was she still drunk? She didn't feel drunk, but she did have a headache starting to form. Maybe a hangover? She let herself into the flat and locked the door behind her, remembering to leave the chain off so that Scarlet could let herself in, and looked at her torn and bloody reflection in the mirror. Well one thing was certain, she admitted. She needed to start buying more clothes.

# Chapter 20

The cavern was blacker than pitch and she couldn't see her hand in front of her face, but the smell of the dragon was heavy and choking. A continuous drip, drip, drip echoed around her, betraying the great size of chamber she was in. She turned, frightened, and a gust of warm air caught her full in the face, carrying a cloying, rotting odour that made her gag. The breath of the dragon. She stepped back, the rock beneath her feet worn smooth by countless years of the worm's passage. Her eyes strained ahead, searching for something. Then, a light blazed before her, dazzling and penetrating. She squinted as the light grew in size, rancid yellow like a low summer moon, split in the middle by a vertical black void. It was the slit-like pupil of a monstrous eye. She found herself cemented to the spot, paralysed as the dragon opened its eye, and sought her out, delving into the very depths of her being, and stripping away her secrets, leaving her naked and helpless under its gaze...

"Why do you always keep the curtains closed?" asked Scarlet, reaching up to open them.

"No!" shouted Roxy, groggily, holding up a hand to stop her. She was lying on the couch in the front room and had only dimly been aware of Scarlet letting herself in a few minutes earlier. Roxy struggled to open her eyes and sit up. Daylight filtering through the curtains made her wince and look away from Scarlet, who was standing in front of them.

"Okay, okay, I'll leave 'em," grumbled Scarlet and walked past her into the kitchen where Roxy could hear the kettle roaring. Her head throbbed, but she couldn't tell whether it was from the alcohol the night before or from tiredness. A bit of both, she suspected, shaking away the last remnants of a persistent dream. "What time is it?" she asked

"Late. It's after eleven," called Scarlet from behind her. "I thought I'd give you a lie in. It looks like you needed longer though," she joked. "Coffee?"

"Uh sure," replied Roxy, now sitting up properly and rubbing her face. Claudia and Leah were on the floor in front of her playing with a pair of stuffed bunnies. Claudia looked up at her and raised her hands, wanting to be lifted up. Roxy pulled her onto her lap and hugged her. She was wearing only her bra and panties, and noticed last night's ruined clothes discarded in a corner. With a groan she stood up, holding Claudia in one arm and picked them up. She didn't want Scarlet to see them.

"I'm going to get dressed," she called towards the kitchen, and headed to her bedroom. Dumping the tattered clothes in a corner and settling Claudia on the bed, she pulled open her closet and tried to find something to wear. She had only one pair of jeans left, her favourite hipster stonewashed ones. She really ought to go back to Clive's and get the rest of her clothes. And her phone. Reluctantly she pulled them out, promising herself that she wouldn't ruin these. Grabbing another t-shirt and a change of underwear she dressed, wishing that her head would stop throbbing. Claudia giggled as she played with the pillows on the bed and Roxy sat down beside her to tickle her when she was done. Claudia babbled away, earnestly explaining something very important to her mother. "Uh huh? Really? You don't say?" encouraged Roxy, rolling on the bed beside her. She looked at Claudia, who was happily burying herself in the bedding, and a wave of despair washed over her. What will become of her, she wondered. What if I don't come back one night? Even if I manage to stay alive what about when she gets older and goes to school? How can I look after her if I have to spend my days sleeping? She rubbed her eyes. She didn't have any answers, apart from the one she refused to consider. Adoption.

"Coffee's ready!" yelled Scarlet, making Roxy wince.

"Come on then munchkin," she said, chasing Claudia down, "let's go and play." Roxy and Claudia returned to the front room where Scarlet had placed the coffee. The smell of it made Roxy's mouth start to water. God she missed it. Maybe she could try just a little? Hesitantly she took a small sip, held it in her mouth for a moment savouring the taste, and then swallowed. Her stomach immediately cramped up, but she fought back the rising bile and managed to hold it down. She put the cup back on the table, flushed with her small success, but not willing to push herself too far.

"So how did you do last night?" Scarlet asked

"Mmm?" Roxy looked up

"You know...the special gig?"

Roxy recovered herself. "Oh it was okay. Nothing special in the end."

"Oh," Scarlet's face fell and she sat back on the couch. "Well never mind. Better luck next time."

Roxy nodded. She remembered her promise, and also that Wolfe had told her to meet at the club later. Roxy closed her eyes and cursed mentally. "Uh, you know I said I'd baby-sit Leah tonight and tomorrow?" she started.

"Yeah, well actually my mum is coming over tonight so she will do it." Scarlet made a grimace, "She is bringing over a friend's son, a 'nice Hong Kong boy'," she said, assuming a Chinese accent in an impersonation of her mother, "as she calls him, to take me out. She is still hoping to marry me off and rescue me from my debauched lifestyle."

Roxy made a sympathetic face, at once relieved that she didn't have to look after Leah that night, and wondering what to do with Claudia. There was no way Scarlet's mother would agree to look after her while Scarlet went out on her date. "Well, maybe he'll be ...," Roxy paused, searching for the right word.

"Bearable?" offered Scarlet sardonically. Roxy looked at her, and they both started laughing.

"Well Scar what can I say? It sucks to be you," Roxy grinned.

"I know, but look at the company I keep," Scarlet retorted with a smile. She glanced at her watch, "I should get going."

Roxy nodded, eager to get back to sleep. Her head was still aching. Scarlet gathered up a few things, picked up Leah and let herself out. Roxy didn't dare go anywhere near the front door.

# Chapter 21

Roxy woke as the sun was starting to set. She had managed to stay awake for several hours until it was time to put Claudia down for a nap. Then she stumbled back into the front room and passed out on the couch. Roxy jerked awake as Claudia let out a feeble cry and swung to her feet. She felt a pang of shame as she opened the door and found Claudia sitting up on the bed clutching a teddy bear, her face red and shiny with tears. She flung herself into her mother's arms and laid her head against her shoulder, gripping her tightly as though she wanted to never be left alone again. Roxy walked slowly back to the front room, cooing softly and stroking Claudia's back until she settled.

I can't keep doing this, she thought. It's not right. Vivid memories surfaced of being left alone in her room for hours at a time while her mother and stepfather drank and took drugs. She had felt intolerably lonely, bitter and angry as she knew her younger step-brothers were allowed to do as they pleased, and even join in, no matter that they were only nine or ten. When she had fled her home at fifteen she'd made a vow to herself that she would not bring up her children in the same way, yet here she was, abandoning her helpless daughter to fear and confusion. Unbidden, she felt a sudden, violent anger towards Wolfe for his unreasonable demands on her. It subsided to a dull loathing of whoever it was that cursed her with vampirism, which she knew would never fade completely. Some things cannot be forgiven, no matter how much religion you find.

She arrived at Wolfe's club an hour later with Claudia carefully protected from the wind by her jacket and a scarf. It was a foolish thing to do, bringing Claudia, but she suspected not quite as foolish as not showing up at all. Besides, they all knew about her now so what more harm could be done? This small act of defiance might get them both killed, but she needed to do it to stop herself slipping away, to regain control of her life again. She'd spent so much of it refusing to let others dictate to her how to act or what to do, that allowing it to happen now made her uncertain and hesitant. Traits which would certainly not help her survival. She lifted her chin, squared her shoulders, and walked purposefully into the club, which was not yet open to the public.

Inside were Ruth, Marty, Dave and James, standing in a loose group in the centre of the dance floor. Roxy noticed at once that they were dressed in formal wear. Ruth was wearing a glittering ruby ball-gown, and the men were in tuxedos. Roxy's heart shrank and her stomach knotted with embarrassment as she glanced down at her jeans and t-shirt. Dave looked up at her as she entered and broke into a smug grin, but it was the pitying look in Ruth's eyes that really touched her. Damn Wolfe for not telling me, she thought. Did he do it on purpose?

"Come in Roxy," said James in a controlled voice, "the others should be here soon."

"Should I go home and get changed?" she asked, trying to ignore Dave.

James shook his head, "There's no time. It doesn't matter. I think the last thing people will notice is your clothes," he continued, glancing meaningfully at Claudia.

Roxy braced herself for an argument, but James turned away and went to sit at a table near the empty bar. Ruth came over to her, closely followed by Marty, who seemed to find her appearance humorous, but not in a malicious way, she sensed.

"Are you mad?" Ruth hissed in a whisper.

Roxy assumed she was talking about Claudia and shrugged, simply holding Ruth's gaze challengingly. Ruth stared at her for a moment and then shook her head with a sigh.

"Let's hope Catallus is in a good mood tonight," she muttered.

Marty, on the other hand held out his finger to Claudia and tried to tickle her cheek. Claudia looked at him warily at first, but then responded with a giggle. Roxy let Marty play with her daughter, feeling cold and numb inside. She was going to die, she knew, and Claudia with her. She should leave now, run away and maybe she could survive for a few years until Claudia was old enough to take care of herself, or at least to remember her mother. That was the worst thing about contemplating adoption, Roxy realised; that her beautiful, precious daughter would not know her, even as a memory.

She had been older than Claudia was now, perhaps two, when her father left her mother, and she had no memory of him at all. She only knew what he looked like from an old photograph she had found once behind the fridge. The colours had faded to give it a reddish-brown tint, but it showed a young man, about the same age as she was now, wearing a Royal Air Force uniform. He was attractive, with the same unruly black hair and cocky smile that Roxy had. He looked very smart and responsible, but a few adolescent pimples on his forehead betrayed his youth. As a twelve year old girl, she used to imagine him as a brave fighter pilot, protecting his country from its enemies, and living a normal life, with a loving family. She had long since learned not to ask her mother about him. All she would admit to was his name, John and that they had been married, but she had replaced him within months by a grifter called Tom Watts and refused to tell her any more.

Sarah and Jessica arrived with a flourish that Roxy already knew was typical of Jessica. She had to be the centre of attention, who demanded to be seen and admired. They were both wearing expensive designer dresses, and Jessica had pinned her hair up on top of her head to form a kind of spiky fan. Sarah spotted Roxy and gave her a welcoming smile, but the room was abruptly filled with Jessica's mocking, ugly laughter.

"Oh my dear Roxy, what *are* you wearing? Is this Stepney-chic?" she cackled happily.

Roxy barely glanced at her and turned her head away, hoping she would leave it that. She was wrong, and Jessica continued to make caustic comments, circling around to see the reaction on her face.

"Oh and look, she's brought her child-thing with her too. A fashion accessory, no doubt? Couldn't find a handbag at Harrods to go with your polyester?"

Roxy turned to look at her finally, struggling to control her anger. "Yeah that's right Jessica," she found herself saying casually. She had meant to tell her to piss off and get out of her face, but something else had taken over, and put different words into her mouth. It wasn't like her at all. It was more like Simon, she recognised with a shock. In any case Jessica seemed even more surprised than Roxy. She was obviously expecting some sort of counter-insult or angry retort, rather than the friendly agreement Roxy had offered, and it totally wrong-footed her. She opened her mouth to say something, then blinked and closed it again, looking remarkably like a floundering fish.

Desperate to recover and aware of the curious looks from the others, Jessica attempted a laugh, rolled her eyes, and turned away as if she couldn't be bothered to waste any more time on her. Roxy caught a delighted expression on Marty's face, which he deftly masked when Jessica turned in his direction, but just that momentary glimpse made

Roxy feel a whole lot better. She still wasn't sure she liked the idea of someone else's words in her mouth though. Memories were one thing, but did that mean her thoughts were now partly his too? She'd never considered that her very identity would be at risk, along with her life.

Wolfe and Natalie arrived a few minutes later, both dressed impeccably, and dashing Roxy's last hope that he would be wearing something rebellious. Wolfe scanned the room, evidently in a good mood, and only briefly lingered on Roxy, before leading the group outside. He did not take them to their vehicles, as Roxy had expected, but instead led the way to the tube station down the road. Roxy fell into step alongside Marty, who simply exchanged a glance with her which she fancied was welcoming and tinged with newfound respect.

They walked in silence, which suited Roxy well as she tried to calm her jangling nerves. There was a curiously tense atmosphere among them as they mounted the train carriage, which was almost empty save for a couple of youths wearing baseball caps and bomber jackets, who kept their eyes to themselves after an initial guarded evaluation. Roxy didn't ask where they were going. She really didn't care. Her world seemed to have contracted to just a few minutes either side of the present. Anything else was irrelevant. She listened to the steady thrum and squeal of the train on the rails as it headed south, letting her body sway in response to the turns it made.

At Tottenham Court Road, Wolfe led them off the carriage towards a disused part of the station which was blocked off by a padlocked iron gate. Roxy recognised the gate; she passed by it every time she came up to Central London to work in the Soho clubs. She had never given it any thought before but now, beside the gate, waited a bored looking underground official, who stood straighter when he saw them approaching. Without a word, he pulled a key from his pocket and unlocked the gate. Wolfe passed through with barely a glance at the man, as did the others. The guard locked the gate behind them and Roxy found herself in a dimly lit passage which emerged onto an old platform which clearly had not been used in decades. Wolfe turned to the group.

"Right. You know the deal. Be careful what you say. Don't trust anyone. And remember, say nothing...nothing," he repeated for effect, "about what happened last night with Craven. We were never there. It never happened."

Wolfe looked each in the eye in turn to make sure they understood, before making for a plain wooden door at the far end of the platform. Roxy looked down at Claudia, who had fallen asleep against her chest and wondered if it was too late to back out. Feeling as if someone else was controlling her actions, she turned and resignedly followed Wolfe into a service tunnel that ran parallel to the track. Illumination came from a series of dull lights set into the ceiling at regular intervals. They walked for about fifteen minutes, occasionally breaking out in conversation, which Roxy didn't listen to, and eventually they came to a door which opened onto another disused platform. Roxy looked at the tiled walls and read the name of the station: "British Museum".

"I didn't know there was a station for the museum," she whispered to Ruth.

"It was closed in the thirties. It's between Tottenham Court Road and Holborn. You can still see the white tiles from the trains if you know to look for it."

Wolfe walked quickly towards some concrete steps leading up. They climbed two flights and then passed into a well lit passageway with clean walls and floor. Roxy squinted against the sudden brightness, noticing with some satisfaction that several of the others were too.

"Where does this lead?" Roxy asked Marty.

"It is a secret entrance into the Museum. That's where the Gathering will be tonight."

"Is it always here?"

Marty shook his head, "No, it moves around depending on the whim of the elders. I guess it keeps things interesting for them."

Roxy nodded and fell into step behind him. After a hundred yards or so, they came to a secure metal door at which Wolfe stopped and knocked. It was opened by a tall, emaciated figure flanked by two menacing looking men who had somehow squeezed themselves into dark suits.

"Domus Wolfe, here for the Gathering," Wolfe declared. The tall figure scanned the group with a dispassionate gaze, which fell on Roxy and his eyes moved down to look at the infant cradled in the carrier strapped across her chest. Roxy thought for a moment that he might question her presence, but he merely looked at Wolfe and nodded, moving aside to allow them in. Roxy followed the others through and found herself standing in the high-ceilinged, marble-floored lower halls of the British Museum. Around her were dozens of vampires dressed in their finery and all turned as one to look at the newcomers, and especially at Roxy.

# Chapter 22

Roxy felt desperately self-conscious under the glare of the vampires, acutely aware of Claudia in her arms and her inappropriate attire. Wolfe sauntered into the hall, flanked by James and Natalie. Sarah trailed after Jessica, who was enthusiastically greeting a small group of women clustered by some ancient Greek statuary. Ruth seemed to recognise someone, and crossed the floor to talk to them. Dave and Marty hung about for a few moments, then drifted idly away in different directions, leaving Roxy standing alone.

Roxy tried to ignore the curious, disdainful glances cast at her, and headed for a quiet spot near a flight of stairs. She tried to affect a nonchalant attitude, as if this kind of thing happened to her all the time, but her insides felt like shards of flint, piercing her heart with every step. Once again she found herself hating Wolfe for putting her in this situation without any guidance. Well fuck him, she decided, it's not like you haven't been taking care of yourself for years anyway. This is just the same kind of thing, with different rules. All she had to do was learn the rules, the first of which seemed to be everyone for themselves.

Claudia mewled, woke up and craned her neck to look around. Roxy cooed at her, trying to ignore her embarrassment as several pairs of eyes turned in her direction, attracted by the sound. She looked up to see a man and a woman gliding towards her, with unfriendly smiles forming on their faces. Both were very beautiful and they looked like negative images of each other. They were of similar build and height, and moved in unison. Her hair was platinum blonde, straight and silky and her clinging white gown only emphasised her pale skin, making her look like one of the statues on display. In contrast, the man was wearing a black tuxedo, and had thick black hair and eyebrows and dark eyes which were fixed on Claudia.

Roxy knew she was going to be tormented, so she stood up straighter and tilted her head back, making full use of her height, and looked down at them. She was pleased to see a slight narrowing of the man's eyes as he looked up at her. She had learned long ago that a simple change in posture could alter people's attitude to her, although it was difficult to predict in which way. Some reacted to the intimidation with anger or violence, but most reverted to a wary respect, which was what she was hoping for now.

The woman looked up at her with an amused smile, "You must be Wolfe's new stray? How wonderful. It must be so exciting for you?"

Roxy stared back at her levelly, not committing herself to an answer. She noticed that the man had stopped frowning and was now smiling again. Well so much for intimidation she thought.

"Did you forget to dress? Or is this a statement you are making?"

"Leave it out Brooke," came a voice from above. Roxy looked up to see Vicky coming down the stairs, and felt a sudden surge of relief. She was dressed in a simple blouse and jeans, and her hair was pulled into a ponytail on the top of her head, which along with the shaved sides gave her a slightly ascetic look. She wasn't wearing a ball-gown either, which made Roxy feel better too.

Brooke looked at Vicky, and made a face, "Well here's another one the cat dragged in."

Vicky narrowed her eyes, "Careful what you say love, Standing works both ways."

Brooke hesitated, and opened her mouth to respond, but then turned to her companion and said in a tight voice, "Come on Gerald, we want to be careful who we are seen with."

Roxy watched them leave then turned to face Vicky, who looked up at her. "I'd forgotten how tall you were. How are you getting on Roxy?"

"It could be better."

"You never mentioned you had a baby."

"It was a busy night. James seems to think it will be a problem. Will it?"

Vicky stuck out her bottom lip in thought before answering, "Well it makes you vulnerable. People like Brooke over there will be sizing you up for weaknesses and that's a pretty obvious one. What's her name?"

"Claudia," Roxy replied, stroking the child's hair.

Vicky gestured to a bench a few paces away, "Can we sit down and talk? I'm getting a crick in my neck."

Roxy sat down. "I feel a bit underdressed. Wolfe never told me this was going to be formal."

Vicky sat down beside her and held a finger out for Claudia to grab. "That doesn't surprise me. He only thinks about himself. Plus he's getting so powerful now he probably thinks you'll be accepted straight away, so why bother making the effort to create a good impression?"

"That Brooke woman didn't seem too accepting." Roxy muttered.

"No, I mean accepted by the Comitia Curiata and the Primus. Ultimately it will be them who decide whether you are allowed to live."

"The Comitia-what?" asked Roxy.

"Curiata. It's like the inner circle, made up of the heads of the Patrician houses. Above them is Catallus, the Primus Inter Pares, who is the Lord of the City." Vicky paused and glanced at Roxy. "Wolfe never even told you this?"

Roxy shook her head. "No, the only one who spent any time with me was Sanjay, and he is–" Roxy broke off, remembering Wolfe's warning not to speak of what happened.

Vicky glanced round the room at the increasing number of vampires now in attendance. "He's what? Where is he anyway?"

Roxy cursed under her breath and lowered her voice. "He's dead, and no I can't talk about it."

Vicky raised her eyebrows in surprise, but not, Roxy sensed, in shock. She nodded slowly and to Roxy's relief didn't pursue the subject, but her eyes flicked toward Wolfe.

Roxy tried to pick up the conversation again, "So what is this meeting all about then?"

Vicky turned her attention back to Claudia and Roxy let her take her onto her lap as she spoke, "Once a month or so Imperator Catallus calls a gathering of the Houses. The heads of the houses, who are called Paterfamiliae, get a chance to raise any issues they think are important and if there is enough interest, a debate and a vote might be scheduled. It's sort of a government if you like," she added helpfully.

"How many houses are there?" asked Roxy. There were perhaps two hundred people thronging the hall now, with more arriving all the time.

"There are six Patrician, or noble houses, which are Catallus, Lambeth, Walpurga, Aelric, Plantagenet and my own, Thorkel." Vicky smiled, "So you see I am really important and you should bow when you see me."

"Really?" blurted out Roxy, suddenly worried, but a bigger smile from Vicky stopped her from apologising.

"No not really. I'm not very important at all, but the Paterfamiliae should be addressed as Lord or Lady if you are ever unlucky enough to have to speak to them. I do get some standing just due to the fact I am in Domus Thorkel though."

"Is that what you said to Brooke?"

"Yeah. She and Gerald are pretty young members of Everett, which is only a plebeian house. Well," Vicky corrected herself, "it's actually one of the most powerful of the plebeian houses, so they are not to be messed with if you can help it."

"Am I in a plebeian house then?" Roxy asked, trying to hold all the names in her head.

"Um...well officially you are, but Wolfe is usually called a Parvenu, which is the name given to young upstarts who defy the traditions."

"What traditions did he defy?" asked Roxy, curiously.

"He's too young to head a house. You're not normally allowed to create another vampire until you are five generations old, which is a hundred years. Now technically he hasn't created a vampire, but he has managed to set himself up as paterfamilias of his own house, which normally means creating a brood. A lot of people are angry about how he has managed to sidestep the rules the way he has. You are not really going to help matters to be honest," she added apologetically.

"I'd kind of gathered that."

A gentle gong sounded and people started to make their way through an archway across the room towards a larger hall containing Sumerian and Akkadian artefacts.

"Here we go," muttered Vicky, passing Claudia back to Roxy and standing up. "Don't worry," she smiled, "they won't kill you tonight. Nothing is ever decided that quickly."

"Great," replied Roxy acidly, "just what I need. More uncertainty."

Vicky tipped her head to one side and gave her a small smile, "Just stick close to me tonight."

Roxy smiled back, clutching Claudia to her breast. "Thanks."

As they walked toward the far hall Roxy asked "So it's okay to see you then?"

"What do you mean?"

"I don't just have to stick with Wolfe and the others?"

Vicky snorted "No you can do what you like. I'd advise not wandering around on your own though," she added thoughtfully, "at least not until you are accepted."

They reached the hall, which was filled with smartly dressed people. Here and there were waiters that Roxy realised were mortals, carrying trays of glasses containing a dark red liquid.

"Is that what I think it is?"

Vicky nodded grimly, "Yeah, they always provide blood at these things. Sometimes they don't bother with the glasses and just have people strung up from the ceiling for people to feed from. Those nights are very popular."

Roxy struggled to fight down a rising horror. "How do you get the waiters not to freak out?"

"You mean the mules?" Vicky asked, idly reaching for a couple of glasses from a waitress. She handed one to Roxy, who took it after a moment's hesitation.

"I guess. The non-vam...er...taken."

Vicky chuckled, taking a sip of the deep red liquid in her glass, which left a residual sticky stain on the rim as she lowered it. "It's okay, you can speak freely in here. The mules are all slaves. They've been hypnotised to serve us."

"How do you do that?" Roxy tried to affect a casual attitude as she raised her glass to her lips. She could smell that it was blood straight away, and felt a strange abhorrence at herself for what she was about to do, so she lowered the glass without tasting it.

"Not everyone can. It takes practise and a bit of talent, but you do the whole, staring-into-their-eyes thing and exert your will on them. Apparently. I've never been able to do it myself. I suppose I should learn how to one of these days. It can be quite useful occasionally just to get little things done, like getting the cops to let you go with a warning, or tell them these are not the droids they're looking for," she smirked.

"Does it work on vampires too?" Roxy was thinking of Sarah and Jessica.

"Well supposedly, but that's even harder, and it's easy to spot, so it doesn't usually happen. What's the point of having a vampire mule that no one will respect? Someone might do it for kicks, but you pretty much destroy the person you do it to. Eventually they can't even feed without your permission. Humans don't tend to last more than a few years unless you are quite experienced at it, like the elders. Some of them have servants who are hundreds of years old."

Roxy frowned, "How does that work? Aren't they mortal?"

Vicky explained, "Yeah, but close proximity to a vampire can do strange things to a person. Plus you can share your blood with them and give them some of your powers. We call them Renfields. They are really loyal, but sometimes they can get carried away and start thinking that they *are* vampires; eating flies, sleeping in coffins and stuff."

Just then the low hum of chatter ceased, and Roxy looked up to see six figures enter and make their way towards some chairs arranged on a dais at the end of the room. The first to enter was a man with a long plaited beard. Beside him sat a brute of a man, very tall and built like a barn. Next was a serious looking man sitting in the largest chair, who Roxy assumed was the Primus, Catallus. Next was a tall handsome man who wore an amused smile, then a woman in a shimmering pink dress and lastly; Roxy gasped – Reyne! The man who had visited her house yesterday was a patrician. Roxy nudged Vicky and nodded towards him, "Who is that?" she whispered.

Vicky looked, then tiptoed up to whisper back "That's Reyne, paterfamilias of Domus Plantagenet. He claims to be the cousin of Mathilda, and an advisor to Henry the Second." She named each of the vampires in turn, "The woman is Walpurga, the third most powerful, then Lambeth, who is second,

Catallus the Primus, then Aelric the Saxon, who is fourth, and finally Thorkel, who is fifth."

Catallus started to talk, and Roxy frowned as she realised he was speaking in Latin. She glanced around to see everyone paying respectful attention, clearly understanding what was going on. She turned back as he concluded his short speech and sat back down. As he did so, a gruff-looking, bearded man took the stage and started reciting something from a leather-bound book.

"That's Harold," Vicky whispered, "he is older than pretty much everyone apart from the Curiata, but because Catallus hasn't released him, he doesn't get to vote."

"Who decides who gets to vote?" Roxy asked quietly.

"Only the heads of the houses can vote," Vicky replied. "Important decisions are normally made by the patrician heads, and a simple majority wins. Catallus has a veto, but it is generally politically safer for him to appear to be dictated to by the others. Primus Inter Pares is only First Among Equals, after all. Less important decisions, such as inter-house disputes, are sent down to the plebeian court, the Comitia Tributa, made up of the heads of all the other houses. Again, a simple majority vote wins, but it can be overturned on appeal by a vote of the Curiata."

Vicky paused to let Roxy digest the information, and was about to say something else when Wolfe's name was mentioned, causing them both to turn their attention back to Harold.

"Here it comes," muttered Vicky.

"What, something about me?" Roxy whispered nervously.

Vicky shook her head. "No. Last month one of the other houses raised a vote to accuse Wolfe of murder. The head of the house will now be brought forward to repeat the claim and then the Comitia Tributa will vote on it."

"What evidence do they have?" Roxy asked, a knot forming in her stomach.

Vicky shook her head, "No evidence. That's not how justice works. Someone makes an accusation, which needs the support of three other houses, and then a vote is scheduled at a later date, during which time both parties lobby the other houses to vote for them, offering bribes and promises or calling in favours as necessary. Then the vote happens, and whoever loses is considered guilty."

Roxy felt cold. Domus Wolfe wasn't very well regarded as far as she could tell. She doubted a vote would go his way. "What is the punishment for being guilty?" she asked quietly.

Vicky pursed her lips, "In this case, the destruction of the accused and his house. If the accuser loses the vote, they might suffer the same fate instead."

Roxy started to feel dizzy and faintly sick. "Did you know about this the other night, when you took me to see Wolfe?"

Vicky hesitated and avoided Roxy's gaze. "I did. But I had no choice. Sorry kid."

Roxy's vision blurred and she couldn't stop her legs trembling. She felt like she needed to pee, and was distantly grateful that she seemed to lack the ability to do that now. Harold was calling out a name for the third time. People were starting to get restless and look about curiously. Roxy looked over at Wolfe, who was standing slightly apart from everyone else with a smug grin on his face.

"What's happening?" she asked Vicky.

"The accuser isn't here. If she doesn't come forward to repeat the accusation, the matter will be dropped."

Roxy felt a slow realisation form in her head. "Who is the accuser?"

"Kate Craven," Vicky replied looking around the crowd with a frown. "Actually I can't see any of her house. Roy was supposed to return my CD tonight."

Roxy took a step back towards the wall. "I need to sit down," she mumbled, nearly dropping her almost forgotten glass. She looked up at the stage and straight into Reyne's piercing gaze, a faint, knowing smile on his lips. Roxy turned away quickly and found a bench to sit on, setting her glass on the floor clumsily. Claudia started to fuss, and Roxy distracted herself by soothing her. Vicky came to sit beside her as the proceedings moved on to another topic. Roxy didn't pay attention, and focused instead on suppressing the panic swirling around inside her.

She couldn't believe Wolfe's audacity. Was this kind of thing common, she wondered?

After another few minutes, Wolfe caught Roxy's eye and beckoned to her.

"I think Wolfe wants me," she muttered to Vicky.

"Good luck," she whispered softly, a troubled look crossing her face.

Roxy didn't have time to ask her what she thought was going to happen, and walked nervously over to Wolfe who stepped forward to receive her. She was aware of a hundred pairs of eyes on her as Wolfe led her to the open area directly in front of Catallus. She looked up at him, tightly clutching a subdued Claudia to her chest. The Primus glanced briefly towards her, but focused his attention on Wolfe with a faint curl of contempt on his lips. Wolfe boldly stepped forward, bowed formally and began to recite an introduction in Latin. Roxy recognised some Latinised versions of his name and hers, and kept her face impassive. Wolfe concluded and stepped back to stand alongside her. Catallus stared at her for several drawn out seconds during which all Roxy could do was to concentrate on not fainting, and finally he barked a single word reply.

Out of the corner of her eye, Roxy noticed Wolfe grin broadly, but the audience behind her broke into angry murmurings of resentment. One of the Patricians on the dais, the tall brutish man called Aelric stood up.

"Nay, Lord, I protest!" he said in English, "I'll not suffer another spawn swelling the nest of this infamari. It is bad enough that you allow his abominable house to exist at all, despite all our objections, but this time you go too far!"

Reyne chuckled, "Come, Aelric. Surely one as powerful and potent as yourself does not fear a Parvenu house, even one with a hundred members?" he said mockingly.

Aelric scowled back, "Your pitiful attempts to insult me will not change my mind. I am set on this."

"But who will support you? Clearly the rest of us are not as insecure as you." Reyne smiled patronisingly back at him, spreading his hands to encompass the other Patricians.

"Actually Reyne, I happen to agree with Aelric this time," spoke the woman icily.

Reyne turned to look at her, "Walpurga, you jest, surely?"

Aelric smirked "There! I call a vote demanding the destruction of the neophyte."

"Seconded." Walpurga responded.

Reyne glanced about at the others frowning, "Someone join me in opposing this ridiculous proposal so that we can move on."

Roxy saw that neither Thorkel nor Lambeth were going to support him. Both were regarding Reyne with careful disinterest. Lambeth glanced at Roxy then turned to Reyne.

"You are outvoted, Reyne." Lambeth looked at Catallus, who had remained silent throughout the exchange.

"Very well," Catallus declared, "a vote on the destruction of the orphan will be taken two days hence, at the unveiling of the Menes Tablets."

"Two days!" blurted out Wolfe, stepping forwards, "my Lord that is not enough time-"

"Silence!" interrupted Catallus angrily. "This is a matter for Curiata, not Tributa. Dixi."

Wolfe stepped back abruptly, head bowed. Roxy glanced at Reyne, who was sitting back in his chair with a defeated air. Roxy didn't thank him for his defence of her. No doubt he was just trying to protect his investment. Wolfe guided her back into the crowd and Roxy walked numbly back to where she had been sitting, dimly aware that Vicky was still there.

"Here, drink this," she murmured, holding a glass to Roxy's lips.

Obediently, Roxy drank. The cool liquid immediately warmed her, setting a fire in her chest.

"So go on then," she turned to Vicky, "tell me how likely it is I'll survive the week?"

Vicky shrugged, "Fair to middling. Catallus won't vote, so assuming Reyne still votes in your favour you just need Thorkel and Lambeth to side with you. I can't really help you with Thorkel, but he'll probably vote in your favour because he doesn't like Aelric. Lambeth is really the decider, so it depends how he is feeling on the night.'

Roxy sighed. "What is this Menes thing that Catallus mentioned?" She wondered why she was even bothering to ask, but she found it difficult to accept her imminent fate. Maybe when it sunk in she would be suitably panicked.

"Menes was an ancestor of Catallus. He was the first pharaoh of Egypt back in three thousand BC or something. Anyway, about thirty years ago someone found some stone tablets supposedly detailing the life of Menes after he was Taken. Catallus got hold of the tablets and has been having them translated ever since."

"It's taken thirty years to translate?" Roxy asked surprised.

"Well they're in an obscure dialect and written in an unusual script. Catallus is really proud that his people have managed it and he is planning a special evening to show them off. He's fanatical about anything to do with his ancestors, and Menes is one of the most famous."

Their attention was drawn back to the proceedings as Reyne stood and addressed the gathering.

"I have one final matter to bring to the attention of the Curia," he began, gesturing to an attendant who hurried away through a doorway alongside. "My sources in the police department have uncovered a sloppy case of murder by a vampire during feeding."

There were murmurs of surprise and indignant shock throughout the listening crowd. Roxy closed her eyes briefly, wondering if Reyne had decided to cut his losses with her already. When she opened them, she thought she saw him glance fleetingly in her direction as he continued.

"Fortunately, the perpetrator was a fool, and the police efficient. They managed to detect the attacker's identity quickly, and my spies made sure that the matter was passed on to me."

"Who was responsible, Reyne?" Catallus asked with a darkened expression.

Roxy looked down at Claudia again, unable to face what was coming. There was nowhere to run to, nowhere to hide, and she wouldn't stand a chance of being able to fight her way out. All she wanted to do in these last few moments was to look lovingly down at her daughter, stroke her hair and apologise to her for not being able to give her more than a few short months of life. She made a decision that before the first attacker reached her, she would kill Claudia herself, so that she would be spared any horrors they might inflict on her. She barely noticed the rising clamour around her until Vicky spoke.

"Here he is,"

Roxy looked up to see that Reyne was presenting a young man to Catallus. He was clearly terrified, his clothes were torn and dirty, his hair dishevelled and his bare feet were raw and bloody.

"I give you the viator named Jasper, my Lord," Reyne said, bowing to Catallus.

Catallus glared at the unfortunate man, who Roxy guessed was a vampire, "There is only one punishment I can give," His steely voice rang out, "I give you to the masses." With that, he stood, grabbed the vampire by the throat, lifting him off the ground and tossed him toward the watching throng in one smooth motion.

"Don't look, Roxy," whispered Vicky, who was licking her lips unconsciously.

Roxy saw him fall to the ground, then he was lost to sight as dozens of vampires swarmed around him. She looked away when his screams started, putting her hands to her ears and squeezing her eyes shut. The attack seemed to last much longer than it should have done given the agonised pitch of his screams. She supposed that being nearly invulnerable had its disadvantages too, as torture could last much longer and be more brutal. Eventually, his cries ceased, and were replaced by a host of slurps and sighs. Trembling, she lowered her hands and kept Claudia facing away from the carnage she knew was just over her shoulder.

"That could have been you," Vicky spoke softly to her.

Roxy looked up with a start. "What?" She searched Vicky's face for some sign that she knew the truth, but saw only a grim bitterness.

"Jasper was a viator, a traveller, just passing through. He had no house to support him, so he was easy to accuse. No one seriously believes that he was responsible, but as long as justice is seen to be done, it secures everyone's standing in Society and serves as a warning to others. If you had not been accepted by Wolfe, you would have been vulnerable to accusations like that too."

Roxy nodded slowly, trying to ignore the heavy smell of freshly spilled blood drifting over from where Jasper fell. "Will there be much more going on tonight?" she asked weakly.

Vicky shook her head. "No I think that's it. And since Craven never showed up, that means that Wolfe is in the clear too. She won't find it easy to accuse him again."

She gave Roxy a sidelong look, "Assuming of course, that she ever shows up again. Like Sanjay, perhaps?"

Roxy looked away, then looked back. Vicky had guessed already, and she seemed more trustworthy than Wolfe. Roxy acknowledged her questioning look with a faint nod. Vicky broke into a triumphant smile and raised a warning finger to stop her from saying anything further. It wouldn't do to voice an accusation like that in a place like this, Roxy realised.

"Do you want me to show you out?" Vicky asked.

Roxy nodded wearily. As she stood to follow her, she caught Reyne's eye. He nodded mockingly at her and then turned his gaze meaningfully toward the bloody mess on the floor. Roxy pulled Claudia close and hurried after Vicky.

# Chapter 23

Roxy arrived home and was just about to walk up the short path to her door, when she heard hurried footsteps approaching from behind, and turned to face them. They belonged to the young man she had nearly bumped into the other night. He pulled up sharply, somewhat surprised, then took a few more paces to reach her. She watched him warily, his scent reaching her and confirming that it was the person who had apparently followed her. He was older than her, probably in his mid-twenties and fairly attractive with careless blonde hair. He was wearing a shirt and tie that had spent too long crumpled against a car seat.

"Amanda Harker?"

She narrowed her eyes, "I know you," she said softly, hugging Claudia to her chest. "You were here the other day, weren't you? What do you want?"

The man seemed taken aback for a moment, then recovered himself.

"I'm Detective Sergeant Anderton. You are Miss Harker, correct?"

She nodded warily, "Yeah, so what?"

"Can we talk inside?" Anderton asked.

"I'd rather not actually, and I'm getting cold, so be quick about it."

Anderton tightened his jaw. "I know that you were involved in the death of Simon Trent, and I know you are also involved with criminal organisations headed by Rupert Wolfe and William Reyne..." He broke off as she started to chuckle humourlessly.

"Do you have any idea what you're getting yourself into?" she asked.

Anderton frowned at her, and unconsciously clenched his fists, "These are dangerous criminals miss. I've been following them for years. All I want is Wolfe and Reyne. I don't care what your role is, or was. If you help me, I'll see to it that you won't be held accountable for the murder of Simon Trent."

Roxy stared at him. "This is all I need. I thought this had all been cleared up?"

"What you do mean?" asked Anderton sharply, and a little too quickly, Roxy thought.

Roxy sighed and turned back to her door, "Go home detective. Get some sleep and don't come back again. I'm not in the mood."

"Not in the mood?" Anderton said angrily, "I can take you in on suspicion right now if I have to, so you'd better start being a bit more bloody cooperative."

Roxy unlocked her door, stepped inside, and turned to smile tiredly at him, "No, trust me, you can't, and believe me, you don't want to. Please, do us both a favour and leave me alone."

Roxy shut the door gently and leaned back against it rubbing her eyes. Great. Now the police knew about her too. Maybe it was Reyne's way of reminding her that she was in his debt? She had better write him a letter soon.

She put Claudia to bed and fished out a notepad from a drawer. She needed to write enough to keep Reyne happy, but not enough to put her in danger. She chewed the end of the pen for a while in thought, and then started to write. She decided to include the attack on Craven, as Reyne had hinted that he knew about it anyway, and it might reassure him that she wasn't holding back. She excluded most of the details though, including her suspicions about Dave and Sanjay, and the real way that Craven died, instead simply relating the story Wolfe had told them.

She re-read it when she was done. It wasn't very long, but then not much had really happened regarding Wolfe, and she had no desire to give Reyne any more information than he had asked for, particularly about herself. She placed it on top of the gas fire so that she wouldn't forget about it.

She ought to go round and get her stuff from Clive, and maybe see about getting some more work. It was a bit late, but he would still be up. Roxy tilted her head to the side and listened for Claudia. She quickly focused on her steady breathing from her bedroom down the hall. Only a few days ago she was getting headaches from hearing and smelling everything that came her way but now she had somehow learned to control her senses to filter out things that were not necessary. She closed her eyes and slowly started to investigate her surroundings using her nose and ears. She could pick out Scarlet's scent from the places she had sat or walked, as well as Claudia's and what she now knew was her old, slowly fading scent. She could hear her neighbours"conversations through the walls and roof of her flat, and could hear them walking about, drinking tea or reading a paper. She likened it to sight, in the way she could see everything in a 180 degree arc ahead of her, but only focused on a narrow zone and distance at any one time.

She stood up abruptly, coming to a decision. She would go and see Clive and get her stuff, and start building bridges. She went into Claudia's room, the thought of leaving her alone in the house never entering her head, and wrapped her sleeping form up in a warm blanket. She lifted her carefully and stepped outside into the night.

The pub was locked when she arrived, but lights were still on inside, so she knocked on the door and called Clive's name. He opened it with a look of surprise when he saw her.

"Well look who it is? I thought you were dying or something?"

"Yeah, something like that," Roxy replied tartly, "can I come in?"

Clive stepped back from the door and let her in, locking it behind her. "Don't expect to get your tips back. I had to use them to fix the sink."

"Fine. I'm sorry about that, but it was on its last legs anyway. You should thank me. If it had broken when a customer used it you might have had a lawsuit on your hands," Roxy placed Claudia down on a broad cushioned bench to sleep and perched herself on a high stool beside the empty bar.

Clive opened his mouth to object, then shrugged. "So I suppose you want your gear back then?"

Roxy nodded, "Yes please."

He disappeared into a back room and reappeared with her bag.

Roxy opened it to see that all of her clothes seemed to be there, if a little crumpled where they had been unceremoniously shoved inside. Her mobile phone was there too, but it needed recharging. She closed the bag and dropped it at her feet.

"So are you better now?" Clive asked her in a casual sort of way, "because I've had loads of requests for you all week."

"Oh really?" Roxy asked, a slight smile forming on her lips at the memory of her last performance.

"If you're interested you're welcome back. I might even advertise it."

Roxy put her head to one side and thought for a moment. She had promised to baby-sit for Scarlet tomorrow, but she might be able to hire a babysitter to watch both of them while she went out for a few hours. She looked at Clive calculatingly, "Make it worth my while. Thirty quid."

Clive stared at her with bulging eyes, "Fuck me woman, you should be glad with the deal I give you now, being able to do it for nothing. Girls up West have to pay the clubs a hundred quid just to work there."

"Sure, but they take home three times that in tips. I'd be lucky to clear fifty. C'mon Clive, I need it for the babysitter, unless you want to do it yourself?" Roxy fluttered her eyes at him, willing him to agree. He opened his mouth to refuse, then a strange expression passed over his face, and he nodded slowly.

"Okay, Roxy. Thirty quid. Deal."

Roxy narrowed her eyes in suspicion, then noticed that he was still staring placidly at her. She had a sudden inkling what might have happened, and decided to test it. "In fact, I want the money in advance."

Clive immediately went over to the till and pulled out three ten pound notes and held them out to her. Roxy took them, now convinced that she had somehow hypnotised him, and wondered how to break it. She pocketed the cash and reached down to pick up her bag. When she straightened again, Clive was busily stacking glasses in the dishwasher. She hesitated, then said "Well I'm off then."

Clive looked up at her with a scowl, "Fine. Make sure you're here on time tomorrow. I want you here from eight 'till midnight."

Roxy nodded. She could just about manage that as long as Scarlet was on time, and she usually was.

She slung the strap over her shoulder, picked up Claudia and left as quickly as possible.

Roxy hurried home and wondered what to do about getting a babysitter.

From the flat upstairs she heard movement and a woman talking. She knew it was Julie, a young mother who lived with her boyfriend. She listened idly to her talking to him on the phone, her words unmuffled by the intervening ceiling.

"...again? Why are you always covering for him? ...yes but he's always sick....okay fine, so it's just tomorrow right? What! The night-shift? For fuck's sake Neil, what am I supposed to do about ...? ....I can't keep calling in sick....no...okay, fine!"

Roxy closed her eyes, trying to block out the sound of her neighbour slamming the phone down, then opened them and stood up. "Damn useful, this hearing stuff," she thought as she grabbed her keys and headed for the door. Julie worked as a night cleaner several days a week, and relied on her boyfriend to look after their child. Roxy strode over to the door to the upstairs flats and pressed the buzzer for Julie's.

"What?" Julie's voice was still taut from anger.

"It's Roxy from downstairs, sorry about the time, but can I ask you a favour?"

"Come on up," came the response after a pause. The door buzzed and Roxy pushed it open and took the stairs up to the first floor. Julie was standing in a faded blue dressing gown with the door ajar waiting for her. She looked very tired, Roxy thought, and not just from the late hour. Lines had formed on her face and her hair, once blonde and soft had turned dry and dull. Roxy didn't really pay much attention to her neighbours and probably hadn't exchanged more than a couple of dozen words with Julie since moving in a year ago. Just enough to say hello and exchange names when they'd first met, and since then only a brief nod if they bumped into each other on the street.

"Thanks," said Roxy, stopping outside in the hallway.

Julie pulled her dressing gown around her more tightly and glanced around the stairwell before looking up at Roxy, "Do you want to come in for a cup of tea or something?"

"No thanks, it's a bit late."

"Yeah, tell me about it," interrupted Julie, "but the kettle's on anyway."

Roxy waved away the offer again, "No, I've kind of gone off tea. I just wanted to ask you a favour."

Julie gestured for her to continue.

"I've got to be out tomorrow night until after midnight and I said I'd look after my mate's kid, but now I can't, so I was wondering if you could baby-sit for mine and hers for a few hours?"

Julie screwed up her face in annoyance, so Roxy hurried on, digging into her pocket for the money she'd received from Clive, "I can pay you. Would thirty quid be okay?"

Julie didn't have to think too long. "Sure Roxy," she smiled, holding out her hand for the money

Roxy had produced, "Your little one is only a toddler isn't she?"

Roxy nodded, "They both are. It should be pretty easy. They'll both be tired and will probably sleep most of the time."

Julie absently counted the money and then stuffed the notes into her pocket. "What time?"

"I'll be leaving about ten to eight and I'll be back, probably around two." Which ought to give me a bit of time after I finish to get something to eat, thought Roxy.

"Okay, do you want me to go downstairs or do you want to bring them up here?"

"Your choice," Roxy shrugged.

"Well," Julie thought for a moment, "I'll bring Gary down with me to yours and he can sleep on the sofa. He's only two and they'll probably enjoy playing together for a while."

Roxy smiled gratefully, "Thanks a lot for this."

Julie smiled as she shrugged, "It's okay. I was going to have to be home tomorrow anyway. I'll see you later then."

"Okay, bye," Roxy turned to head back down the stairs to her flat. She heard Julie close her door and then give a little laugh and clap her hands. It made Roxy smile to realise that she had actually made someone happy for a change.

# Chapter 24

Claudia woke her in mid-morning. Roxy rolled out from under her bed with a groan, hearing her daughter's frantic screams for attention. She stumbled to Claudia's room and found her sitting in the middle of the floor clutching her teddy bear and a small blanket. At the sight of her mother she raised her arms and cried out pitifully. Roxy picked her up and hugged her gently, her daughter's distress banishing the last of her tiredness. She took Claudia to the front room, checking that the curtains were securely closed and went into the kitchen to get her some breakfast. The milk had gone off and the bread was starting to mould at the corners. Roxy trimmed the bad bits away and put a couple of slices under the grill to toast. It probably wasn't very good for Claudia to eat, but it was all she had.

She looked in the rest of her cupboards and made an inventory. A couple of packet soups, a can of peas, some cornflakes, a few sprouting potatoes and some butter and jam in the fridge. Roxy made a mental note to go to the supermarket later. There was one about half an hour's walk away that was open twenty-four hours during the week. Roxy paused and checked the calendar. Shit, it's Saturday today, she thought, which meant they closed at ten, two hours before she finished work. She'd have to take a break during her performance and go to the more expensive convenience store across the road from the pub.

Next she sat down and counted out how much money she had. That was even more depressing. After putting aside money for her rent and bills she had ten pounds and fifty-four pence. Well it would get her some milk and some vegetables for Claudia. She should get some tips later as well. She sighed and put the money back into her purse. Claudia was playing on the floor. Roxy got up, finished making the toast and gave it to her with some orange squash, which was also nearly empty. She went into Claudia's room to get her a dry nappy. There were only four left, so she added those to her list too, although she wouldn't be able to afford them until she got some tips.

She glanced at the curtains with the threatening daylight beyond and wondered how other vampires dealt with these kinds of things. She hadn't appreciated before, being a night-worker, how much she actually did during the daytime. She wondered if there was a way to go out into the sunlight without getting hurt. She got up and retrieved the costumes bag she'd recovered from Clive. There were some satin gloves in it, the kind that stretched all the way to the elbow, which she thought might be tightly woven enough to block the sunlight. She pulled one on and approached the curtained window nervously.

Just a finger, she thought, trying to summon up the courage to draw the curtain aside. It will only be like touching a saucepan, she encouraged herself, and standing well to the side, she reached out and stabbed her index finger through the parting where the curtains met. Nothing. Tentatively, she put her finger through again slowly. There was still no pain, so she parted the curtains slightly and allowed the sunlight to fall on her gloved hand and wrist. The brightness stung her eyes and made her squint, but she felt no burning on her hand. She let the curtain fall back and returned to her seat triumphantly rubbing her eyes to clear the brightly coloured after-images swimming across them.

If she could find the right kind of heavy clothing, she could probably go outside, but she would need some very dark sunglasses. They would be useful anyway, to tone down the dazzling headlights of cars and the strobes at the nightclub.

She stayed up with Claudia for the rest of the day, dozing occasionally on the couch. At about seven in the evening, she started to think about going out again. The light was much weaker now as the sun drifted downwards. She still had to squint, but she could at least keep her eyes cracked open enough to see. She got dressed and put on a hooded running top to protect her neck. She pulled the elbow-length gloves on and covered them with the sleeves of the top. It would look odd as people didn't tend to wear black satin gloves to go shopping, but there was nothing she could do about that. She completed the outfit with a baseball cap pulled down over her face, and a scarf to protect her cheeks and nose. Hopefully it would be enough. Claudia noticed her mother getting ready to go out and ran to the hallway to find her coat.

Roxy smiled at her eagerness, but wanted to test her protective efforts before she got Claudia all dressed up. Clenching her fists to strengthen her resolve, she prepared to face the sun. She tightened her muscles ready to leap back if she felt any pain, and slowly opened the door. The late evening daylight was made weaker by a thick cloud covering. Roxy opened the door wider, pulled the peak of her cap lower over her face and eased her way into the light. Her face tingled slightly, but it wasn't a painful tingle. She buried her chin deeper in her scarf and stepped out of her door. She was doing it! She was outside in the daytime, and she was safe!

Claudia burbled behind her and tried to follow so Roxy turned and ducked back into the hallway and closed the door behind her. A great feeling of security and relief descended on her and she realised how terrified she had been and how much willpower it had taken for her to stand out there even for a few seconds. Her plan had been to quickly go to the nearest convenience store and buy the groceries she needed, but now she wondered if she could make it that far. She shrugged inwardly. She had to. Claudia would need something to eat when Julie arrived. Roxy bent down to help Claudia into her coat and shoes, repeating, *it's for Claudia,* over and over in her head like a mantra. She stood up, carrying Claudia, who was excited about going outside with her mummy, and opened the door, trying not to think about the punishing sunlight about to surround her.

She walked quickly, almost running, squinting against the painful light, holding Claudia in one arm and covering the exposed part of her face with the other hand. Her heart was pounding with irrational fear, even though she knew she was physically protected. The fear struggled for supremacy with a sudden lethargy, which made it even harder to open her eyes. She struggled with her mantra, desperately resisting the compulsion to turn back to the safety of her home. It seemed to take longer to get to the store than it normally did, even though she was going much faster. After an agonisingly long time, she squinted open her eyes and saw it up ahead. Once inside the store, away from the plate glass windows and bathed in artificial strip-lighting, she felt better and lowered Claudia to the ground with trembling hands. She let Claudia ramble between the aisles and tried to get a grip of herself.

Eventually she relaxed enough to pick up a shopping basket and get the few things she needed and could afford. She browsed through the sunglasses on display, trying several pairs on. They were all tacky and unflattering, so she settled on the darkest pair she could find that weren't too outrageous. A quick glance at the price told her she wouldn't be able to afford them, even without all the food Claudia needed. She checked to see if anyone was near, picked up a second pair in her other hand, then under the pretence of fussing over Claudia, slipping the ones she wanted under her coat. She stood up, holding her in one arm and made a show of replacing the dummy pair before picking up her basket and heading to the checkout. The shop assistant was a bored teenage girl, who barely looked at her as she passed the goods over the barcode reader. Roxy bagged up and paid and prepared herself for the outside again.

Any thoughts that the return journey would be easier were quickly dashed. Even though the sun was below the height of the surrounding roofs, Roxy was a quivering wreck by the time she got home. She took off her stolen sunglasses and collapsed in the armchair after setting Claudia down to play. She doubted that she would ever get used to going out in daylight, but it was useful to know that it could be done in an emergency.

Scarlet arrived half an hour later with Leah and left quickly for a gig in Central London. Julie knocked on the door five minutes afterwards, and Roxy kissed Claudia goodnight and hurried out. The pub was busy when she arrived and Clive jerked his thumb to the stage as soon as she stepped inside to indicate that she get started.

She performed her usual routines, but found herself getting more excited than usual, picking up on the lusty pheromones of the audience. She finished with the much-requested "vampire" routine, selecting a good looking man with nice straight teeth.

She was much more careful this time and though she wasn't planning on feeding, the encouraging calls from the crowd persuaded her to pin him down and bury her face in his neck. He gave a small gasp as her teeth pierced his skin, and his body tensed in her arms. His blood flowed gently into her mouth. The taste surprised her, as it had every time she'd fed. Each time was different, each person and situation produced different flavours and subtle variations that her sensitive palate could now pick up. She wondered what a woman would taste like. She felt her thoughts drifting as she fed and forced herself to concentrate. The tension in the room had reached fever-pitch by the time she released him, and lowered him gently to the stage to recover. He looked up at her with a silly gratitude, too dazed to speak. Roxy blew a kiss to the crowd and slipped off to the bathroom to change.

Clive had closed the bar by the time she returned but there were still a fair number of customers drinking up before the pub closed. Roxy sat down at a table and stowed her jug takings in a large furry pencil case and zipped it up, planning to count it later. She was joined by a few smiling customers who complemented her on her performance and slid her some more coins. She pocketed them with a smile and tried to memorise their faces so she could single them out if she saw them again. Customers appreciated that.

At twelve-thirty Clive locked up, and Roxy left with her kit-bag over her shoulder. The night was clear and crisp, a light breeze rustling the leaves of the small fume-blackened trees lining the road. The moon was waxing almost to full and cast a milky glow on the concrete buildings. Roxy wandered aimlessly at first, letting her cluttered mind drift and enjoying the night. She wrapped her arms around herself and after a time tried to organise her thoughts.

She was due to return to Wolfe tomorrow, and he would then take her to Catallus who would decide her fate. More than likely she would be killed. Oddly, that didn't bother her. It probably hadn't really sunk in yet. Hell the whole vampire thing hadn't really sunk in yet. What did bother her though, was what would happen to Claudia. She had no one to turn to except perhaps Scarlet, for a while, but eventually Claudia would be turned over to the state and if she was lucky, fostered out to a loving family. Well that was something, she supposed, blinking back a welling tear. They couldn't do a worse job than she had.

# Chapter 25

The next day she arrived at Wolfe's and parked in the alley behind the club. She had left Claudia with Julie again, along with another thirty pounds she couldn't really afford despite pulling in quite a lot the previous night. She'd held Claudia for a long time before kissing her goodbye, unwilling to let her go and memorising every strand of her hair and the way she felt in her arms. Claudia had been too excited to see Julie's son again to want to cuddle with her mother for too long, and Roxy had reluctantly let her go, a sense of injustice filling her as Claudia rushed away. She'd asked herself again why she was going back to Wolfe and not running away as fast as she could, but no answer came.

As she walked to the main door of the club she glanced across the street and spotted the detective, Anderton, sitting in his car. She let her eyes unfocus and pass on, pretending she hadn't seen him. Damn, she thought. If Wolfe spots him he's going to go ballistic at me. She hurried into the club where Wolfe was waiting with James. Ruth and Marty were also there, but not the others. Roxy felt a little relief at not being the last to arrive again, and made her way over to where Ruth was sitting.

Ruth looked up from her book, "Hello, Roxy. How are you feeling?"

"I dunno. I just want to get it over with I guess."

"I'm sure it will be all right. Wolfe is very good at persuading the Primus."

Roxy said nothing. Ruth started to read her book again. Roxy heard the main door open and Dave's heavy footsteps approaching.

"Good," said Wolfe, "Are we ready to go?"

Everyone stood up, once again dressed in their fine clothes. Roxy had guessed this would be a formal occasion and had come prepared. She unzipped her jacket and pulled down her jeans, letting the dress she had tucked up around her waist fall down to her ankles. She was wearing low heels to match the dress. She bundled up her clothes and walked over to Wolfe.

"Can I leave these in your office please?"

Wolfe took a brief look at them and nodded.

Roxy pushed open the door and was about to toss them in a corner when she noticed Natalie sitting on a chair, staring at the far wall. Roxy dropped her clothes by the door and cleared her throat. "I think we're about to go now."

Natalie moved her eyes to look at her, the rest of her body remaining motionless. A sudden chill ran down Roxy's spine, then Natalie blinked and gave her a wry smile, "Very well."

Roxy hurried back to where Wolfe was gathering everyone together.

"So tonight is when Catallus finally unveils the Menes Tablets," he was saying. "Supposedly they reveal some great secret about his ancestry that he feels he must share with us."

"Whoopie-fucking-do," sneered Dave loudly.

"I know, but it means he'll be in a good mood." Wolfe looked directly at Roxy, "Which will be good for you, won't it?"

Roxy started to shrug, then nodded, not wanting to ruin Wolfe's good mood.

"Is it at the museum again?" Ruth asked.

"Yes, so let's get going. You all know the way, so we split up and meet there separately. We'll leave in ones and twos, a few minutes apart."

There was no surprise from the others. This must be something they were used to. Roxy edged over to Marty and said in a low voice "Why is he being cautious tonight?"

"It's just Wolfe being random. He likes to avoid routines as much as possible. It makes it more difficult for his enemies," he added.

"Oh."

"Roxy, you go first." Wolfe said. "Do you remember the way?"

Roxy considered for a moment then looked back at him, "Yes."

"Good answer," said Wolfe. "Off you go."

Roxy made sure she hadn't left anything, then headed outside. The detective was still there, she noted as she turned toward the underground station. She walked steadily, listening for and finally hearing the snick of a car door opening and closing. Well, let him follow her. She pretended not to notice him as she bought her ticket and descended to the platform. He waited at the base of the escalators until the train pulled in, and then took the carriage behind hers. At Tottenham Court Road she waited until the doors were about to close then leapt out and started running down the platform towards the disused part of the station. She didn't know if he had been able to follow her, but didn't look behind to check. It took her a few seconds to remember the correct passage, but then she saw the security guard beside the locked gate and rushed towards him. He nodded at her and immediately reached for his key. Roxy let out a mental sigh of relief. She wasn't quite sure how she would have persuaded him to let her in if he hadn't recognised her. She took the opportunity while he was unlocking the gate – why was he being so slow? – to glance over her shoulder to see if Anderton had caught up with her. She couldn't see him, and silently congratulated herself.

"There you go ma'am," said the security guard, stepping aside for her.

Roxy ran through without bothering to say thank you, which she felt bad about half a minute later when she was safely in the tunnel and had calmed down a bit. Well I guess he gets that a lot anyway, she thought. Wolfe hadn't been very polite either. It took longer than she remembered to walk down the passage, but eventually she reached the disused

British Museum underground station and retraced her steps of a few nights ago.

At the final door she paused and gathered her thoughts. Was this really such a good idea? Well she might be fucked if she went in, or might not, but with Reyne out there knowing where she lived and everything about her, she would definitely be fucked if she didn't. Besides, it was in his interest to ensure she was accepted. The odds were probably better than even. She knocked on the door.

It opened smoothly, revealing the same creepy-looking tall thin man and his two heavies. They all glared at her in a hostile way.

Roxy grinned, "Evening fellers, nice night for it, wouldn't you say?" She stepped through the door and gave one of the bodyguards a look up and down. "Nice suit," she said as the door was closed behind her. None of their expressions changed, which made her smile more. "Bye then." She headed up the stone steps to the museum gallery.

There were perhaps a dozen vampires in the room. They looked at her curiously, now recognising her. Most looked away quickly, as if she were an unclean thing, which might infect them if they stared too long. She looked around, hoping to see Vicky, but she wasn't there. Maybe she would turn up later? She decided to wander round by herself, feeling less self conscious now without Claudia, and wearing suitable clothes. Most people avoided eye contact, but she noticed several sideways glances in her direction. She looked at the exhibits with interest, having never really had much of a chance to develop an interest in archaeology before. She was struck by how old everything was, with some of the relics dating to three thousand years before Christ. She found herself wondering about immortality. Would she still be alive in five thousand years? What would that be like? Would she still be on Earth, or on some alien world? Unbidden, part of her mind started calculating how long it would take a conventional spacecraft to travel to the nearest star. She frowned and suppressed the thought. She didn't need to be reminded of Simon right now.

"Hey babe," came a voice from behind her.

She turned round to see Vicky, and blinked. Gone was the punk haircut and casual clothes. In their place was an elegant blonde wig falling to her shoulders and a clinging dress revealing a shapely slender body.

"Wow! You look good."

"Yeah I scrub up pretty well don't I?"

"Why? I mean-"

"Why tonight and not before?" Vicky shrugged. "You've got to know how far you can push things. Besides, I couldn't let you be the only one that wasn't dressed up. You looked so confused and vulnerable I decided to get changed."

Roxy gaped in gratitude, "I can't believe you did that for me. Thanks."

"Don't worry about it. It was fun. I see Wolfe is working your case already," she continued.

Roxy followed her gaze to see Wolfe talking with a woman in a white dress. "Who is that?"

"Edmeé. She's Lambeth's eldest child. Pretty high up. Probably the next best thing to talking to Lambeth himself."

"Nice. I feel so special."

Vicky chuckled. "I'll have my fingers crossed for you." She looked at a slim expensive-looking watch on her wrist. "I wonder where Catallus is."

Evidently that question had occurred to several others, and Roxy became aware of a growing undercurrent of acid comments and impatience. She watched as a heavy set man addressed a senior member of Domus Catallus and ask loudly and pointedly whether the Primus would be joining them anytime soon.

"The natives are getting restless," remarked Roxy.

Vicky nodded, "Yeah, but no one will leave for a while. No one will dare insult Catallus on his night of glory."

"You'd have thought that vampires would have more patience," said Roxy, "being immortal and everything."

Vicky chuckled, "It's an ego thing. We like to think that we have no masters, which is a load of crap really. Everyone serves someone."

"Even the Primus?"

Vicky nodded, "Yeah; his parens for a start, or if you want to be obtuse about it, he also serves the patricians. If they all pull together they could remove him."

A disturbance made them both look around. Two men were arguing.

"That's Harold and Lawler," murmured Vicky, "Harold is Catallus" elder child, and Lawler is Walpurga's eldest."

"What are they saying?" Roxy could hear the angry exchange, but it was in a language she didn't recognise. Vicky shrugged.

Harold turned on his heel and took a step away. Suddenly, he stumbled and collapsed to his knees. At the same time, several other vampires around the room collapsed too, many crying out in shock and pain. Vicky gasped. Roxy shot her a worried look, but saw that she was merely reacting to the drama around them.

"They're all Domus Catallus," Vicky whispered.

"Aiieeeeee" wailed a diminutive young woman, "Catallus mortuus est!"

Everything went black. It wasn't that the power had simply gone off, because even the candles placed artfully around the room couldn't be seen. Screams filled the air and Roxy dropped into a crouch, holding her hands loosely in front of her in case someone blundered her way. The screams changed character, from a reedy panic to deep-throated agony which cut through to the core. She heard a wet sucking sound worryingly close behind her and another scream, definitely male. She tried to scuttle forward, but her legs and arms felt as though they had been immersed in ice-water, and didn't respond. She felt a coldness rushing over her shoulders and belly, and she clutched at her chest, knowing with unnerving certainty that she couldn't let it reach her heart. All around she could hear pounding footsteps, frantic scrabbling, cries and curses, broken by screams which lasted only a few seconds before trailing off pitifully. She moaned, now on her knees, inexplicably drained of strength and trying to remember what it was she'd been doing when someone slammed into her, sending her sprawling and sliding across the polished marble floor.

At once the coldness disappeared and she leapt to her feet and ran, not caring what was in front of her. She heard another scream behind her, and that slurping, sucking sound and ran faster. She collided with something, a display board perhaps, sending it scattering away and causing her to turn slightly. She ran on, acutely aware that she might be running back the way she'd come but unwilling to pause and get her bearings. The screams had stopped now, but she could hear distant sounds of running and banging. Her foot collided against an obstruction, and she tumbled forwards, flinging her hands out in front of her. They hit a hard, sharp edge earlier than she was expecting, which cracked the underside of her forearms painfully. When her knees struck a similar edge a moment later she realised she was at the foot of a flight of stone stairs and hurried upward, nearly faint with relief. She trailed her fingers along the wall, taking the steps two or three at a time. The wall curved away from her as the stairs changed direction and she followed.

Abruptly the darkness vanished and she saw that she was nearly at the top of a wide staircase leading to the Egyptian room. Long glass cabinets lay ahead, encasing the withered remains of long dead kings and priests. Roxy cleared the remaining steps in a single bound and glanced over her shoulder. She nearly collided with the side of the doorway as she did a double-take. The staircase led down a short way into a wall of blackness which extended from floor to ceiling and spanned the whole width. It was difficult to focus on, like a rip in a canvas, and unlike any shadows Roxy had ever seen. It was simply black. A hand grabbed her shoulder and she started.

"Careful babycakes, it nearly had you again," Vicky pulled her back towards the Egyptian room. She allowed Vicky to lead her past the glass coffins, trying not to look at the desiccated figures inside in case they suddenly came to life. Vicky had lost her wig and her hair hung raggedly around her ears.

"What the hell is going on?" blurted Roxy.

"Hang on," Vicky pulled up short just before another archway, listening intently. Then she was suddenly ten feet inside the room facing to her left, with a hunting knife in her hand. Roxy took a step and saw a male vampire glaring at Vicky. His teeth were extended and his fingers were tipped with inch-long claws, like those of a panther. His eyes flicked to Roxy, then back to Vicky with a hiss.

"Forget it Ryan," Vicky warned. He narrowed his eyes, glancing again at Roxy, who stared back in what she hoped was a threatening manner.

"Another time Victoria," he snarled, and jumped backwards into another room.

Vicky watched long enough to make sure he didn't change his mind, then gestured for Roxy to follow her down the hallway. They hurried along the corridors and through large rooms, and finally arrived at a massive hall with a vast glass roof. Beyond was a pair of large doors leading outside, one of which was hanging on its upper hinge, the lock shattered. On the floor in the middle of the room were a pair of bodies which Roxy would have taken to be Egyptian mummies due to their dry and withered appearance, but for the tuxedos that each was wearing.

"Vampires," muttered Vicky, somewhat unnecessarily.

"What killed them?" whispered Roxy.

"Probably another group who escaped like us."

"But why? Aren't we all running from the same thing?" asked Roxy

"That's just how we are. Exploit any opportunity, any weakness."

They reached the bodies, and Roxy saw that they had both suffered decapitation and a number of large wounds across their torsos and limbs. Vicky crept up to the broken door and peered out.

"All clear, come on."

They ran down the sweeping stone steps into the cool night outside, Vicky leading the way. A couple of minutes later, after putting several streets and turns between them and the museum, Vicky stopped. The street was empty.

"What happened back there?" Roxy asked in a hushed voice.

Vicky reached down and secured her knife in a sheath belted around her thigh. She adjusted her dress to conceal it and stood up straight before answering.

"I dunno for sure, but I think Catallus is dead. All his line collapsing at once like that, well that was pretty weird, but I've heard of sympathetic links between masters and their line – it's how they keep control, and Catallus liked to control everything tightly."

"What about the darkness?" Roxy clutched herself, shivering at the memory.

Vicky frowned and shook her head. "Beats me. There are a lot of strange things in the world. It could have been a mind trick I guess. Pretty powerful though. I don't know who was doing the killing. There must have been a lot of them. Maybe..." her eyes widened, "maybe it was a coup? An attack on Domus Catallus? But no other house is strong enough to challenge them."

"Maybe it was a joint effort? If a few houses joined together could they do it?" Roxy asked.

"I don't know. It could only be the Patrician houses. If so they'll be wanting to consolidate their position, which means..." she trailed off, "Oh Christ Roxy. I've got to find Thorkel. You should get back to Wolfe too. Things are going to get rough for a while."

She started to cross the street. Roxy called after her, "Vicky, what's going to happen?"

Vicky looked back briefly, "War."

# Chapter 26

The road leading to Wolfe's club seemed darker somehow. She kept to the shadows, watchful for any threats. The bouncers were gone and a hand written sign taped to the door read *"Closed for repairs"*. She opened it and slipped inside.

James and Ruth were standing alertly by the bar, facing her as she entered.

"You made it then?" James said quietly, more of a statement than a question. Roxy walked over to them.

"Did you see anyone else?" Ruth asked.

"Only Vicky and a guy named Ryan who was about to attack us for some reason," replied Roxy.

"Vicky of Thorkel?"

"Yeah"

"Ryan was probably just taking advantage of the chaos to settle a few old scores. He and Vicky have had arguments in the past. We'll probably see a lot of that in the next few days." James suggested.

"What do you mean?"

"The city is without a Master now. Until a new one is chosen people will try to get away with anything they can – murder, treaty violation, creating new vampires..."

"How long will it take to choose a new Master?" asked Roxy.

James shrugged, "I don't know. Catallus was Primus for a thousand years, so there's no recent precedent. Before I met Wolfe, I spent a few years travelling around, and in smaller towns when this happened one or two of the most powerful vampires laid claim to the title and people lined up behind them as they wished. The one with the most support won."

"It is also the way in France," Ruth volunteered, "Lille had a new Master about twenty years ago, and it took about a week to sort out."

"So who is likely to become Master now?" asked Roxy.

"That is the question on everyone's lips, Roxy," Wolfe boomed from the doorway, grinning widely.

Roxy looked at her watch for the sixth time in half an hour. It was about three in the morning. She was already late to collect Claudia. She would have to apologise to Julie. The club was full of nervous vampires and their mules, as if the human slaves would be any use if the darkness came again. Maybe they plan to use the mules as a distraction, thought Roxy cynically, while the vampires run off in the other direction?

They had started showing up a little after Wolfe had arrived. Mostly young vampires, confused and frightened. Roxy was glad she wasn't the only one who felt that way. They talked in hushed, furtive voices, trying to stay both out of earshot and within sight of each other. Roxy had mingled a little at first, trying to get to know people, but she had only received icy stares or acid comments so she'd given up. Most of them knew her as "the one with the baby". She'd intended to leave earlier, but Wolfe had spotted her and told her not to run off. She'd presumed he was going to make some sort of statement or talk to her, but after four hours she was still waiting.

She looked over to the far corner of the room where Wolfe and James were holding court. All night a procession of vampires had taken a place at their table, and engaged in an often lengthy discussion. Roxy gathered that Wolfe was talking to the heads of the minor houses, who were working out deals and trying to gauge which of the Patrician houses they should support. The penalty for backing a failed candidate would be disastrous, and conversely supporting the winner would bring favours and rewards. All of Domus Wolfe had returned from the museum, and they were now mixing with the other taken, no doubt engaging in their own micro-politics.

A disturbance caused Roxy to lift her head. Like the ripples from a stone dropped into a pool of water, people moved away from two men who were facing off against each other, long knives in their hands. Roxy glanced over at Wolfe to see if he would interrupt, but he merely stood to get a better view and watched. Roxy recognised one of the men as the paterfamilias of Domus Price, a man called Jordan.

The other had arrived with him, along with two men and a woman. She'd assumed that they were all from the same house. The men circled each other, fangs exposed, looking for an opening.

"You just made a big mistake Liam," said Jordan.

"You've been making mistakes for years," Liam replied grimly.

"I certainly made one when I created you," Jordan slashed out backhanded towards Liam's face. Liam swayed out of reach and immediately brought his knife down on Jordan's arm, striking it just behind the wrist. Blood spattered across the room and Jordan hissed in pain. Liam stepped back as Jordan healed the wound. Roxy looked at the faces of those watching and felt her stomach turn over. Each face was distorted by a ghastly grin, many licking their lips in expectation of an impending murder.

Jordan dived at Liam again, but this time Liam didn't move backwards but instead stepped into the attack, forcing the rising blade to enter his stomach, rather than his heart, trapping Jordan's weapon. With a swift movement, Liam grabbed a handful of Jordan's hair, tilted the head back, and brought his knife down against the side of Jordan's neck, sawing frenetically through a fountain of blood as Jordan screamed and tried to pull away. His struggles were short-lived as Liam's knife reached his spinal cord and sliced through it. Jordan went rigid and collapsed to the ground. His head, still in Liam's hand, made a sucking sound as he fell. Liam made a final grand sweeping gesture and hacked through the remaining strip of skin and muscle joining it to the body.

Roxy turned away and doubled over, consumed by dry retching as Liam held up the head and declared "Domus Price is dead. I claim authority and declare myself Paterfamilias of Domus Halloran. I extend an invitation to former members of Domus Price to join me, challenge me, or else depart."

The former members lined up to bow before Liam and kiss his knuckles. The wound in his stomach was already healed. There was a slight jostling of position as they organised themselves into the appropriate hierarchy that would be continued within the new Domus Halloran. Roxy looked down at the body on the floor, then wished she hadn't. Already the body and head were showing signs of advanced decay as Price's age caught up with him. In a few more seconds, there was only a withered skeleton wrapped in a tight shroud of skin, the soft tissues disintegrated, the once luxurious hair now wispy and grey.

Roxy lurched away as several of the watching throng stepped up to congratulate Liam and offer promises of support.

"It is a bit gruesome isn't it?" A soft voice below her shoulder offered.

Roxy glanced down and was surprised to see Natalie at her side. She slid into a chair, not trusting her legs to hold her up for much longer and Natalie took a seat opposite, regarding her under heavily made up eyelashes.

Roxy cleared her throat experimentally and asked "What will happen now?"

Natalie flicked her eyes towards the victorious Liam and then back to Roxy, "Liam will petition the Tributa to recognise his claim. They will vote on its legitimacy and then he will be allowed to take his seat with them and Domus Halloran will be born. All of Jordan's possessions and mules will also pass to Liam."

"Will the vote pass?"

"Almost certainly. This is the way things are done. Besides, Liam is right now promising future favours in return for their votes. Most likely he'd already negotiated enough votes before challenging Price. His offer for the other members of Domus Price to leave is an empty one. They will have nowhere to go, no voice and no protection."

"In other words, no choice," muttered Roxy.

Natalie gave her a lop-sided smile, "Precisely, my sister."

Roxy tried to swallow, but her throat was too dry. Did Wolfe know about this? She wondered.

"Of course Wolfe knew about this," continued Natalie, making Roxy look up sharply. "He would not have allowed it otherwise." Natalie lowered her eyes and sat quietly for a moment, seemingly lost in thought and lightly tracing a finger across the table, "So tell me Roxy, who took you?"

Roxy hesitated for a moment, confused by the sudden change in topic, then shrugged. "I have no idea."

"Come now, we all had to make the Choice. Even if the implications were not fully explained, the law is quite clear. Only those who choose can be chosen. He must have given you a name."

"No one gave me a choice!" Roxy snapped, "and I didn't get a name. I barely got a look at him."

"Never gave you a choice?" Natalie mused, "Perhaps it was disguised, as a proposal, or a letter?"

Roxy shook her head, "No, in fact I think it was an accident."

Natalie raised her chin delicately, tilting her head to one side questioningly.

Roxy found herself obliged to explain, feeling slightly uncomfortable as she remembered Vicky's warning not to tell anyone about herself, "Well, I was attacked. I think he just wanted to feed, but he must have been drunk or something, because he was really clumsy. He let me bite him, so hard I drew blood. Just as I died, I drank some of it."

Natalie started to smile, a twinkle in her eye as she imagined the scene.

"Oh my," she whispered, "a self-born." She pressed a finger to her lips to prevent herself from laughing and composed herself. "Do you know about the prophecy of the self-born?"

"No."

"Have you had any dreams?"

"What?"

"Who else knows about this?"

"I don't think I've told anyone else," replied Roxy quietly, feeling oddly as if something was wrong with that statement.

"Probably for the best," said Natalie, struggling not to smile again. She stood up. "I'll see you later Roxy."

Roxy watched Natalie walk away, her shoulders shuddering with repressed laugher, and suddenly felt unbearably lonely. She stared unseeing at a distant point ahead of her, crippled by the isolation which was thrown into harsh contrast by the dozens of chattering, pale figures around her, their eyes still gleaming from the spectacle of the bloody fight, their voices loud and pressing as they discussed the ascension of the next Primus. She struggled to her feet. To hell with Wolfe, she thought, I'm going home. She didn't notice the eyes following her to the door, or the dark figure slipping out after her.

# Chapter 27

Roxy snapped awake with a start. Every nerve in her body tingled with tense anticipation. She opened her eyes and looked around cautiously. She was in her bedroom, the curtains tightly closed against the late afternoon sun. She could hear Claudia playing quietly in the front room and wondered if that was what had woken her. She'd tried to stay awake as long as possible after collecting Claudia from her neighbour, but the pull of sleep had become too much to resist and she had set Claudia up with food, drink and toys, and went wearily to bed. Roxy rose silently, acutely aware that something was wrong, when she heard a noise. It was soft, but deliberate and unmistakable. Someone was in her house.

She closed her eyes, stretching out her senses. She heard the faint sound of breathing – two people, in the kitchen beyond the front room. Claudia! They would find her in seconds. Roxy stood and swiftly opened the bedroom door. She was dressed only in an over-sized t-shirt. The hallway beyond was dim, and the door to the front room was half-open, showing the curtains still drawn and keeping out the threatening sunlight. The smell of men drifted though the door, heavy with fear and excitement.

Claudia burbled a greeting and one of the men gave a contemptuous chuckle. Roxy realised she was wasting time and bolted though the door into the front room. The two men were in the room, one of them bent over Claudia. They froze, looking up at Roxy in shock. Roxy's eyes were drawn towards the heavy sports bag carried by one, and by the heavy automatic pistols clenched in each of the men's hands.

"It's not possible," spluttered the one crouched by Claudia, his eyes flicking to the window.

"Back off boys," warned Roxy menacingly, noting the sudden terror gripping both men. They knew. They knew what she was, not bothering to raise their guns, and tensing ready for flight. Roxy felt charged with energy, drinking in their fear, feeling it strengthen her limbs and sharpen her senses. She bared her fangs and felt an additional frisson of delight at the panic it caused.

They both took an involuntary step back, then the one nearest Claudia seemed to find some inner strength and regained control of himself. He sneered at Roxy and raised his gun, not toward her, but at Claudia.

Roxy's smile froze, and her eyes turned hard. "You're dead," she whispered, "and so is whoever sent you."

"No woman, you may be able to resist daysleep, but the sun is strong outside. You'll never leave this house alive."

Roxy clenched her teeth, feeling the stolen energy start to slip away. But not entirely. She readied herself for action, knowing she had only seconds, and barely noticed the second man reach inside his bag. She ducked out of the way as he pulled something out and threw it at her. The object passed over her shoulder and struck the wall behind her, the shattering of glass followed moments later by an ominous roar of deflagration.

Roxy moved, diving headlong into the man threatening Claudia, her speed and strength stimulated by the fear of the men before her and multiplied by her rage. She hit him square in the chest and felt his ribcage collapse beneath her fists. She rolled to her feet behind the second man, who was still staring at the spot where she had been standing, and slammed her open palm into his back, shattering his shoulder blade and sending him crashing to the ground in front of the burning curtains. Roxy stooped to pick up Claudia, and backed away from the methyl-fed flames, which were rapidly consuming the drapes and allowing terrifying beams of sunlight to lance across the room towards her. The men moaned in front of her, winded and in terrible pain, but not dead. Roxy briefly considered finishing them off, but decided it wouldn't be worth it. Besides, now that she had Claudia in her arms, her anger was gone.

She backed into the kitchen, glancing at the rear door that led out into a small, untidy yard behind her house. She could get out, but it would do her little good, at least until the sun set. She wouldn't have that long, she knew, looking back into her front room. The fire had now reached the armchair by the window, and the thin nylon carpet was melting, a growing blackened region creeping inexorably towards her tattered couch. The sun was blaring through the now completely uncovered window, slanting across the doorway into the hall. Her clothes were in her bedroom, and she would have to pass through the beams of sunlight to reach it.

Roxy squinted against the dazzling light and clutched Claudia tightly. Thick brown smoke started to rise from the armchair, carrying a bitter acrid tang, and Roxy wrinkled her nose and stopped breathing. Claudia started to cough, however, which spurred Roxy into action. She turned into the kitchen, grabbed a tea-towel and ran it under the tap. She wrung it out and wrapped it carefully around Claudia's face, trying to soothe her struggles with encouraging happy noises. The flames had reached the couch by the time she returned to the doorway. The two men had recovered slightly, and were desperately trying to crawl towards her, away from the heat of the fire. Roxy reached down and pulled them one by one into the kitchen, dumping them unceremoniously by the back door, which had been forced open and was slightly ajar. She turned her back on the men, wondering at her act of mercy, and told herself that she was just clearing a path to make a run for the hallway.

Thick smoke curled up around the ceiling and started to descend, slinking down the walls like a mass of wary spiders. There was a wall of flames on front of her and a pool of sunlight beyond. She felt herself shrink back, unable to move closer, but then a panicked gurgle from Claudia snapped her out of it. She leapt forwards, reaching the doorway in one bound. She landed with a hiss, her naked legs reddened and stinging from the sunlight, her forearms tingling with promised pain. She stumbled into her bedroom, setting Claudia gently onto her pillow. In a blur she gathered together some clothes, a cap, sunglasses and a blanket and was wearing them in seconds. She gasped, feeling her blood burning from the exertion, but wasted no time in picking Claudia up and racing to the front door. She threw the blanket over her head, checked that her gloves were pulled all the way up to the elbow, and flung open the door.

She ran, her eyes closed for most of the time, only opening them to check she was still on the path. She hurtled down the road, outpacing a startled cab driver, and collided with a post box, jarring her shoulder painfully. She found a pool of shadow and gratefully sank into it, pausing to look back at her flat. Smoke was pouring out of her windows, and people were streaming out of nearby houses to watch. She wondered if Julie would be okay, but knew there was nothing she could do about it. She turned and hurried away, cradling a frightened Claudia in her arms.

# Chapter 28

Roxy reluctantly awoke, protesting against the demanding consciousness pulling her away from the blissful oblivion of sleep toward a harsh cruel world where her body screamed in agony from countless burns covering her legs, arms and back. She groaned, turning onto her side, and opened her eyes grumpily. Everything seemed to hurt at once. Apparently fire couldn't be healed straight away either. She sat up gingerly and looked around. It was dark, though a faint flickering yellow light filtered in from a shattered doorway and illuminated a broken, foul-smelling toilet and a vandalised wash-basin by her head. She crawled towards the door and peered into the room beyond. She was in an abandoned house, the carpets removed to reveal warped floorboards, the plaster on the walls crumbling and covered with graffiti tags. The light came from a damaged streetlamp outside that kept cutting out, alternately plunging the room into darkness and glaring unmercifully through the broken windows.

Roxy pulled herself to her feet, wincing when her arm brushed against a tender spot on her thigh, and stood silently, trying to work out what was nagging her. She'd found the house only a few streets from where she lived, in a row of similarly decrepit houses normally inhabited by squatters and junkies, and had broken in, desperate for the welcome relief from the sun. The blanket had not proved to be the most ideal protection from the sun, which had found its way through the coarse weave to scald the back of her neck and head. She had checked every room downstairs, and spent a few seconds listening for sounds upstairs, before deciding that the house was empty and retreated to the toilet. She had wrapped Claudia in a – Claudia!

She looked round frantically, and limped further into the room. "Claudia," she called, "Claudia, where are you baby? Claudia!" She hobbled to the kitchen and, finding it empty, made her way to the rickety stairs leading upwards. They were missing risers in places, exposing twisted, rusted nails and the banister had been torn away leaving a nasty drop on one side. Roxy leapt up the stairs, four steps at a time, ignoring the protests from her legs, and swung into the hallway at the top, which was blackened from old fires and heavy with the stale odour of urine. There were three bedrooms, and she found Claudia sitting down in the middle of the second, surrounded by scraps of silver foil and used needles, playing with a blackened teaspoon.

Roxy rushed inside "No!" She whipped the spoon away from Claudia and threw it into a corner. Claudia smiled up at her mother and reached up her arms to be lifted. Roxy picked her up and started a thorough search of her body, looking for pinpricks or injuries. Apart from soot and dirt on her hands, legs and face, she seemed unharmed, but there was no telling what she had put into her mouth. Roxy looked at Claudia's tongue just in case, but saw nothing. Claudia giggled, and Roxy held her close, trembling as she made her way slowly downstairs, away from the drug paraphernalia, mouldering mattresses and empty sharp-edged food cans scattered around the walls.

This can't go on, she told herself, stripping off Claudia's sodden nappy and throwing it carelessly into a corner. She didn't have anything to replace it with, and a quick check in the kitchen confirmed there was no water to bathe her reddened bottom, so she merely sat on the floor with Claudia on her knee and let it air-dry while she stared into space and tried to think. For the moment Claudia was still happy to see her mummy, and was burbling quietly as she played with the small silver hoops in Roxy's ear. It wouldn't be long before she realised that she was hungry and started to become more demanding. Roxy thought back to the fire and how quickly it had spread. There was no way any of her stuff would have survived. She had lost everything.

She bit her lip, fighting back the threatening tears and focused instead on the two men who had come to kill her. Who were they? Or more to the point, for whom did they work? Not Wolfe, she felt sure. No matter how annoyed he was with her for leaving without his permission, she was too useful to him to just discard. Or was she? With the Primus dead, who would enforce the law restricting the creation of vampires? Probably no one, she thought, which would mean that other houses were likely to take advantage of the chaos to increase their numbers. It was possible that Wolfe would desert her. No, she decided with a slight shake of her head. Wolfe wouldn't waste time or effort in killing her. Not like that. He would wait until she came to see him and then set the rest of the house on her for sport if he wanted her dead. It must be one of his enemies, trying to reduce his power by killing off his house. As she was the newest and weakest, she was the natural choice. They'd probably decided that a couple of humans could complete the job, and normally they might have been right. Only the fact that she could wake and act in the day had saved her life.

She ran a hand through her hair, matted and stiff from the gel she hadn't yet washed away and looked down at Claudia in the blinking light. She hadn't lost everything. She had been worse off when she'd first run away from home. Home. It would be so nice to be able to take Claudia back home, to her mother, and let her help to look after her. A tear finally broke though the mental dam she had constructed and rolled down her cheek. She had no-one. Her only friend, Scarlet had withdrawn from her, and Roxy couldn't blame her. Maybe she should give Claudia up? Take her to a hospital and let the state find her a place where she could grow up safely?

She wished that would be true. More than likely she would find a foster home more interested in what benefits and handouts they could get than loving her. Perhaps she could hypnotise someone to look after Claudia, and visit every night so she would never lose her? She wiped away her tears. That was a fantasy too. What kind of monster would that make her? Besides, she needed Claudia as much as Claudia needed her. If it weren't for Claudia, she suspected she might easily give up, and walk out into the sun. Everything was just too hard. Why couldn't she get a break, just once?

Claudia leaned in and wrapped her arms around her mother's neck, and Roxy hugged her close gasping quietly at the pain above her shoulders, but needing the loving touch of her daughter more than anything.

"Come on baby, let's go and find something to eat shall we?" she whispered, getting to her feet. She realised that she was hungry too, but it was something she could ignore. She wrapped the blanket around Claudia and walked outside.

The air was fresh with the scent of recently fallen rain, and contrasted pleasantly with the stale reek of the filthy house. She wandered back toward her flat, barefoot, drawn by a compulsion to see the damage and a natural desire to try to retrieve some of her belongings. Her heart sank when she turned the corner onto the street where she used to live. The entire block of flats had been gutted, the walls blackened with smoke, windows shattered, and the paint on the frames was blistered and cracked. A police notice had been pinned to her door, which was loosely boarded shut with fresh pine planks. She circled around the building to the alleyway behind, making her way to her back door, the point where the arsonists had entered. She passed through the gate and up the concrete path to the door which was warped from the heat and no longer fit the frame. Hoisting Claudia in her arm, she pushed open the door and stepped into the kitchen, dismayed by the thick black dust coating every surface.

The front room beyond was completely destroyed, the furniture now nothing more than charcoal and ashes, held together by once-molten polyester. Her mobile was a twisted mess. She saw no sign of any bodies, or silhouettes where bodies may have lain. They must have escaped. She walked across the room to her bedroom. The fire did not seem to have reached here, curiously, but the thick smoke had filled the room, coating everything in sticky soot. Her clothes, scattered about on the floor, were filthy and partially singed from the heat. Fortunately, those in her battered chest of drawers seemed to have fared slightly better.

She found a slightly cleaner spot on the bed, under the sheets, to sit Claudia on, and started to go through the clothes. She found a few t-shirts, the pair of stained jeans she'd been wearing when she killed Simon, a couple of discoloured bras, four pairs of socks and a handful of cotton panties which she set on the bed next to Claudia. Along with the jeans,

Pooh Bear nightshirt and the gold leather jacket she had thrown on before she left, she had nearly a week's worth of clothes.

She crouched down and reached under the bed for her boots, pulling one out and looking at it. It was covered with grime, but she managed to wipe some off with the edge of the sheet and decided it was retrievable. She reached back for the other one and her fingers brushed something hard, metallic and unfamiliar. She pulled it out with a frown. It was Sanjay's sword. The varnished scabbard had cracked and was no longer a smooth calfskin brown but was wrinkled like the face of a weathered old sailor. Roxy pulled it from the scabbard and was surprised to find the blade still a polished, shining silver. She stared at it, unblinking, and then pushed it back into its housing and placed it on the floor beside her before reaching back under the bed for her second boot. She also pulled out the bag containing her costumes and looked inside. The clothes inside looked largely undamaged, apart from the smell of smoke, so that was another few dresses, some lingerie and high-heeled shoes and boots.

She stuffed her normal clothes into the bag and looked around for some clothes for Claudia. She tended to leave them in a pile at the foot of her bed, and they had all been affected by the smoke in some way. She found a dozen items that were less damaged than the others and dressed Claudia, squeezing the rest of them into her bag. She had kept Claudia's nappies in the front room, so they were all destroyed. She would have to get some more. She looked for her purse which was normally beside her bed, but it was gone.

"Damn police," she cursed, wondering how she could get her last remaining hundred pounds out of the bank now.

Claudia cried out, trying to reach her.

"Are you hungry?"

"Yes, hung-wy" sobbed Claudia. Roxy stood up and looked around one last time.

"Come on then," she soothed, picking up her daughter in one hand and the sword and bag in the other. A quick check in the bathroom confirmed that there was nothing she could salvage apart from, ironically, her tampons which she kept in an old tin. She didn't need those any more, she supposed. She'd lost track of when her period was due and was suddenly wracked with indecision. She knew so little about vampires. A few seconds later she thrust the tin in the bag, just in case, and headed back outside through the kitchen. Pausing once more at the door, she turned and opened a cupboard. There was her tip jar, still containing some silvers and the occasional pound coin. She grabbed it and left her flat for the last time.

# Chapter 29

Claudia was screaming. The poor thing was starving, Roxy knew. So am I she thought, shuffling her daughter onto her shoulder with her bag and moving the sword into her opposite hand. Why am I carrying this thing around? She looked up and down the litter-strewn street. There were plenty of people about as it was still early evening but they all refused to meet her eye, or hear her plea for any spare change. The best she got was an embarrassed "Sorry" from the occasional passer-by before they stepped around her and walked on at a slightly faster pace.

This is stupid, she thought angrily. You're a fucking vampire Rox. You shouldn't be begging like this. Yeah but what's the alternative, her inner conscience asked, mug someone? You could hypnotise them, her other voice argued. It's still theft, her conscience admonished. Roxy stroked Claudia's hair in an unsuccessful attempt to soothe her. She should go to a shelter. There she could get food and maybe a bed for the night, no questions asked. She'd need it for during day though, which they didn't normally offer. It was worth doing though, if only to get some food for Claudia. She started walking, knowing of a place not far from Leicester square, but it would take her almost an hour to get there. Maybe another option would present itself before then?

It didn't, and Claudia was in a bad state by the time they arrived. She was sobbing pitifully, her throat too puffy and swollen to cry any more and her clothes were wet with urine, her bottom covered with a painful red rash. Roxy was faint with hunger, weary and footsore. The fires of her anger had simmered down to a slow, raging hatred of those who had put her in this position. Not just the ones who had burned her house, but also Wolfe for attracting such enemies, and the one who had taken her in the first place. Especially him.

The volunteers at the shelter helped to clean and feed Claudia, and gave her a plastic bag containing half a dozen nappies and some baby wipes. They pointedly ignored the sword, for which Roxy was grateful. After Claudia calmed down and started to fall asleep on her shoulder, she turned to the volunteer helping her, a middle-aged woman with slightly greying hair and asked if she could hold her while she went to the bathroom. The woman eyed her warily.

"Don't worry," Roxy reassured her, "I'm coming back."

"Okay, but don't be long, and you'd better not be doing any drugs in there!"

"I promise," said Roxy, passing Claudia gently across to the woman, "I'll be right back." She crossed the floor of the community centre toward the toilets, but after a quick look over her shoulder to make sure the woman wasn't watching, veered off to the dormitories. There were five huddled shapes in the women's room, sleeping on rough mats with foam pillows and thin blankets. Roxy crept over to the nearest sleeper.

It was a young woman, her bleach-blonde hair dark brown about an inch up from the roots. Her face was relaxed in sleep, but grimy lines about her eyes betrayed her normally bitter expression. Roxy forced sympathetic thoughts from her mind and bent down to bite gently though the soft skin of the girl's wrist. The girl stirred slightly and moaned but didn't wake. Roxy felt the warm flow of blood in her mouth as a healing balm, calming but insistent, tasting of flowers and light spring days. She was ready for its demands though, and pulled away immediately after only a mouthful. She couldn't risk losing control and killing her. There were plenty more to feed from and she hoped that taking the edge off her hunger first would prevent any accidents.

She moved on, taking three or four mouthfuls from each as she worked her way along the room. There was a definite difference in the flavour compared to men's blood; softer, smoother somehow, more like strawberries and cream than meat and gravy. She thought she preferred it. She wiped her mouth after the fourth, feeling much better and wondering if she needed to stop by the fifth before she left. She turned around and saw a pair of rheumy eyes on her. It was the occupant of the fifth bed, an old woman with a weatherworn face and damaged grey hair.

"Yer one o' them ain't you?" muttered the woman, non-judgementally.

Roxy stared back at her in surprise, "How do you know that?"

The woman chuckled throatily, "It's a bit bleeding obvious, if you'll excuse the pun!" She laughed again at her own joke, which quickly turned into a coughing fit.

"I mean you haven't forgotten, or...gone mad?"

The woman shrugged under her covers, "I ain't completely sane neither, you know. Else I wouldn't 'ave been on the streets for forty years. You see too many things in that time that don't do you no good."

Roxy shuffled forward on her knees until she was within touching distance. She wrinkled her nose against the smell of the woman, who regarded her calmly.

"Aren't you worried about what I'll do to you," asked Roxy curiously.

The woman shrugged again. "Don't suppose I care so much, really, but you don't seem the type to do no-one no harm anyway."

"How can you possibly know that?"

"Well you're still sat there talking away at me for a start. Plus you was careful with them girls, an' I can see it in your eyes. You're a new one, ain't you?"

Roxy smiled, "Yeah, I'm new. I'm also full now, so you don't need to worry about me. I'd probably gag at the smell anyway."

The woman gave a chortle and lay back down on her pillow. "Don't you come back here too often. The girls ain't strong enough to keep losing blood like that. They have enough problems as it is."

Roxy promised not to come back if she could help it and stood up. She looked down at the woman, who had closed her eyes and was trying to get back to sleep, and then turned and went to collect her daughter.

# Chapter 30

Roxy found herself at Club Obsession not long after midnight. She knew instantly that she had been foolish. She spotted the detective a hundred yards down the street almost immediately. The bouncer on the door gave her a hard stare, his eyes flicking disapprovingly across Claudia, but then his colleague whispered something in his ear and they both stepped aside to let her in. Roxy headed upstairs where it was quieter and spotted Ruth and Marty standing beside the large arched windows.

"What's up Roxy? You look a bit scorched," ventured Marty.

Roxy touched her reddened skin and gave him a crooked smile, "Someone tried to burn down my flat while I was in it."

"When? Tonight?" Ruth asked.

"Well, this afternoon actually. Shut your mouths both of you, you look like fish. I'm okay, just a little cooked."

Marty and Ruth exchanged a look and then Marty checked to make sure no one was listening nearby.

"You need to tell Wolfe," urged Ruth quietly. "He will be furious."

Roxy dropped into a chair and rubbed her face with her free hand. "I don't think I can cope with this. Every time I turn around I find someone who hates me, or wants something from me." She set the sword down between her legs and shifted her sleeping child onto her lap. Her arms were sore, her feet ached and her back was stiff. Just a thought and a tingle, and I can make the pain stop, she told herself, but she didn't. The physical pain helped to distract her from her emotional pains, and she welcomed it. Ruth sat down next to her.

"You are doing well, Roxy. You have survived the first week."

"Yay for me. What do I win? Another week?"

"And then another. And then a month."

Roxy stared down at Claudia, trying to force out her words through a swollen throat, "It's too hard," she whispered finally.

Ruth exchanged an inscrutable look with Marty.

"Do you have anywhere to stay?"

Roxy shook her head. "I was hoping Wolfe might let me stay here."

Ruth made a negative-sounding noise. Roxy raised her eyes to look at her.

"Wolfe is very...particular...about who stays here during the day." Ruth said, choosing her words carefully.

Roxy's lips curled into a tired smile. "I see. Well I wouldn't want to bother him at such an important time. I guess I'll sort myself out somehow." She stood up, shuffling Claudia onto her shoulder and picking up the sword. "I'll see you later, perhaps?"

"Roxy-" started Ruth, but broke off when their eyes met.

Roxy shrugged, "Thanks anyway," turned and walked away.

"Au revoir, Roxy," said Ruth softly, watching her depart.

A cold rain had started to fall outside, so Roxy pulled her jacket over Claudia. Her eyes blurred, having little to do with the rain. She walked away from the club, not thinking where she was going. The rain started to beat down faster, bringing a cleansing aroma to the roads, and running off her matted hair in cold streams down her face and neck. She didn't care at first, but became increasingly aware of Claudia, not quite covered by her cropped leather jacket. What if she caught a cold? What if the cold became a fever because she couldn't take her to the doctors during the day for medicine? What kind of life would Claudia have anyway? Hardly seeing the sun, always in danger of being snatched by some malicious enemy of her mother's, just to make a point or force a promise from her.

What if she gave Claudia away? Not to her family. Not into a house with that abusive step-grandfather, strung-out grandmother and violent uncles. Nor to a care home, unloved, unwelcome and lonely. Maybe she'd find a foster family that would love her? She was young after all, and highly sought-after. Maybe they'd adopt her? And she'd grow up, never knowing her mother. Roxy clutched her tightly, the thought of Claudia calling someone else "Mummy" tearing at her soul. Better to die. And Claudia too? Why not, she reasoned, it could be quick – while she was sleeping. And then to follow her into the dawn. Easy. Easy? Roxy wondered if it would be that easy. Her arm still throbbed from the pain the sunlight caused. It would be the hardest thing in the world not to lose her nerve and run and hide. "If you are brave enough to kill yourself you are brave enough to live," someone had once told her. She had thought it excessively pretentious at the time, but now she felt she knew what they were trying to say.

She brushed the rain away from her face and looked up, straight into the detective's car only a few paces ahead of her. He was furiously hiding behind a newspaper, but she knew it was him. She pressed her lips together and strode up to the passenger door, opened it and sat down next to him before he could utter a startled response.

"Well since you're following me, you might as well give me a lift too, and save us both a lot of effort."

He stared at her warily, his eyes resting briefly on the sword in her hand and then put his paper on the seat behind him, all pretence gone. "Are you okay?"

Roxy followed his gaze to her reddened face and hands, "Yeah I guess so."

"Who burned down your flat Amanda?"

"Don't call me that!" she snapped.

"You prefer Roxy right?"

"It's safer." She turned to look at him. He looked as though he hadn't been sleeping much. "What was your name again?"

"Anderton."

"Have you got a first name? We might as well get to know each other."

Anderton looked away, apparently embarrassed, "Just Anderton will do."

Roxy raised an amused eyebrow. "Well you definitely don't get to call me Mandy if you won't tell me."

"It's not important okay?"

Roxy started to smile crookedly, "Now I'm really interested."

"Maybe I'll tell you later," he suggested, "but first I want to help you. Who's after you Roxy?"

Roxy looked out through the windscreen at the club before answering quietly, "Trust me, you really don't want to know.'

"I've heard that before, but I promise you'll be safe if you talk to me."

Roxy stared at him for a moment, considering her words, then said quietly, "I think the people you work for also work for the people I work for. You can't keep me safe Anderton."

Roxy saw a group of vampires emerge from the club and turn down the road towards them. "It's not safe to sit here. Drive somewhere," she said, sinking down into her seat.

Anderton followed her gaze, but didn't appear to recognise them. He started the engine and pulled away from the side of the road. Roxy kept her face turned away from the vampires as they passed them.

"Well?" he prompted after they had driven for five minutes in silence.

"Anywhere along here will do." The rain had eased off a bit.

Anderton sighed and slowed to a stop at the kerb. "That's not what I meant."

"I know, but you wouldn't believe me anyway. Thanks and everything, but this is my mess, and I'll get myself out of it. Somehow."

"Have you got anywhere to stay?"

"I'll find something."

Anderton studied her stony face, as if searching for a way to soften it. She pulled up the corner of her damp t-shirt and tenderly dabbed at Claudia's face and hair to dry it, despite being about to go out in the rain once more.

"Here," he said, pulling something from his pocket.

She turned and saw that he was holding out the keys to Sanjay's bike.

"I found them in your flat."

She took the keys and shoved them into her jacket pocket.

"If you change your mind, give me a call."

Roxy gave him a look which told him how unlikely that would be and climbed out of the car without a word.

# Chapter 31

She hurried away, trying to soothe a stirring Claudia and not paying much attention to her surroundings. She nearly ran into a gang of youths loitering under a rail bridge around the next corner. There were about a dozen, dressed in hooded tops, including a couple of young women sitting on the kerb out of the rain. Roxy hesitated only a moment before ploughing on, already in their midst and too late to pull back. They stared at her with a mixture of surprise and contempt, a couple finding their voices a few seconds later to call obscenities after her. She ignored them and tried to avoid eye contact, but just when she thought she was getting away, a female voice behind her called out "It's the Wolfe girl!"

Roxy shot a look back, despite herself, catching the gaze of a woman who had an intense gleam of excitement in her face. Two men turned pale faces towards her triggering a shock of recognition. They had been at the museum the night Catallus had died. Swearing to herself, Roxy turned and started to run, not caring about pride and hoping they would be too lazy to follow. A series of shouts and whistles behind her put that idea to rest. Stealing a look over her shoulder she saw four or five figures detach themselves from the group and run after her. She put her head down and sprinted, hugging Claudia to her breast and frantically looking for a hiding place.

The calls behind her grew louder and more enthusiastic, taking on the character of a hunting party flushing game from the terrain ahead. They were gaining on her. She jumped across a side street and pushed herself harder, feeling her blood burn. A line of small, closed shops loomed up ahead, facing onto a small open area with a park beyond.

Knowing she would never make it to a safe area in time, Roxy made for the recessed doorway of a newsagents. At least she could restrict the number of lines of approach. She set Claudia down on the thin, dirty mat in front of the door, waking her up in the process, and turned to face her pursuers. They were grinning in expectation. Three of the men were carrying wicked-looking Japanese swords. Roxy gripped the hilt of her sword tightly and stepped towards them. Four men and a woman circled her, stopping just out of reach.

"You're in the wrong place, infant," said the woman.

"I don't want any trouble," began Roxy, knowing that her words would make no difference.

"Too bad," sneered one of the men holding a sword, his eyes flicking past Roxy to where Claudia was sitting up and rubbing her eyes. The tip of his tongue swept over his top lip.

"You're dead, girl, and we're going to have some fun with your baby too," said another man, "maybe we'll make it a chew toy out of your ears?"

Roxy snarled at him and raised her sword.

He laughed and casually tapped Roxy's inexpert lunge away with the flat of his blade. "Do you even know how to use that?" he asked.

Roxy held his gaze. He was right. She would make better use of it by ending it quickly for Claudia. How could she be so stupid? A bitter hatred stirred inside her, directed at Life and the unfairness of it all. She hardly cared what happened to her now, but the hardest pill to swallow was how much she had failed Claudia. With a scream of frustration, she swung her sword in a wide arc straight at the man taunting her. He jumped back, letting the momentum of her swing carry her round and deftly brought his sword down onto her exposed back. Pain flashed through her as it cut through her waist to her hip. She dropped her sword and pulled herself away, feeling her body tingle as it struggled to repair itself. She barely ducked under an attack aimed at her head from her left, and leapt at the man who had hit her, hoping to grapple him to the ground but a thrusting attack from behind drove a foot of steel completely through her upper thigh. She screamed and fell to the ground, feeling the sword tear out of her, causing even more damage.

She looked up into the faces of the men around her, their swords held lightly at their sides as they saw the chance to play with her, and tried to summon the courage or rage to stand up again and at least give them a hard time. Claudia was crying nearby, confused and scared, but even that failed to rouse her. She propped herself up on her hands and uninjured knee. One of the men swept her hands out from under her with a foot, sending her crashing painfully onto the concrete. She heard chuckles and a kick was delivered to her ribs that made her vision swirl. She was dimly aware of the woman stepping round her towards Claudia and made a feeble grab at her ankle. The woman shook it off easily and reached down to pick Claudia up.

A couple of wet thumps sounded in rapid succession out of Roxy's sight. She turned her head to look and received a shower of cold blood in her face as the severed torso of one of the men fell across her. She caught a brief blur of motion and out of the corner of her eye a moment before the third swordsman's head rolled down his chest to land with a crunch at his feet. Roxy turned back to the woman, who still crouched with one hand poised over Claudia. Roxy made a desperate lunge to pull her away from Claudia. The woman tumbled on top of Roxy, who locked her hands around her, holding on tightly. Roxy dug her fangs deep into the woman's shoulder repeatedly, becoming covered in cool, coppery blood but intent on reaching the back of her neck and her spinal cord. The woman screamed and bucked wildly but Roxy didn't let go, despite receiving a vicious blow from the back of the woman's head which shattered her nose, and finally gnawed her way to the spine.

A couple of attempts was all it took to reach the bony ridge of the spinal column and Roxy bit down as hard as she could, her efforts bolstered by the small amount of blood trickling down her throat. Her head cleared, forgetting the pain as she paused to suck in a larger mouthful, sending ripples of warmth through her body. The woman brought her elbow back hard into Roxy's ribs, nearly causing her to lose her grip. Roxy thrust aside the temptation to continue drinking and with a final savage bite, tore the top of the woman's spine out of her body. The woman went rigid, spasmed a couple of times and then went limp.

Roxy continued to hold her, taking the opportunity to lap up a couple more mouthfuls of blood from the ruin of her neck before it started to taste bitter and dead as it rapidly decayed and congealed. Roxy spat out the last mouthful as she rolled the woman away and looked around. A fifth headless body lay a few yards away – evidently caught trying to escape. She spun to check on Claudia, and saw that she was untouched, sitting on the doormat and gazing up at something over Roxy's shoulder. Roxy turned and saw a large, powerful-looking man watching her. He had long brown hair framing his head and shoulders and was wearing a suit and tie beneath a heavy trench-coat. He held a thin rapier in one hand with an elegant basket hilt, which he was carefully cleaning with a large linen handkerchief.

# Chapter 32

His dark eyes held hers as she rose to her feet. She was a good five inches taller than him, and she unconsciously lowered her head and stood back on one leg to appear less intimidating.

"Don't slouch child," his rich deep voice was inflected with a subtle but delightfully sexy accent which she had never heard before – not exactly Spanish, but it settled in the back of his throat in a similar way. "You are who you are. Be proud."

Roxy straightened up and he turned his attention back to cleaning his sword. She took advantage of his distraction to bend down and pick up her own sword. It made a sharp metallic grating sound as the tip slid across the paving slabs, causing him to glance up at her. He gave his blade one last check and then slid it under his overcoat and secured it in place. Then he took a step toward Roxy and gave her a small bow. "Forgive me, my name is Juan," He held out a business card, which she took hesitantly.

"Hi Juan. I'm Roxy Harker." She said awkwardly, stealing a glance at Claudia, who was staring at Juan in fascination. She resisted the urge to pick her up although she didn't think she had anything to fear from this newcomer.

"May I suggest if you insist on carrying that weapon," he said with a smile, "that you learn to use it."

Roxy felt foolish and looked down at the sword in her hand. "I was given it when ... someone died. I'd never even seen one before."

Roxy looked down at the bodies, which were now withered and decayed, but still whole enough to have hair and cracked grey skin stretched tightly across their faces. "What are we going to do with them?"

Juan reached into a pocket and withdrew a mobile phone. He made a call, speaking to someone in a language Roxy didn't recognise, then put the phone away. "It is done. We should withdraw, however. Caution is a habit of the wise." He inclined his head towards the park, inviting her to join him. Roxy bent down to retrieve Claudia, who was yawning again and snuggled her face eagerly into her mother's shoulder.

"So who are you?" Roxy asked after they had walked for some way into the park, "and why did you save my life back there?"

"I have been watching you for some time Roxy," he said softly. She got the impression he hardly ever raised his voice in anger, and if such a thing were to happen, it would be followed by a devastating violence she hoped never to witness. Something stirred in her memory.

"Back when Wolfe took us to attack Domus Craven, you were there! You saved me then, too?"

He gave a little twist of his head in acknowledgement, "I did not want you to fall at the hands of that arrogant whelp. You are too important."

Roxy looked at him in surprise. "What do you mean? I'm nobody."

"Precisely. Afterwards I talked with you for a long time in order to confirm that my suspicions were correct."

Roxy frowned, "What are you talking about? I've never seen you before."

He dismissed her comments with a flick of his hand, "I caused you to forget the conversation. It was necessary to fool her. I was sure that I had waited long enough, but one can never be too careful."

Roxy looked at him blankly. "Long enough for what? And who is '*her*'?"

Juan paused under a large sycamore tree, and scanned their surroundings carefully before dropping cross-legged to the ground amongst the rain-damped roots. Roxy sat too, thankful for the opportunity to set the sword down and manoeuvre Claudia into a more comfortable position. She wrapped Claudia snugly in her leather jacket to protect her from the chill morning wind. It didn't bother Roxy in the slightest, although she could feel its bitter sting through her thin t-shirt.

"What I am about to tell you will change you Roxy. I will not lie to you. I am doing this for my own purposes, not necessarily to help you, but I would ask that you hear me out before making your decision, and I hope you will choose to help me."

Roxy's shiver had nothing to do with the chill draught that slid down her top.

He composed himself, organising his thoughts and then asked "How many times has Wolfe fed from you?"

The question caught Roxy by surprise, "I ... I don't know. A couple I guess."

"Do not allow him to bite you again. He is slowly enslaving you to his will. Each bite strengthens his influence and allows him to make suggestions to you that you will find yourself unable to resist."

Roxy stared at him, "You mean, like Sarah and Jessica?"

Juan nodded. "It is an ancient technique for ensuring loyalty. The parens shackles his child when they are taken, and then uses the power to maintain it so that they will not betray them. Traditionally they visit the human over the course of several nights prior to the take, drinking shallowly to ensure obedience before infecting them."

Roxy recalled the silent, watchful looks from the other members of her house during the times that Wolfe had drank from her. They had known what was happening, and they hadn't told her. Not Sanjay, not even Ruth. She felt sick. What kind of people were they? Well, you haven't told Sarah, she reminded herself. No one has. That's different though, she argued, Sarah is already lost. I still had a chance to escape. Roxy's lips curled in a bitter smile as she remembered Jessica's refusal to save her from the Little Death and forcing Sarah to feed her instead. Jessica was scared of allowing Roxy to gain any control over her. Another memory surfaced, and she looked up with a frown.

"I've drunk from Wolfe too. Every time he drank from me. Doesn't that mean I'm shackling him too?"

Juan shook his head. "Think – he would have poured his blood into a receptacle first for you to drink. Only through the bite can you subvert their will. Every time you feed, you draw part of your victims' soul into you. This gives you intimate knowledge of their motives and fears which can be used against them. Humans are easier to shackle than vampires, but no one is safe, and no one knows if one is shackled to another. Sometimes it is obvious, but spies can be created without the subject even knowing, ready to be activated at the right time. Only very powerful Annunaki have the skill to trace the presence of a shackle and deduce who holds the chains."

Roxy shrank back from him, wondering what else he had done to her before wiping her memory.

"Relax child. You are as yet uncontrolled. I had to make certain of that. It makes you very dangerous though, and a rarity. When you first appeared I was curious about you. Who created you, and why? Such things are seldom left to chance, especially where Wolfe is concerned."

"Wolfe? Wolfe had nothing to do with me until Vicky introduced us. She said no one else would have me."

Juan chuckled. "It seems that her deception has been a little too successful for its own good, and has taken on a life of its own. She must have been curious about you too."

"Who? That's the second time you've mentioned 'her'." Roxy wondered if he was talking about Vicky.

"She calls herself Natalie."

Roxy laughed, caught off-guard "Natalie? She's almost as young as I am."

"It is true that she only joined with Wolfe a few months ago, but Domus Wolfe is not what it appears," replied Juan, "It is unheard of for a ragtag band of infamari and orphans to form a house which has persisted as many years as Wolfe's. He first arrived nearly thirty years ago and quickly teamed up with James to form Domus Wolfe. Within a couple of years he had recruited Ruth, Jessica, Sanjay and Marty, all of whom were alone and fleeing persecution elsewhere. Each time he was summoned before the Curiata to answer charges of breaching tradition, and each time he made an impassioned speech about strengthening the power of the community, and through breathtaking skill for one so young, he managed to secure secret deals with the patricians and major plebeians to vote in his favour.

"He then bided his time, slowly securing his power base and managing to gain a seat on the Tributa, until Dave and Sarah arrived – young lovers as wild as Bonnie and Clyde. They tore a trail of destruction and death through the city which caused an outcry among the comitia, who demanded their death. Wolfe managed to persuade the Curiata to allow him to adopt them if they could be tamed. No one thought it possible, but within a week he had secured their allegiance and was granted *in loco parentis* over them."

Roxy couldn't keep quiet any longer, "Sarah? Okay I can believe that of Dave – he's a psycho, but cute and dainty Sarah? No way!"

"She was the worst of the two. Where she led, he followed. That is why Wolfe made Jessica shackle her."

Roxy was puzzled "Why not do it himself?"

"She is Jessica's responsibility now." Juan explained with a shrug.

Roxy smiled gleefully "Wolfe was afraid of her?"

"More of being held responsible for her actions."

"But that doesn't make sense. Why ask to adopt her if he wasn't sure he could control her?"

"Ah now," whispered Juan, "we come to the final piece of the puzzle. The first part of the answer is that with Dave and Sarah now part of Wolfe's house, none dared challenge him. Certainly not the parvenu houses, but also many of the plebeian houses too. The second part is that it was not his decision to make. He was but a pawn in an elaborate plot to manoeuvre the house into a position where a new member could slip in without much more than a murmur of protest."

"You mean Natalie?"

"Yes. She had slowly gathered together the members of Domus Wolfe, using her influence across the world to sever their connections with their original kin and make sure they were totally isolated and desperate. Then she summoned them to London to join Wolfe and directed his actions so that he managed to persuade Catallus and the other patricians to allow them to live. Every member of Domus Wolfe claims to experience prophetic dreams from time to time – a rare, highly sought-after power among us – but these were merely telepathic suggestions sent by Natalie, as she calls herself, designed to provide the illusion of free will."

Roxy shifted uncomfortably, "I've had some strange dreams too. I don't know if I'd call them prophetic though. They were more immediate, and they had a dragon in them..." she trailed off, feeling somewhat foolish.

Juan eyed her keenly, "Interesting. A dragon, you say? Tell me."

"Yeah, it was sleeping, and then it woke up and looked at me, as if it had just realised I was there."

"When did you have this dream?"

Roxy thought for a moment, "The day after the attack on Craven I think."

Juan thought for a moment. "Interesting. That was just after I questioned you. Have you told anyone about this?"

Roxy shook her head.

"Well I don't suppose it would matter if you did," he admitted, "People expect it from Wolfe's house now."

He fell silent, pondering what she had just told him. Roxy leaned forward, "You were telling me about Natalie?"

Juan folded his hands in his lap. "Indeed. Her real name is Na'amah, and she is in fact an extremely old Annunaki, bitter and twisted with hatred. She has existed at least since the time of Ancient Greece, although I believe she was originally Persian. That she has persisted so long is testament to her cunning and power, but she is one of the most evil creatures on the planet."

Roxy took this in slowly, strangely unsurprised. "Why is she doing this? I mean why hide herself like this?"

"The tale goes back millennia, but do you remember what ancient artefact Catallus was so proud of before he died?"

Roxy frowned "Some sort of writings wasn't it?"

"Yes," he said, "the Menes Tablets. Supposedly the words of Menes who was the first Pharaoh to unite Upper and Lower Egypt, and one of the earliest recorded Annunaki. He was the grandfather of Catallus, which is why the Primus was so excited when the Tablets were uncovered. He has had experts translating them ever since, both living and undead. No one knows what they say, but their significance is beyond imagining to Annunaki society.

"Wolfe arrived in London soon after Catallus announced the discovery of the Tablets. It is my belief that Na'amah wanted to acquire them for herself. You see, Menes and Na'amah were once lovers, and ruled Egypt together as king and queen for a time, until she betrayed him. She joined another powerful Annunaki called Mangala and they drove Menes out of his homeland. Then she turned on Mangala, betraying him in turn and nearly killing him. That was the start of a three-way feud that has lasted for over two thousand years, fought by proxy through vampire progeny, mules and even whole civilisations. Alliances have occurred at times, with two sides banding together to oppose the third, especially when one has gained more power than the others, but the partnerships never lasted and invariably ended in another cycle of betrayal."

Roxy ran her fingers through her hair, noticing that the rain and old hair-gel had conspired to make it matted and untidy. She needed to wash it. And find some clean clothes. And some make-up. She sighed.

"So how do you fit in?" she asked tiredly.

Juan tilted his head, "I like to think of myself as an independent agent, but if truth be told, I side with Mangala. Menes I have not met, but Na'amah and I have had many dealings, none of which I have found pleasant. I have assisted Mangala from time to time, mostly indirectly through my opposition to her. I became aware of her again only last year and since then I have been trying to find out what her latest scheme is. Now we know."

"We do?"

"She has slain Menes" most powerful pawn and stolen his writings. She must be exultant." Juan said, scowling.

"I'm not sure," mused Roxy, "Wolfe was happy, but Natalie was...odd."

"In what way?"

"Well she came over and spoke to me for a start. She'd never taken an interest in me before."

"What did you talk about?"

Roxy scratched her nose, "There was a fight in the club. Then she asked who had taken me. She called me a 'self-born', and seemed to find it quite funny. Oh yeah," Roxy remembered, "she asked me if I knew about the prophecy of the self-born."

"Did she tell you what it was?" asked Juan.

Roxy shook her head.

"It is not really a prophecy, but more of a warning, or a fable. The self-born are those that manage to take themselves without the consent of their creator. As such they are uncontrolled and have the potential to cause havoc, bringing doom to all those around them, before dying gloriously."

"Great," muttered Roxy.

Juan smiled, "It is only a tale to scare the young. Doubtless it has happened once or twice, but such creatures are usually killed out of hand when it becomes known what they are. I suggest you do not tell anyone else."

"No shit, Sherlock." She stroked Claudia's hair softly and looked back at Juan. "So you think Natalie...Na'amah...killed Catallus?"

"I am almost certain. Few others have the power to do so, and I know that it was not Mangala; he is not yet ready to reveal himself." He hesitated, "Yet I feel that I have missed something. If she did indeed do it, then why is she still here? She is not one to linger to see the results of her plans once they have come to completion. She must have another purpose yet."

Roxy wrapped her arms around herself. Her skin was colder than she realised. She was also getting hungry after the exertion of the night. She needed to find somewhere to hide for the coming day, and get food for Claudia. Her earlier self-destructive determination had now given way to a weary persistence. She knew that she couldn't take her own life, or Claudia's. It wasn't as if it would be hard to do though. Between Wolfe, Reyne, Natalie and Dave (she still couldn't accept what she had learned about Sarah), she just had to upset one of them and they would happily kill her. Juan was watching her impassively. She wondered what he was thinking. Judging me probably, she decided. She knew what he wanted from her.

"So what you really need," she said quietly, "is for someone to find out what it is she is planning next, and to confirm whether she really killed Catallus."

"That would be good," said Juan.

Roxy smiled to herself, "Well I'll try to remember to ask her the next time I see her." She stood up, carefully cradling Claudia in her arms.

Juan rose to his feet in a smooth, catlike motion.

"Do you know who trashed my flat?"

"You are upset about that?" he seemed mildly amused, which annoyed her.

"Damn right I'm upset. I'm fucking pissed off."

"You must let it go. You are alive. They failed. Move on. Revenge is not healthy."

"Revenge has nothing to do with it. I just want to know who to look out for."

"It was nothing personal. Just one of Wolfe's enemies trying to weaken him. They are unlikely to try again for a while."

"You're not going to tell me who it was?" Roxy asked heatedly.

"Not today. I will see you again, Roxy Harker."

Roxy opened her mouth to speak but the words died on her tongue as he appeared to disintegrate in front of her eyes, leaving only a cloud of tiny swarming insects which moved rapidly away.

# Chapter 33

Roxy carried Claudia all the way across town and eventually arrived at Scarlet's house. It hadn't been easy. She worried about forcing herself on her friend and causing her more problems, but in the end she decided that Claudia's need for food, warmth and a bath was greater, and a couple of days probably wouldn't do Scarlet much harm. As it turned out, Scarlet was overjoyed to see her, despite the late hour.

"Where have you been?" she cried, throwing her arms around Roxy. "You've not called, and I saw your flat got burned down. Are you okay?"

Roxy nodded wearily, "It's complicated, but I've lost pretty much everything now. Can we stay with you for a few days until I can work something out?"

"Of course you can," scolded Scarlet and pulled her into the house. "Sit down, I'll get you a cuppa, and then you can tell me all about it."

Roxy let herself be thrust into a chair in the kitchen and watched Scarlet fussing around her, getting a drink and a snack for Claudia and filling the kettle.

Claudia ate her biscuits greedily and Scarlet set a mug in front of Roxy before sitting down at the table with one of her own. Roxy picked it up and pretended to take a sip. It smelled good, and a sudden pang of loss swept over her, threatening to bring her to tears.

Scarlet was watching her with a look of concern. "What happened?"

Roxy shrugged, "There was a fire. Luckily we got out okay, but now we don't have anywhere to go."

"You are welcome here," interrupted Scarlet firmly, "Why don't you go and get cleaned up? I can wash your clothes tomorrow."

"Thanks. A shower would be nice. I'll get myself sorted out soon though, I promise."

Scarlet reached over and squeezed her hand, "Hey, it's not your fault. I know it's going take a few weeks. My place isn't big, but you can have the couch whenever you want," she smiled.

Roxy smiled back. "Thanks, but I'll try not to overstay my welcome." She made her way to the bathroom, stripped off her grubby clothes and left them in a heap on the floor while she indulged in a long, hot shower. It felt good just to stand there and let the water caress her, and she spent more time than necessary scratching her head as she washed her blood-stiffened hair several times. Her clothes were encrusted with dried blood and her jeans had a hole in them where she had been stabbed in the thigh. She didn't want to put them back on.

She emerged wrapped in a towel to find that Scarlet had put the exhausted Claudia to bed with Leah. It was nearly dawn outside.

"Can I stay here during the day?" Roxy asked hesitantly.

"Of course," said Scarlet. "Do you mind the couch?"

Roxy looked at the window opposite it and said quietly, "I'm going to need somewhere dark. All day."

Scarlet paused, a strange look momentarily in her eye and nodded slowly, "Oh...yes...well you'd better use my bed then. I'll make sure you're not disturbed."

Roxy wished she could hug her, but the moment felt wrong. "Thanks Scar. You're the best."

Scarlet smiled, "I know. Go on then. Do whatever it is you do. I'll see you tonight."

Roxy gratefully sank into Scarlet's bed, comforted by her familiar smell and quickly fell asleep.

She awoke at sunset feeling refreshed, but still faintly sore from her burns.

Scarlet knocked on the door. "Are you awake yet?"

Roxy rolled out of bed and opened the door. Scarlet was carrying a shopping bag. "I went out and got some clothes for you. I think they'll fit."

Roxy hugged her and took the bag, "I don't deserve you."

She dressed and returned to the living room and sat with Scarlet for about five minutes, watching Claudia and Leah play and making idle conversation. Then Roxy rose from her chair.

"I guess I should get going. I've got a few things to do."

Scarlet stood up to embrace her, "Sure babe. I'll look after Claudia. You go and sort yourself out."

Roxy gave Claudia a kiss and a hug goodbye and then made her way back to her flat to collect her bike.

# Chapter 34

The club pulsed with energy and heat. Overhead spots bathing everything in red light, pierced every few seconds with dazzling white strobes like lightning at sunset. Roxy picked her way through the throng of dancers, conscious of every movement they made, every scent plastering their bodies, and every touch as she brushed past them. She spotted a vampire she didn't recognise, circling around a young girl who didn't seem to notice him. He flashed a look at Roxy, warning to keep her distance and then, a heartbeat later, moved behind the girl and wrapped his arms around her waist. The girl leaned into him as he nuzzled her ear, whispering something that made her smile. Roxy saw Wolfe sitting with James and Natalie at the rear of the club. Wolfe caught her eye and raised a beckoning finger.

She passed Jessica who was allowing a tall, good looking young man chat her up. Jessica smiled dangerously and watched Roxy pass before reaching out to her companion and pulling him in for a kiss. A trio of female vampires Roxy recognised from the museum were dancing together, attracting a lot of attention from most of the men nearby. Roxy realised there were several more vampires in tonight.

She paused, turning on the spot and swept the club, counting at least eleven immediately, most of whom she didn't think she'd met. They were all hunting, and there was an atmosphere of barely suppressed excitement and anticipation which made her blood rise. She tried to ignore the lust rising inside her, turning instead toward Wolfe in his booth.

Wolfe looked up as she approached and narrowed his eyes in annoyance. Not a good sign, she thought absently, still struggling with a desire to get back to the dance floor and join in the games. James stood and took a step to the side, a blank look on his face as he cleared a space for her. Roxy took the invitation and slid onto the bench seat opposite Natalie. James sat down next to Roxy, opposite Wolfe, blocking her exit, she noticed apprehensively. Wolfe stared at Roxy, his face dark, while Natalie regarded her, inscrutable as ever. Roxy tried not to look at her, and attempted to appear calm.

"Hi Rupert. What do you want?" Roxy asked cautiously.

Wolfe blinked slowly and deliberately, and steepled his fingers in front of him. "Roxy, Roxy, Roxy" he began, his soft tone all the more menacing in contrast to the anger simmering behind his eyes. Roxy found it difficult to remind herself to be scared of him however, with Natalie, or rather Na'amah sitting beside him. It was like worrying about the sting from a wasp perched on a crocodile's snout. "Where have you been?" he continued, snapping her attention back to him.

"What do you mean?" Roxy shifted nervously.

"I want you by my side, Roxy. How can I give you the benefit of my wisdom if you hide from me?" Roxy jumped as he suddenly shouted the last few words and thrust his face towards her. His calm facade was gone now, and rage played across his face, his eyes glowing slightly red from within. Roxy shrank back into the bench, gaining only a couple of inches before being stopped by the high backrest. Wolfe sat back, immediately calm again and smiled reassuringly. Roxy flinched at the sudden mood change, and cowered in the corner, not sure what to expect next.

"I forgive you though. I am a kindly parens, and you are still but a babe. You do not understand the importance of a strong house, or the parts we must all play to maintain it." He smiled again at Roxy, who glanced helplessly at James and Natalie, trying to gauge her reply from their reactions, but they were both staring at her blankly.

"Uh, I'm sorry. I've been busy, sorting things out. You know?" Roxy attempted weakly.

"I know, I know," Wolfe was all smiles and encouragement now, but Roxy wasn't fooled for a minute. Any second he might reach over and tear out her throat for looking at him in a funny way. "Do not worry, Roxy. Come, show me you truly mean what you say." He held out a hand to her.

Roxy looked at it in confusion, "What?"

"Give me your hand. I wish to share of your blood."

Roxy shook her head reflexively, despite herself. Right now she feared that more than Wolfe's temper. She wouldn't be anyone's slave. She wouldn't be another Sarah. Wolfe stared at her in disbelief, his eyes widening in growing wrath.

"Give me your wrist," he snarled, staring into her eyes hatefully.

Roxy felt an overwhelming compulsion to hold out her wrist to him, but a flittering presence in her mind soothed the urge like a gentle breeze cooling her skin on a hot day. She shook her head. "No," she said flatly.

She watched as Wolfe did a double-take, barely comprehending what had happened. Nothing and nobody opposed him, and with two bites on her, she ought to have been almost under his control and unable to resist his hypnotic command. He shuddered, his eyes flaring red, his fangs lengthening. James scrambled to his feet, desperate to get away from the coming outburst, but became caught up by the table and fell back onto the seat with a panicked cry. Roxy squeezed her eyes shut, unable to escape, and unwilling to spend her final seconds looking at Wolfe. She tensed, her body coiled painfully tight as she waited for the blow, but after several seconds it still hadn't come, so she opened her eyes. Wolfe was sitting quietly, turned slightly toward the rest of the club and watching the dancers. James had also relaxed and had turned his back to her. They were quietly talking, Wolfe chuckling at James' suggestion that he tax the vampires for every human they fed from. They were both ignoring her completely. She sat up slowly, eyeing Wolfe in confusion. His moods were erratic, but she never expected anything like this. She glanced across at Natalie and started when she saw her shining black eyes fixed intently on her. Gone was the bored, apathetic demeanour, and a cunning, calculating intelligence radiated from her. Roxy glanced back to Wolfe and James in sudden comprehension.

"Do not worry yourself with them," Na'amah whispered, though her words carried easily to Roxy. "They have forgotten that we are even here."

Roxy stared at Na'amah, then back to Wolfe. "How can that be? We're sitting right here."

"The weak-minded are easily swayed." Na'amah replied, a slow smile forming at the corners of her full lips. "Pay them no mind." She paused and regarded Roxy through her long lashes silently. Roxy shifted in her seat. Every sense screamed at her to leave, but she knew that was as pointless as wishing she wasn't there. She would only be able to go if Na'amah permitted it.

"What do you want?" asked Roxy as the silence between them grew too painful to continue. Na'amah tilted her head to one side and rested her chin on laced fingers, her elbows on the table.

"You puzzle me, Roxy. I am not accustomed to being puzzled. Nothing happens here that I am not aware of. I know every thought and every desire of those around me, I dream of things yet to occur and I know what someone's actions will be even before they know themselves. Yet I did not dream of you. Why not?"

Roxy remained absolutely still as she returned her gaze, to terrified even to wonder if she would survive this night. Na'amah fell silent again at what Roxy assumed was a rhetorical question, but she felt the need to answer anyway. "I don't know. Maybe you're under some sort of stress?" Roxy marvelled that she could be flippant at a time like this. The immediate possibility of death seemed perversely to have removed her fear of it, as if her mind rejected the notion rather than let it cripple her.

Na'amah seemed to find it amusing, however, and waggled her head briefly as if considering the statement. "Maybe so. Tell me, Roxy, who helped you to resist Wolfe's will?"

Roxy considered brazening it through, but quickly decided that honesty was the only thing that might save her now. She didn't really owe Juan any loyalty anyway. "He called himself Juan." She hesitated, and then went for broke." He told me who you were, Na'amah."

Na'amah smiled, "Did he now? I'm flattered. Did he also warn you that I have a heart as black as sin and as cold as ice?"

"Something like that."

"Well I can tell you one or two dozen atrocities that he has been responsible for in the last eight hundred years. Don't trust him Roxy. Everything he tells you is a lie."

Roxy smiled tiredly, "Funny. He said the same thing about you."

"He was right. Nothing you hear is completely true, you should know that. Juan is merely the mouthpiece of an older, more ancient power. Did he tell you about Mangala?"

Roxy nodded her head slowly. "He said he was an associate of his."

"Mangala is an old enemy of mine," said Na'amah, "He is known to most as The Dragon. We go back to what you'd now call Ancient Egypt. We used to be allies once, but those times are gone." She sounded wistful, but her eyes were as hard as ever. "Mangala was responsible for Catallus' death."

Roxy frowned and shook her head slowly "I don't think so. Juan seemed to think it was you."

"Why would I kill Catallus? I owned him. I broke his shackle and installed my own years ago." Na'amah narrowed her eyes, "So Mangala doesn't have the Tablets then?"

"No. Well...unless Juan was lying of course. He wanted me to find out if you had them. Do you?" Roxy asked pointedly.

Na'amah smiled broadly at Roxy's audacity. "No, Roxy. I do not. And I cannot scry them either, which presumably means that neither can Mangala...unless..." her eyes widened as a thought occurred to her. She sat upright and looked at Roxy. "I need to see Juan quickly."

"I don't know where he is," Roxy protested, "Honestly. If you could only read my mind you'd know." Roxy felt a pricking of renewed fear slide down her spine.

Na'amah waved her hand absently, "I did that already, I know you don't, but he will contact you again. When he does, tell him that I want to see him."

Roxy thrust aside the sudden revelation that her thoughts were not safe, and concentrated on a more immediate question, "What if he refuses? He seemed to want to avoid you."

"Well of course he would," Na'amah replied soothingly, "Tell him I have not forgotten Madrid, and that this will balance the scales."

Roxy gave her a sceptical look. "Just that?"

Na'amah nodded "Then send him here. I would be most grateful." She smiled sweetly, but the underlying menace was unmistakable.

Roxy sighed inwardly, "Okay."

"There is another way you might be useful to me." Na'amah continued, in a more business-like tone.

"Great," said Roxy dryly, "if that means less chance of you killing me."

Na'amah smiled again, "I don't kill superfluously. Especially someone as amusing as yourself."

Roxy sat back with a tight smile and waited for Na'amah to continue.

"There is a man I want you to see," she began, "called Darius. He may be able to find out where the Tablets are."

Roxy gave her a puzzled look, "How will he be able to find them if you can't?"

"I think I am being deliberately targeted by a scrying ward. Darius will not be."

"Darius is a vampire I take it?" asked Roxy.

Na'amah smiled, "Not exactly. They call themselves Eternals, but everyone else calls them witches."

"He's a witch...?" Roxy said flatly.

Na'amah gave her a playful nod.

"And he'll be happy to talk to me?"

Na'amah rolled her eyes sideways, "Not...entirely. The witches have certain...philosophical differences with us. However, you are young and still reasonably pure of heart, despite your recent mindrape of that poor boy, so I don't *think* he'll kill you. Not straight away, in any case. Not like he would if I tried to approach him."

Roxy rubbed her hands down her face slowly and looked back at Na'amah resignedly, not surprised that she knew about Simon. "Where will I find this Darius?"

"He has a little shop in Soho. It might take you a while to find because it has misdirection charms to hide it from vampires, but keep concentrating on finding it, and you will."

"Right. Anything else I can do for you? I could stick a broom up my arse and sweep the floor while I'm at it."

Na'amah looked at her in surprise, unused to being insulted. "Not at the moment, no."

Roxy studied Na'amah for a moment, suddenly struck by a question, "Do you know why Dave killed Sanjay?"

Na'amah regarded Roxy with raised eyebrows, "My, my, you are a curious one aren't you? Do you think that I had something to do with it?"

"It had occurred to me," admitted Roxy. "You must have known what he was going to do, and you didn't stop him.'

"You're giving me more credit than I deserve, Roxy," smiled Na'amah. "If I controlled everyone's actions that tightly it would soon become obvious and my little disguise might be uncovered. The fact is that Sanjay was attempting to manipulate Dave, and underestimated him. Sanjay, rightly believing himself intellectually superior, expected Dave to be unable to think of a way to stop him. However, Dave had a more primitive solution.'

"What a waste," muttered Roxy sadly.

"Don't worry, you seem to be doing quite well without him," said Na'amah.

Roxy turned her head to look at James and Wolfe who were still in deep discussion and wondered how to get past them. Na'amah chuckled and waved a dismissive hand at them. Immediately, they both stood up and walked over to Wolfe's office.

Na'amah turned back to Roxy. "Be a good girl and run along now. Try not to get yourself killed, and stay away from Wolfe if you can help it. You've really upset him."

Roxy slid out of the seat to leave, but hesitated and looked down at Na'amah.

"Have you been sending me telepathic dreams?"

Na'amah considered her quietly for a moment as if phrasing her response, then said "No, Roxy. Your visions are your own."

Roxy turned and walked swiftly away without looking back. She could feel dark eyes drilling into her as she went, which made her increase her pace. All she wanted was to get away as quickly as possible.

# Chapter 35

Outside, the wet ground gleamed orange under the reflected streetlamps. Roxy inhaled deeply, relishing the smell of the rain-washed concrete, and knowing that she had avoided death narrowly once more. She didn't think the air could taste much sweeter.

"Hello Roxy." Roxy spun around and saw a beautiful woman with shoulder-length dark hair, dyed red at the tips, standing a few paces away.

"Who are you?"

"I'm Cadence," smiled the woman. "Cadence Plantagenet, filia Reyne"

"What do you want?" asked Roxy cautiously.

"Just to help you."

"I find that hard to believe."

"Now, now," pouted Cadence, "we hardly know each other. But I do know that Reyne is protecting your little secret."

Roxy stiffened, "What about it?"

"Well," Cadence glanced round theatrically before continuing in a soft voice, "there is a problem. It seems that you have acquired a detective that refuses to do what he is told and drop the case."

Anderton, thought Roxy. "He's harmless. He doesn't know anything."

"That may be true, but while he was poking around after you, he caused the death of one of Harold's mules, the guard at Tottenham Court Road. The guard was forced to throw himself under a train to avoid questioning."

Roxy's mouth felt dry, "So is this detective going to be killed then?"

"Oh, it is worse than that I'm afraid." Cadence continued in a concerned voice that didn't fool Roxy at all, "Harold's child Bronwyn has had him captured, and it won't be long before they find out what he was doing." She looked at Roxy meaningfully.

"You mean they'll find out about me?"

Cadence nodded, "I'm afraid they will blame you for the death of the mule."

Roxy felt faint. "What can I do?"

"Well if you're quick, you might be able to get to him before Bronwyn does. I happen to know where they are keeping him. It's not far away."

Roxy's mind raced, trying to decide what options she had. Would Na'amah or Juan save her if Harold came for her? Would Reyne? She wondered if Reyne *was* helping her, in an arms-length kind of way. More likely he was protecting his own skin if they forced Roxy to talk. Which they would easily do.

"How do you know where he is?" asked Roxy suddenly.

Cadence flicked her eyes away uncomfortably, "I have my sources."

Roxy stared at her. "You told Bronwyn about Anderton, didn't you?"

Cadence turned back to her with a snarl, "I didn't know he was connected to you! Bronwyn asked me for the report on her mule's death and I gave it to her. That's what I'm supposed to do."

"You control the police department for Reyne." It was more of a statement than a question. Things were becoming clearer now. Cadence had fucked up. She had passed the details to Bronwyn, hoping to earn a favour, and then realised that Anderton was connected to Roxy.

"Reyne doesn't know, does he?" asked Roxy softly.

Cadence glared at her, "Do you want to save yourself or not? I can't really waltz in there and do it myself can I? I might be recognised. But fine, we are doing each other a favour so we'll end up even. Don't worry about owing me."

Roxy almost laughed. "Okay Cadence. No choice right? Tell me where he is and what I'm up against."

Cadence forced herself to calm down. "They're holding him in a lock-up near Hampstead Heath. It's just a couple of thugs – mortals at the moment, but Bronwyn is due there at midnight."

Roxy considered this for a moment, then grabbed Cadence by the arm and half-pulled her to where she had parked her bike.

"Hey, get off me!"

"I need you to direct me."

"Forget it," hissed Cadence, "I can't be seen there."

"You can jump off at the end of the street if you like, but unless you come there's no way I'll be able to find the place in time, and then it's both our arses."

Cadence opened her mouth to reply, but seemed to realise Roxy was right. "Okay, but you're on your own when we get there."

Roxy pulled up at the end of a short cul-de-sac. Cadence jumped off, smoothed her skirt down and pointed towards a row of garages.

"Over there. The one on the far left. That's where they're holding him," she said, already backing away. Roxy let her go, and swung her leg off the bike as she studied the street. It was dimly lit, and a high steel fence separated the garages from a railway line, beyond which rose a line of dark trees. The garages were covered with graffiti and the nearby houses looked abandoned. There was a battered white transit van parked opposite. Roxy didn't see any sign of movement as she walked softly towards the lockups, her sword unsheathed in her hand. She wasn't sure quite what she was going to do, but felt oddly calm. Committed.

As she drew near, she heard faint sounds coming from within. She slowed her pace and listened. She heard someone speaking in a hushed voice, too low to make out the words, and a grunted reply. She studied the access door and considered smashing through it, but a sudden uncertainty made her hesitate. She only had Cadence's word that someone was holding Anderton here, and she doubted that Cadence was at all trustworthy. She listened for a while longer, and decided that there were only two men inside. She couldn't hear anything that might be Anderton, but after a few moments of concentration, she thought she could smell traces of his scent around the door. He had been here earlier at least.

Roxy raised her hand and knocked on the door. The voices inside stopped immediately. Roxy heard the jangling of keys and the door was unlocked. It opened inwards and she was faced with a brutish bald man whose surprised expression was quickly replaced by one of suspicion. Roxy's doubts vanished as a powerful smell of blood assaulted her, mixed with Anderton's scent, still detectable under the heavy odour of machine oil and petroleum.

"Who the fuck are you?" demanded the man.

Roxy stepped over the wooden surround below the door, pushing him aside easily. She saw Anderton, slumped unconscious and naked in a chair under a strong arc-light. His hands and face were covered with blood, and his legs and feet were covered in weals, burns and dried blood.

She turned at a sound just in time to see that the man had picked up a shotgun and was pointing it at her, thrusting the muzzle close to her head before pulling the trigger. Roxy spun to the side as the shot went off, narrowly avoiding decapitation, and swung her sword into the man's chest. The blade cut nearly through to the other side, stopping just below his armpit. His chest cavity exploded, sending a gout of frothy blood in all directions, covering her face and body. Roxy yanked the sword back, blinking blood out of her eyes, and turned to where the second man was reeling towards a bench at the back of the room.

She reached him in seconds, while he was scrabbling on the floor for a large knife. Roxy let the sword slide from her hand onto the ground beside her, and reached down to pick him up. He was tall but skinny, and weighed nothing at all. The smell of blood had roused something inside her that she knew would not easily be sated unless she fed. One part of her mind protested against what she was going to do, but another reasoned that she had already killed one person, and she was going to have to kill the second anyway, so why not gain some benefit at the same time. She bit into the back of his neck roughly. His struggles continued weakly for a few moments, then he went limp as she sucked the blood from him. This was not a time for enjoying the taste. She gulped down the warm fluid, intent only on easing the craving that suddenly consumed her. She could hear the man's heartbeat getting faster and weaker as she fed, and knew he was near death. The last flutterings gave way to silence, then she sensed a familiar elusive pull somewhere deep inside him and broke off abruptly. Never drink after the heart stops, Sanjay had told her. Now she knew why. She didn't want this sadist inside her head. She sat back and wiped her lips, though it was a pointless gesture with all the blood soaking her face and hair.

She looked at Anderton. He was staring at her in horror, his lips moving wordlessly over a row of broken teeth. Roxy felt faint at the sight of him. Bruises dappled his face and chest, interspersed with burns from heated metal instruments, but Roxy's attention was drawn to the bloody stumps at the end of his hands. His severed fingers were scattered on the floor at his feet, which had been punctured through the soles by skewers. Roxy felt bile rise but bit it back and gritted her teeth. She briefly wondered whether to kill him. It might be a mercy. She knew she couldn't, even before she completed the thought. The heat of righteous anger was different from the frosty resolution needed to do that, and it wasn't in her. Not yet. She stood up, collected her sword and moved over to the detective. He kicked his legs feebly, trying to back away, but succeeded only in making the chair wobble. Roxy went behind him and used the sword to cut through the cord binding his waist to the chair. The moment the restraint was gone he slid off and collapsed to the floor. Roxy moved around and said in a soothing voice, "I'm not going to hurt you. I'm here to help. Come on, we need to go."

Anderton mumbled something, his eyes wide with panic as he looked up at her. Roxy knelt on something and looked down to see that it was a finger. She clamped her lips closed and took a moment to fight back the threatening vomit. After she recovered she glanced around and spotted what she was looking for – Anderton's shirt. She reached over and spread it out on the floor. Then, with trembling hands, she picked up each of the fingers and laid them on the shirt. She forced herself to count the stumps on Anderton's hands, making sure she had them all. They had cut off all four fingers from each hand, leaving only his thumbs. Roxy double-checked she had found them all before carefully wrapping them up. She knew they could do some amazing things with surgery, but you needed to have all the parts. She checked his toes were all still there. They were, but the tendons in his feet had been severed. He wouldn't be walking any time soon. She turned her attention back to Anderton, who had passed out.

Acutely aware of the time, Roxy thrust the package of fingers into her jacket pocket and retrieved her sword before stooping to pick him up. She carried him outside, not bothering to look for his clothes, and wondered how she was going to get him help. She couldn't take him on the back of her bike. Her gaze fell on the van. It probably belonged to the abductors. She hurried over to it and tried the rear doors. They were unlocked. She set Anderton inside, then after a quick check to make sure they weren't in the ignition, went back into the garage to look for the keys. She found them in the pocket of the bald man, and took a second to scan the room for anything she had left behind. She saw Anderton's wallet on a bench, and grabbed it.

She slid behind the wheel of the van and started the engine, then tried to remember what to do next. She had only driven a car a few times, usually stolen ones, which she had not cared about wrecking. After a few false starts, she got the hang of the clutch, and turned the van around. At the end of the street she pulled up and stared at her bike. *Shit.* After a few indecisive seconds, she jumped out and grabbed it, picked it up with a grunt and carried it to the back of the van. She was pretty sure it would fit inside, but it would have to lie on its side which probably wouldn't do the faring much good. She'd have to move Anderton to the front seat too, otherwise the bike might move around and crush him. It took her three or four nerve-jangling minutes to rearrange everything, but eventually she could drive off again. Bronwyn hadn't arrived. Roxy drove carefully away, her heart pounding, concentrating on putting as much distance between herself and the garage as she could.

# Chapter 36

Roxy drove past a hospital less than a minute later, but ignored it, fearing she was too close to the lock-up. She headed south, occasionally glancing across at the unconscious detective. He was pale, his heartbeat weak, his breathing shallow. She regretted her decision a few minutes later as she drove past Euston Street station and into Bloomsbury. There were quite a few hospitals in the area, she knew, but she wasn't used to driving and the one-way system seemed intent on thwarting her. Anderton moaned next to her, but didn't wake up. He wouldn't last much longer.

Roxy found herself driving west along Oxford Street and pulled over to stop at the side of the road to get her bearings. To the south was Soho, still bustling in the hour before midnight, before the raunchier clubs would open and the people on the streets became less savoury. She stared out of the window, wondering if she was even doing the right thing. If she dropped him at a hospital, then surely because of the nature of his injuries the police would be called, and then his name would come up on whatever database they used and before the sun rose, the vampires would find out. Would Cadence protect him? Unlikely. She would have him killed to protect herself, and even if she didn't, Bronwyn would find him. Roxy saw that his eyes were fluttering open.

"Hang in there mate," she said, looking past him towards Soho. Na'amah had wanted to her find someone in Soho. The witch. A crazy thought struck her. Soho wasn't particularly big, but it was made up of lots of small streets. It could take ages to find the store Na'amah had told her about. She shrugged. No choice. She'd find it. She put the van into gear and set off. She knew Soho well; she'd worked it long enough. There were narrow streets and pedestrian zones to contend with, but she drove slowly and scanned the shops carefully, paying special attention to the darker, unobtrusive ones.

After forty minutes and three complete circuits she started to get frustrated, and stopped the van. Anderton was unconscious again. She stepped out onto the pavement and looked around. She was sure she was close. She closed her eyes, trying to put the dying detective out of her mind. You can do anything you want, Vicky had said. Fine, she thought, I am going to find the Witch. She stood silently for a few moments, then opened her eyes. She walked towards a nondescript alcove nestled between a drainpipe and a billboard plastered with fly-posts for local bands and strip-clubs. The alcove extended back some fifteen feet and ended at a mouldering wooden door, held together with chipped green paint. Some feeling deep inside told her this was the place. She hurried to get Anderton and carried him back, half-expecting it to have vanished, but it was still there. She walked down the darkened passage with slight trepidation and as she raised her hand to knock on the door, it opened.

"Come in," a rich male voice beckoned. It was warm and welcoming, but held a commanding edge that Roxy knew wouldn't take refusal kindly. She stepped across the threshold into a dazzling white light. She suddenly felt very vulnerable and struggled to force her eyes open, blinking rapidly to get them accustomed to the light. She heard the door close softly behind her, but could tell that no one was near her.

"What have we here?" the voice asked jovially, "Homo Nosferatis Rex. A young one I'd wager."

"I'm Roxy," she said, squinting into a modern-looking room decked out with computers, monitors and electronic devices, interspersed with leafy-green ferns and coloured crystals embedded into the walls.

"Hello Roxy. What can I do for you?"

She could make out his shape now and focused on it. "Are you Darius?"

"Ah, so you didn't just stumble in here by accident then? Still, I'm surprised you found me. Not many can."

"I need help. I'm not sure if you can, but I don't know where else to go. If I take him to a hospital they'll kill him. Is there anything you can do for him, please?" She knelt down and set Anderton on the varnished wooden floor. Her vision seemed to clear, or maybe the light became less intense, but she found she could open her eyes fully. She looked up at Darius and was surprised to see a fairly young-looking man, perhaps in his thirties, dressed in jeans and a faded AC/DC T-shirt, looking coolly back at her. He was clean-shaven and had wavy blonde hair pulled back in a pony-tail.

"What happened?" he asked.

Roxy pulled out the shirt from her pocket and unwrapped it, showing him the fingers. "He got a little too close to some of my...peers, or whatever you call them. They were trying to find out about me."

"Is he one of your slaves?" Darius asked casually.

Roxy shook her head, "No, he's just an annoying policeman who's been following me around and getting himself into trouble."

"Why are you helping him then? Surely you would be better off with him dead?"

Roxy looked at Darius suspiciously, "I just want to. I feel bad that this has happened to him because of me. Can you help him?"

Darius bent down and studied the detective for a while, picking up his hands and looking at the bloodied stumps thoughtfully. Finally he stood up, tucked his thumbs into his pockets and shook his head.

"No, I can't help him."

Roxy dropped her head in despair. She had convinced herself that everything would turn out all right. She took a steadying breath and ran through her options again. She'd have to take him to a hospital. If she stayed with him until near dawn, then she might be able to protect him. But no longer than that. She looked up fiercely at Darius. "Will you look out for him during the day then?"

Darius looked back, re-evaluating her. "You really want to save him, don't you?"

Roxy nodded. "I'll owe you."

Darius smiled broadly, "That must have been hard to say. Do you really understand what that means?"

Roxy shrugged, "I guess not, but I'll stand by it anyway."

Darius pulled at his lip and came to a decision. "I said I can't help him, but you can."

"What do you mean?"

"The blood of a vampire is pretty funky stuff," he explained. "It has all sorts of uses, especially to mages like myself, and one of them is that is can heal almost any wound. You've probably seen vampires heal themselves, but it works for others too."

Roxy felt her heart leap at his words. "How do I do it?" she asked excitedly.

Darius squatted down beside her, "You need to cut yourself and pour the blood over the wounds. Unfortunately they've already started to clot over, so we'll have to scrape the scabs off and get the blood flowing again. It's going to hurt him like a bitch, but I'll be able to help there."

Roxy looked around for a knife, but didn't see anything sharp, so she extended her fangs and pulled her jacket off, exposing her bare arms. "Tell me when," she said, lisping slightly around her teeth.

Darius took in her sharp teeth with a glance, picked up one of Anderton's hands and produced a black-bladed knife from somewhere. "Get his index finger. No, the other one. Right, when I say, let a few drops of your blood fall on both sides of the wound, then press them together. Try to line them up as best as you can."

Roxy bit into her wrist and allowed the blood to well out and run down her arm. Darius took the knife and poked the point into the severed end of the finger, agitating a small trickle of blood, and then handed it to Roxy, who dipped it in the pool of blood on her wrist. Then he did the same to the stump on Anderton's hand, making him moan in pain.

"Quickly," Darius said, and Roxy held her wrist over the newly opened wound, coating it with her blood. She fumbled with the finger, dropping it on the floor, but quickly recovered it and held it against the hand. Anderton screamed and started to buck and writhe.

"Hold him down," Darius commanded, and Roxy threw her body across his, preventing him from moving and holding his wrist tightly in one hand and the finger in the other. She stared in fascination as the flesh started to knit back together and twist to correct a slight misalignment of the finger. Within seconds, it had curled up into the beginnings of a fist, wrapped in the remaining thumb and was turning from a pasty ashen colour to a flushed red. Anderton's screams turned into a moan, and he went limp again. Roxy looked across at Darius and realised that she was trembling with exertion. Darius gave her an encouraging smile.

"One down, seven to go."

When they had finished, the floor was covered in Roxy's blood. She was exhausted and felt much weaker than she thought she ought to. Darius stood and started to clean the knife with a damp cloth. Roxy noticed he didn't seem to have any blood on his clothes, and in fact looked as fresh and alert as ever. In contrast she looked like an extra from a Tarantino film. Anderton was sleeping. His face didn't appear to be as swollen as before, but his cracked and broken teeth hadn't healed. The bruises on his body were less aggressive, and his feet were merely red and swollen, rather than bleeding and torn.

"Your blood is in his system now, so his other injuries will heal faster," remarked Darius, observing her study.

Roxy sat back and leaned against the leg of a desk. "Thank you," she said. Her head felt light, as if she might faint. She looked at her wrist and as if by command, it healed over immediately with barely a tingle.

"You'll probably need to feed shortly, so I'd appreciate it if you would leave now," said Darius conversationally.

"Why do I feel so tired?" asked Roxy.

"It was your energies that healed him, even though the blood had left your body," replied Darius quickly. Roxy looked up at him, feeling that he wasn't telling her everything, but was too tired to argue.

"You don't look much like a witch," she muttered.

"What were you expecting, a pointy hat and broomstick?" he chuckled.

"Yeah, something like that," Roxy answered, climbing unsteadily to her feet. She looked at the crisp furnishings around her, totally at odds with the impression given by the shabby exterior. "Nice place."

"I think so too," he said immodestly. "Now you were about to leave?"

Roxy felt a sharp stab of pain in her stomach and realised she was hungry. "Okay, but I want to come back afterwards, if that's okay?"

Darius shrugged in a non-committal way. "If you must. Come alone though."

Roxy nodded and reached for her jacket. "Sorry about the mess," she gestured to the blood-stained floor. Then she walked out.

# Chapter 37

An hour later, after dumping the van on the edge of London and feeding from a couple of sleeping beggars, Roxy returned on her bike. The streets were emptier now, populated mainly by drunks and prostitutes. She found the alcove easily, and made her way to the tattered green door. It didn't open on its own this time, so she knocked on it.

"It's open," called Darius from inside.

Roxy turned the handle and pushed the door. It wasn't as bright inside as before. The room was totally bare. There were no bloodstains on the floor.

"Darius?" she called.

"In here."

Roxy walked through a doorway into a comfortably furnished lounge area. Darius was sitting in a large leather armchair, swirling a whisky idly in one hand. On a matching couch sat Anderton, perched on the edge of the seat, clutching a rather larger whisky in both hands. He was wearing a thick bathrobe and looked up at her warily as she entered.

Roxy hovered in the doorway, not sure what to do, until Darius indicated with a motion of his head for her to sit on the couch with Anderton. She crossed the thick carpet and sat down. Anderton immediately shuffled to the far end, away from her.

"Are you okay?" Roxy asked him.

Anderton gave a barely perceptible shrug, "I guess."

They sat in an uncomfortable silence for a while, then Anderton cleared his throat, took a large swig of whisky, and said, "Thanks, for...you know?"

"No problem," replied Roxy softly.

"I told him what you are, darkling," said Darius.

Roxy looked at him, "Why?"

Darius toyed with his glass, "It seemed the thing to do. I think he's taking it very well."

Roxy scowled at Darius and turned her attention to Anderton, "How do you feel about that?"

Anderton gave a loud bark of laughter, "Oh, fine! Of course! I'm just waiting for the alarm to wake me up." Then he winced and tenderly touched his jaw with his fingertips.

Roxy could see he was barely holding himself together. He started to rock back and forth slowly, his trembling hands making the amber liquid slosh about in the crystal glass. "Well if it's any consolation, you'll think this was all your imagination in a few days. I suggest you try to forget about it as soon as you can."

"It's not quite as simple as that," remarked Darius. "You see, your blood is in his veins, so there's a link between you now. All sorts of interesting things may happen."

"Like what?" asked Roxy.

"You may share each other's dreams, feel each other's pain, that sort of thing, but it also means he won't be affected by the Denial and forget about you."

Roxy and Anderton exchanged a glance, and then quickly looked away. Roxy leaned back and crossed her legs. She fingered the bloodstains on her jeans and t-shirt and knew she had ruined Scarlet's clothes too. She looked across at Darius, who was regarding her shrewdly over the rim of his glass.

"I have something else to ask you," she said, wondering how to say it.

"I thought you might. Go on."

Roxy stared at the floor for a minute, her mind oddly blank as she tried to form the words. Darius waited patiently for her. "Do you know a vampire called Na'amah?" She asked finally.

Darius froze momentarily, his eyes narrowed, then he resumed the gentle swirling of his drink. "We've met, once or twice," he admitted.

"Well she's here, in London, and she wants your help."

Darius"face broke into a knowing smile. "Ah, I wondered how you found me. And what can I do for the Mistress of Deception?"

"She wants you to find something. Something she says is hidden from her." Roxy relaxed into the soft couch, a sense of safety enveloping her for the first time in months. It was perhaps Darius' easy manner, but she felt no threat from him. Anderton was curled in the corner of the couch seemingly ignoring them.

She felt a sudden need to comfort him but made no move to do so, knowing it would upset him.

"What something?" Darius asked in a neutral tone.

"Some ancient artefacts, with writings on them by someone called Menes."

"Ah, the Menes Tablets," crooned Darius. "Did Catallus translate them at last?"

"Catallus is dead," said Roxy. Darius raised his eyebrows.

"That," he said quietly, "explains a lot."

Roxy waited for him to continue. When he remained silent, she prompted, "What do you mean?"

Darius seemed suddenly a lot older than her first impression had suggested. A hardness in his violet eyes hinted at experiences and knowledge that was best kept hidden and unspoken.

Roxy felt she had to say more, "No one seems to know how he could have been beaten. He was too strong. So who or...or what, killed him?"

Darius regarded her with a little more respect. "That is a good question." He paused, looking up at the ceiling and drumming his fingers on the arm of his chair. Eventually he lowered his gaze to her. "If you find the answer, would you let me know?"

"So much for the all-knowing witches," said Roxy sarcastically.

"Do you want to know where the Menes Tablets are?"

Roxy sat up straighter, "You can tell me?"

Darius shrugged, "Not yet, but I can find them. It might answer some of your other questions too."

"How long will it take?"

Darius cocked his head to the side, "Come back tomorrow."

"Is this going to cost me anything?"

"No," said Darius slowly, "I think our interests lie together for the moment."

Roxy looked at Anderton, who was now sleeping against the arm of the couch, "What about him?"

"I'm not his keeper," replied Darius. "He can go when he pleases. I've made sure he won't go into shock and I'll sort out a dentist for him, but it may take him a while to get over what he's been through."

"I meant can you protect him? They'll still be looking for him, even more so now."

"I'm sorry, there is only so much I can do. I suggest that he go away until things settle down, but with vampires that could take years. They have long memories and don't tend to forgive."

Roxy bit back her frustration. He was a dead man. Another corpse to add to her pile? She stood up and looked down at Darius. "I'll be back tomorrow."

"I'll be expecting you," he said with a slight smile.

Roxy hesitated once more, threw a last glance at Anderton, then left.

# Chapter 38

Roxy awoke, hungry and wet. She had slept in the cellar of a disused pub, not wanting to return to Scarlet's in her state. She groaned and tried to work out where the water was coming from. It puddled around her and smelled fetid. A steady drip sounded behind her and she guessed it was rainwater filtering down from the street. She rubbed her stiff limbs and vowed not to sleep on bare concrete again. The cellar was completely dark and she gingerly felt her way around the room until she found the stairs and made her way up to the bar.

She caught her smeared reflection in a broken mirror and paused to rub the grime away to stare at herself. She looked a mess – soaked through and wearing the bloodstained clothes from the previous day. Her face was smudged and stained with dirt and dried blood. She ran her fingers through her matted hair and tried unsuccessfully to pull it into some sort of shape. She needed a shower and a ton of make-up. Her thoughts drifted back to the hard days when she was homeless and used to wash in public toilets, trying to look presentable enough to attract someone willing to pay her to sleep with them.

"God don't let me go back to that", she groaned, resting her head on the mirror and closing her eyes. Unbidden, the bloody memory of the previous day came back to her. She had killed again. Twice. They'd deserved it, perhaps, but the look in their eyes when they'd realised death was coming chilled her. How many more would there be? Should she bother to keep count? She opened her eyes to banish the memory and stared at her reflection.

"Come on Mandy, get a grip," she muttered, wishing she had some clean water to splash over her face. She took a moment to compose herself, then reached up to a dirty part of the mirror and drew four parallel lines with her finger.

The street was strewn with deep puddles, but it wasn't raining. Heavy clouds soaked up the light from the city, darkening the night. Roxy started up her bike. The low-fuel light came on as she pulled away. She rode vaguely in the direction of Soho, thinking to visit Darius, but carried on past it, not feeling ready to face him yet. She needed someone to talk to, someone to distract her from the guilt she was feeling; from killing, to causing Anderton's torture, to dragging Claudia into her fucked up life – unlife – whatever.

A familiar silhouette appeared on the side of the road, and Roxy grinned and pulled over. Vicky was standing a few paces away, swaying slightly with a glazed look in her eyes. Roxy approached her hesitantly. She saw that there was an air of rage in her stance, nearly animal and barely controlled. It was not directed at her, but she kept her distance nonetheless as she called out "Vicky?" Roxy repeated her name a few more times, until Vicky blinked and struggled to focus on her.

"Roxy?" she said finally.

"What's happened?"

Vicky shook her head slowly, unable to speak. Then her eyes rolled back into her head and she collapsed. Roxy rushed forward and knelt beside her. Vicky opened her eyes and looked up at her.

"The vines ... the black vines ... everyone gone. Sucked out from the inside." Then she passed out.

Roxy stared at her in confusion. For some reason she didn't expect vampires to faint. She noticed that Vicky was colourless and needed blood. So do I, she told herself, but raised her wrist to her mouth. She hesitated before presenting the bloody wound to Vicky's lips, remembering about the shackle. Would this mean Vicky would gain control over her? Was that wise, when she might recover on her own anyway? Roxy shrugged the thoughts aside and held her wrist over Vicky's mouth, allowing some blood to drip into it. Vicky stirred almost immediately and moved her head up to try to clamp her teeth around Roxy's arm. Roxy was ready for that and pulled away, keeping just out of reach of Vicky's fangs. She didn't think she would do herself any favours to risk the Little Death. Vicky opened her eyes, her tongue extended to catch the drips. She licked her lips and turned her head away to control her urge to feast.

Roxy withdrew her arm and healed the wound absently as she raised Vicky to a sitting position.

"Come on girl," she whispered, helping her to stand.

Vicky leaned on Roxy, clutching her stomach tightly. "I need to eat," she gasped.

"I know." It was still early enough for there to be several people about and she looked for someone for Vicky. She spotted a couple of young men looking around uncertainly, trying to get their bearings.

"Excuse me," she called, "can you help us?'

They looked at each other and Roxy felt that they were about to walk off, so she flashed them her most dazzling smile, which made them reconsider.

"What is it?" asked one, as they walked over.

"My friend has had a little too much to drink. I just need help getting her to a taxi–"

Vicky leapt at the closest, sinking her teeth into his exposed wrist. He stumbled back and sank to his knees. Roxy grabbed the other and wrapped her hand over his mouth to keep him quiet while Vicky fed. He struggled, but she held him easily. She had intended to save him for Vicky, but the smell of blood reached her and her stomach contracted painfully. His warm body wriggled in her arms and his manly scent teased her. Brushing her lips against the back of his neck sent a tingle rushing from her head to her crotch. She tenderly bit into the side of his neck, freeing his rich, healthy blood and allowed the stream to flow over her tongue. Her thighs squeezed together as a sexual lust overcame her and she clamped her mouth over the wound to drink deeply. Remembered to count her mouthfuls, she reluctantly withdrew when she reached ten, giving the wound a final farewell lick. Her victim had stopped struggling the moment she started to drink and now collapsed. She lowered him to the ground and breathed in his mouth to wipe his memories. Vicky was still drinking and Roxy moved over and eased her away. Vicky resisted at first, but her experience kicked in and she forced herself to pull off. The colour had come back to her face and her skin was warm to the touch. Roxy breathed into his mouth too and checked to make sure no-one was watching.

"Thanks," whispered Vicky. She looked weak. Her troubled expression mixed with despair. She pulled herself to her feet and looked down at the bodies. "We should get out of here."

"Okay. We can take my bike." Roxy started to walk back to where she'd parked, but Vicky grabbed her arm in panic.

"Don't go back there!" she gasped.

Roxy allowed herself to be dragged away. "What happened?"

Vicky was silent, leading Roxy through darkened streets far away from where they started. Finally, she looked up at Roxy and said "The city has gone insane. I know I said there would be a fight for the throne, but it's much more bloody than I expected. Whole houses have been wiped out, or more bizarrely, vanished without trace. Maybe they're in hiding, but I don't think so."

"So vampires don't normally do this kind of thing?" said Roxy.

"You mean the violence? Well yes and no. I've never heard about anything on this scale before, but it's one of the ironies about being a vampire that although you are immortal, you'll probably die earlier than you would if you'd never been taken. Your chances of dying by violence are pretty much one hundred percent. You've either got to deliberately commit suicide or else you're murdered. Very few of us make it past fifty. That's the mad thing about this war. Normally when houses fight, it is human proxies that die, followed by the youngest members, like us. The elders escape unscathed. Not now. I heard that Mallory and Gilmer have been killed, and several members of the patrician houses are missing."

Roxy waited until Vicky had stopped rambling, and asked softly "What happened to you?"

Vicky shuddered. "I don't know," she replied quietly, "I saw only a glimpse of something growing out of thin air, like a misshapen tentacle that pulsated and bubbled, never holding a fixed shape. It made my head ache to look at it. I remember feeling cold and I couldn't move. Then it expanded into a ball around Lucy, like a massive hand snatching her away, and they were both gone. Thorkel shouted something and the next thing I remember, I was on the street and you were there."

"Do you think Thorkel is okay?"

Vicky closed her eyes and steadied herself, concentrating on something within her. "I don't think he's dead," she said.

"What are you going to do?"

Vicky set her jaw and looked up at Roxy, "I'm going to look for the rest of my House. What about you? I hear Wolfe has managed to gather quite a following."

"Wolfe and I don't really see eye to eye at the moment," said Roxy. "I've got someone I have to talk to anyway. I'd better get going."

Vicky reached up and stroked Roxy's cheek. "Well I owe you one, so whatever side you end up on, you don't have to worry about me." Vicky smiled grimly, full of new resolve, and hurried away.

# Chapter 39

It was nearly midnight when Roxy finally made it back to Soho and Darius. She had walked most of the way, making a diversion to break into a store to steal some more clothes. She'd opted for a gypsy-style skirt and woollen shrug over a V-neck t-shirt. The skirt wasn't the most practical thing she could have chosen, but she felt a need to express her feminine side for a while. She prudently stuffed a few spare t-shirts and a couple of pairs of jeans into a carrier bag. The only shoes they sold were strappy designer heels, but they were too small for her size nine feet, so she kept her boots but changed her socks. She washed her face and hands in the restroom and left feeling a lot fresher and happier.

She smelled Anderton before she saw him. He was at the mouth of the alley leading to Darius' place. She studied him quietly before she let him see her. He was pacing nervously up and down, rubbing his fingers as if to reassure himself that they were still there. She edged up to him slowly.

"What are you doing here?" she asked.

Anderton started, and spun to face her. He eyed her warily, as if trying to gauge her mood. "I couldn't sleep."

"You need to run away. It's not safe for you here."

Anderton shrugged, feigning an indifference that fooled neither of them, "What's the point? Do you think they'd never find me? I want to find out who was responsible."

"I can't tell you that," said Roxy tiredly, "I have things to do. Please go home."

"I can't do that either, and you know it." Anderton pressed his lips together to remain calm. "For whatever reason, I'm involved now, whether I believe that stuff Darius was telling me about vampires and witches or not."

Roxy winced at the volume of his voice.

"Let me help you," Anderton stepped forward earnestly. He held out his hands, "You helped me. Please, Amanda. No-one is so strong that they don't need help occasionally."

She looked at his desperate face. She could smell his fear — fear of her as well as fear of his abductors — but she could also see the resolution in his eyes. He would not back down if she said no. He would simply follow her and get in her way until he got himself killed. "Fine," she sighed, "you can help, but call me Roxy, okay? I don't need everyone finding out all about me."

"No problem. Thanks Roxy."

Anderton hovered behind her as she knocked on the door. It was opened by a young waif-like girl who was clearly expecting them. She beckoned them inside and led the way to the sitting room where

Darius was sitting cross-legged on the floor, surrounded by half a dozen men and women. Roxy felt a warning shiver pass through her, but sensed that the danger was not immediate; more a threat of power which could be unleashed if she pushed too hard. She gave the people a cursory glance and saw that they were a diverse group. Young and old in a variety of fashions. There was even a collared priest. She turned her attention to Darius and sat down boldly on the floor opposite him. Anderton hung back in the doorway uncertainly, studying everyone carefully.

"You came back then?" said Darius lightly. He extinguished a candle between his legs with a soft blow. He looked at Anderton, "I didn't think you'd do the smart thing. Come in and take a seat. We won't bite."

"I'm okay standing, thanks," replied Anderton.

Roxy tilted her head to the silent watchers standing near the walls, "Friends of yours?"

"We are Eternals, yes," conceded Darius.

"They don't look like witches either," said Roxy tartly.

A couple of the figures behind Darius bristled and clenched their fists. Darius raised a placating hand without looking round.

"Am I interrupting?"

Darius considered the question before answering "There's an important matter we are discussing, but we believe that it concerns your kind."

"What do you mean?"

"What do you know of the Dark?"

Something in his tone sent a shiver down Roxy's spine. She shook her head slowly without taking her eyes off him. "I guess you're not talking about the absence of light?"

"Did you ever wonder where vampires came from?" he asked.

"Give me a chance, I've only been at this a couple of weeks."

He gave her a brief smile. "The Dark has many names – X'ecunda, Formori, the Great Old Ones – but the one you will be most familiar with, is Demon."

Roxy gave him a sceptical look, "You mean like fire and brimstone and pitchfork demons?"

"That is merely a desperate interpretation by medieval scholars, but they were attempting to describe the same entity, yes."

Roxy stole a look at Anderton who was still lurking by the doorway. "What has this got to do with me?"

"The Dark is the ancient evil, spawned when time began. It feeds on hatred, anger and fear. As with all things, it had its opposite, the Light, which opposed it and kept the balance. We believe that balance was maintained for aeons, until humanity appeared. Their consciousness awakened both the Light and the Dark, and they become self-aware. With this awareness, the Dark became greedy and sought to destroy the Light and for millennia the Light and the Dark fought, but with each as strong as the other, a stalemate persisted. Then the Dark realised it could use humanity as a tool and tip the balance."

One of the men behind Darius took half a step forward, "Why are you telling it all this?" he snarled.

"Is there a reason not to?" asked Darius calmly, keeping his gaze fixed on Roxy.

"It will use it against us somehow. It's in their nature."

"I have a name you know?" said Roxy testily, glaring at the man behind Darius. He glared back, grinding his teeth.

Darius waited a moment in silence, then continued as if there had been no interruption. "The Dark gained strength from the fear it engendered when it broke into Earth's vector space, but the Light also gained strength from our hope and laughter, so the Dark never truly gained the upper hand. Then, it did something unexpected. It sent a splinter of its essence into a handful of early humans, warping their souls and infusing them with some of its power. These abominations could stay permanently in the material plane, and cause continual suffering, increasing the strength of the Dark."

"Let me guess," said Roxy when he paused for breath, "they were the first vampires right?"

"Correct," he said, ignoring the sarcasm in her tone, "and they learnt a clever and devastating trick. They found they could further split their essence and create more vampires, initially weaker, but quickly gaining in power, and all adding to the despair in the world at a geometrical rate. Every cry of pain, every frightened child, every angry young man or suicidal maid caused by the unthinking actions of the vampires added directly to the strength of the Dark through mystic channels into the higher dimensions where it dwelt."

Roxy felt a sudden bitterness inside. "Why are you telling me this? It's a nice story, and I'm sure it helps you sleep better at night, but what has this got to do with me?"

"You are a vampire. You are part of the dark design of the X'ecunda. Your very existence threatens humanity and the whole of creation. Everything you do is tarnished by negative energies. Nowhere you go will escape your destructive, entropic touch."

Roxy shook her head, "No, I can do good things too. I've helped people, I saved Anderton, I can make my daughter smile. And I know vampires who have helped me too. You're wrong about us."

Darius made a dismissive gesture, "You may struggle at first, and resist the descent into evil, but ultimately you are doomed. Anger and hatred will dominate everything you do. Look at the elders. Look at Na'amah. She is the psychic equivalent of a black hole, draining the life and spirit out of everything around her as surely as if she sucked on their necks." He paused to fix her with a steely gaze. Roxy felt uncomfortably like he was seeing into her deepest thoughts. "I can see that you have already killed, and worse. You have disrupted someone's

Karmic journey, cut their soul from the cycle of reincarnation and rebirth, just as your creator did to you."

"What do you mean?" Roxy felt uncomfortable, and suppressed a notion in her mind that sounded like Simon screaming in anguish.

"You are immortal. Did you think that there wouldn't be a price? You are now cut out of the Great Cycle. When you die, your soul will not pass on and be reborn. It is already being devoured. When you are destroyed, all the hope and energy you have taken from the world will pass to the X'ecunda, and you will fall to oblivion, never reaching your final peace.'

Roxy felt an overwhelming sense of loss at his words. She tried to tell herself they were untrue – just speculation and propaganda, but deep down, she knew he spoke the truth. "So I'm the bad guy?" she whispered.

Darius looked at her, not unsympathetically. "I'm sorry. You might resist for a while, possibly even centuries, if you live that long, but the Dark will take you in the end."

Roxy stared at the ground in front of her, unable to respond.

"So where do you fit in?" interrupted Anderton, "You seem to have just caused quite a bit of despair yourself you know?"

"Touché," smiled Darius, "however, I am one of the Eternals. Just as the Dark created the vampires through shards of itself, so the Light created soldiers too, but in a different way. It created hundreds of seeds which combined with human souls in much the same way as the Dark, but these seeds did not consume the souls, and did not grant immortality as such. Instead they encouraged the growth of the soul towards enlightenment, and aided its progress through the Great Cycle. The seeds could not create new seeds, but they persisted from one life to the next and so the humans they inhabited became magi."

"Sounds like some sort of Buddhist Sect," said Anderton.

"Close," admitted Darius. "Most of the world religions were influenced by our guidance. However because our souls are enlightened, I can remember many of my former lives, and with concentration I can access the skills and memories of my spiritual ancestors. Eternals are at one with the universe, and can feel its patterns and ripples as if it were a physical thing. With a thought we can locate the hidden, or learn the truth behind a lie. The strongest of us can manipulate the fabric of existence and perform what most people would call magic. Nothing is beyond our power, and when combined, the will of many is inconceivable."

"Well, I dunno," said Roxy, feeling a perverse need to pierce his ego, "I'm not convinced. After all, you couldn't fix this guy's fingers back on. Or stop him feeling pain."

"I helped more than you realise, but perhaps now you see my point – if it were not for you, he would not have suffered."

"Hey, you can't blame me for that?" cried Roxy indignantly.

"Your actions triggered a series of events which led to his pain. This is the insidious way the Dark works. Your kind do not even realise the casual negative energies they spread."

Roxy slumped back. Darius looked at her calmly, seemingly unconcerned at the effect his words had on her. Roxy wondered briefly if it would be easy for her to kill him, then quickly admonished herself for the thought. Maybe that was the Dark talking, leading her towards negative thoughts and actions? They sat quietly for several minutes. Finally, Roxy stirred and asked "You still haven't told me why all your friends are here."

"I mentioned that when a vampire dies, their essence flows back to the Dark. Well the older a vampire is, the greater their power, and the stronger the Dark grows upon their death. Several nights ago, presumably the night Catallus died, there was a violent surge in the strength of the Dark in London, which was felt all around the world. It has attracted several interested parties, but more importantly and dangerously, the barrier between our world and the other has weakened, and the Dark is starting to manifest here."

"Manifest? You mean it's creeping around outside somewhere?" Roxy asked, remembering the strange encounter that Vicky described.

"Yes, and it is hungry. The first thing it will do is feed itself, by seeking out vampires, and consuming them."

"Great. I obviously picked just the right time to be made into a vampire then," muttered Roxy. "So what does this thing look like, so I'll know when to run?"

"You are unlikely to get the chance. The first thing you will feel is an utter despair which will paralyse you. The X'ecunda appear as black, formless blobs, for want of a better word, constantly changing size and shape. They are unhindered by doors or walls and can fly at tremendous speeds or simply teleport from place to place."

Roxy licked her dry lips. "How you do defeat them?"

"The first thing to understand," lectured Darius, "is that they are all connected through higher dimensions, so anything experienced by one will be felt by all. If you are seen by one, then expect others to follow rapidly."

"What do you mean, connected through higher dimensions?"

"Imagine you lived in a two dimensional world, as if you were a stick figure drawn on a piece of paper. Your house would be made up of lines that you couldn't climb over, and doorways would be gaps in the line. You would have no concept of up or down, because you could only ever move or look from side to side. Now imagine that a three dimensional ball were to fall on the paper and pass through it. As far as you would be concerned, it would look as if a dot had suddenly appeared and become a rapidly expanding circle, which then started to contract as it got half-way though, until it became a dot again and disappeared."

Roxy frowned. "Yeah, okay, because you only see the bit of the ball that is touching the paper. Like slicing a tomato into circles."

"Precisely. Now imagine that instead of a ball, it was a hand passing through the paper. At first, only a single dot would appear, expanding into a slightly circular object as the first finger touched. Then a second, third, fourth and fifth would appear. You would think they were all separate entities, each with a slightly different shape and size. But if the hand passed lower, all of a sudden they would merge into a massive hand-shaped object, no longer circles, but five long rectangular creatures joined at one end to a squarish lump. But that is still not the whole picture, because the hand is joined to an arm, and the arm to a body with legs and a head. You could never see or hope to understand how such a thing could possibly exist, or what it would look like. That is what the Dark is to us. It exists in many dimensions above our paltry three. All we see are occasional projections into our world, which tell us nothing about its true nature."

"There must be a way to kill it, or drive it off," said Roxy.

"Many folk stories and old wives tales describe traditional wards which are based on teachings from the Eternals. Religious symbols are another example, created to help people resist the Dark and counter despair with hope."

Roxy held his eye for a while and then said tonelessly, "Are you saying the best way to defeat the Dark is to all join hands and kill it with love?"

Darius laughed. "There may be hope for you yet."

Roxy found herself smiling, despite herself. She wondered how Anderton was taking all this. He was finding out about vampires and witches and demons in a very short space of time. She wondered how long it would be before he started to deny it all, like Scarlet had. "Did you find those Tablets, by the way?" she asked, suddenly remembering why she had come.

Darius nodded briefly, "I know where they are, but I cannot retrieve them."

"Why not?"

"They are guarded by vampires. I have no wish to enter the reincarnation cycle again quite yet."

"Well can you tell me where they are at least? Please?"

Darius chewed on his lip for a while as if considering the wisdom of telling her, then shrugged and replied, "As you wish. They are deep underground in a large room filled with boxes containing very old objects."

"Well that's helpful. How old?"

"Ancient. Thousands of years I should imagine."

Roxy thought for a moment. "It sounds like some kind of museum. How far away?"

Darius cocked his head to one side, "They are only a few miles from here."

"Don't tell me they are under the British Museum?" said Roxy dryly.

"Actually, you might be right," smiled Darius.

Roxy frowned, "That's where they disappeared from."

"Well they obviously didn't move very far. You'll probably find them in one of the storerooms in the basement."

"You said they were guarded by vampires. Do you know how many?"

"No. But I would exercise caution if you decide to go looking for them. There is something not quite right with the guardians."

"Right. Well thanks a lot for that. Maybe I'll see you around some time." Roxy rose to her feet, noting with surprise that her sudden action had prompted several defensive changes in posture in the watching Eternals. They were clearly treating her with caution. It made her feel guilty about upsetting them at the same time as making her feel powerful and intimidating. She picked up her carrier bag of clothes and her sword and walked calmly out. Anderton gave Darius a brief nod of thanks, and followed.

# Chapter 40

"Do you have your car?"

"Sure, over here." Anderton led the way to where it was parked and unlocked the doors. Roxy slid into the passenger seat, depositing her spare clothes and sword on the back seat. Anderton climbed behind the wheel and put the key in the ignition. "Where to?"

Roxy stared at the poorly-lit road outside. "I dunno."

"Do you want to check out the museum?"

"Not really. I'm supposed to find out where these things are for someone, not to get them. I suppose I should go and tell her."

"Who?"

Roxy turned her head towards him. "Why are you getting involved? I'm not exactly the safest person to be around, you know? All that bollocks about the Dark and vampires being evil aside, I know you'll come to a sticky end if you hang around with me. Probably just before I do."

"You talk pretty tough, but you and I both know that you need help. I've read your file and I know a lot about you, Roxy. I know you've been alone for a long time, and you've had to put up with a lot of crap-"

"Fuck you! You don't know shit about me. You don't know what it's like to be homeless, to be raped, to have to let stinking old men shove their dicks in your mouth just so you can afford to eat!"

"Yeah okay..." started Anderton.

"Fuck okay!" Roxy was in full flow now, finally having someone to lash out at after years of suppressed anger, "I've been on the streets since I was fifteen. I had to run away from home to stop my step-father fucking me while my mum was drunk unconscious in the next room. Even my step-brothers were starting to eye me up, and they were only twelve. Do you know what it's like to have your mother, who is supposed to be the one person in the world you can rely on to protect you, tell you that you shouldn't expect men to behave themselves if you act like a slut?

"I only ever wanted to live a normal life. To see something of the world, maybe go to college, have a boyfriend – whatever? People like you screwed that up though. I just fell through the cracks in the system and no one came to rescue me. And, just as I was clawing my way out, fortune vomits on me yet again and gives me bloody fangs!"

Anderton, who had been quietly weathering her assault, couldn't suppress a smile at her inadvertent pun. Roxy saw his lips twitch and opened her mouth to lambaste him again, but found that she had run out of steam. She dropped her head into her hands and struggled to contain a sob. Anderton put his hand on her thigh but removed it when he felt her stiffen.

"I'm sorry, but don't you think you deserve a little help now?"

"I'm poison Anderton," she replied dejectedly. "You'll either be killed or go insane if you hang around with me. I can't deal with that."

"Let me worry about that. It's my choice. Besides, you saved my life, and according to an old Chinese proverb, that means you are forever responsible for me. Anyway, if I walk away now, how do I know some nasty vampire won't track me down and eat me in the future?"

Roxy felt her anger melt away at his innocent tone and smiled tiredly at him. "This isn't China, and if you don't shut up, I'll eat you myself."

Anderton smiled at her reassuringly "Come on Roxy, what do you have to lose?"

Roxy rolled her eyes and gave in, "All right, but do what I say okay?"

"Sure. So where to now?"

"Let's go to Wolfe's. I need to tell Natalie what Darius said."

"Who is Natalie?"

Roxy thought for a moment before answering. "She is pretending to be Wolfe's lover, but in fact she is a really old vampire called Na'amah who is manipulating him, and possibly many others as well. Needless to say if she finds out you know this she'll kill you."

"As long as she does it quickly," muttered Anderton, flexing his fingers unconsciously. "What are those tablets you asked Darius about?"

"I didn't realise you were paying such close attention."

"I'm a detective. I'm trained to do that."

"Right, duh, of course. The way it was explained to me, the Tablets of Menes are the writings of an ancient vampire called Menes, who was involved with Na'amah once, along with another ancient called Mangala. They were discovered by one of Menes' descendents called Catallus, who happened to be the lord of all the vampires in London. Someone killed Catallus the other day, and now everyone is scrabbling around looking for a replacement, while also trying to find the Tablets. Clear?"

"Menes, Na'amah, Mangala, Catallus, leadership battle and lost artefacts," intoned Anderton, "got it."

Roxy blinked in surprise. "I take it back. You're good."

"I'm just good at remembering things," shrugged Anderton, starting the engine. "Shall we go?"

Anderton parked near Wolfe's club, and at Roxy's request stayed in the car as she made her way inside. A couple of minutes later she hurried back.

"They're at a meeting," she said as she sat down. "Do you know the way to Kings Cross?"

Anderton nodded and pulled away from the kerb. They sat in silence, both wrapped in their thoughts until Anderton brought the car to a stop in front of the station.

"We need to go into the tunnels," said Roxy

They made their way down the steps to the underground. Their way was barred by a security gate.

"Damn, it's closed," said Roxy.

"It *is* after one," said Anderton, "It closes at twelve-thirty."

Roxy peered though the bars and exclaimed "Someone's there. Hey! Over here!"

A man in dark overalls called out "We're closed. Go away."

"Do you know Lord Catallus?" asked Roxy, not quite sure if there was a password or something to get in.

"What?" asked the man, already starting to walk away.

Roxy rattled the gate in frustration, wondering if she could break it.

"This is a police matter," called Anderton, pulling out his identification. "Open the gate."

The worker hesitated and then said, "I'll get the super."

He was back a minute later, following a blustering man with a silver moustache.

"What's going on here?"

Anderton held out his ID, "Could you open the gate please?"

The supervisor studied the ID carefully, then pulled out a large bunch of keys and unlocked the gate. "What's all this about?"

Roxy smiled at him seductively. "We're here for the meeting."

His eyes glazed over and he nodded mutely. He turned and led them into the station. The worker watched them go, his curiosity in conflict with his duty, but ultimately duty and fear of reprisal won, and he returned to his cleaning trolley. Roxy and Anderton followed the supervisor down a motionless escalator to an unobtrusive wooden door at the bottom. He wordlessly unlocked the door and stood aside to let them through. Roxy passed him without saying anything, and Anderton followed, somewhat bemused. The door was locked behind them.

They were in a dimly lit tunnel. Roxy led the way down a long flight of stairs. Anderton followed closely behind Roxy, occasionally glancing over his shoulder. The stairs came to an end and the tunnel changed character, becoming cleaner and more finished in appearance. The walls were painted and powerful strip-lights replaced the weak bulbs. Roxy squinted but before her eyes became accustomed to the light, she heard voices up ahead and stopped.

"What is it?" asked Anderton.

Roxy hushed him and tilted her head to listen. There was a large gathering in a room up ahead, she realised. Possibly fifty or more vampires. She started to question to wisdom of bringing Anderton with her. She turned to face him.

"Okay," she said in a low voice, "there are going to be a lot of vampires around you in a minute. They'll smell your fear, but try to stay calm. I'm going to claim you so they shouldn't touch you. At least I think that's how it works."

Anderton tightened his jaw and nodded. Roxy took his hand and gave him a moment to compose himself. He squeezed it gently, and let out a nervous laugh. "You're cold," he said. "Funny, how that seems to bring it home to me what you are, more than anything else so far."

Roxy said nothing as he took a couple of rapid breaths, then held it for a count of five. He nodded his readiness to Roxy, who turned and led him to the meeting room.

They passed through a set of double doors and entered a chamber hung with tapestries and lit with electric chandeliers. The marble floor was littered with agitated vampires, many of whom Roxy recognised. This was no formal occasion though, and there were no ball-gowns and few suits to be seen. The clothes were a garish mix of styles, as each chose to wear what felt most comfortable and familiar to them. Roxy admitted that she would still prefer jeans and t-shirts to whatever sparkly jump-suits became popular in a hundred years.

Arguments and threats flew between many scattered groups, which were mostly organised by house. As Roxy searched for Natalie and Wolfe, she also realised that the room was loosely arranged into three large factions. She spotted Vicky beside

Thorkel, in quiet conversation with a petite woman wearing a simple woollen dress. Roxy remembered that she was Edmeé, Lambeth's progeny. She saw Wolfe, flanked by James and Natalie, clustered around the Patricians Walpurga and Aelric. Wolfe was trading insults with a third group that contained Reyne and Harold. She pulled Anderton close behind her and marched purposefully towards Wolfe.

"What do you think you're doing?" hissed a voice at her ear. She turned and saw Cadence glaring at her and Anderton venomously. Roxy saw that she had attracted a small amount of curious attention from those nearest, but generally people were too busy in their own arguments to care.

"I won't be long," she replied, pitched in a voice so only Cadence could hear her.

"If Bronwyn recognises him you're dead," snarled Cadence, keeping her voice low.

Anderton regarded Cadence through narrowed eyes and followed her nervous glance across the room towards Bronwyn. The barest hint of a grim smile touched his lips.

Roxy took a closer look at Cadence and saw the remains of heavy scarring across her face as if her skull had been crushed and had not quite healed.

"What did she do to you?" she asked.

"Never mind, I didn't tell, but you are risking everything! I don't know if she's seen his photo."

"You're just drawing more attention to him," said Roxy brusquely. "Keep away from me and I'll be gone soon."

Cadence clamped her mouth closed furiously, but saw that Roxy was right and spun on her heel to march back to Reyne's group. Roxy continued towards Wolfe, ignoring the stares she was getting as people started to sense she had brought a human with her. She could see nostrils twitching and tongues dart out to moisten dry lips in anticipation. She circled around to approach Natalie from the rear, not wanting to talk to Wolfe if possible. Jessica saw her first and moved to intercept her.

"You've come back to us darling," gushed Jessica, staring at Anderton, "and you've brought us a gift!" She held out her hand to him invitingly. Roxy pulled him close.

"I've claimed him. He's mine!"

"Oh dear, but that's not good enough. Don't you know that you can only protect what you are strong enough to defend?" She smiled nastily at her.

Roxy stared down at Jessica "I'm here to see Wolfe, not his lackeys."

Roxy looked at Natalie, trying to catch her eye, but she was staring into space, a startled expression on her face. All attention turned to Edmeé, who had stood up on a table.

"Fellow Annunaki," she began, shouting over the clamour, "I have called you here to try to break the violence of recent days and agree on a new Primus."

"You mean that you want to be Primus!" shouted someone angrily.

"I consider myself worthy, but there are many who may have the capacity and support to rule. This bickering is unbelievable. We have never before seen such dissent. That we cannot even agree on candidates is inconceivable."

"Tell us why your sire refuses to take Catallus' place? He is the oldest of us." Bronwyn called out.

"Lambeth does not share his reasons with anyone – even me, but everyone knows he enjoyed the sparring that Catallus offered. No doubt he sees no challenge in remaining."

"Yet he does not leave! Nor is he here."

Edmeé looked flustered, then opened her mouth to reply. She was drowned out by jeers from the audience. Jessica looked back at Roxy.

"Wolfe doesn't like you any more. You have disappointed him my dear." She smiled up at Roxy smugly.

"Get out of my way Jessica. It's between him and me. If you think you're being scary you're wrong. You are barely annoying." Roxy glared at her, feeling a lot less brave than her words implied. She readied herself in case Jessica took a swing at her. The tension in the room might spill into violence at any moment and conventions be damned. All around people were shouting and pointing and pushing at each other. Roxy and Jessica stared at each other, each unwilling to back down.

Then the atmosphere in the room changed abruptly. The shouting ceased and arguments faltered. Roxy became aware of a pressure on her thoughts, forcing her to drop her eyes and turn towards the doors. They swung open slowly and a figure strode through it, a familiar fluidity of gait that Roxy recognised as Juan. He was followed by a menacing figure who walked purposefully through the parted crowd to where Edmeé stood. Roxy found it difficult to look directly at him, and later couldn't recall what he looked like. There was silence by the time he reached the centre of the room. Roxy looked for Natalie, suddenly realising who this was, and couldn't see her at first. She took a second look and saw her cowering behind Wolfe, smaller and more inoffensive than ever. Then she was gone again, like a mote in the eye swimming out of vision. Roxy gave up trying to find her again.

"Attention Annunaki. I am Mangala." Even his voice resonated power. Roxy knew he wasn't speaking English or Latin, but she understood his words nevertheless. "I am now your king."

# Chapter 41

Confusion erupted but violence was held at bay, both by the tradition that Gathering was sacrosanct, and the obvious display of power by Mangala and Juan, who were joined by Thorkel, Edmeé and a scattering of other Houses. The rest clustered around either Aelric and Walpurga or Reyne and Harold.

Roxy searched for Natalie and although she knew where she was, focusing on her was like trying to juggle soap. The moment she saw her she led Anderton up to her and whispered, "I know where they are."

Natalie looked at her sharply then glanced around, her eyes coming to rest on Aelric. He immediately stepped before Mangala and cried out, "I'll not be dictated to by an outsider! You will have to fight to prove your worth. I will linger here no longer."

With that, flanked by the members of his house, he strode from the room, with Mangala glaring at his back. Natalie shifted her gaze to Walpurga, who smiled broadly, gave a contemptuous wave to Mangala, and led her house after Aelric. A wave of similar departures followed, as several plebeian houses took the opportunity to leave. Wolfe slid in amongst them and Roxy found herself and Anderton being swept along in the tense crowd back to the underground station. At the top of the stairs, the various houses split away from each other, some heading towards the tunnels, some rushing up to the street, ripping the gates from their hinges as they went.

Natalie pulled Roxy to one side and pushed her roughly against the tiled wall. Roxy felt something snap in her back and gasped in pain. Natalie didn't appear to notice and standing on tiptoes, reached up and pulled Roxy's head down level with hers. "What do you know? Quickly child."

Roxy winced against the burning sensation in her healing spine and quickly relayed what Darius had told her. Natalie released her and stepped back, her dark eyes clouded in thought. "Why can I not see them?" she mused to herself. Then she gave a dismissive shake of her head and looked up at Roxy, a faint smile on her ruby lips. "I need them. Get them for me."

"What?" Roxy protested, "I can barely feed myself. How am I supposed to get them? They're guarded."

"Assuredly they are, but you have that secret advantage over the rest of us, don't you? Use it."

Roxy stared at her in confusion.

Natalie stepped away from her and rejoined Wolfe, who was waiting a few feet away, apparently unaware of Roxy. As Wolfe led the way up into the street, Natalie looked back and her voice echoed in

Roxy's mind, "Remember that the Dark abhors the Light." Then she was gone.

Roxy straightened rubbed her tender back. Anderton came over to her, "Did you talk to Wolfe?"

Roxy gave him a puzzled look, "No I was talking to Natalie. Weren't you watching?"

"Natalie?" Now it was Anderton's turn to be puzzled. "I just saw you standing by the wall..." he hesitated, not sure now what he had seen. "Was she the blonde?"

"Never mind," said Roxy, "we can't stay here." She hurried up the steps to where Anderton had left his car. She was just opening the door to climb in, when she heard her name being called. She saw Reyne standing alone, beckoning her with a pale finger. She briefly considered ignoring him, but prudence took over and with a quick gesture to Anderton to wait, she walked cautiously over to him.

"Roxy, my dear. You are starting to disappoint me." Reyne's tone was that of a kindly uncle, quietly admonishing a niece for not offering a kiss. "You have given me nothing, yet I sense that you have learned a great deal." He cast a glance at Anderton, sitting tensely in the car. "You have found a pet I see. It will not help you. I can have him destroyed along with you."

"I know. Things have been a bit manic, in case you hadn't noticed?"

"I am here now," he said warmly, the smile never reaching his eyes. "Tell me the secret that Wolfe is hiding."

Roxy shifted her weight to one side pensively, wondering what she could get away with, and a sudden thought struck her so hard she nearly lost her balance. She turned it over in her head, wondering if she were really that brave, or that stupid. He waited patiently, looking up at her with a relaxed expression. Can you read my mind? She wondered. He gave no indication that he had heard her unspoken question, so she took a steadying breath before speaking.

"All right, I'll tell you. Do you know who that was back there? Mangala, I mean?"

"Of course. The influence of the Dragon is legendary. And from the way Edmeé and Thorkel behaved, they are clearly shackled to him, and have been for years. Possibly centuries."

"Do the legends speak of his enemies?"

Reyne narrowed his eyes, "Many have opposed him; few still survive. But I am not about to give you a lesson in history. Speak now, or I'll cut out your tongue and nail you to a post to greet the dawn."

"Na'amah is here too," she said simply.

Reyne took a step backwards as if slapped. "The queen of the Triad," he whispered. "It cannot be. The Pharaoh, the Dragon and the Queen have fought for centuries. They would not be careless enough to find themselves in the same city. Only something of utmost importance would bring them together."

"Like the translation of the Menes Tablets?" asked Roxy.

He stepped towards her excitedly, his eyes blazing passionately, "What do you know? Where is she?"

Roxy smiled lopsidedly, getting a perverse pleasure out of doling out the information slowly. "She's been here about thirty years, as far as I can tell. Ever since Wolfe appeared and started forming a house. She helped him get established and then had herself adopted. Probably so that she could see the Tablets first-hand."

Reyne's eyes darted about her face, trying to work out what it was she wasn't saying. Roxy let him struggle for a few moments, and then said quietly, "Natalie is Na'amah."

Reyne froze. His eyes lost focus and he stared unseeing through Roxy's chest. Roxy watched him warily but he gave no sign that he was aware of her. She stepped back nervously, wondering if Na'amah was somehow controlling him. He appeared to be completely paralysed. She hurried back to the car, keeping an eye on him as she climbed in. Reyne still hadn't moved.

"Drive. Quickly." Anderton pulled away with a squeal of tyres.

"That was Reyne! What did he want? Is he a vampire too?" Anderton asked when they were half a mile away.

"The usual blackmail stuff, and yes he is," replied Roxy distantly. She wondered whether she had extended her life or shortened it. It probably only amounted to a few days either way. She felt a strange dread creep over her, which had nothing to do with the threat of retribution by Na'amah, or Reyne either. It was an unsettling feeling that she had just turned another cylinder in the lock of fate. Reyne's reaction had spooked her. She sat in silence as Anderton drove. Eventually he cleared his throat.

"So where to now?"

Roxy shook her head to clear her thoughts. "We've got to get the Menes Tablets. God knows how though."

"What's the problem? We know where they are."

"They'll be guarded, stupid!" Roxy shot back angrily.

"Not in daytime," replied Anderton mildly, "all the vampires will be sleeping won't they?"

"In case you hadn't noticed, I'm a vampire too-" Roxy stopped abruptly. My secret advantage, she thought with a smile. How did Na'amah know? Roxy dismissed the question. Na'amah could know anything she wanted. Anderton waited, seeing the excited look on her face.

"We'll do it." Roxy declared. "As long as I keep out of the sun I should be able to stay awake long enough to get us in and out. You'll have to help me on the outside though."

"As long as you help me if we bump into anything inside," muttered Anderton, turning down a street to take them to Bloomsbury.

# Chapter 42

Anderton drove to an underground car park near the museum. "We can stay here until morning," he said, turning off the engine.

They had a five or six hour wait ahead of them, and Roxy wondered if she should take the opportunity to feed.

"So how often do you have to, you know, drink blood?" asked Anderton, echoing her thoughts.

Roxy gave him a lop-sided smile, "Getting nervous?"

"No, I've been nervous for a while. Not about you though."

"I do have to drink blood, yes, but not every day. If I've had a big feed I'm usually okay for several days."

Anderton cleared his throat hesitantly. Roxy knew what was coming. "Do you, um, kill every time you...feed?"

"No," she replied softly. "Only twice. Once on purpose with the guy who hurt you, which you saw, and once by accident, which was Simon Trent."

Anderton swallowed. "How do you mean by accident?"

"I'd only been a vampire for a few days. I wasn't ready for the intensity of the hunger. I wasn't in control. I've learned to be careful since then. Most of the time I only drink a few mouthfuls, less than you'd give as a blood donor, then I wipe their memory and send them on their way."

"It sounds almost harmless," Anderton forced a chuckle.

"It isn't of course, but I have to tell myself it is, otherwise I think I'd go mad."

They sat in silence for a while and then Anderton tilted his seat back, lay down and closed his eyes. She watched his breathing become deep and steady, touched that he felt he could sleep beside her without fear. She suppressed an urge to smooth out his unruly hair and lingered in the caress of his familiar scent before slipping quietly out of the car.

She changed into a practical pair of jeans and set about fashioning the skirt into a headscarf to protect her face. She found a pair of sunglasses in the glove box, and tried them on. They weren't as dark as she'd have liked, but they were better than nothing. She didn't have any gloves, so she would have to keep her hands in her pockets. Anderton's overcoat which was slung across the rear seat completed the outfit and covered her arms.

Satisfied with her daytime precautions, she took the opportunity to get something to eat. Unwilling to resort to homeless drunks, she played the prostitute again and found two men to feed from before returning to a gently snoring Anderton. She found a newspaper beside her seat, turned away from the completed crossword and settled down to read.

Eventually, she started to feel drowsy and knew that the sun must be creeping over the horizon. She waited until the clock on the dashboard read eight-fifty, then nudged Anderton awake.

"It's time."

Anderton rubbed his face wearily.

"You don't look too good," said Roxy, noting the dark circles around his eyes.

"You should look at yourself."

Roxy looked in the mirror. She was very pale and her normally rich brown eyes looked washed out. "Well I think I look damn good for someone who's been dead for two weeks. Come on."

Roxy donned her makeshift headscarf, put on the dark glasses and led the way up the ramp. As the sunlight came into view, she stopped.

"Are you going to be able to do this?" Anderton asked in a concerned voice.

"I'll be fine as long as no sunlight touches me," she replied tightly.

Roxy jerked forwards. Just keep your head down and you'll be okay, she told herself. Anderton hurried to keep up with her, taking her arm as they emerged onto the street. Roxy felt a warm prickling on the top of her head and fought down the rising panic. She let Anderton guide her towards the museum, keeping her eyes mostly closed except for occasional peeks at the ground before her feet. Anderton kept up a low patter of encouragement, telling her when they were about to cross a road or dodge a group of pedestrians.

"Almost there," he said after what seemed an age, and Roxy opened her eyes briefly to see the large wrought iron gates surrounding the Museum. Anderton led her up the steps to the hastily repaired entrance and joined the short queue that was starting to file inside. Soon the welcoming shade enveloped them and Roxy shuddered with relief. She kept the glasses and scarf on to avoid stray light from the high windows, but found she could open her eyes without pain.

"Where to?" asked Anderton quietly.

"Downstairs. To the storage rooms."

"We could be looking for hours. There must be thousands of items down there."

Roxy didn't say anything. They made their way through the Egyptian rooms and found a set of steps by the Persian statues which led down. A simple rope sealed the steps from the public. Anderton nonchalantly unhooked the rope without glancing around and ushered Roxy through before snapping it back into place. No one called out to them and they were soon out of sight on the floor below. The stairwell was well-lit and led to a modern windowless door with an electronic keypad entry. Roxy gently pushed against the lock until the wooden frame around it split. Beyond was a large room filled with hundreds of boxes. A cool breeze came from several faintly whirring fans set in the ceiling. Anderton started to read the labels on the sides of the boxes, but Roxy ignored them and strode deeper into the room, looking for a way to the deeper storerooms. She saw what she was looking for – a service lift in the far wall and beckoned Anderton over.

"You don't think they're up here then?" he asked hopefully.

"Darius said they were guarded and deep underground." Roxy pressed the button to call the lift. She was tired, and a pressure was building behind her eyes. She rubbed her temple to ease the throbbing.

"Are you okay?" Anderton opened the lift door.

"I dunno. I guess I'm not as good at staying awake in the day as I thought. This feels...different though." Roxy waved his concern away and stepped inside. There were four basement levels below them. Roxy hit the lowest button and pulled the sword out from its hiding place within the overcoat as the lift made its slow descent.

Anderton eyed the sword apprehensively, but held his tongue. The lift shuddered to a halt and the doors opened to reveal an unlit room, several times larger than the one they had left. The light from the lift illuminated an avenue of crates stacked almost to the high ceiling. Anderton peered into the darkness beyond the puddle of light.

Roxy stood motionless, staring at nothing. Her head was really pounding now. She felt weak and nauseous too. She blinked to clear her head and held out her hand to Anderton. "I think this is it. Do you want to stay here and wait for me?"

Anderton licked his lips involuntarily, then took hold of her hand and shook his head.

Roxy looked into the valley of crates, her eyes adjusting to the low light. They were arranged in rows, creating narrow corridors through which they walked. The hairs on the back of her neck prickled as she moved into the room. She saw that Anderton was staring blindly ahead, his gaze unfocused as he relied on his hearing to guide him. His hand felt warm in hers. Their steps made too much noise on the concrete floor and the sibilant hiss of the air-conditioning created unpleasant draughts which caught them from unexpected directions causing Anderton to look over his shoulder more than once. Roxy could hear nothing beyond the fans and Anderton's breathing and heartbeat. The light from the lift was little more than a glow reflected from the ceiling as Roxy came to a T-junction. She headed left knowing somehow that their target lay at the far side of the room. A soft thump sounded somewhere off to the right, behind the crates. She stopped, raising the sword defensively.

"What is it?" asked Anderton in a whisper.

Roxy winced inwardly. He was being too loud. She should never have brought him. She squeezed his hand warningly and listened. Nothing. Cautiously she started walking again, making as little noise as she could. Anderton tried to walk softly, but Roxy thought that a cow in clogs would be quieter. The thump was not repeated, but the sense of something stalking them grew stronger. Roxy kept Anderton close behind her as she led him towards the rear of the room. The maze of crates came to an end, opening into a large space containing a stone table flanked by four long, slender boxes lying on the floor. They were the same size as coffins. On the table rested a case the size of a shoebox.

Roxy squeezed Anderton's hand gently and guided it to rest on one of the crates. She patted him briefly on the arm as she let go of his hand. Anderton opened his mouth to say something, but Roxy put a finger to his lips, stopping him. The last thing she wanted was to wake the vampires that were certainly inside the coffin-like boxes. Anderton closed his mouth and Roxy slid quietly over to the stone table, reciting her mantra in her head – I can't be seen, no one can see me. The light was too dim for her to see any details on the case. She explored it with her fingertips, feeling cool metal and a small keyhole. A bitter smell caught her attention. At first she thought that Anderton had broken wind and started to smile but then a scraping sound made her spin around.

One of the coffins was opening. She took her sword in a two-handed grip and held it up, ready to bring it down on whatever came out. She almost missed her chance. The lid was suddenly flung away and a shadowy figure sat up, hissing loudly. Roxy had to alter her aim mid-swing as it moved to a squatting position, but caught it square in its side. There was a sickening crack and wet sucking sound as her sword cut three-quarters of the way through, severing the torso under the ribcage. A piercing scream filled the air as the thing flopped about like a landed fish, its arms flailing desperately against the hard floor. Roxy steeled herself and wrenched the sword free for a second swing. It was just as clumsy as her first. Although she aimed for the head, the figure lurched to the side at the last moment and she severed the thing's arm just above the elbow. She swung again and again, knowing she couldn't give it time to heal itself. Anderton's shouts of concern slowly filtered in, the smell of his fear giving her strength and mingling with the fresh scent of rich, hot blood. She stopped hacking at the figure, now motionless at her feet. Something was wrong, she realised, but the truth was unable to break past the numbness in her head.

"Roxy?" Anderton's voice cracked. He was cowering at the base of the crate where she had left him, blind and helpless, not knowing if she was alive or dead. She fell to her knees, dropping the sword with a clang. Vampire blood didn't smell like that. It wasn't hot either. *Oh my god!* She put her hands to her mouth, listening to Anderton's desperate pleas for her to answer and unable to speak. She stretched out a hand to touch the still, warm body. With a sick sense of shame she stood up on unsteady legs.

"I'm okay," she croaked.

"Jesus Roxy, you scared the shit out of me. What happened?"

Roxy reached down and picked up her sword. "I got confused. Never mind."

A violent splintering sound shocked her into action.

"My mule!" A man's voice raged. She turned to see one of the other coffins had burst open and a dark, slender figure was standing amidst the ruins, his clawed hands ready to strike. Roxy stumbled back, slipping in the spreading pool of blood she had spilled. Her assailant lurched forward, almost faster than she could follow, but his movements were uncoordinated and oddly sluggish. Roxy scrambled past him and felt something grab her ankle but she shook it loose and ran over to Anderton. The figure behind her swayed.

"You will not leave here, whelp," His voice was strained and slurred. He had not fully awoken. Roxy stood her ground in front of Anderton, ready to receive the next charge and expecting pain this time. The smell of bad eggs rose again more strongly, making her gag so that she almost didn't see the vampire ahead of her lose his head. It wasn't severed, but instead disappeared from the top down, as if swallowed by a black fog. There was a faint shriek as though from a great distance as his body was slowly enveloped by a shapeless, rippling form, totally black against the heavy gloom of the room. His legs disappeared next, and then his body, shrinking inwards until it vanished with a wet sucking sound. Roxy gaped at the dark form remaining, which towered eight feet high, vaguely humanoid, but shifting every second into obtuse dimensions that made her head spin. She couldn't move, her legs were ossified, her arms refused to obey her. The form half-glided, half-lurched towards her and then, mindless as a shadow, it veered away and descended on one of the undisturbed coffins, consuming it like a hand passing in front of a distant tree.

"Our Father, who art in heaven," Anderton, nearly catatonic, babbled inanely to himself, yet his words had a liberating effect on her. She turned her head and saw that the thing had stopped. It hovered over the final coffin, regarding them blindly. Roxy joined in with Anderton, dragging the words from memories of school assembly.

"...Hallowed be thy name. Thy kingdom come, thy will be done..."

It grew smaller. Roxy looked at the case on the table. She had to get it. As long as the creature stayed where it was she would have a chance. She edged closer, mumbling the prayer around an uncooperative tongue. The form lurched away from her, giving her the courage to dart in and grab the case. It didn't respond, so she leapt back to Anderton, the case clasped under her sword arm and her other arm ready to pick him up. The shape seemed to jump forwards without moving, suddenly only inches away, then it shrank to the size of a football and retreated to the final coffin. Roxy didn't wait. She threw Anderton over her shoulder and ran, the sound of the creature feasting on the last vampire ringing in her ears.

Every frantic step back to the lift she took expecting it to be her last. She didn't think she would remember the way, but then the lift was there, its dim light dazzlingly bright after the darkness behind her. She leaped in, dropped Anderton unceremoniously on the floor and pulled the lift doors closed. The door didn't close properly at first, making her sob in frustration. She hauled it back and tried again, the smell of sulphur rising around her. The door closed and she stabbed at the ground floor button desperately, feeling her limbs grow numb with cold. She clung to the wall, expecting the dark shape to emerge from the floor and swallow her up, but second after second passed, and the lift continued to rise. The thing below, whatever it was, had not pursued her.

The lift came to a halt and the doors opened to reveal the main exhibition floor, slightly away from the public area. She turned to help Anderton and let out a gasp of shock. His hair had turned completely white and his pale face, lined around the eyes and mouth was that of a man thirty years older.

# Chapter 43

Anderton staggered out of the lift, wracked by a dull terror and shaking uncontrollably. He collapsed to his knees, staring at the wrinkled, liver-spotted backs of his hands.

Roxy lifted him to his feet and pulled his arm over her shoulder, half-carrying him through empty halls towards the exit. They stopped just short of the main foyer and Roxy turned his face to hers with gentle fingers.

"Anderton, you're going to have to help me now. The daylight is too strong for me to see properly. You'll have to guide me back, do you understand?"

Anderton nodded dazedly. He concentrated on her as she pulled the scarf over her head and adjusted her sunglasses.

"Ready?" she asked, "we don't have much time."

"Okay," Anderton found his voice, but it was hoarse and broken. He licked his lips and tried to swallow. Taking Roxy's arm, he led her out under the curved glass roof towards the exit, gasping with pain every step.

"That's it," said Roxy, "you can make it. Just another few minutes, and we'll be there."

She kept up a constant stream of encouragement all the way back to the dark safety of the car park. They fell into the car gratefully, both exhausted from their respective ordeals.

"We can stay here for the rest of the day," said Roxy, pulling off the headscarf wearily.

"Wouldn't it be safer to put some distance between us and the museum?" asked Anderton weakly.

"Yeah, but you're in no fit state to travel, and where would we go?"

Anderton started the engine, "I know a place," he said grimly, "put your scarf on. I'll be okay."

He drove up to the street into dazzling sunshine. Roxy cowered in the passenger seat as he took them to a small hotel on the outskirts of London.

"Come on," he opened the passenger door and helped a trembling and drowsy Roxy into the dingy reception and then up to the room. He pulled the curtains together securely before he let her sink onto the battered double bed and covered her with a thick blanket.

She squinted up at him, looking into his eyes searchingly.

"You'll look after me?" she murmured.

"Of course," he forced a smile, "sleep now."

She slept.

She stood on a wide, featureless plain bathed in the deep red glow of sunset. Purple and yellow clouds lingered over the point where the sun had just dipped below the horizon. She was alone, but a distant howling filled her ears. She scanned the horizon for the source of the sound, but saw nothing. A door slammed behind her. It was standing freely in space, the only object on the plain apart from her – no walls prevented her from walking around it but she hammered against it, knowing she had to get through. The howling grew louder and the red glow deepened to black, chasing towards her from the horizon at her back. Her pounding grew more frantic. She couldn't let the shadow reach her. She couldn't–

Roxy jerked into a sitting position, wide-eyed and trembling from the imagery of the dream. Anderton was curled up on the armchair, illuminated by a table-lamp, his brow furrowed. His lips were moving in his sleep, clearly tortured by dreams of his own. Roxy swung her legs over the side of the bed and tried to stand but her they wouldn't support her and she collapsed to her knees on the thin carpet. Her whole body felt weak. She knew she was hungry but this was different. She shook her head, unable to clear the lingering dream. She was smothered in an overwhelming sense of being trapped and some great danger that she couldn't place.

"Roxy?" Anderton rubbed his eyes and peered down at her. He slid off the chair and shuffled over to her on his knees. She looked at him and tears welled in her eyes.

"What have I done to you?" she whispered. He looked like a man on the far side of middle age. The lines around his eyes multiplied as he smiled carelessly,

"At least I still have my hair," he joked.

Roxy saw that his clothes were faded and threadbare. His watch was tarnished and the glass face was cracked. Her own clothes were faded too, the t-shirt baggy where the material had lost elasticity.

"The clothes aged too," said Anderton, following her gaze. "You're still as perfect as ever though," he added quietly.

Roxy looked at her hands. They were smooth and unwrinkled. "It must be because I'm a vampire. I'll look like this forever."

"That's what I thought. Your eyes look funny though. Are you okay? Don't you need to drink blood or something?"

Roxy struggled to her feet and pulled herself over to a mirror. Her irises were silvery in colour, the pupils large and unnatural in the pale expanse of her eyes. "I don't know. I'm a bit new to all this. I don't think it's because I'm hungry though." She turned to face him, "We need to get out of here. Something is very wrong."

Anderton moved over to a table to retrieve the case. "I opened it," he said, showing her the broken lock before lifting the lid. Roxy gingerly walked over to him, still weak. She reached in and pulled out a small hard clay object about five inches by three and an inch thick with strange crabbed symbols carefully etched on either side.

"I was expecting something bigger, like Charlton Heston had in that movie about Moses," she said. "How many are there?"

"Seven."

Roxy pulled out another and looked at them both side by side. "I can't believe these have caused so much trouble."

Anderton took them from her, set them back in the foam pockets where they'd rested and closed the box. "Are you going to take them to Wolfe?"

"No." Roxy decided, "Natalie or Na'amah or whatever-the-hell her name is can wait. I think we should go back to Darius. I want to ask about what happened to you too."

Anderton shrugged her concern away, "Don't worry about it. You warned me away, so it's my fault."

Roxy started to reply, but a sudden dizziness arose and she fell forward in a faint. Anderton caught her and guided her into the chair.

"Are you okay?"

"I don't know. It feels like something is stealing my strength. Like a vampire, feeding on me. I'm getting another headache too."

Anderton hesitated then spoke in a rush, as if not trusting himself to finish unless he got it all out at once, "You can feed on me if you like? If it would help?"

Roxy smiled and touched his face tenderly. "I don't think that would help. Besides, it's dangerous for you. It would start to twist your mind. You'd become enslaved to me."

"I can think of worse things," he said. Their closeness suddenly became uncomfortable. Anderton stood up awkwardly and offered her his hand. "Come on then. We might not have much time."

Roxy accepted his hand and let him pull her to her feet. She felt better now, but the headache was lurking just beyond reach, threatening to descend at any moment. She gathered up her bloodstained sword and the case, and followed Anderton to the car.

# Chapter 44

The night air was cool and smelled of gardenias. Roxy stared out of the window as Anderton drove, trying to ignore the growing hunger clawing at her stomach and thought of Claudia. She missed her so much the emptiness in her heart hurt more than the void in her belly. By the time they reached Darius she had managed to suppress the feelings, but a tiredness had replaced them which made it difficult to concentrate. Anderton helped her down the dark passage to the paint-chipped door. Roxy felt a shiver of warning run down her back as they knocked. The door was opened by an aggressive-looking young man who looked startled when he saw Roxy.

"What are you doing here?" He growled.

Roxy gave him a flippant smile, "Just stopped by for a friendly chat with my mate Darius." She peered past him, hearing the urgent chatter of several voices. "You having a party or something?"

"Cade?" A woman came up behind the man to see who was at the door. Roxy recognised her as one of the eternals that had been with Darius earlier.

"It's the leech and her puppet," Cade answered bitterly.

"It's Roxy actually. Mind if we come in?"

The woman narrowed her hazel eyes and pursed her lips.

"It's not a good time."

"Okay, we'll just take the Tablets to Na'amah instead," Roxy hefted the case in her hand and started to turn away.

"You have the Tablets?" the woman said in surprise.

Roxy opened the case briefly, watching her carefully. She could smell the sudden excitement from her and the fear from Cade who regarded her as if she were a poisonous snake.

"You'd better come in."

"Louisa, are you insane?" Cade hissed.

Louisa waved him away and stepped back, indicating that they follow her. Roxy couldn't resist giving Cade a toothy grin as she passed, nearly gasping in delight at the sudden wave of fright that it provoked. She felt better immediately. Louisa led them into the main room where they had been before, but now it was now three times the size, and in place of the comfortable sofa and armchairs stood a round table, empty in the middle like a ring doughnut and large enough to accommodate twenty people. Darius was sitting on the floor in the centre with another man and a woman, chanting softly. All three were dressed in ceremonial gowns embroidered with arcane symbols. Seated around the outside were about a dozen more men and women, all in regular clothes. The idle chatter stopped as Roxy and Anderton entered and everyone turned to stare.

Louisa walked up to the table and slid over it, swinging her legs around in a dainty arc and hopped down next to Darius. She touched his shoulder and spoke in a low voice that Roxy heard anyway.

"The vampire neonate has come back. She has the Menes Tablets."

Darius opened his eyes and stood up swiftly with a smile. The other two robed figures stopped chanting and looked round. Their eyes quickly found Roxy, who became acutely self-conscious as their gaze seemed to penetrate her very soul. She gritted her teeth.

"Roxy. Good to see you," Darius was saying, smoothing down his robe. He turned to greet Anderton and his eyes widened slightly, then narrowed under a concerned frown. "Ah, I was afraid you would ignore my advice. I see you've had a close encounter with the X'ecunda. I'm impressed that you survived."

"What happened to him?" Roxy asked, then pushed on without waiting for an answer, "I mean I know he's aged – our clothes did too, and I guess I did as well, but you just can't tell, but why?"

Darius held up a hand to stop her rambling. "First let me introduce you to everyone. There are some strange and disturbing things happening in the city tonight."

"It is her fault!" the robed woman declared suddenly. "I can see it. What did you do girl?"

Roxy didn't know what to say, taken aback by the vehemence and certainty in the woman's voice.

"I...I got the Menes Tablets," she stammered.

The woman shook her head briskly, "It wasn't that. Something else. I sense your fate is strongly tied to what is happening, and what is yet to happen."

"Hush Lillian," said Darius, but he regarded Roxy with a new speculative air. "You have the tablets?"

"Yeah." Roxy hefted the case in her hand. Darius vaulted athletically over the table towards her. Roxy gave him the case, which he set on the table and opened to reveal the small clay objects nestled in their foam pockets. Everyone moved around to see. Roxy and Anderton hung back until the curious crowd had finished looking. Darius and his two colleagues were poring over them, studying them closely without touching.

"Can you read them, Benito?" Lillian asked the man.

"Yes, but...these cannot be the right tablets."

"Oh I think they are," replied Darius. "I can feel the touch of a powerful Darkness about them." He fixed a piercing glance on Roxy, "they were guarded were they not?"

"Yes. A...a few vampires and that...shadowy thing. It ate the guards."

Benito stared at her. "You faced a manifestation and survived? How?"

"She has a strong fate, Benito." murmured Lillian, as if that explained everything.

"The tablets, Benito," insisted Darius impatiently.

"They are worthless. They talk of cattle and grain inventories. Who they were bought from and for how much. Nothing mentioning Menes or Annunaki, let alone the personal thoughts of the first Pharaoh."

"What about on the back?"

"I'm not touching them. Get her to turn them over."

They looked at Roxy. Since she had already handled them with no apparent effect, she shrugged and started to turn them over one by one. The mages once again bent to examine the writings on the rear, but Benito snorted in disgust.

"The same. They cannot be the right ones. That's what you get for sending a cripple to get them."

"No, Benito." Lillian whispered. "These are what Lord Catallus has been translating. I am certain of it. Perhaps he was mistaken?"

"Impossible. This is Classical Sumerian, not fully understood by mortal scholars agreed, but certainly enough to translate most of the meaning. A college graduate could read them."

Darius, Lillian and Benito fell silent, lost in thought. Roxy saw that Anderton had a far-away look in his eyes that had started to appear in unguarded moments ever since his torture, and reached out to give his hand a reassuring squeeze. She was about to speak when a pain like she had swallowed an ice-cube the size of her fist struck her chest. She collapsed with a cry and crumpled to the floor like a rag doll, her mouth wide in a silent scream. Anderton dropped to his knees beside her, still clutching her hand, and gathered her head to cradle it in his lap. Her skin had turned grey, as if a shadow had fallen over her and her silvery eyes became translucent so that the nerves of her retina could be seen behind the tiny black pupil floating on the surface.

"Help me!" he spluttered, but Darius was already beside him, studying Roxy with a dispassionate curiosity.

"She is being subsumed," he said. "Lillian, Benito – we must be quick."

Anderton gripped Roxy tightly, "She's slipping away – like wet soap!"

The three witches joined hands in a ring around them and closed their eyes in concentration. They began to sing a gentle lullaby in a language he didn't recognise, but it immediately calmed him. Painful seconds passed, as Roxy seemed to pulse in and out of shadow, then her colour returned and she sat up in a rush, knocking him aside unconsciously. Her eyes had regained their rich brown colour and they were wide with terror. Anderton crawled back to her and put a tentative arm around her. She stiffened momentarily, then relaxed into him, closing her eyes to shut out the fleeing nightmare.

"Come, Roxy," said Darius softly, holding out his hand, "we haven't much time."

Darius and Anderton helped her to her feet, but apart from a ravenous hunger which she knew she would find impossible to ignore, she felt strong again. They led her to the table and made her sit down. Darius sat on one side of her and Anderton on the other, holding her hand possessively. Everyone took that as a signal to sit too.

"The reason so many eternals are gathered here tonight, is that a terrible magic is affecting the city. We all woke this morning with ominous dreams, especially Lillian, who is highly skilled in prophesy. A great barrier has appeared, encircling the city, invisible and impotent to mortals, but like a stone wall to enlightened beings, such as vampires and ourselves. It prevents entry and more importantly, exit. We don't know what it is. We know that it comes from a very powerful and ancient source, possibly vampiric, but certainly channelled by the Dark. We have been trying to break it down, but so far we've had no luck. It has been growing stronger as night deepens.

"That is not our only concern; for in conjunction with the wall another effect is occurring, which you have just experienced. The X'ecunda is recalling its scattered elements and reabsorbing them. All of the vampires in the city are suffering. Their essences are being drained, their strength adding to the Dark with every death. The weaker ones will succumb first, and the strongest will grow progressively more feeble and wretched until they too, are subsumed. In the meantime they will give in to their base urges, becoming violent and uncontrollable."

Roxy gripped Anderton's hand, making him wince until she realised she was squeezing too hard and relaxed her grasp. "What happens if all the vampires are subsumed?"

"We cannot be certain, but some of us suspect that the X'ecunda may be able to break through to our dimension in unprecedented numbers. The effect would be catastrophic to all life. The ageing effect our poor friend suffered is due to the multi-dimensional nature of the X'ecunda. One of the dimensions they inhabit is time, and they warp it in uncontrolled and often lethal ways wherever they manifest. Some suspect that this is the source of vampire immortality, but we are drifting into metaphysics now. I shan't bore you with vector spaces and Riemann geometry.'

Roxy suddenly became aware of Simon's presence again. Vague, fading memories of complex variable mathematics and eigenvectors drifted across her thoughts. "You're talking about General Relativity, aren't you?"

Darius paused to give her a bemused smile. "Partly. How did you know?"

Roxy dropped her eyes, unable to look at Anderton. She said softly, "I can remember things that someone I killed once knew."

"You ravished someone's soul." It was more a statement than a question. "That is a terrible act, as I'm sure you are aware."

"I still hear him sometimes. In my head." She felt Anderton stiffen, but he kept holding her hand. She was glad he did.

"Your stronger will is keeping him at bay. Be thankful it is not the other way around."

"Darius," interrupted Benito, "I still don't think there are enough vampires in the city to weaken the Barrier. It would take two or more likely three very powerful vampires to lower the potential enough for the Dark to tunnel through."

"We know that Na'amah is here. Maybe she is enough?" suggested Darius.

"No, even with her, the energy density is still too low."

Roxy shot a glance at Anderton. He raised a questioning eyebrow at her, seeing the look in her eye, but not able to guess its meaning. There was not enough energy in Na'amah, thought Roxy, her head suddenly light, but there was another source of energy in the city. Something just as powerful as Na'amah. It couldn't be a coincidence that this ritual had started so soon after the appearance of Na'amah's old adversary. In fact the only question was why hadn't it started earlier? Nearly all the vampires in the city had seen him march in and take over. She cleared her throat with a nervous cough.

"Mangala is here too," she said quietly.

Darius and Benito fell silent. Roxy looked up at them, "He announced himself last night. In front of everyone. He claimed the throne, but not everyone accepted him. Some of them gathered around Natalie – I mean Na'amah. I guess she's shackled them. The rest seemed to just mill about, or follow Harold and Reyne."

"I don't imagine Na'amah would bow before him," said Darius. "Was she there?"

"Yes, but she was hiding. I don't think she expected him to turn up like that. She probably wasn't ready to face him." Roxy frowned. "I'm confused though. He must know she is here. His follower Juan told me about her in the first place."

"We are missing something," said Benito. "However, the presence of two ancients in the city is concerning. The power they will return to the Dark if they should die in quick succession would be devastating. Combined with the loss of the elder vampires, it might be enough to let the Dark through."

"We need to find out who is behind the ritual," said Darius. "Not Mangala or Na'amah, certainly. The Dark is powerful, but it has not the focus to work this itself. It is being manipulated by another. Perhaps even an eternal gone bad?"

"Which makes it important that we investigate now," said Lillian. "It must be someone very strong indeed to challenge Na'amah and Mangala. They must be warned. They have worked together in the past. Maybe they can be persuaded to do so again?"

Roxy felt a dozen sets of eyes rest on her. She smiled grimly at Lillian, in an attempt to lighten her mood, but she wondered if she'd ever feel happy again. "I'll go. I'll need to take the tablets though."

"Take them," said Darius, pushing the case towards her, "they are useless to us. Dangerous even."

Roxy stood and closed the case. "Will I...make it that far? How long have I got until that thing gets me again?"

Lillian rose and spread her hands, "Who knows? The enchantment on you will help for a while longer, but you will do as well to keep your thoughts from despair. Apart from that, trust to luck. You seem to have it in abundance."

Darius led her and Anderton out. "We will do what we can here, but in truth there is little we can hope for. We cannot fight the Dark directly. That is not our role. To use violence, even to prevent violence, still causes pain, which merely strengthens our foe. We'll let you know if we uncover something important however. Good Luck."

# Chapter 45

"Give me your phone," said Roxy as they got to the car.

"Do vampires use mobile phones?" asked Anderton.

"I do," Roxy ignored his playful sarcasm. She rooted around in her pockets and finally found what she was looking for. A small business card containing only an eleven digit number.

"Here," Anderton passed her his phone.

Roxy dialled the number. She hoped it wouldn't go to voicemail. It didn't. She only had to wait two rings before an unfamiliar voice answered.

"Yes?"

"Juan?" Roxy wasn't sure it was him. When he didn't answer straight away, she continued, "This is Roxy. From Domus Wolfe."

"Ah yes, hello," It sounded more like Juan now.

Roxy let out a silent sigh of relief, "You had your posh phone voice on. I thought it was someone else."

"One can never be too careful," replied Juan in an amused tone. "What can I do for you Roxy?"

"A meeting. You, Mangala and me. It's important."

There was silence on the other end of the phone.

"I have the Tablets of Menes."

"Ah," breathed Juan. "Has Na'amah seen them?"

"No. I'll be in Green Park at midnight." She hung up before he could respond. She felt her heart beating twenty to the dozen. She couldn't believe she was doing this. She turned to Anderton, "Take us to Wolfe's. Do you have any paper?"

"There's a notebook and pen in the glove box," said Anderton.

Roxy dug them out and started to write a note. *Natalie. I have them. Meet me in Green Park at midnight, alone. Roxy.* She tore it out of the notebook and folded it twice.

"I don't suppose you have an envelope?"

"No, but we could get one if you want?"

Roxy chewed her lip for a moment. "Yeah, okay. But if we're going to stop and buy something I have a better idea."

They stopped at a convenience store and went in together. The harsh lighting hurt her eyes a little, but she thought that Anderton looked a bit better. Not so many wrinkles were visible and his hair wasn't as white as she thought. She found what she was looking for and Anderton paid for it.

It was nearly half past ten by the time they reached the club and Anderton pulled up sharply. The street ahead was teeming with leaping figures, circling and attacking each other with preternatural grace and speed. Blades flashed in the streetlights and blood splashed in lazy arcs onto the slick tarmac.

Roxy recognised several of the vampires who had lined up with Wolfe and Walpurga fighting some who had stood with Mangala. She saw James and Dave amongst the melee and suspected that Wolfe was around somewhere too.

"This isn't helpful," she muttered, opening the door.

"You can't be serious," blurted Anderton. "You can't go out in that."

"No choice," said Roxy, collecting her sword. "I won't hang about though. In and out. You stay here."

"Not a chance. I'm coming with you."

"You don't get it, do you?" Roxy leaned back inside the car, the point of her sword waving threateningly in front of Anderton's face. With a swift motion she ran her free hand down the length of the blade, causing thick, dark blood to well in her palm. She held the flowing wound in front of Anderton and he watched in horrified fascination as it sealed itself up and stopped bleeding.

"I can cope with a few stabbings. You can't. Please, stay here."

Anderton clamped his teeth together and for a moment she thought he would refuse, but he nodded stiffly.

"Don't be long."

"I won't," she grabbed the compact disc they had just bought and slid the note in between the pages of the booklet inside. It was a bit tight, but would pass cursory inspection. She willed herself invisible, not sure if it would work against vampires, but figured it was worth a try.

Roxy circled round to approach the club from the other direction. She hoped to find a side door or a window she could use to get inside. Roxy slipped down a darkened alley too narrow for vehicles. She could hear the sound of fighting around the corner up ahead but saw what she was looking for. An unmarked fire door led out of the club into the alley. She heard low female voices behind it and recognised them as Ruth and Sarah, clearly nervous. There was no way to open the door from this side, short of smashing it in, so she raised her hand and lightly drummed against it with her fingertips. The hushed talking ceased and Roxy dared a loud whisper, "Ruth, it's Roxy,"

There was no sound for a moment, then she heard the slide of a bolt and a click as the door was pushed open. Ruth peered out suspiciously, glancing first at Roxy and then beyond her to check she was alone.

"Inside, quick," she opened the door just wide enough for Roxy to slip in and closed it behind her. Ruth and Sarah were both dressed in heavy leathers and holding weapons. They looked tired and their eyes were a washed out shade of their former selves.

"What are you doing here, Roxy?" said Ruth. "Wolfe has cast you off. He has declared you a traitor. He will kill you if he sees you."

"Yeah I guessed that. I'm not staying. What's happening outside?"

"It is Mangala. He has sent his followers to destroy us. We have called Walpurga for help, but it is the same all over the city. A madness has seized everyone. No one is prepared to talk any more."

"You shouldn't have upset Wolfe, Roxy," said Sarah weakly. "I liked you."

"I'm surprised Jessica lets you have an opinion," replied Roxy tartly. She regretted her words the moment they were out of her mouth, especially when she saw the confused, hurt expression on Sarah's face.

"Sorry, Sarah. I'm just mad at Wolfe, not you. That was unkind."

Roxy thought that Ruth hid her disapproval well, "What do you want?"

Roxy held out the CD, "Can you give this back to Natalie? Call me stupid but I'd hate to piss off any more people than I have to."

Ruth frowned and took the CD from her. "She lent this to you?"

"Yeah, believe it or not, we share the same taste in music. Probably because we're both about the same age." Roxy was grasping at straws now and pretended to be checking to make sure that Wolfe wasn't coming so that she didn't have to look Ruth in the eyes. It seemed to work. Ruth shrugged and started to put the CD in her pocket. Roxy stopped her.

"Uh, actually, is she here?" she asked.

"Yes I think so, with Wolfe," said Sarah.

"Do you think you could go and get her? I'd like to tell her thanks and goodbye."

Sarah looked at Roxy like she'd asked her to set fire to her hair. "Get her?"

Ruth shook her head, "We can not just go up to her and say 'Roxy is downstairs'. Wolfe will hear."

"Just give her the CD then. She'll know it's me and Wolfe won't realise."

Ruth and Sarah exchanged glances. They were both terrified of doing anything to upset Wolfe. No, they were simply terrified of him, Roxy thought.

"Please," she addressed Sarah, hoping that the slight hold she had on her from drinking her blood, would sway her. As added insurance, she looked into her eyes and tried to reproduce what she had done with Clive when she had forced him to obey her. Sarah hesitated for a moment, then held out her hand to Ruth for the CD. Ruth narrowed her eyes and didn't take them off Roxy as she pulled it out of her pocket and passed it to Sarah. She said nothing until Sarah was out of hearing then said in a hostile voice, "I do not know what this is about Roxy, but get out. Now." Ruth raised her sword defensively.

Roxy kept her sword low, "Okay. I'll explain one day. I hope."

She opened the door and slipped out, hearing it bolted behind her. She hadn't gone more than two steps when a faint scuffle from above made her tense. A heavy boot fell on her neck and sent her sprawling. She rolled over, trying to hold onto her sword and bring it up defensively, knowing that she wouldn't be quick enough. She saw a small figure crouched at her feet, a long knife held high and ready to strike, but the blow never fell. Roxy froze, her sword at her side, not wanting to do anything to provoke her attacker and wondered why they had stopped.

"Roxy?" It was Vicky.

Roxy focused on her blood-splattered clothing and crazy hair. Vicky had a lop-sided smile on her face which didn't quite hide the tinge of madness in her eyes. Roxy slowly got to her feet. "What are you doing here?" she asked.

Vicky gave a dismissive shrug, "Wolfe chose the wrong side. His house must be extinguished."

"Are you going to kill me?" Roxy kept her sword low.

Vicky looked up at her, "No. I owe you one. But someone will I guess. I'm sorry about that."

"Yeah I'm sorry too." Roxy just felt tired now. She could still hear the sounds of combat at the end of the alley. "Are you winning?"

"Not really. There are a lot of dead vampires tonight."

"Vicky, this is wrong, can't you feel it?" Roxy wanted to tell her about the ritual, but doubted Vicky would believe her.

Vicky was quiet for a moment. Roxy thought that she looked tired. "I don't know Rox. I just do what I'm told. Nuremberg Defence. We're all shackled to someone, aren't we?"

"I'm not," said Roxy quietly.

"Well that makes you even more dangerous." Vicky smiled again, but this time there was a bitterness to it. "You should go now before anyone comes. I won't kill you, but I won't defend you either. I can't."

Roxy nodded, and on impulse stepped forward and hugged her. It surprised them both, but it made them both smile.

"Good luck," called Vicky as Roxy jogged back to the main street. Roxy turned to reciprocate, but Vicky had gone, vanished into the shadows.

# Chapter 46

At ten minutes to midnight Roxy and Anderton arrived at Green Park to wait for Mangala and Na'amah. Anderton refused to stay in the car, so Roxy let him carry the case containing the tablets. She felt strangely calm. She was swept up in a raging torrent, unable to do anything except cling to any driftwood she could find to avoid being sucked under. The tablets were her driftwood, but having seen the waterfall ahead, she no longer cared about drowning. She led Anderton to the centre of the park, which was deserted and eerily silent and waited motionless, holding Anderton's hand. He was quiet too, but she could smell his fear and hear his heart racing at a hundred and twenty beats a minute.

A few minutes later a cloud darkened the sky overhead, accompanied by a sudden gust of wind that circled around the park, whipping up litter and fallen leaves into a loose barrier, cutting off the roads beyond. Roxy's skin prickled and her legs turned to ice. She squeezed Anderton's hand warningly, but he was already staring into the middle-distance, his mouth hanging open in numb terror. Roxy was impressed that he was still standing. She couldn't see anyone, but she knew they must be near. Probably

Mangala, she reasoned, because Na'amah wouldn't have bothered to try to scare her like this. Roxy tried to say his name, but her lips wouldn't move.

Abruptly, the wind dropped and was replaced by a heavy, chilling fog that blanketed the park and reduced visibility to only a few paces. Roxy's legs felt stronger as a second wave of power clashed with the first and drove it away. Another gust of wind cleared an area of fog about thirty feet in diameter around Roxy, beyond which a wall of white mist hung. At the edge of the clearing on either side of her three figures appeared, two on her right and one on her left. Mangala, Juan and Na'amah. Crunch time, thought Roxy.

"What is the meaning of this Na'amah?" Mangala's deep voice demanded.

"I suspect our young friend here is indulging in a little game of her own," Na'amah said with a touch of humour. She walked towards the centre where Roxy was standing, her eyes on the case. Mangala also approached, eyeing Na'amah suspiciously. Juan followed slightly behind, regarding Roxy with a smile.

"I have the tablets," said Roxy, taking the case from Anderton and opening it, "but they are worthless," with that she turned the case over and scattered them onto the damp grass.

Mangala reached out a hand and all seven tablets leapt into the air and hovered a foot off the ground. Two of them suddenly shot off towards Na'amah, who caught them nimbly in each hand and started to read them. Mangala made a gesture and the rest floated over to him, suspended before him so that he could read them. Roxy waited, hoping that the witches knew what they were talking about.

"She's right," hissed Na'amah, turning them over and reading the back. Mangala snarled and swept them away. Na'amah diverted them towards her before they hit the ground and scanned the rest. Then she let them all fall at her feet.

"You killed Catallus for nothing, my dear," sneered Mangala.

Na'amah narrowed her eyes, "That was not me. If not you then who?"

"The same person responsible for the ritual," said Anderton, suddenly, "Menes."

Roxy stared at Anderton. He'd obviously been listening harder than she realised, but it made sense somehow.

Mangala gave a barking laugh, "Nonsense! Catallus was the jewel in Menes' crown."

"Quiet Mangala," snapped Na'amah "What do you know about the ritual?"

"Can't you feel it?" asked Roxy.

"Of course I can feel it! How can I not miss the sapping of my strength and the presence of the Dark all over the city?"

"Is this also what is preventing us from leaving?" asked Mangala.

"According to Darius, yes," replied Roxy. "It's a trap. Menes wanted to lure you here so he could finally kill you. And he's getting the Dark to do it."

"He doesn't have the power to perform this ritual. Who is helping him?" demanded Na'amah.

"Maybe the Dark?" Roxy was on dodgy ground here.

"No," said Mangala thoughtfully, "the Dark can only communicate with this plane through proxies. I think we are underestimating our old adversary."

"Menes is being tricked," a new voice announced from the edge of the fog.

"Hello Darius," acknowledged Na'amah with an enticing smile.

Mangala studied him, "That is a good incarnation for you."

Darius approached, flanked by Benito and Lillian. "We think there is a sentient manifestation of the X'ecunda involved. A powerful one. No doubt it has promised Menes power in addition to killing you. Menes doesn't know what will actually happen. He cannot, otherwise he wouldn't allow it. Unless he is insane."

Na'amah and Mangala exchanged a meaningful look. "I don't think he is insane," said Mangala slowly.

"But he has not gained a victory against either of us for a long time," finished Na'amah. "He must be feeling trapped and frustrated. It might have affected his judgement."

"He must be stopped," said Darius. "This will affect our kind as well as yours."

"Where is he?" said Mangala.

"We do not know for certain, but it is a critical time for him. He would make sure he was guarded."

Na'amah closed her eyes and tilted her head in concentration. "Reyne and Harold have gathered in Bloomsbury," she said.

"The museum," said Darius and Mangala together.

"Hang on," interrupted Roxy, "are you saying that Reyne is shackled to Menes?"

"Yes," said Na'amah absently.

"Would Menes know what Reyne knows?"

Mangala turned his attention to Roxy, "Perhaps. If he wished it. Why?"

"Oh my God," said Roxy, "I know why the ritual started last night." She glanced from Darius to Mangala, trying to avoid looking at Na'amah, "When I told Reyne about Na'amah yesterday he suddenly went blank, like he was paralysed."

"So that was the trigger," said Darius, "Menes must have known that Mangala was in the city, but he was waiting for Na'amah."

"Of course it didn't help that you marched in and took over, without thinking, as usual," commented Na'amah lightly. She caught Roxy's eye and gave her a strange look. Roxy felt as if she had been caught in a lie, even though she hadn't promised anything. She sensed that Na'amah wasn't angry with her though, which left her somewhat confused.

Mangala ignored the pointed remark and turned to Na'amah, "We need to work together."

"It wouldn't be the first time," said Na'amah slowly, considering her position. She came to her decision quickly and nodded, "I'll send mine to the museum. Call off your dogs."

Mangala's gaze unfocused for a moment, then he said, "It is done. But they will not be enough."

"I know. We will need to go in person." She turned to Darius. "Are you coming? Roxy and Juan will protect you."

Nice to be asked, thought Roxy, but she knew she would have agreed anyway. Darius nodded at once. "We will come. This has implications beyond our personal survival."

# Chapter 47

Na'amah and Mangala disappeared, leaving Roxy, Anderton, Juan and the witches alone in the park.

"Come," said Juan, "we must make haste."

Roxy looked at Anderton, unwilling to be separated from him, but knowing that she must go alone. "You have to stay here." She put her fingers to his lips to stop his protest.

"She's right," said Darius softly, "there will be demons there, minions of the Dark, whose presence will be too much for you. We will not be able to protect you."

Anderton looked into Roxy's eyes, and she could tell he was wondering if he would ever see her again. "Here," he said, rolling up his sleeve, "you'll need the strength."

Roxy put her hand out to stop him, but Anderton thrust it towards her again, his eyes moist. "You know you have to. Please. It's the only way I can help now."

Roxy felt the hunger stir inside her, and glanced longingly at his arm. She was dimly aware that the others had moved discreetly away, giving them time to say goodbye. She took his wrist, and guided him to the ground where they knelt beside each other.

She shifted slightly to allow his other arm to wrap around her. The close contact comforted them both, but Roxy knew they didn't have much time.

"So what is your name, anyway?" she whispered.

"Trace," Anderton replied, hesitantly.

"Trace? That's not so bad."

"It's actually short for Tracey," he said with a faint shrug, "it's kind of embarrassing."

"Don't worry, I won't tell anyone," Roxy gave him a smile and bit gently into his wrist. He gave the briefest of gasps, and held tightly onto her as she drank. Hot blood slipped down her throat and sent fiery tendrils of energy into every pore of her body. It was charged with a passion she hadn't experienced before, so different from the lust of the young men she'd danced for or the terror of the torturer. It warmed her from the outside in, not as immediately satisfying as before perhaps, but more wholesome, comforting and fulfilling. She felt an unfamiliar sense of protection encircling her, unconditional and loving. Her fingers gripped Anderton's wrist possessively, but gently, careful not to hurt him. She listened to his breathing getting heavier, more ragged. His pulse quickened, and she knew she was taking too much. For a brief moment she tried to convince herself that Anderton had tacitly told her to end his life, but she pulled away abruptly. She couldn't. Anderton collapsed in her arms and she laid him gently on the damp grass. Anderton smiled at her weakly. Roxy felt a panic rising. She didn't want him to die. She didn't want to have killed him. She felt a light touch on her shoulder and looked round to see Darius leaning over her.

"He'll be okay. I'll make sure he's looked after," he said.

Roxy looked back at Anderton and stroked his hair.

"See you later, maybe?"

"You'd better," croaked Anderton. "Good luck."

Roxy leaned down and kissed him softly on the lips. Anderton returned the kiss, then gave a sigh and closed his eyes. He was asleep seconds later.

Roxy glanced up at Darius in surprise, but he looked unconcerned. "Come on. He'll sleep until morning. Louisa will be here soon to look after him."

Roxy gave Anderton another kiss on his forehead, and got to her feet. "Let's go."

They ran down Piccadilly towards Shaftesbury Avenue. Roxy felt strong, confident and free from doubt for the first time in weeks. Juan set a punishing pace, which she was surprised Darius and the others managed to match. They obviously had hidden reserves of their own. As they crossed the theatre district she became aware of dark figures running along adjacent streets and leaping from rooftop to rooftop overhead, all converging on the museum like water flowing into a plughole. The ancients were summoning their thralls to fight.

They reached the high gates of the museum and stopped abruptly. The plaza beyond was swarming with battling vampires, tearing at each other in unconstrained frenzy.

"Oh my god," gasped Roxy, stunned by the violence. They were literally being torn limb from limb.

"The proximity of the Dark has driven reason from their minds," said Benito grimly.

"Why aren't we affected?" asked Roxy.

"We are shielding you from the effects Roxy," said Lillian softly, "and your companion is old and is controlling himself well."

Roxy gestured to the melee before them. "How do we get through that?"

Juan hefted his sword in response, but Darius held up a cautionary hand. "We cannot kill any."

Juan turned to stare at him incredulously.

Roxy stepped between them, sensing that things might escalate. "Darius is right," she said, "he told me that every vampire death strengthens the Dark." She glanced at the fighting, "This is probably exactly what it wants us to be doing."

Juan grunted. "As you wish. Follow my lead."

Juan turned and ploughed through the throng, scattering those in his path with a flurry of steel and blood. Roxy opened her mouth to protest, then realised that his apparently wild swings were actually carefully aimed strikes, severing arms and legs, leaving the opponent helpless, but alive.

Roxy stayed close to the witches, keeping them between her and Juan. A wild-eyed female swept up and Roxy deflected the murderous lunge with her sword, nearly severing the woman's hands and sending her sprawling to her knees. Roxy levelled a kick at her head to knock her back, and hurried after Juan, shepherding the mages towards the entrance.

They had just reached the huge columns at the top of the steps when Roxy felt a cold shroud fall upon her, gripping her heart and freezing her in place. Cries sounded all around and the fighting faltered briefly. Over her shoulder she saw a multitude of black shapes materialise, writhing and nebulous at first, then assuming a variety of vaguely humanoid forms, unnatural and disturbing.

They descended on the vampires, passing through their pale bodies like ghosts, drawing an eviscerative, watery scream from an unfortunate victim. Roxy stared in numb fascination as a wispy, tortured shadow seemed to emerge from the crumbling vampire only to be absorbed by the disturbing, tenebrous spectre.

The fighting resumed with increased ferocity. Some tried to strike at the creatures, but their blows passed though the rapidly changing figures like flailing hands grasping at smoke.

Roxy struggled against a consuming terror, her limbs weak and her senses numbed by a barrage of stimulation. She experienced a vertiginous sensation of falling, and swayed, expecting any moment to feel the frigid touch of the Dark and the emptiness that was certain to follow.

"Roxy," a light touch on her shoulder snapped her back and she looked shakily down at Lillian.

Roxy felt a fierce warmth burning within her and her strength returned. She nodded gratefully at

Lillian, and followed her and the others inside the museum.

Juan led the way in a confusing race along dark body-strewn corridors, down slippery stairs and through cavernous rooms, they finally arrived at a huge vaulted chamber deep underground, decorated with ancient statues and tapestries. In the centre of the room was a magnificent golden sarcophagus, decorated with lapis lazuli and jade. It was guarded by vampires from what was left of Domus Catallus and Domus Reyne. In opposition stood Mangala and Na'amah, flanked by Thorkel, Edmeé, Walpurga and Aelric. No one moved, except Juan, who slid in behind Mangala. Other vampires flickered in from the street above, crouching near the edge of the room, awaiting their next command.

At an unspoken signal, both sides fell upon each other in brutal combat. Roxy stayed close to the witches, prepared to fend off any attack that came their way. They were clasping each other's hands in concentration. Roxy stared open-mouthed as the elders fought, unable to see the intricacies of their moves due to their sheer speed. Bodies were flung across the room, crashing into the stone walls with bone-snapping cracks, only to leap back into the fray, claws and fangs flashing.

Roxy felt a familiar coldness and her limbs felt sluggish and heavy once more. The fighting slowed and people fell back in confusion. The witches started chanting in low voices, but no one paid them any attention. Na'amah and Mangala moved towards the sarcophagus. It shuddered, and the lid slid slowly to the side. No one was fighting now. All eyes were on the sarcophagus, which seemed to be in shadow, as if it were sucking the light from the room.

Roxy couldn't look at the pale man that emerged from within it. She surrendered to an uncontrollable compulsion to drop to her knees and lower her head. The memory of her brief glimpse of the radiant figure burned like sunlight.

"You cannot win, Menes," she dimly heard Mangala say.

"Lord Menes!" sneered the man. His voice carried so much power she wondered how Mangala didn't capitulate immediately. "I have already won," the commanding voice continued, "You cannot escape me now."

"You don't know what you are doing," hissed Na'amah.

"I am finishing this," replied Menes. "I have waited millennia for this moment and you will forgive me now if I am enjoying it." Roxy twisted in revulsion as she realised that his honeyed voice danced with madness. "Soon the X'ecunda will come, and its power will be mine. The world will bow before a risen God once more."

Roxy felt the hold on her abruptly fall away and snapped her head up to watch him stretch his arms to either side. The darkness around him deepened, spreading away from him like probing fingers. The nearest of his followers was caught in the path of the creeping shadow, and instantly doubled over with a piercing shriek. Roxy saw a dark stream of fog leave the screaming vampire's parted lips and streak toward Menes, swirling around the ancient before being absorbed into his body.

Mangala and Na'amah sprang at him, jumping high into the air. Menes leapt to meet them, and they became three blurs of motion flying high above the heads of the watching assembly. Vampires around the room suddenly collapsed to the floor as Mangala and Na'amah called upon the chains of their shackles and demanded their strength. Blood exploded from the eyes, noses and mouths of the stricken vampires and rose up to orbit the raging stars, adding to the strength of the ancients. Menes' shadow pulled at the souls of the remainder of his followers, creating a swirling ribbon of black fog that mingled with the streams of blood and feeding him.

Roxy stared around her, shocked at the way dozens of vampires had been laid low at a stroke. She knew that she was unaffected because she was the only one who wasn't shackled to anyone.

A hateful roar made her spin around.

"Roxy!" Wolfe was glaring at her. His eyes burned with a violent rage that Roxy instantly knew was beyond reason or sanity. Na'amah was focused entirely on Menes, her protective control on Wolfe discarded.

# Chapter 48

Wolfe swayed and blood poured from his ears, dripping upwards towards Na'amah like water flowing into a pool. Roxy felt a sudden vertigo, as if she were upside down, then Wolfe charged at her. She brought up her sword but Wolfe knocked it away with his hand, not even bothering to draw his.

The madness in his face was overwhelming. He reached for her throat with a feral growl. Roxy brought her fist up under his chin, shattering his jaw and then felt something in her shoulder snap as Wolfe grabbed it and squeezed. She pulled his hair and yanked his head sharply to the side as she crashing to the floor beneath him. Her broken arm burned with pain, and lay limply at her side. He thrust his face violently forward, leaving her holding a large clump of his hair and she jerked her head to the side to avoid his gnashing bite. Her arm recovered with a painful tingle and she punched him hard in the side, breaking several of his ribs. He hardly noticed but moved his hands to her throat and started to throttle her.

Roxy felt her windpipe collapse with a disturbing popping sound, and for a distracting few seconds couldn't work out why he was doing it. She didn't need to breathe after all, or was he too mad even to remember that? Then she suffered a momentary loss of feeling in her legs, and realised that he wasn't trying to suffocate her at all. He was trying to destroy her spine. She bucked underneath him, raining panicked blows and scratches into his sides and face, but Wolfe's leering face never wavered.

She managed to get a leg under him, and raised it quickly, pushing herself into a backwards roll to land on top of him. His grip loosened slightly as he tried to reposition himself, which was all the opening she needed. She grabbed his thumbs and pulled them back, breaking them and rolled away, searching for her sword. He was slow to follow. Blood now gushed from his eyes and nose. Roxy saw her weapon and scrambled towards it on hands and knees. Wolfe reached out, grabbing for her. She pulled her feet away and closed her hand around the hilt of the sword. Wolfe rose to his knees, screaming in rage and agony as he searched blindly for her.

His face was a bloody mass, joined by a thick crimson cord to the maelstrom overhead, feeding his uncaring mistress. Roxy rose to her feet, raised the sword high and brought it down onto his head with all her considerable strength. It split in two like a melon, spraying blood and brain matter everywhere. Roxy collapsed to her knees, staring at the ruined mass as it rapidly dried and turned to a shrivelled corpse before toppling sideways to the ground, her sword still jammed in the top of its spine. A dizziness swept over her, followed by a sense of euphoria as a burden she hadn't realised she was carrying was suddenly lifted.

She looked up and saw a sliver of pure darkness appear vertically above the sarcophagus, only a foot in length and less than a hand-span wide. Then it started to grow in random, spastic jerks.

# Chapter 49

All around her were the scattered remains of desiccated corpses, and others which looked whole, but as pale as ivory and lost in the agony of the Little Death as the last of their blood was stolen away.

The sliver of Darkness increased to the size of a doorway and Roxy sensed a terrible intelligence lurking beyond, waiting for it to grow large enough to step though. There was an ugly cry of triumph from above and Mangala fell to the floor, his face twisted with pain. Moments later a swarm of dark shapes materialised around him and covered him like locusts, sucking up the last of his energy until all that remained was a faint outline of dust where he lay. The gateway doubled in size, and Na'amah and Menes dropped to the ground before it, facing each other. Na'amah was favouring one leg and her left arm hung limply at her side. Menes was covered in scratches and half of his face was missing, simply a bloody pulp with white fragments of shattered bone peeking through. Neither had the energy to heal themselves, and they circled each other, exhausted but resolute.

The thing beyond the gateway was restless now. A black claw the size of a canoe emerged, eager to pass through. Menes looked at it and smiled at Na'amah.

"It is nearly here. Soon it will join with me, and all my ambitions will be realised. All it needs is your death to open the way."

Na'amah said nothing but changed direction, keeping Menes near to the dark gateway. Menes waited for his strength to return, fed from the souls of vampires throughout the city who were succumbing to the draining ritual. Na'amah looked tired, nearly defeated, and trembled as she limped away. No more blood was available from her shackles to aid her. Menes grinned. His face knitted itself back together in a clear show of superiority – he had strength to spare. His next step took him within a pace of the gateway, and the claw emerged again, greedily searching for more power. It impaled Menes from behind. He stared at the huge spike jutting from his chest and opened his mouth to howl a protest, but the cry never came. The claw pulled him swiftly through the opening into the black void, which doubled in size yet again. The claw returned at once, joined this time by three others. Na'amah stared helplessly as it scratched at the ground just beyond her.

"It's stuck," cried Darius. "It cannot get through. It needs the power from all three ancients to complete the passage."

Roxy looked at Na'amah, swaying in front of it. Only hate had kept her alive while facing Menes. Now the ritual set in place by Menes was drawing the last of her strength and when that happened, the gateway would open fully. Na'amah dropped to her hands and knees and turned her head towards Roxy.

"Not like this," she whispered, and collapsed to the floor, her black eyes wide, as if staring into the approaching void.

The idea hit Roxy like a train. She shook her head in mute protest. She couldn't. She looked around fearfully. Everyone in the room was unconscious or dead apart from Roxy, Na'amah, the witches, and a few of the strongest elders who were watching with weary, helpless horror. Darius and the witches were on their knees, buckling under the strain of the encroaching Darkness, their faces twisted with despair. She wondered why she hadn't been subsumed by the Dark like so many others, and realised that Darius and the other two witches were still protecting her. Would that be enough? She didn't know, but it was better than nothing.

Thoughts of Simon rose unbidden. She had consumed his soul. Almost forgotten now were his memories along with everything he was, brutally suppressed by her will and denied any chance of an afterlife. How much greater was Na'amah's will than hers? A hundred times greater? A thousand? It would be worse than death. To be trapped in her own mind with less and less power until she was merely a blind, deaf and dumb consciousness desperate for release.

"I can't," she whispered, unable to move. It would only delay the inevitable anyway.

The gateway grew larger and Roxy shuffled forward on her knees, zombie-like along the floor towards Na'amah. Her mind was numb, her thoughts too fractured to make sense. She tried to focus on something, anything, but all she saw were faces of people she knew and places she'd been. She thought of Anderton, but he was quickly snatched away into the vortex of her thoughts, and then something stuck. Claudia. Her beautiful Claudia, whom she'd almost given up hope of ever seeing again. Now she probably wouldn't but a world shrouded in darkness would deny her the chance of a life more surely than merely losing a mother. It wasn't much, but it gave Roxy the strength she needed and she held the image in her head as she bent over Na'amah and bit into her outstretched neck.

It was like gnawing through steel, but she clamped down as hard as she could, and with a snap, the resistance was overcome. A few traces of blood spilled into her mouth. It burned like alcohol mixed with menthol. The pain made her gag, but she forced herself to suck and swallowed another mouthful. Her nerve endings lit up and a dull heat swept over her body. She felt as though thousands of knives were piercing her body time and time again. The next mouthful was smaller as the last of Na'amah's blood left her body, and Roxy sensed an ephemeral presence just beyond. She pulled it in, knowing that this was her last chance to draw back. Goodbye Amanda, she whispered a mental farewell to herself and sucked once more.

She was falling, slipping into a terrifying turbulence of sights, sounds and textures which flashed across her mind with startling intensity.

Roxy clutched herself in agony as wave upon wave of Na'amah's diabolic experiences buffeted her. The six people she had killed were nothing compared to Na'amah's count. Not six hundred or six thousand or even six hundred thousand, but over a million deaths had been caused at her own hands and teeth. Who knew how many tens of millions more had died indirectly, through her shackles and mules and intrigues. Nameless faces strobed across her vision, their screams resonating in a discordant dirge, begging for justice, each sharing their ghastly manner of death, until all she could perceive was a sea of blood rising up over her head to block out the stars.

Roxy reeled under the weight of memories flooding through her. She saw the chains linking Na'amah's shackles – Aelric, Walpurga, Wolfe, Halloran and countless others around the world. She sensed them collapsing as the powerful bond shattered, but knew that she could renew it if she chose. She also saw the hidden lines of force between others. She saw Thorkel's hold on Vicky and those that survived between the paterfamiliae and their houses. She even saw the tight coil around Sarah held by Jessica, both lying unconscious in the museum above her. With a flicker of thought, she broke it. Gone. See how Jessica liked that!

Then she became aware of a screaming all around her. Not real screams, from flesh and blood throats, but a psychic scream that pierced deep into her subconscious and stirred up a nameless rage and hatred. It was the call of the Dark, singing to her. It knew she had stolen its prize and it was angry and frustrated.

She rose to her feet, noticing idly that all her wounds had healed and turned to face the gateway, although she did not need to. She could sense the whereabouts of everything in the room as if she were floating above it. Thorkel and Walpurga were staring at her in shock. Their thoughts were as clear to her as if they were shouting them out. They knew what she had done. It was the greatest secret the elders held, jealously kept and protected by the Patricians alone. They wove stories for the masses of the perils of drinking after the heart stopped, and it was the first lesson that a new parens taught their young. But Roxy had never been told. Not really. Sanjay had tried, but she hadn't listened.

Darius, Benito and Lillian stood behind her, staring at her, but Darius held them together and maintained their chant. She could see a halo of pale light around each of them – the true eternals inhabiting their bodies, as old as time. She stretched out her thoughts and found Anderton, lying in the back of a van on a makeshift bed, staring into space. His thoughts were clear to her too, wondering if he would ever see her again.

She shushed him, touching his mind tenderly. I am alive, love. Rest now. She saw him smile as she put him to sleep. She saw the faint bond tying him to her pulse with slow, gentle persistence. Just another bite or two, and he would be hers. Unquestioning and obedient. She knew she could break it if she wished and started to do so, but something made her hesitate. It might be useful, she thought. I'll need help if I get through this, and he is already half-way there. She could complete the bond now, in fact. She could reach out and ensnare the remnants of Domus Wolfe. How would that be? To have Dave and Jessica answer to her? Domus Harker? Why not?

No! She struggled, feeling herself sinking in a rising tide of emotions and desires that were not her own. She wrenched back control and found Claudia, sleeping restfully in Leah's bed at Scarlet's house. My Claudia. She nearly wept. So beautiful. She felt an insidious feminine presence in her mind back away reluctantly as the love for her daughter washed over her.

*As you wish*, it said, sulkily, *but we have not yet finished and you need my help.*

Roxy knew it was true. Dozens of black shapes started to materialise around her as the X'ecunda attempted to retrieve the much-needed soul. Roxy turned slowly on her heel knowing they would soon overwhelm her, when a calmness descended, washing over the tense places inside her and relaxing them. She looked at Darius and understood. They couldn't challenge the Dark directly – it was too strong now – but they were giving her the power to resist it, to strike back. She felt herself leaving the ground, rising into the air with arms outstretched – a dark angel to oppose the demons that flew screaming to meet her. It was at a piercing whining pitch far beyond human hearing which would once have crippled her, turning her limbs to stone while she waited for it to subsume her and draw her soul back to the Dark. Not now.

She spun on the spot, time stretching out limitlessly, and lashed deliberately out at one manifestation after another, her fists and feet connecting solidly with the extra-dimensional beings and catapulting them back to where they came from. She was a rock deflecting the crashing waves of the dark figures, impervious to their rage and turning away their attacks easily. Her blood sang with a blistering, exhilarating intensity as her body moved with terrifying speed and precision. It was as if she was merely an observer, watching herself whittle down the horde of attackers until only the gaping maw of the gateway remained.

She circled in the air to face it and sent a barrage of thoughts streaming at it, unleashing a psychic blast of hatred and anger that would kill a human and stun all but the strongest vampire. The creature beyond merely absorbed the blast and grew larger, thrusting another claw through the widening portal.

A snarl escaped her throat.

*No*, thought Roxy. *You can't fight it like that, it just makes it stronger.*

*What do you know?* A familiar feminine presence spat back.

*You're going to need me too, Na'amah. You've forgotten that the opposite of anger is patience, the opposite of despair is joy. You have forgotten how to love.*

*Love never brought me anything but pain and I feel joy every time I destroy an enemy.*

*That isn't joy, that's just bitter satisfaction and yes, opening yourself to love will invite pain. I know about your baby sister – little Enanna. It wasn't your fault she died.*

*I know that! I was shackled to my parens. He made me do it as a lesson. I learned it well.*

*I have a different lesson. I know that Claudia will grow old and die one day while I live on, still strong and beautiful. I know that it will hurt more if I hang on tight than if I let go now, but it will be worth it to hear her talk and teach her to read. A single one of her smiles makes all the bad things just fade away. You never knew. You were taken as a virgin. You can never understand, and for that, I pity you.*

*Keep your pity to yourself bitch. But I will concede this point. We do not have much time. Think your happy thought and let us finish this.*

Roxy held her hands to her head and closed her eyes. It wasn't hard to summon the sound of her daughter's giggles and the memory of her warm snuggles. She relaxed, drifting in the air, relishing the freedom of lazy flight, and let the feeling swell out from her in a bubble. It swept over the beast in the gateway, pummelling it with soft caresses and gentle kindness. Her tolerance and understanding shredded it into rags, curling it in upon itself like a slug under a mound of salt. It screamed in impotent, mindless rage, retreating in terror from the divine strength of her mind, enhanced by the light of the eternals. The gateway snapped shut after it and the screaming was shut off for good.

Roxy twisted slowly in the air, her eyes still closed but seeing everything clearly. *I am everything. I am everyone. I can do anything.*

*Yes you can. Anything you like. And the more you use your powers, the stronger I shall become. Eventually your love will turn to hate and you will be bitter too. And when that happens I shall be waiting. I will take your place and push you to one side.*

Roxy closed her out. *No. This body is mine. You have had your time.*

*Then prove it. Break Anderton's shackle. It would be easy for you. You can do anything, remember?*

Roxy shook her head in confusion. No, she couldn't. Not yet. She wasn't strong enough to resist Na'amah yet. Yes, that was the reason. It was a trick, to make her weaker. She needed more time to build up her will to act as a barrier. It had nothing to do with power, or her dominance over him. She wouldn't abuse it anyway. Not ever. Not really. Not unless she had to. Or wanted to.

She clamped her hands over her ears, trying to block out the confusion that was resurfacing and fell to the ground painfully, but she welcomed it. She opened her eyes but she was already inside the shrinking tunnel that led to blackout. She saw Darius peering down at her.

"She's passing out," his voice was distant.

"Will she die?" Was that Walpurga?

"I don't think so."

"That's a pity."

"We cannot kill her. Not yet. It would be too dangerous."

"We owe her a great debt," said Thorkel

"I know. But we cannot suffer her to live either. It will only be a matter of time."

"I know."

"We all know."

Mercifully, oblivion came.

# Chapter 50

Roxy hugged Claudia. She didn't think she would ever put her down again.

"I'm glad you are back on your feet again," said Scarlet, handing her a coffee. They were in Scarlet's small house. It had been two days since the confrontation with Menes, and the city had returned to some sense of normality. As much as Roxy could define "normal" anyway. Over half of the vampires in the city had died in the days leading up to the Night of Rage, as the survivors were calling it. The Patricians had quickly selected a new Primus. With the Triad's influence gone, Walpurga had renounced her support for Aelric and Thorkel had switched his vote from Edmeé to Reyne. Harold was a mistrusted reminder of Catallus, and as Lambeth had disappeared it was Reyne who assumed the mantle of Imperator. His first act was to summon Roxy to a secret meeting of the Curiae.

She had stood before them, feeling small and weak once more. Na'amah had withdrawn and the power she had briefly wielded had slipped away like a summer dream. Only fragments remained – confused memories of Ancient Egypt and foreign shores she had never visited.

"We have a problem with you, Roxy Harker," said Reyne, flanked by Thorkel, Walpurga and Aelric. "By right, as an unsanctioned Take, unshackled by a recognised parens, your life is forfeit. But your actions have saved the lives of us all, as well as freeing us from the shackles of our Masters."

Roxy stared back at them nervously, trying not to fidget. She said nothing.

Reyne rubbed his chin thoughtfully. She knew he was playing with her. They had already decided her fate. She tried to learn something from the faces of the other three, but they were as impassive as stone, except Aelric, whom she felt was suppressing annoyance or anger. She returned her gaze to Reyne with just a hint of defiance, and was rewarded by a slight smile from Walpurga.

"We owe you a life debt. You may not be aware, but this means that you have immunity from us until we can repay you. However, you also carry the spirit of Na'amah, which makes you dangerous. If you die too soon, her essence will return to the Dark, finishing the task that Menes began, but if you live too long she will eventually overwhelm you, and rise again to spread destruction and revenge. It is something of a dilemma for us, as you can see. However, the debt takes precedence. It is our oldest law, but it carries a price, which is your silence."

Roxy understood. If any of this became known to the other houses, the power of the patricians would be diminished. Questions would be asked anyway, about the death of Catallus and the events of the past two weeks. They had given her the right to life, and more. Since she had defeated Wolfe in single combat, she was granted his trappings as the law allowed. His club was now hers, along with his mules and his possessions. She was visited by a Mr. Filton who introduced himself as Wolfe's accountant and showed her some of her new assets. The balance listed at the bottom of the page was longer than the account number at the top. He gave her a business card and told her he would return the following week when she'd had a chance to read her new portfolio.

It hadn't really sunk in yet, but she had plenty of time. Reyne had given her the option of taking a place in the Tributa. What remained of Domus Wolfe could be hers if she wished, or she could cast them aside, sending them back to the orphans where they would be vulnerable and without a nomen. She hadn't said yes straight away, but she figured she would. Domus Harker would start out stronger than most, but she would need to watch her back, not least from those within.

"So what are you going to do now?" asked Scarlet, snapping her back from her reverie.

Roxy curled her legs underneath her and kissed Claudia who was now struggling to get down and play. "I think I'll be okay. First I need to find somewhere to live. I might need your help with that."

Scarlet stirred restlessly, "Still having...problems... in daytime?" she asked, hesitantly.

"It looks like it." Roxy didn't press the point. Scarlet knew the truth, but preferred to interpret it in her own way. It was enough. I'm going to get you out of here too, she thought, into a decent place.

A whispering presence in her mind chuckled. Of course. We cannot have any weaknesses for others to exploit, can we?

Roxy shut it out. She knew she would spend the rest of her life struggling with Na'amah for control. Her personality hadn't changed radically, as she had feared, but she was definitely viewing the world through different eyes. Four and a half thousand years of memories do that to you.

The vast chronicle of Na'amah's life had unfolded before her, as if it were her own. She remembered standing at the base of the mighty ziggurat adorned with flowers - barely a woman - ready to be given to the God of the Night and trying not to show her fear. Her beauty had attracted more than just the young warriors, and now she was to be granted the honour of everlasting youth and power. She didn't, couldn't, fully understand the cost though. The God was cruel, his first command to her was to kill her family. He forced her to drain them one by one, even poor Enanna, not yet two summers of age.

Then he abused and beat her, subjecting her to every depravity imaginable, until she was a shell of her former self, empty except for the hatred of him and his kind. He channelled that hatred outward against his enemies, making her a tool of destruction that knew no fear or mercy or remorse, and she made him proud. For five hundred years she served him, nursing her anger in a quiet corner of her mind, the embodiment of loyalty, until she saw her chance. Seducing the powerful stranger from the east had not been easy, but Mangala had finally fallen for her charms and she twisted and teased his strings with the skill of an artist until he flew into a wild rage and brought down his army upon her sire, killing him and his brethren and freeing her from his oppressive shackle.

Mangala had taken her away from the shattered empire which would never again achieve the same glory and they travelled south, along a mighty river to the city of Ineb Hedj, ready to carve out a new empire. But Menes was there already. The wars they fought over the following centuries caused untold suffering to the people of those lands, but neither Menes nor they could gain the upper hand. Eventually, tiring of the conflict, she had made a secret deal with Menes, guiding Mangala into a trap and nearly destroying him. But her treachery was even more devastating and cunning. As Menes gloried in his victory, he was discovered by the priests and sorcerers she had tipped off, and they called upon the spirits of the sun and the hearth to drive him into the sea, unable to rise again for a hundred years.

She had ruled alone for generations until Mangala and Menes returned as allies at the head of an unstoppable army from a city of seven hills and so the war began again; over a thousand years of shifting alliances across nearly every continent using whatever civilisation that existed at the time. And then, Menes had vanished. His pawns still ruled some of the mightiest cities in the world, but the most obvious signs of his influence were absent. She had formed a brief, uneasy alliance with Mangala to search for him, but it quickly disintegrated through distrust and mutual hatred and they resumed their battles once more.

The announced discovery of the Tablets of Menes was a beacon to both her and Mangala. It seemed an obvious trap, but neither could resist its lure. It was trivial to find a new pawn in the form of Wolfe and move him to London as her spy. To protect her asset she built up a house around him, guiding them all with telepathic visions and gentle mental prompts. Her powerful shackles in the Patricians made sure he survived censure, and she even managed to gain control of Catallus, a fact which led her to believe that perhaps Menes was truly weakened. Now it was obvious that Menes had allowed her to influence Catallus simply to draw her in. She had been so careful! Now she was trapped inside the whelp's feeble mind. To end like this? At least she had been the last. The winner!

The doorbell rang. Roxy stretched out her thoughts and knew who it was even before Scarlet had reached the door. She waited until a smirking Scarlet led Anderton into the room.

"Someone to see you Rox."

Roxy looked at him and smiled. He smiled back and with an awkwardness that she found cute. He held out a bunch of crimson flowers.

"Roses? I like the colour," she grinned.

He shrugged, "It seemed appropriate somehow."

She studied him curiously. It seemed that his face was smoother, the wrinkles fading away. Perhaps his grey hair would grow out and become blonde again? The blood that she had given him was healing the ageing just as Darius had suggested might happen.

"Are you sure you can handle someone like me?" She rose to her feet to accept the flowers. "I have a few issues you know? I sleep late, I'm a fussy eater and my feet are always cold."

"I think I'll manage," he smiled, "I'm pretty tough."

So am I, thought Roxy, allowing herself to sink into his arms and looking at her friends and family, content for the first time she could remember, but I'm glad I won't be alone.

Somewhere in the back of her mind she thought she heard a chuckle.

*Don't worry, you won't be.*